ONCE UPON A TIME THERE WAS A MAN

Peter Scholes

Text ©Peter Scholes
Edited by Veneficia Publications
Additional editing by Julia Krzyzanowska
Cover image public domain images
SnapStock and bones 64
modified by
Veneficia Publications.

ISBN: 978-1-914071-96-6

Veneficia Publications
October 2023

VENEFICIA PUBLICATIONS UK
veneficiapublications.com

For John and Yvonne Scholes
The best parents a lad could wish for.

DEDICATED TO THE MEMORY OF ERNIE GRIMSHAW. RIP.

ONCE UPON A TIME THERE WAS A MAN

CHAPTER 1
One step ahead of the game

10.1.19

Information note (case 4360). Urgent.

Contact Mrs. N. regarding observations at Beech Grove.

Mr. N. reinforces suspicions and backs up previous findings. Video evidence taken at 11.52 a.m. on 9th January 2019. Mr. N. seen in a compromising position with unnamed female outside (the front door) of number 15. Lady in question was dressed in short black negligee with no underwear visible. As usual I refrain from making opinion or offering suggestion, but the video clearly shows flirtatious behaviour towards Mr. N. Her hair was ruffled, and her use of makeup considerable. Said anonymous female appeared to be very affectionate towards Mr. N. and kissed him on the lips and cheek eight times in total. Mr. N. did not refuse her advances and appeared to enjoy the attention. He smiled and embraced the lady. They both stood in the doorway of number 15 in full view of any passersby, making no attempt to hide. Before Mr. N. returned to his Ford Focus car, which was parked on the driveway of number 15, he instigated a final kiss (on the lips) before hugging unnamed female and grabbing her bottom, making her giggle and blush. Mr. N. returned to his car (pulling up his fly zip) before blowing a kiss to unnamed female and driving away from Beech Grove. The exchange lasted no more than six minutes.

Diary updated at 1:12 p.m. today after a thorough study of the video evidence and the digital photos taken before, during and after the meetings; times, movements and pattern of behaviour all correlate. This information will be relayed to Mrs. N. now in the form of a telephone call at the stipulated time of 2:20 p.m., when Mr. N. is assumed to be at his place of work. Hard copies to follow at the discretion of Mrs. N.

Yet again, I feel I need to emphasise to my diary the importance of thoroughness. Treat each case on its own merits and never presume you know anything based on the experiences of other similar cases. I have found that, in this job, no two cases are *ever* the same. People are not the same.

I realise, Mr. Diary, that I repeat myself every year, but this is a reminder to myself to stay sharp. Stay focused. Stay right. Competition is rife in this job, and only the best will stay in the game and make a healthy living from it. Too many fall by the wayside. Too many get bored with the tedium of the majority of the cases. Few are prepared to go that extra mile. To me, that extra mile is the mark of a professional. Reputations are built and contacts are developed if the job is done right.

Mr. Diary, you and I go back a long way. This year, our eleventh year together, we can be proud of our achievements – and our prosperity. Back in 2003 you were a shadow of your present self. Cheap and tacky, shabby and shoddy. Look at you now – leather bound, encased and sturdy. I have grown, and you have grown with me, but, Mr. Diary, we must never forget our roots or our principles that have held us in good stead all this time. You are my Bible. Welcome to 2019.

11.1.19

Initial letter drafted to Mrs. N. (case 4360) and memo for Ms. Cannon re: father-in-law and misuse of vacuum cleaner (case 4339).

Copies of discs included with letter to Mrs. N. Further information will follow letter (including photographs and copies of relevant paperwork). This will show copies of receipts for items purchased in the last two weeks. These include two bouquets of flowers (Carnation, Chrysanthemum, Freesia, Forsythia, Gypsophila, Gentian, Holly Berries, Iris, Lily, Orchid, Rose, Stephanotis, Snow Drop and Winter Jasmine), perfume (Chanel perfume) and various items of an adult nature from Ann Summers which, Mrs. N. confirms, have failed to see the inside of their marital home.

Again, avoiding assumption, I later discovered that, whilst tracking unnamed female acquaintance of Mr. N., the stockings and suspender belt had been an exact match of those acquired by Mr. N. only hours earlier in town. Video evidence shows that Mr. N. did visit 15 Beech Grove with purchases from the 'Ann Summers' store in hand and left the house without.

With regards to Ms. Cannon (case 4339), advise client that evidence such as this is unlikely to stand up in court if a civil action is taken, and therefore recommend she pursues a different course of action. Do not guide or advise beyond this as it is beyond your jurisdiction, as she is definitely a lady who could put more business your way. In total, after checking accounts, Ms. Cannon had contributed £4398 to the 2018 gross profit. She is a very suspicious lady with a lot of money. **DO NOT RISK**.

Bill payments and direct debits to leave account before the end of January total £8,987. Estimated income (should all clients pay on time) should reach £13,500. A good month's work.

With the books in order and not much to fluster about through February, I think you and I, Mr. Diary, could treat ourselves to a few days' relaxation. There are enough irons in the fire to see us through to spring without even stepping up the quest for new work and, with March to October being our busiest period (if the last ten-year trend is anything to go by), we may as well take advantage of the lull. Where do you fancy? France? Spain? Greece? Germany?

They all appeal to me, Mr. Diary. Anything to escape the greyness of the Lancashire skyline. God instilled many a great quality in the people here, but He could not stretch to welcoming weather. Still, a holiday would not be a holiday if you stayed at home. I think you will make a fine travelling buddy too. To invite Karen, who I haven't seen for weeks now since the fish and chips incident in Grimsby, would be foolish.

For someone who prides themselves on being so meticulous, I cannot begin to understand my lack of judgement in women. As someone who spends so much time studying and following them, I chastise myself on a daily basis for failing to understand what makes them tick. Perhaps one day the penny will drop, and all will become clear. For now, Mr. Diary, we will enjoy hotter climes without the companionship of a female and return fresher and more eager.

I feel that this is going to be a good year. Let's make it so.

Reminder: Call Tom. Criminal history file of John Weston needed (case file 4011). Case records (2016 to 2018). Remember to ask Tom about behaviour patterns. (Last thing I want is a knife in my back before I pack the passport and shorts.)

12.1.19

Tragedy strikes in a faraway land. Sri Lanka to be precise. An earthquake of horrific proportions by all accounts. Thousands of innocent people suspected injured or dead. It amazes me how I can stare at the screen watching a disaster unfold in front of my very eyes and, although I know it is awful and devastating, I am still somewhat impassive towards it all. I was always quite an emotional child, but age thickens the skin, and the more I seem to experience the less I seem to care. It is wrong, and I am ashamed of my apathy, but here I am watching TV and, at the same time, logging trivial thoughts as a whole nation literally crumbles.

It is hard to pinpoint why I should feel this way. They say we are no longer shocked by what we see on the screen. We have been desensitised by it all. Our spirits crushed by over exposure and sensationalism, and yet I cry every time I watch *Schindler's List* or *The Elephant Man*. Why is this real suffering on the TV in front of me any less upsetting than a film?

I feel guilty for myself. I should be feeling selfless and guilty for my lack of drive and determination to help. I know I will turn over when the charities plead for my £2 a month. How have I developed such a callous streak in my soul? Is it the job? I need people's suffering, pain, suspicion and hatred to thrive in order to pay my wage. Am I immune from normal human feelings after years of tracking society's sludge and slime? Even as I write, I am managing to turn off from the disaster.

Can I even justify thinking of my upcoming holiday?

Yes, I think I can.

France and Germany seem to be topping the list at the moment, Mr. Diary. How do you fancy Munich and Bavaria? I can picture myself stereotypically wolfing down a bratwurst and washing it down with a stein of beer, overlooking the glorious Alpine peaks. Or even a winter stroll down the tight-knit Parisian back streets on the hunt for nothing but relaxation.

I am in the zone. Selfishness over compassion. I need a holiday, and, looking at the TV screen, I don't think Sri Lanka will be on the shortlist.

Cheque for £430 received and deposited from Mrs. N. (case 4360) with accompanying letter attached below. Another job well done with another angry but 'satisfied' customer. That money will go towards the holiday, and if Mr. Thompson (case 4299) eventually pays what he owes, I won't have to dip into the savings.

Dear Mr. Brunskill,

Please find enclosed a cheque for £430 (in final settlement) as payment for your services. It is with regret that this money should be spent in order to uncover such tragic news but,

I fear, the longer-term cost could have been much greater had I kept the cheating bastard as my husband. Allow me to congratulate you on a thorough and professional job. In the unlikely event that I find myself in this position again, I would certainly seek out your number and screw another man as he has screwed me.

Yours honestly, – Mrs. (soon to be Ms) Fiona Niles.

Tragic news? Try watching the news, love – that's tragic, not your husband's extramarital shenanigans. Having said that, if Mr. N had kept his bratwurst in his pants, I might not be quids in, and be heading off to Munich. Yes, Germany is the winner. Right, Mr. Diary, I think we should tie up one or two loose ends here and look to fly before the end of the month.

What d'ya say?

13.1.19

John Weston (case file 4011). Good man, Tom. They may take an age to call round to your house when you have been raped, burgled or attacked, but ask them to delve through old records and pass on confidential personal information on any given individual, and the police always come up trumps – for a price. Mind you, a pack of Guinness and a pork pie was enough to bribe old Tom.

So, Mr. Weston, what have we found out about you? Well, apart from a spate of petty thefts you only have one notable conviction worthy of my attention, it seems. Assault. Serious enough,

7

though, for a concerned judge to send you down for twelve months with three suspended.

Mr. Diary, I think we should mull over this one. This case has sat in the background for a long time now. Can we afford to give it a miss? His sister is prepared to pay above the usual rate, but my own safety is worth more than that. I have a suspicion this one is not worth the hassle, and as you know, my paper friend, my hunches are normally accurate. Weston has avoided the radar of the local rags and TV, and yet he is a serial offender, which leads me to believe he has friends in places he shouldn't. That would place my anonymity at risk as I would no doubt be digging in the same places where he is trying to fill the holes. His sister is very pretty too, and I think she has a crush on me, but I must never mix business with pleasure. Perhaps that is why she is prepared to pay over the odds. Or, more likely, she knows her brother is a bit of a psycho, and no other man or woman has been prepared to touch this case.

This job really does make a man paranoid. Maybe this joint wasn't such a good idea after all. Three espressos, half a bottle of Merlot and a cannabis joint is not a good mix, Mr. Diary. I don't know whether to panic or pass out. I will consider this case with a clear head tomorrow. In the meantime, I will pack up now and get to bed.

14.1.19

Sri Lanka. This is getting worse by the day. Hundreds proclaimed dead already. Poor souls. Yet again, my compassion lasts for the length of the broadcast before I am sucked into my own selfish bubble to concentrate on my own life. Providing the

Alps don't burst open, spraying volcanic ash over Austria and Southern Germany, I can rest assured that my holiday will be the relaxing jaunt that I am ready for.

I will have to do some serious clothes shopping before I go. It is alright for you, Mr. Diary, your cover will suffice, but I need half a new wardrobe to even pass as acceptable in normal society once again. Days spent cooped up in a transit van spying on perverts, paedophiles and prostitutes, pissing in an old lemonade bottle really takes its toll on your self-esteem and only decent pair of jeans. What would the Germans think if I entered their proud land stinking of takeaways and stale sweat?

This is a chance to dust myself down and forget all about my neighbouring world of sleaze and scum. It has been four long years since my last holiday, and, as short as this one may have to be, I need to leave this green and unpleasant land behind for a while and check in on my European neighbours.

Internet. What a wonderful tool. How did we manage before this, Mr. Diary? I appreciate that you and your relatives took a knock when the internet entered our lives, but even you must admit it is one hell of an invention. I would never abandon the pen and paper, but writing is a dying art for the masses. Why write when you can email? Why scribble when you can click? Why flick through a magazine with staples in the centrefold when you can access worldwide porn thanks to broadband and a healthy search engine?

Also, who needs a travel agent when you have the internet? Just look at the choice of cheap holidays. Hotels, hotels with flights, transfers, inclusive food and trips, car parking, car hire – it is all there, and I don't even have to leave the house or talk to Malcolm Patel in a call centre in India.

Booked. Flights, a one-night stay in Munich on arrival and three nights in Fürstenfeldbruck including sightseeing trips to the Bavarian Alps. All for under £500. Printed.

All appointments to be cancelled or rescheduled between 28th January and 3rd February. According to you, Mr. Diary, there is nothing out of the ordinary to worry about during those days and nothing that cannot be shuffled around to suit. There is something incredibly satisfying about booking a holiday. That initial worry about money soon disappears only to be replaced by a sense of excitement. I wonder if I need new shorts.

15.1.19

John Weston (case file 4011). Meeting with Sheila Thompson at 12:15 p.m., The Circle Club, Barton Square, Manchester, (Senior News Editor – The Telegraph). Take one line of enquiry before making final decision on case. Go no further than Sheila unless the vibe is right. Trust instinct as ever. No payment taken from Julie Clarkson (Weston's sister).

Take Tom's notes, newspaper clippings and witness statements.

Bob Fletcher (case file 4320) completed. Final payment received for £231. No further action necessary. Satisfied by her explanation following surveillance reports. If she is a lesbian, I am Adolf Hitler.

Susan   Tomlinson   (case   file   4299).
Rescheduled visit with Susan following break in
Germany. No urgent action required. Ms.
Tomlinson assures me that the new padlocks are
sufficient for now and the sedatives will work their
magic while I am away. Offer discount of 10% for
the inconvenience but be sure to complete
programme of observation until Ms. Tomlinson is
satisfied. I am enjoying this one.

Late mail delivery. Two bills, two offers for
laser eye treatment, one welcome cheque and two
handwritten letters – one post marked Rochdale
and another Plymouth (Devon).

Possible work. Skimmed both – nothing out
of the ordinary. Will action later this evening
following meeting with Sheila.

16.1.19

God can that woman drink! 12:15 p.m. soon
became 12:15 a.m. What is it with journalists?
They live and work on the streets. Literally. She was
out of her head by last orders – all on expenses. I
am not complaining, Mr. Diary – I was out of my
head on her expenses account too. No wonder
newspaper front pages are filled with snappy
headlines. They are all too pissed to write a good
story after that.

That said, she was not completely useless.
My initial hunch was right. Weston is not without
friends in high, and indeed low, places. Caution
needed. Is the money worth the risk? Again, my
hunch says no, but the thought of seeing Julie's
breasts again coupled with a higher-than-normal
wedge of cash is starting to cloud my normally
razor-sharp thought process. I will give this one

11

some more thought, but she does need a decision by Wednesday.

Letters from yesterday. Both possible leads for work.

Letter 1. (Rochdale) – Typical affair. Suspect male, 34. Usual surveillance and bank checks should uncover the necessary. Letter (below) sent from workplace of wife (presumably to avoid trace – paper watermark and choice of stationery typical of large chain insurance company). First impressions typical. Language used formal but with hints of panic and urgency. Not a wealthy woman, but the worry is weighing heavy on her shoulders, and the outlay of a couple of hundred pounds is worth it for her. No address details in letter.

Mobile telephone number only. Workplace easily ascertained from choice of stationery and franking machine used should the need arise to contact in person. Always cover your back before you cover someone else's, that's my motto.

Husband's behaviour has prompted understandable concerns. Actions of a concerned wife, not a hysteric.

As usual, reproduction of the letter for the diary noted below. Identification details removed. Records kept in safe with original paper copy plus the usual back up scans taken.

Mr. P Brunskill
Mrs. Kathryn Fitzgerald
Rochdale
XXXXXXXXXXXXXX
XXXXXXXXX XXXXXXXXXXX
Tel: 079XX XXX XXXX XXXXXX

Dear Mr. Brunskill,

It is with much sadness that I feel the need to seek your services.

After much soul searching and nail biting, I have decided to take positive action in order to save both my sanity and the sanctity of my marriage.

I have, for some months now, suspected my husband of having an affair. After nine years of marriage, one would expect periods of tension or boredom but, until the summer of this year, I had no reason to suspect my husband of any wrongdoing.

In August, following a work party in which he stayed out all night, he has become far more secretive and sly.

He is working much later than usual in the evenings; he will snap at me and look for an argument over the simplest things and our own sex life has diminished. These traits may not be unusual and may simply be the result of a marriage on the wane, but I fear he is seeing another lady. For my own peace of mind, I need to know one way or another, and I am willing to pay to uncover the truth.

These may be the ramblings of an overweight, paranoid wife but for my own peace of mind I would be obliged if you could consider my request.

I look forward to hearing from you soon. I would be grateful if you could use the mobile number listed above to contact me. As you will understand, I am reluctant to give my home address. On your advertisement you assure professionalism and discretion. I trust this is the case.

Yours sincerely, K Fitzgerald.

Note: contact tomorrow. Unless there is anything untoward not noted in the letter, this case can be taken. I see no more than two weeks' work here (perhaps 20 hours at £30 per hour – mainly consisting of surveillance). Find husband's job, shift patterns, age, doctor, income, some relationship history – loves, likes, interests.

Letter 2 (Plymouth, Devon).

Another straightforward detection. Short, brief letter. Very formal. Style indicates elderly gentleman. Copy of birth certificate enclosed – I will check that out in a week or so.

Cumbrian family - this would explain the desire to seek the help of a Northwest investigator, although the search for birth records is not difficult to trace. One-off standard fee (£150) for work. That said, the money is better in my pocket. This one can be done and dusted before Germany.

No noted concerns, and his flattery will get him everywhere.

Again, reproduction of the letter for the diary noted below. Identification details removed. Records kept in safe with original paper copy plus the usual back up scans taken.

Mr P Brunskill
XXXXXXXXXXXXXX
XXXXXXXXX
XXXXXXXXXXX
XXXXXX
XXX XXX

William Green
XXXXX XXXX XXXXXXX
XXXXXXXXXXXXXXX
XXXXXXXX
XXXXX

Dear Sir,

I am writing in the hope that, after careful consideration of my request, you would consider offering both your time and expertise. I have never had the need to approach a Private Investigator before, but, after carrying out some research of those in the local area, you come highly recommended. As I am limited in my abilities to use modern technology, please reply to me directly by letter at the above address. Any monies invoiced by you I will honour immediately in the form of cheques by return post.

If you choose to accept the work, I would be thankful if you could contact me as soon as possible with your response and I will write again soon.

Mr. Brunskill, I want you to help me find a man.

Yours sincerely,

Mr. William Green

CHAPTER 2
Priorities

17.1.19

Fourteen cases active. Four long-term. Most can be cleared before the break with what looks like one with potential for two weeks' work and wages (Rochdale) and a day on the paper trail (Plymouth).

Looking at the job specifications over the last twelve months, it appears that we have a growing trend, Mr. Diary. Family trees. It seems like the immediate family are no longer enough for some – they want to know how far that bloodline stretches beyond the grave.

TV is to thank for that too. Dozens of C-list celebrities chasing around the country, delving into old documents and waking up the priests in village churches hoping to find evidence of a legacy greater than their own. Still, who am I to complain? The knock-on effect on the general public is proving to be quite a bonus for me. Too lazy to trace their own darling deceased, they are quite prepared to pay for me to do it. Looking at the time spent on each case and the money earned, it appears that people are more than happy to part with their hard-earned cash, then sit back and watch their histories unfold. To be fair, it is amazing what you can uncover with a bit of digging and, more often than not, the lines of enquiry are easy enough to follow.

I must admit I am finding quite a bit of enjoyment in it, and the contacts and enquires made may very well hold me in good stead for all the other cases. The change in hospital records, police case files, civil service personnel records, births and deaths, wills and testaments, marriages and registrars etc. – so many lines of enquiry.

People are strange. Mr. Shaw (case 3468) was delighted to find out that his great grandfather served eight years in prison for a serious sexual assault.

Ms. Taylor (case 3997) could not contain her joy when one line of enquiry (alongside DNA records) proved that her ex-husband, after a long-term affair, was about to marry his half- sister. Confidentiality decrees that I only need to pass on the information, not expose it.

What Ms. Taylor chooses to do is her business. A large part of me hopes she passes on the information – but only after the wedding has taken place.

Dame Joyce (case 4001) was convinced she had thick royal blood only for the truth to reveal she hailed from gypsy stock.

I hope this is not just a fad. Family trees are far more exciting than affairs. Other people's, that is. I have no intention of hunting down my own family ghosts. They are best left in the past.

To do:
Travel insurance to sort out.
Airport car parking.
Maps and town plans.
Book Flea into the cattery.
Ask Mother to water the plants.

18.1.19

Excited for the holiday but always stay professional and stick to your own rules. Reply within three working days of receipt.

1) Mrs. Kathryn Fitzgerald, Rochdale. Allocated new case number (4501). Called once to check voicemail message matched the caller. Check. Second call to leave voice message on mobile to give conditional acceptance. Outlined payment plan, expected time span and standard contract between the two parties. Message brief as ever. Formality essential to reassure client and promote professionalism and discretion as required. Await response.

2) Mr. William Green, Plymouth. Allocated new case number (4502). Short formal letter drafted and posted recorded delivery accepting case and stating costs.

19.1.19

Final email confirmation for flight times received. Nine days until the flight. Ridiculously early but relatively cheap. The compromise will be worth it, and I should have the best part of the day to enjoy the city.

Call received from Kathryn from Rochdale accepting my terms without asking for information on my methods or track record. Those that accept straight away without seeking trust should not be trusted themselves. Perhaps she is more desperate than her letter first intimated. Should I take this one on? - A paranoid middle-aged housewife with a desire to hold on to her cheating hormone-driven husband.

Of course I will.

Returned call. No answer. Left message. Left the ball in her court to arrange meeting time and place.

20.1.19

Met with John Weston's sister (Julie Clarkson - Weston case 4011) against my better judgement. A pretty but hard-faced woman with a passion for revenge. Little was given away during the meeting and I got the feeling she was trying to assess me over a latte in Starbucks. I didn't give much away, but then again, I don't really know what she was looking for me to give.

She dressed very business-like in a black power suit. Her knee-length boots and figure-hugging blouse enhanced her sex appeal, but her demeanour was assertive enough to ensure I kept my distance. This was a woman used to being in control of herself and her space. I didn't encroach once. I suspect she would have liked me to, if only to put me in my place. It was very much a game of emotional chess, and until, or if, we reconvene, we are both in a position of stalemate. I am a tough nut to crack, but she is too.

I do not need this – or the money – but I like a challenge.

The only snippet of relevant information I gleaned from her was that the case revolves around money. I expected nothing less. How much money could also indicate how much risk is involved, especially when dealing with a man such as Weston. The money is good though. £1500 up front, £40 an hour and a final payment of £5000 if I prove her to be right. Whatever 'right' is. Vagueness scares me. Money drives me. Which emotion will win out? Cash or cowardice?

Another meeting scheduled for 24th January 2019. Same time, same place. Perhaps I will find out then.

21.1.19

Received call from K. Fitzgerald (case 4501) at 4:45 p.m. She would like to meet tomorrow at Manchester Piccadilly train station at 12:30 p.m. She will be wearing a red skirt and a black sweater with red jacket. I hope it doesn't have a hood or I will be keeping one eye out for a wolf.

She promised to bring along any evidence she has gathered so far. I wonder what this will include. Dental records? Fingerprints? The poor man doesn't stand a chance. Schedule in two hours maximum for the meeting with Mrs. Fitzgerald. Trainspotting in Manchester Piccadilly with a fairytale character from Rochdale is no way to spend your 37th birthday.

Booked *Romario's* for 7:30 p.m. Table for three on the off chance my unreliable sister can make it.

Thank God for a mother's love. My only other female company for the day will be a cheating man's wife.

22.1.19

I have lived on this planet now for approximately 13,150 days, and I am none the wiser when it comes to understanding the complicated world of marriage. After two hours in the company of the delightful Mrs. Fitzgerald, I cannot see for the life of me why Mr. Fitzgerald (Robert) would choose to 'play away'.

This woman was beautiful, charming, sensitive, caring and humorous. Two hours became four.

This evidence could come in very useful. I curse myself for being so judgemental. I should know better.

I will give this case priority on my return from Germany.

If first impressions count for anything, and I believe they do, Mr. F does not know what he is throwing away here. At the same time, I wonder how a woman of such integrity can allow herself to fall for such a man. Alas, the complexities of love will continue to amaze and annoy me, I fear.

I hope the rascal is up to his eyes in marital affairs. Some women deserve to be set free. I'd better get a wriggle on. I am meeting Mum in an hour.

23.1.19

God can that woman drink. Two bottles of red polished off before the dessert menu even reached the table. Why did I even bother trying to keep up? Years of peer pressure I suppose. At least she bothered to turn up, which is more than can be said of my sister.

My head is banging today. These hangovers are taking longer and longer to shake off, Mr. Diary. Not for my mother it seems. A text received at 8:30 a.m. telling me to get up and join her at the garden centre. Sod that. A text alarm clock from my hyperactive mother is not what I need when I am trying to die.

I knew Gill wouldn't turn up. She doesn't mean to be so flippant and heartless, but she takes after Mother. Mother only turned up because she has already done everything my sister is doing now. My sister is only two years my junior but has the energy of a girl in her early twenties. Lucky cow. It is only jealousy. No wonder Dad died young. It was probably through exhaustion trying to keep up with those two. Well, I have no intention of joining him on his cloud just yet. Certainly not with a trip to Germany just around the corner. Mind you, that can wait too. I am off back to bed.

Text from Julie Clarkson (Weston case 4011) to confirm meeting for tomorrow. I will feel better by then. I need all my faculties when I meet with her. A few extra hours of sleep and I will be as 'right as rain'.

24.1.19

Not the day I expected today. Why the hell didn't I trust my first instincts? Log of meeting with Julie Clarkson (Weston case 4011):

Met in Starbucks as agreed. Ms. Clarkson did not appear to be as assured as she did during our first encounter and tried to hand over a sum of money within the first five minutes of this one. I refused to accept, explaining that an assessment of the job was needed before an agreement could take place. This angered Ms. Clarkson considerably, and she threatened to take the job to another party. Whether or not this was a threat or a promise was neither here nor there, and I calmly refused the money and the job.

I have always reacted on suspicion, and I was happy to walk away.

Following the meeting, I adjourned to the Hope and Anchor on Bell Lane to gather my thoughts and reflect on wages lost, only to be joined at the table by a large, heavy set, shaven-headed, middle-aged man who introduced himself with a firm and meaningful handshake and the words, "Good afternoon, Paul, I'm John Weston".

I nearly laid an egg there and then.

Only on a few occasions have I ever met the people I am employed to track and follow. And, for all intents and purposes, I could not call Ms. Clarkson a client as contracts and monies had not changed hands, and yet, having conducted the initial meetings and sort of discussed terms, I felt like I'd blown my cover. I wasn't prepared for it, and I realised I had not been professional or thorough enough.

I rarely lose my cool, but I must have appeared visibly shaken, and this did not go unnoticed by Mr. Weston.

Had this been a typical business meeting, my Dictaphone would have been on, and the record of the conversation duly logged, but alas, it was not, and I will have to rely on memory to record the conversation. I am writing these notes thirty-five minutes after our meeting. I have returned to the car. The conversation below is not *wholly* accurate and cannot be used as an accurate statement, only a guide to the manner and tone should a transcript be needed for future reference.

Mr. Weston began the conversation along the lines of,

"Paul, I don't suppose you were expecting to see me. I don't suppose you were even aware that I knew of your existence?" I had to agree. Weston had always seemed something of a mythical being. Now I was sat opposite the man behind the many stories. Being in the presence of a known criminal has never really worried me. He did.

"It seems you know quite a bit about me. It may surprise you to know that I already know quite a bit about you too, Paul." He seemed comfortable using my first name, though this familiarity left me feeling decidedly uncomfortable.

Mr. Weston spoke calmly, but I detected a hint of menace. I was not wrong either.

"Paul, your job can be very rewarding, I have no doubt about that, but it is not without its dangers. If you dig, you must be very careful not to fall into one of the holes you are digging." Was he trying to suggest I was going to be buried alive, or was I getting carried away with the severity of the situation? He didn't leave me guessing for long.

"It was your birthday last night, Paul, wasn't it?" I agreed.

"Your mother likes a drink I hear," That sent a shiver down my spine.

"Your sister was... how can I say this... otherwise engaged, I believe." He was staring into my eyes, but there was no affection. Thank God. I stammered a 'yes' and cursed myself for showing weakness.

"I hear you have been tracking my movements for nearly two months now. I have been tracking yours for about one month and twenty-nine days.

How does it feel to be watched, Paul?"

This was a hypothetical question. I didn't reply.

"Your sister did not attend the meal last night because she was with me, Paul. Well, you have been seeing my sister so I thought, perhaps I should see yours. A very pretty and feisty lady, isn't she?"

Hypothetical or not, I felt the need to reply to this one.

"Are you screwing my sister?" I mumbled.

24

"No more than you are screwing me, Paul" he snapped. "She responds to money and charm. I see my sister is trying to entice you with the same to uncover something about me. I would advise you, Paul, the circles you mix in are within mine. You are not MI5. You are a small-time, lonely private investigator with ideas above his station. You live alone with a cat called Flea, you have limited success with females, and you are over reliant on your mother. Your contacts are small fry and unreliable. Now, I suggest you swim in the small pond, because if you venture into my slipstream again, I will crush you. Mark my words. Enjoy your lonely little holiday with the Krauts, Paul. I suggest you leave this case to gather dust and never dare open it again. My sister is a bitch with an itch. She wants more than she is entitled to. This is not your concern. I trust we can leave the matter here.

Especially if you would like your sister to attend your 38th birthday party."

This conversation has been reproduced as accurately as I can remember. I don't intend to take the matter any further. I am not afraid to admit that I am visibly and mentally shaken. I am also feeling a little humiliated. He may be a wrong 'un, but in many ways he is right. I am no Inspector Clouseau. I am actually feeling quite clueless now. I was beginning to believe my own hype. Feet are now planted firmly back on the ground.

I returned home at 3:45 p.m. and texted my sister. She replied at 7:34 p.m., apologising for missing the meal, and asked for my forgiveness and sympathy. She explained that she had just been dumped by her most recent man. I had never felt happier for her. Or for myself.

Only one letter received today from Mr. Green in Plymouth (Case 4502). I am not in the mood for work anymore today. Letter noted below. I will deal with this tomorrow:

Mr. P Brunskill　　　　　　　*Mr. William Green*
XXXXXXXXXXXXXX　　*XXXXX XXXX XXXXXXX*
XXXXXXXXX　　　　　*XXXXXXXXXXXXXX*
XXXXXXXXXXX　　　　*XXXXXXXX*
XXXXXX　　　　　　　*XXXXX*
XXX XXX

23 January 2019

Dear Sir,

Thank you for your prompt reply and your willingness to take time out of your schedule to take on my proposal. I am unsure how much you will be able to garner from a birth certificate, but I hope it gives a man of your talents a decent starting point. Your fee of £150 will not be fair recompense for the work done and the work required going forward. I am sure we can negotiate a more reasonable rate for your services.
It is so, so important I find my man. You have no idea how much I will appreciate your efforts going forward.

Yours sincerely,

William Green

At least someone appreciates me.

CHAPTER 3
Re-evaluating priorities

28.1.19

The flight was as straightforward as they can be, Mr. Diary. A few hours in the air sat beside an old gentleman who shared my love of cricket and a glass or two of wine. It took my mind off the conversation with Weston for a while. Only a while though. Travelling alone gives you a lot of thinking time. Worrying time too. The conversation had been a private one. A short one. Just him and me. No one else knows what he said, and no one would really be that bothered, but I am. I thought I was doing so well. I thought I was making my mark in the whole private investigator industry. I thought I was the best private investigator in the land. It just shows what I know.

Anonymity is vital in this job. The ability to hunt without being spotted. To blend in. To be a shadow. And all this time, I was being watched, followed and studied myself without a clue. I felt – and still feel – violated. It hurts. I have never really stopped to think how it feels to be traced, investigated and ultimately caught.

I work for the victims. Or so I tell myself. But what of those on the other side? The cheaters, the losers, the drunks and drips. Why do they behave that way in the first place? What drives them? What drives me? It is a sobering thought, and the only conclusions I can draw are my motivations – greed and ego.

I thought I was a good man. Doing a job for a greater good: carrying the flag for those who had lost someone or had someone or something taken from them. I am sure, deep down or a long time ago, this was a motivation, but ego and greed seem to have consumed all, and I am not happy with myself. I am ashamed.

I am now sat in my Munich hotel room jotting these thoughts. I hope by doing so, I will feel better for it. To get it out there and on paper might just cleanse the soul a little.

I am going to put the pen down now and go and explore the city. The bustling streets below suggest there is plenty to see. I will leave you here, Mr. Diary, and go and enjoy the start of the holiday. I can leave you – if only I could leave my conscience here as well.

29.1.19

I should never have entered that wine bar. Solo drinking is bad enough at the best of times, but I seemed to be on a mission last night. Too much of the red. My head is banging. I had planned to visit Augustiner-Keller and the Victuals Market Beergarden today. Hair of the dog or just a walk for the fresh air to clear the head? Let's see how it goes.

Where possible, I am ignoring work throughout this trip, but I must record the content of a voicemail message from Mrs. Fitzgerald, the darling of Rochdale – and that is saying something when you are up against Lisa Stansfield and Gracie Fields.

She has requested another meeting at the earliest opportunity. As beautiful and intriguing as she is, I am in no mood to chat, so I replied with a text to say I am out of the country until 3rd February.

She replied almost instantly to ask to meet on the 4th. I confirmed that this would be fine. No other information at this point. Right, back to the holiday. A long stroll and lots of water. I might just be up for a stein when I reach the gardens. It would be cheeky not to. When in Rome and all that...

30.1.19

Lovely evening last night. What a place – what a size! It was surprisingly mild for the time of year. I was expecting the place to be empty, but there must have been a couple of thousand folk dotted around that vast park. Goodness knows what it must be like in the summer or during the Oktoberfest. I am pleased I went along after all. The BBQ sausage helped banish the remnants of the wine too.

As much as I try, I can't seem to leave work back in England. Another voicemail arrived today from a very angry Julie Clarkson wanting to know why I have refused the very lucrative contract to uncover the shenanigans of her wayward and violent brother. As I am not taking on the work, I have no reason to reply nor record the full transcript of the voicemail, but the gist was that I am a lily-livered, timewasting four letter word beginning with 'T'. I think before the meeting with Mr. Weston, I would have taken her criticism to heart, but I would like to think I am a little more philosophical now. I would rather take the wrath of the bitch than the beast. There may be others out there willing to take the coin, and I wish them well.

I have no intention of seeing Mr. Weston again, and I would rather search the family history of twenty families instead of cashing in on her blood money.

For security reasons, the voicemail is saved and will be recorded on my return in case anything comes back to bite me on the arse.

I am actually starting to feel better about myself now. I am enjoying my holiday. I have a few 'normal' cases to get my teeth into when I get back home. A chance to see Mrs. Fitzgerald and a wander up to Cumbria for that chap from Plymouth. That will be a nice way to ease back into work.

Austria tomorrow. A trip to Salzburg and a *Sound of Music* tour. A nice introduction to the beauty of the Alps. The train journey is meant to be magnificent. Can't wait. Early start, Mr. Diary. We'd better get some sleep. Night-night.

31.1.19

I like making notes as I go along, Mr. Diary. A sentence here, a paragraph there. Making a note when I note something of interest. Thoughts on paper. "Don't bottle your thoughts", my dad once told me. "Get them down on paper. You don't forget them then." A lesson I have heeded ever since.

The train has just rumbled out of Hauptbahnhof Station and is now heading for Austria. You really see the backside of a town when you travel by rail. I often wonder how graffiti artists manage to reach the most unreachable places to spray their tags.

It is everywhere – on the backs of buildings, on railway bridge arches, up lamp posts and halfway up chimneys without any ladders. The culprits are never seen but their 'work' is evident in the side streets and slums of every urban hole.

The cathedrals and castles and monuments and fountains are safely ensconced in the centre with the tourists. It is only the tourists who travel by train who really see the scars of a city that the tourist boards try to keep secret. Munich is no worse or better than any big city on this score. Miles and miles of backstreet neglect flies by as the train gathers speed, but we are soon out of the concrete jungle and back into the fresh air of the Bavarian countryside. The outline of the distant mountains can be seen on occasion as the train snakes through the southern German farmlands.

It only takes a couple of hours to reach Salzburg, but the contrast between the two cities was noticeable straight away. Impressive as it was, Munich didn't take the breath away like Salzburg. The air itself is clearer – fresher. The station was cleaner too. Walking out into the plaza, the peacefulness was obvious. I had crossed a border, and the contrast was stark. The rush and bustle of Munich seemed a million miles away. Horse-drawn carriages plodded by, and taxis and buses waited patiently behind them. No rush. I walked along behind them. I made my way into the Getreidegasse to Mozart Square and the Platzl.

I stopped for a coffee and a seat outside. Again, the weather was unseasonably mild; the sunshine brightened the square and gave off enough heat to encourage me to take off my jacket. Church bells rang out somewhere in the distance, and I watched other customers and shoppers come and go. I was at ease at last. The weight of self-doubt had lifted. I'd been taught a lesson, and now I was ready to start again.

My batteries are well and truly recharged. As strange as it sounds, Mr. Diary, I am looking

31

forward to work again. My priorities have changed, though. I want to help. Of course, I am going to get the usual cases where I will be on surveillance duty, but I plan to be more selective with my cases in future. I am good at what I do. I am meticulous and organised. I am methodical, and I am careful. I lost sight of those qualities, and ego and greed got the better of me. Not anymore. The hills are alive, and I want to sing up. I'd better find the hotel and check in, before I walk in the footsteps of Julie Andrews and Christopher Plummer.

Come on, Mr. Diary, let us pull on our warm woollen mittens and see some of our favourite things.

1.2.19

Well yesterday was bloody brilliant. Just what I needed. What a place! I'm in love. The Mozart trail today. Guided tour. Can't wait. I can't say I know anything about the man or his music, but you cannot come here and not be in awe of Salzburg's favourite son.

I also had another text from Mrs. Fitzgerald. She is looking forward to our meeting. 11 a.m. in *Ey Up's* Coffee Shop in Rochdale town centre. I am looking forward to meeting her again too, but for now, all thoughts of Rochdale need to be shunted out of my head.

Rochdale and Salzburg should not be sharing my headspace. The two should never be brought together or used in the same sentence again.

Whatever next? Hull and Venice, Rome and Wigan. Would Mozart have become Mozart if he had been born and brought up in Skegness? Would he have composed work of breathtaking genius had he been reared in Oldham? I fear not, and I needn't fear.

He is here - in this beautiful city, and I must sign off now and go and follow in his footsteps.

2.2.19

My last full day of the trip, and what a day it has been. A trip up to Fortress Hohensalzburg, a jaunt around the cathedral and a pleasant amble through the Mirabell Palace. Breathtaking in every direction. The adjectives I would use to describe the place – beautiful, white, clean and peaceful – are hardly words of wonder, but they sum up the place perfectly.

I am sure there are many more superlatives that could be attributed to such a glorious city and its surrounding area, but these will do for me. Would I come again? In a heartbeat. I am so pleased I chose Austria over the other options available to me. I am sure the other city breaks have much to offer too, but the calm and tranquillity here has been like a shot in the arm for me and just what I needed. I feel at one with nature – chilled to the soul.

The nearby Alps have looked down on me and sheltered me from all the stresses and strains of the world. This is so different from home. So different. I couldn't have asked for more. Salzburg – I have really fallen for you.

Back to Munich tomorrow and the flight back to rainy Manchester. Have I checked the weather forecast? I don't need to.

This trip has certainly stoked a fire in my belly to travel and experience other cultures. We get lost in our own worlds and forget there is a bigger one out there. This time tomorrow I will be thirty thousand feet up in the air and 774.2 miles away from where I am now. I needed this. Thank you, Germany. Thank you, Austria. I have found myself again.

3.2.19

Up early this morning and a fond farewell to my German hosts, Jonas and Mila Fischer. How their place ever found its way onto an internet search history is a mystery. *Trip Advisor* recommendations and a highly commended status by three of the leading accommodation websites lured me to this Munich backstreet. Hotel Lisa (I didn't ask who Lisa was) was its name and, with the red lamp blazing above their front door, I really did have to wonder what their game was.

The entrance was neither grand nor inviting, but after hours of travelling, I didn't really want to have to go looking for other places to lay my head. Any initial fears evaporated when Jonas opened the door and invited me in. He welcomed me like the son he hadn't seen for twenty years. No handshake here. A firm embrace and a smile that could melt the hardest of hearts. A complimentary glass of beer helped too. His own brew, I later found out.

He led me into what I can only imagine was his own living room, he invited me to sit by the fire. His English was superb – it always shames me that I cannot converse in any other language other than my own. I had only been in the place ten minutes and here I was, sat on his sofa in front of a roaring log fire, drinking his beer, watching football on his TV. I hadn't even seen my room at this point. Shortly after, I was introduced to his wife, Mila. It was hard to put an age on the couple, but I would guess they were at least a decade over the usual retirement age.

Mila greeted me in much the same way as her husband and insisted I join them for supper. The smells from the nearby kitchen were intoxicating. How could I say no, Mr. Diary?

The food – some kind of goulash – was mouth-watering. Fresh, home-cooked bread, more beer and a bottle of red wine too. I can't even remember introducing myself as a guest, but they must have been expecting me, and the suitcase would have been a giveaway anyway. By the time I was eventually shown my room, my head was spinning, and I knew more about the Fischer's than I knew about my own family.

My room was basic but homely and welcoming. The furniture, carpets, curtains and upholstery were dated but scrupulously clean, and it was as warm and welcoming as the people who called this place home. It didn't feel like a hotel at all. Both Jonas and Mila were genuinely interested in me and my life. This wasn't false customer service or fake fawning over me. They were genuine, loving, caring people. You can keep your free Wi-Fi, complimentary mints and folded swan serviettes – this was my kind of place.

My two nights here - split by the other two in Salzburg - were first class. Five-star without the glitz and glamour. I sat with the pair for a coffee in their living room before I made my way to the train station and the journey back. I was their only guest that week. February was always a quiet time, I was told. They only had three rooms to let anyway, so to have a third of the rooms occupied was not a shabby return at this time of year, Mila joked. We exchanged phone numbers and addresses. I didn't bother with email - they struck me as writers not typers - and we promised to stay in touch. I hope we do. I hope I do.

We parted with another embrace and handshake which bookended my visit just nicely. I write this on the train back towards the airport and home. This will be my sign-off for the day. I think I will be ready to crash out and go straight to sleep when I eventually navigate my way through two airports, car parks and the slow-moving motorways on the way back home. The journey takes nearly as long as the holiday.

Thank you, Jonas and Mila. Thank you, Germany, once again. Normality looms. Goodnight, Mr. Diary.

4.2.19

No time for rest and recuperation. The flat was as I left it apart from a mountain of post which I will log after my morning meeting with Mrs. Fitzgerald. It is only about fifteen miles to Rochdale, and it is hardly New York, so I don't need to set off much before 10:30am.

I am quite laid back about this one.

She is a nice, genuine lady with an itch needing to be scratched. For all, she is an attractive lady – sweet and warm too – I am not attracted to her, but I did enjoy her company. I think today will be the same. I don't want to be the one that brings her bad news, but I must put on my professional head and deliver any news I get with efficiency and honesty without emotion. She is seeking information. How she deals with that information is her business. I am sure I never used to overthink these things before. I must have softened. I need to get my head back into the job. The holiday is in the past now. I must not leave it so long before the next one though.

Right, have I got what I need? You, my diary, are coming, of course, along with Dictaphone, notepad and pen. Spare pen just in case other runs out. Camera; you just never know when an opportunity presents itself to gather some evidence.

Here we go then. Quick shower and a trip to *Ey Up's* in Rochdale. What a way to spend a Monday morning.

P.M. – It is now 1:00 p.m. and I make these notes sat outside The Cemetery Pub on the outskirts of Rochdale.

Ey Up's was little more than a greasy spoon but served its purpose, and the booths gave Mrs. Fitzgerald the privacy she obviously needed. She looked tired and drained. The strain is clearly getting to her, and she wants this matter put to bed as soon as possible, which is understandable. I won't milk this one. She deserves a quick resolution, and I don't think it will be too hard to reach one. Her husband leads a fairly normal and predictable life, and any changes to his routine will be quick to identify. His work start and end times are set; his routes to and from work are straightforward; his pattern of behaviour is regular; and his hobbies and interests are all within a three-mile radius, so any wandering out of this range will deserve further investigation.

She explained that his movements have deviated from the norm over the last three months. He has been later coming home from work, and he has taken to cycling on a weekend – a hobby he has shown no interest in previously. This on its own is

37

not strange, but when people behave out of character quite suddenly, there is usually a reason why.

His name is Adam Fitzgerald. A civil servant in the local council offices. Not on a bad wage. Good holidays. Boring job. All the elements of a man looking for a spark to reignite his dull existence. Monotony is no good for monogamy, as I have found out after years in this job.

I explained my rates to her, and she was happy to pay. I estimated a cost of around £1,500 for no more than two weeks' work. I reckon I could crack this one within a week, but it is always best to give yourself extra time.

Post time. Bills, of course. Virgin Broadband, BT Broadband, SKY Broadband. Pizza shops leaflets, kebab shop takeaway flyers. Political party leaflets. Even a business card from some guy looking to tarmac my drive. I don't even have a drive!

Only one work-related letter. I will add it to the file and begin work on this one tomorrow. Mr. Green from Plymouth. There could be more work in this than I first thought.

Mr. P. Brunskill   Mr. William Green
XXXXXXXXXXXXXX   XXXXX XXXX XXXXXXX
XXXXXXXXX   XXXXXXXXXXXXXX
XXXXXXXXXXX   XXXXXXXX
XXXXXX   XXXXX
XXX XXX

23 January 2019

Dear Mr. Brunskill,

If you are ready to proceed with this search, then I am too. I trust you have had time to check out the birth certificate. Unfortunately, I have little more to offer you than this. It should at least give you a start and, with your skills and talents, I am sure you can unearth more than I ever could.

I have set aside an amount that I hope will cover your expenses for this job, but this can be increased should the work demand it. I would be obliged if you could notify me weekly of progress, with your invoice for wages. I will, of course, in addition, reimburse you for any expenses accrued (e.g., travel, hotel costs etc.).

Forgive my previous letters. I know they must have appeared vague. I should have been more explicit, but I really wasn't sure I was doing the right thing until now.

I want you to find a man.

I want you to find everything you can about him and his life. From his first days on earth up to his most recent. I want you to find out about his family, his school, his work and his relationships. Who he is? What he is? Why is he?

I would be obliged if you could complete the work at your earliest convenience and give me all you have no later than the end of April. I will explain why nearer the time.

Obviously, the more you find, the more you earn.

Thank you Mr. Brunskill. I know this is an unusual request. I am sorry I cannot offer you any further information, but the birth certificate is the only document I have to go from.

I look forward to hearing from you soon.

Yours sincerely,

William Green

Jackpot. An almost open cheque book. You don't often get a job like this. Real investigation. Not just sitting in a van and eating soup from a Tupperware bowl. Something to get my teeth into.

I confess, Mr. Diary, I did not even look at the birth certificate when it was first sent. It was a job for after the holidays.

Here it is. Not much to go from. An old one. Handwritten. At least I have a starting point. Ernest Grimshaw. Date of birth: 1st March 1929. Place of birth: Greenbank Farm, Prospect, Cumbria.

Father: David Grimshaw. Mother: Mabel Grimshaw. Home birth. And that is that. No more to go on.

Ernest Grimshaw – I am coming to find you.

CHAPTER 4
The search for a man

5.2.19

Two jobs had my attention. The others could either be accessed online or later in the week. Or into next.

I thought it would be a good idea to spend two days on the Rochdale job before travelling up to West Cumbria on the Green case. I've booked into a hotel near Wigton on the Thursday night. According to the map and an internet search, it is a small market town about five to ten miles from the village of Prospect.

On the birth certificate it simply mentions a home birth in 1929. The address is given, but it is unlikely that I can reveal anything at the actual house or farm itself. It is a starting point. Cover every point and never turn your back on any possibility – even more so when someone is paying for the hotel. My mother has even offered to take in Flea. That will save a few pounds. That cattery is getting more and more expensive.

I will take the van to Rochdale today. The trusty van. The old bugger has been a good servant to me. I have lost count of the number of nights I have lost sleep on his floor. A sleeping bag and a mattress thinner than a wafer is not conducive to a good rest, but I suppose, I was never in it to rest. Anonymity of the van was as important as anonymity for me. All white, no adverts or garage contacts. A registration plate with serial numbers covered. No additional features or add-ons. Everything factory fitted. No stickers. Kept clean to avoid any scamp adding their own 'dirty finger graffiti'. I could not compromise myself and risk driving around in a van that could be considered recognisable with a 'wash me now' scar on the back door.

Never leave or park it in the same place for more than two hours either. Any more than that draws attention.

My destination this morning is Drake Street. I have photos and timings. She has already done a lot of my work for me. Watch him. Back at 11:30 a.m. to 1:00 p.m. to watch where he goes for lunch and with whom.

After that, kill a few hours and back for 4 p.m. and follow him home – or wherever he goes.

Voicemail from Mrs. Fitzgerald at 10:15 a.m. Mr. F. has a purple lunchbox apparently. Shouldn't be hard to spot on the way in to work.

Meanwhile, I have been thinking about Mr. Green. Who is he? What is his relationship with Mr. Grimshaw? The man is ninety. Son-in-law maybe? Grandson? What is he so keen to find? Why is he prepared to find out about someone he seems to have no connection with? Has he got the money? I suppose an element of this job is based on trust. Work first, pay later. That is the way it has always been, and to be fair, in all these years, I have yet to have any unpaid invoices.

Instinct again; he seems genuine. He is articulate, and I have his address and details should I ever need to seek him out, which I don't think I will need to do.

I have been on the hunt for missing people for a while now, but I normally have more to go on. A birth certificate pre-NHS is always harder to unravel. Records are usually incomplete or sporadic, and the authenticity is often questionable. The benefits of the smaller communities are the other sources of information that are available. Local pub competition winners, community clubs or Working Men's Institutes, not to mention church records, employment histories and, in the case of farms, animal ownership records.

There will be plenty of other places to investigate, I'm sure.

That is for later. Rochdale, here I come.

10:30 p.m.

A last diary entry of the day. I have been at this job long enough now to realise that every observation could be the one that cracks the case, but there seemed to be little of interest today. All very routine. If he is having an affair, he wasn't at it today – or if he was, it was through texting or emailing. He certainly didn't meet anybody to arouse suspicion (or anything else). I know I am on a metre with this job. Mrs. Fitzgerald isn't made of money, and the surveillance can only last so long. I need to choose my lookouts carefully. Although vital, I doubt Mrs. F. would be too happy to rack up a bill without any kind of news, and that is exactly what we seemed to have today. He was easily identified on the way in. The purple lunchbox was very noticeable, and her photos and descriptions were very clear too. I know my man. Tall but not confident in his own body. Walks with a stoop. A nervous, shy-looking man. He opened the door to let somebody in and ended up letting eight more in without the slightest look of incredulity. Non-confrontational. Non-aggressive. Only two seemed to acknowledge and thank him. Was the choice of a purple lunchbox his? Does it add colour to his life? Does it make him stand out?

His work clothes didn't stand out either. Smart in a suit but not worn with any formal power trip. He was just a middle-aged man in an averagely paid job in a drab town. I almost felt sorry for him. And then there is the job.

I returned to watch and follow at lunchtime, but this proved to be futile in the main. I even had to pay for a car park ticket. He sat and ate lunch on a park bench near the river. He didn't use his phone once. He just sat there staring. Eating. *Staring.* I could note down exactly what he ate but that would be a waste of ink and won't help me solve anything.

Although it did remind me to pick up some cheese on the way home.

At the end of the day, he left on time with three other men. I thought it had the makings of an evening drinking session (I hoped not as I wanted to get home), but, thankfully, the four soon went their separate ways, and Mr. Fitzgerald simply boarded his bus home. Following a bus is never as straightforward as you might think. So many stops and starts and trying to work out who has got on or off and who is sat with whom, but it soon became apparent that there was nothing unusual to see here either. I sat about fifty metres back from their house. He got off the bus, walked the short distance to the front door, took out his key and went inside. He was on time. The only noticeable difference was the lunchbox. He didn't have it with him. I presumed he had left it at work. Still, he won't be hard to spot tomorrow. Average height, average dresser, average looks and average daily routine. In this job, you are always on the lookout for the little differences. Everyone seems to have them.

This chap doesn't seem to be the secretive or elusive type. His routine is so *routine*. It will be so easy to spot even the slightest change in his behaviour, thus making him the easiest man in the world to follow.

Goodnight, Mr. Diary. Not exactly an eventful day. Bed beckons.

6.2.19

Day two in Rochdale. By the time my surveillance ends, I will have spent more time in Rochdale than I did in Munich. I know where I would rather be, but this pays the bills. It certainly grounds you, this job.

Rochdale – tower blocks and tarts, chavs and charity shops. In recent years, the town has been in the news for all the wrong reasons, but, if I am honest, I cannot see much good news coming out of the place. Grey skies hang over the town forming part of its DNA. "It is hard to cope when you have no hope", as my father used to say. Well, there isn't much in the way of hope here. And there doesn't seem to be much hope finding Mr Fitzgerald's Achilles heel either. The man is as bland as magnolia paint.

Perhaps I am being a bit too harsh on the place – and him. Nowhere looks great in the drizzle, and maybe I have let Mrs. Fitzgerald's suspicions about her husband taint my own views. It hasn't taken the cynic in me a long time to return to the surface. I must try to supress it. Who am I to judge anyone? I am here to do a job.

Mr. F.'s journey to work was pretty much the same as yesterday, other than the fact he did not leave the building for lunch. The purple lunch box must have been left at work the previous day as he had it in his hand on the way home. It comes to something when spotting a purple lunchbox is the highlight of a day's surveillance.

He left work on time, boarded the same bus home as the day before and entered the house at pretty much the same time as yesterday.

I don't really want to waste my time (and her money) repeating the exercise Thursday and Friday. I will contact her when I return home and see where we go from here. I need to get up to Cumbria soon, but I hate leaving loose ends. Something is not quite right about this one.

9:00 p.m. – Spoke briefly with Mrs. F. We agreed to follow Saturday afternoon and evening. She is away at her sister's place in Wigan, and she feels he might just take advantage of her absence then. She doesn't want to give up and is convinced that her suspicions are correct. She is also aware of her budget and does not want to exceed the amount discussed. I can understand that – especially when all the work carried out so far has revealed nothing of note. For her to take this step in the first place is a brave move, and I am always honest with the client. If I think I am just chasing shadows, I won't milk it. We agreed to go for Saturday and review everything on Sunday evening. If we are no further forward by then, I will suggest closure on the case.

For her sake, I hope we get to the bottom of this – good or bad.

If I do not unearth anything, then she will have to choose an alternative approach. There are no guarantees in this job, and she understands that. I don't like to leave a job incomplete, but as nice as she is, this is my job. I need to remain professional throughout. Emotionless.

A trip up to Cumbria beckons tomorrow. A nice change and a new case.

7.2.19

An early start, Mr. Diary. As soon as I finish this breakfast and pack an overnight bag, you and I are heading north. It is pitch-black outside, and it will be pitch-black at 4 p.m. too. I hate winter days. I need to make the most of the daylight hours while I am up there. It is not the best time of year to be tackling narrow country roads and farm tracks, but the van should be able to cope with it. The weather forecast is not great – sleet and snow. In fact, the last few days have been pretty much the same. I have absolutely no idea what I am going to find there – if anything – but I need to make the most of the light. I don't expect the weather, or the people, will be very inviting on days like this. I know I wouldn't be.

Some stranger knocking on your door asking questions about a man who was born there nearly a century ago. I know I am going to the countryside, but the term 'needle in a haystack' springs to mind. I need to find a start – a foothold. Something or someone to help open a few doors. Mr. Green seems happy to pay, but he will want something back for his money.

At this time, I should beat all the morning traffic and be there by around 9:00 a.m., all being well. Once you pass Lancaster, there isn't much on the road other than tractors and sheep. The Greenhill Hotel on the outskirts of Wigton is my destination. A nice spot by the looks of it. On a main road too. It boasts 'A beautiful, two-hundred-year-old building set in charming gardens and only eleven miles from the Lake District National Park'.

The pictures certainly look nice. Evening meal on site too. Lovely.

It is £90 a night – I'd better make sure I get that back in my account ASAP. I will file an expenses and wages invoice on my return home. I need to make sure this guy is good for the money before I embark on a long-term project.

Right, time to eat up, pack up and get out.

Another update later when I reach Greenhills. Prospect is about five miles away from the hotel. I wonder what my prospects of finding Mr. Grimshaw are.

10:00 a.m.

Room 6, Greenhills Hotel, Wigton, Cumbria. A lovely, smooth journey to justify my decision to set off not long after the milkmen start their rounds. Most of the journey was spent driving in the dark, and apart from a service station stop for a pee and a coffee near the Lancashire/Cumbria border, the trip was without incident. There is something very satisfying about leaving the city behind and heading into the countryside. I am by no means a spiritual kind of chap, but even I can feel an aura of peace and tranquillity when the pace of life slows. And what a countryside it is. Less than five miles off the motorway and the jagged outlines of the mountain tops tower up to greet you.

There is a job to do here, but it doesn't feel like work. I won't be camping out in my transit van here for hours on end. I have no idea who I am looking for or what I might find, but I will be doing it from the base of a comfortable hotel with a hot meal inside me, all paid for by a man I have never met two hundred and fifty miles away.

The room is lovely. Clean, welcoming, fresh. Here I am, sprawled on a king-sized bed debating whether or not to spend an hour in the bath or get on with the task in hand. I calculate that I have approximately six hours of daylight in which to gather information, investigate and probe, and I shouldn't really waste this time lounging around.

Sod it. I can't resist. I can't resist a soak. It looks so inviting. I can gather my thoughts and make a plan while I am in the tub. If need be, I can work an extra hour in the dark. They have even provided a decent standard of bubble bath. The perfect start to the day.

12:00 noon

Plan of action for day
1 – paper trail.
Visit Prospect. Locate the family house. Photographs to be taken for evidence of any remaining building related to Mr. Grimshaw (e.g., family home, farm, local amenities, pubs, church/cemetery etc.)
Is Mr. Green keeping a scrap book? If he is, what would he want in it?
Check records. Church, library, schools, social media groups of area. Seek out any local historian or community groups for further information.

Identify long-standing sports and social clubs and when they were founded. Role of Honour, Players of the Year, committee members etc.

Return to hotel for updates and evening meal. Lamb looks delicious. I might even treat myself to a few drinks and a dessert, on expenses of course. If only all the jobs were like this one. Update as I go along...

1:30 p.m.

A promising if somewhat unusual start. I cannot say the same about the weather – heavy showers throughout.

Prospect is a strange place. Not really what I expected. A small village just off the main road to West Cumbria. A pub, a small shop/post office, a couple of workshops and a smattering of different types of dwellings. Perhaps because of the weather, it was made to look even bleaker than usual, but it was not the idyllic settlement I had in mind on the fringes of the Lake District. Very much a working-class area with a mismatch of structures surrounded by miles and miles of farmland.

I decided to start with the farm and the birthplace. It was not what I expected to find. Greenbank had functioned as a farm since 1798, according to Google, and is still running as one today. Google can only tell you so much, so a visit to The Miner's Arms, the village's only public house, proved to be worthwhile. From the outside, the place did not look very welcoming, but the warmth of the greeting inside soon lightened the mood. On entering, I was greeted by Stella, an Old English sheepdog, and Sheila (anything but a dog) behind the bar. I wanted to tickle the tummy of both, but I settled for Stella on this occasion.

I sat on a stool beside the bar, ordered a pint and explained why I was in the area. Sheila leaned in and listened intently. So did the other locals gathered around the bar. More on them later.

They seemed fascinated by what I had to say – excited even. I suppose I was expecting a degree of secrecy and reserve - or even suspicion, but they couldn't have been more accommodating and helpful. Perhaps this interlude was a flicker of excitement on a drab day. Maybe a romanticised notion of what a private investigator does. Either way, their enthusiasm and eagerness to help was very welcome.

When I explained what was being asked of me, they began to tell me what they already knew about the farm and who, locally, could help me find what I was looking for.

Greenbank was now run and managed by Keith Brockbank and family. I was informed that he was a cantankerous bastard in the morning, a tight bastard when it came to buying a round and a drunken, friendly bastard in the evening. For a triple bastard they did speak highly of him, though, and his family too. But they had only been on the farm since 2010. They purchased the holding from Robert Robertson – or Bob Bob, as he was affectionately known. He owned the farm for nearly twenty years before the Brockbank's took over.

A serial womaniser and gambler by all accounts. No one could understand the former as, to quote my new friend 'Ronnie', he had "a face like Les Dawson sucking on a lemon".

"He must have had other qualities." Sheila suggested. This caused a ripple of laughter around the bar.

Before Bob owned it, the place was in the hands of a lovely old couple called Harold and Clara Papworth. They had Greenbank for over twenty years, and only old age, and their subsequent death, forced the sale.

This would have taken us back to the 1970s. Mr. Grimshaw would have been about forty at the time. I purposefully did not ask them to tell me about him, if they had anything at all to tell. They were enjoying filling me in on the farm's history, and I was more than happy to listen to their tales. It seemed like they were leading me somewhere, but I didn't know where. My Dictaphone was on all the time. I didn't want to miss a trick.

Alf (what a great name), clearly the oldest around the bar by some considerable margin, chipped in next.

"Harold bought the place from Billy Turnbull," he informed us. "Bill was a nice man. Kept himself to himself though. Never married. Not sure how long he had it for, but it must have been a decade at least. Before him, it sat empty for a while. Derelict. Me and the lads used to play up there as boys. The grounds were lying empty – no doors and windows. Nowt inside at all. I must have been about ten at the time. It was our den.

Our haunted house. Our hideaway. Before Billy, it was empty for as long as I can remember. I was born in 1944 so I am guessing it had been vacant since not too long after the war – early '50s maybe - before Billy stepped in to bring it up to scratch."

At this point, I was estimating the farm to have been lying in a state of disrepair since approximately 1945. My man would have only been sixteen at this point. The memory trail ended there.

I decided to ask the question after all.

"Do you know Ernest Grimshaw?" I asked. They all nodded and smiled.

"Aye, son," said Alf. "Ernie lives in the bungalow next to the farmhouse. Give him a knock. He should be in."

BINGO – this was proving to be easier than I imagined.

I promised to catch up with them later in the afternoon after I had met with Ernie and have another drink with them. I felt at that point I needed to speak with Ernie first out of courtesy before gleaning more from the locals behind his back.

And here I am. Sat in the car outside Greenbank Farm and Greenbank Cottage, the bungalow next door. I hope he is willing to talk. If he is, it could simply be a case of a couple of interviews and the job is done. That's the notes written up, Mr Diary.

I shall update again after this visit then nip back into The Miner's Arms. I'm guessing there will be a lot to report back on here, so I will update you again this evening.

I have found my man!

5:30 p.m.

Back at the hotel. By the time I return to Lancashire I will have quite a dossier on Mr. Ernie Grimshaw and, despite the fact that I started off with only a copy of a birth certificate of a man born

53

ninety years ago, I have done pretty bloody well, even if I do say so myself.

Two trips to a pub and one to a bungalow half a mile down the road, and I have a sizeable file to send to Mr. Green. I will catalogue it all and work out a price for the work done. Considering it has only taken two days of my time and a bit of prep work, I can't charge too much, but I do have a lot of information to send. That will be reflected in the price.

I will update you now, Mr Diary, and then enjoy a nice evening meal and a few drinks to celebrate. Now, where shall I begin? The knock on the door of the bungalow, I think.

It was pouring down again when I approached the house. A slight overhang offered some protection from the rain while I waited for an answer. A man of ninety does not move at pace, and I didn't expect him to open the door quickly. Sure enough, there was the shuffle to the door then a shuffle back to a table to get the key, then a shuffle back to the door again with a muffled apology, and then it opened.

He was taller than I had expected. Nearly six feet tall. He invited me in out of the rain without even asking who I was or why I was there. This was incredibly trusting, but that is country folk for you.

I followed him into the living room, and he offered me a seat. I was not used to such hospitality – twice in one day. You wouldn't get that where I come from.

I didn't really know how to approach it, so I told him the truth. Why I was there and who had sent me. I expected him to be on the back foot or curious as to who was asking about him but, if he was worried, he didn't show it.

"I am an old man," he told me. "I have nothing to hide."

I explained that I knew nothing of Mr. Green other than his request for information.

Mr. Grimshaw just chuckled and told me not to worry – it was maybe a long-lost relative wanting to give him money and, if it was a long-lost relative looking for money, he could bugger off as he didn't have any. He said he didn't know anyone called Green anyway.

I explained that, as the request was a little vague, he could just tell me whatever he wanted. A little of his life and where he grew up. Perhaps a little about his family and where he went to school/worked/lived, etc. He seemed more than happy to share this information on the Dictaphone too. He was quietly spoken and put me at ease straight away. I was meant to be doing that for him.

He told me about his family – his wife. How he lost his wife after a long battle with cancer and how, while they had no children themselves, he was close to two nieces who now live abroad. No regrets though. His nieces keep in touch over the phone, and they have their own lives to live now which he shares, albeit from a distance. He said he isn't afraid of being on his own. He likes his own company. He keeps pigeons out the back, and the neighbours visit often. As for work, he spent most of his adult life helping on the farm with David and Mabel. There were a few years later on working down the pit, but it was never something he enjoyed. Too tall for all that back-breaking work in small spaces, he said. He much preferred the fresh air. He went to school in the nearby town of Aspatria and met his soon-to-be wife there – Sarah.

The two of them made their first home

together in one of the terraces near the pub. It was basic and small, and they didn't have much other than each other. The usual tale. Nothing out of the ordinary. A nice man with a normal background in a close-knit community. There's a bit more information gathered for Mr. Green.

We talked some more over a coffee, and he told me to come back any time, and he would try and remember some more. He said he enjoyed sharing with me. I felt he enjoyed the company as much as anything, and he was a pleasure to listen to.

By the time I left, I was keen to get back to the pub and speak with the locals again for their stories and opinions. They were bound to have a few tales to put a bit of meat on the bones of this nice but fairly ordinary story. They didn't let me down either.

The general consensus was that Ernie was a nice man. A humble man. A 'friends with anyone' type of guy.

Those gathered around the bar were all considerably younger than Alf (I'd guess mid-fifties/early sixties), but even he had some way to go to catch Ernie.

Through the conversation, I later found out that Alf was seventy-eight. He must only have been a boy himself when Ernie was in his teens, so he was not in the same friendship group and did not really have much more to relate than the others, other than tales of hanging around with the older lads which, in this sparse area, did not result in much more than high jinks and adolescent dares.

Alf did not recall much at all from these days and did not get to know Ernie until much later. He remembered that Ernie was a fast runner, a great tree climber and a decent student – good enough to go to university but did not have means to do so. He remembered Ernie being quite shy around girls (and then women), and he 'spoke a bit funny'. The two could have been connected; a speech impediment or stutter can paralyse a young person looking to find their place in the hierarchy with their peers.

The others told tales of growing up, but few of them involved Ernie – he was much older than them and just another resident in the village.

To sum up, he was kind-hearted, athletic, studious and amiable. He was celebrated in the village for his skills as a gardener, crown green bowler, a cricket umpire and crossword specialist. He was a friend to everyone without getting too close to them. In many ways, a social loner but by no means a recluse.

A lovely profile of a lovely man.

I flirted with Sheila over a bag of nuts and a pint of lemonade but eased off when I found out her husband was in Afghanistan on secondment. I played darts with the Mickleson brothers. I discussed the art of making scarecrows with Big Sam, and I played cards with Tom and Barbara. A jolly good afternoon on the job.

I will go back to see Ernie in the morning to see if he has anything more to add before returning to Lancashire. From there, I will write up a profile for Mr. Green with all information gathered – including photographs and copies of documents (if any) I can collect as evidence. I will also ensure I get a few photographs of Ernie himself – now and in years gone by – and generate an invoice for work done.

I did not expect to get so much so quickly. If he is happy with my findings, I will conclude the case.

I will then go to work on the Mrs. F. case over the weekend and, all being well, conclude that by Sunday evening. The hunt for new work will commence then, but for now, Mr. Diary, I am going to head off downstairs and try the roast lamb and local ales.

No rush in the morning. Mr. Grimshaw isn't going anywhere, and I can saunter back at my own pace. What a lovely way to end a very productive day.

8.2.19.

10:30 a.m.

This must be the closest thing to heaven I have had for quite some time. A glorious meal, last night with a few pints of beer and a sleep in the most comfortable bed I have ever slept in. It was like how I would imagine lying on a cloud to be. If I ever have reason to come to Cumbria again, I will certainly seek out this place.

The breakfast just topped it off. I don't think I will eat for a week now. I have only been here twenty-four hours, and I feel utterly refreshed.

I have jotted a few questions down for Mr. Grimshaw and will log his answers after the visit, before I return back down the road. It shouldn't take more than an hour, so I should be on the road by mid-afternoon and avoid the worst of the traffic.

4:15 p.m.

A little later than planned, but I did not take into account the slowness of old folk, nor their willingness to put the kettle on every five minutes. Still, it was another pleasant visit with a very nice man. When his time comes to shuffle off this earth, people will only have nice things to say about him. I wouldn't mind that as my epitaph – Paul Brunskill, born in May 1974, died... (hopefully, not for a few years yet), husband of Sheila from the Miners' Arms – *He was a very nice man.*

By the time we eventually sat on the sofa to talk, I was already halfway through my second coffee and a generous helping of Victoria sponge cake.

We recapped on yesterday – Dictaphone recording to ensure no inaccuracies – and I asked him if he wouldn't mind answering a few questions to pad out my profile to send to Mr. Green. He was more than happy to help.

The questions and answers are logged below. Audio files will be saved on the home computer to back up written content.

Me: "Can you tell me about your early life on the farm?"

Ernie*: "We were an ordinary family, nowt special. Mabel and David were loving and kind. We didn't have many possessions. Farming didn't make us a lot of money by any means, but we got by. My brother and I were close. I worked for many years on the farm – before school and after. It never felt like a chore though, and David was great with me."*

59

Me: "Were you a close family?"

Ernie: *"Very. We looked after each other, and I don't recall many arguments growing up. We appreciated each other. Very much so."*

Me: "How did you meet Sarah, your wife?"

Ernie: *"We met at a dance in Wigton. 'Young Farmers' Night', I seem to recall. She was radiant. I fell for her straight away. She was so bonny. I knew that first night that she was the one for me. I don't think she felt the same. I was hopelessly shy and couldn't approach her in the way many of the other boys could. Thankfully, my friend approached her on my behalf. It nearly knocked me off my stool when she agreed to dance with me. I was so nervous. I could barely speak at first. I had never been to the town before, let alone a dance."*

Me: "How old were you when you met her? Married her?"

Ernie: *"It was 1950 when we met, and we courted for nearly two years before tying the knot. She was a beauty that day – an angel. I remember thinking 'You have fallen on your feet, my boy. You will never find a lady as good as this girl.' We had many good years together. We spoilt our nieces as though they were our own children. It is a shame they don't live closer. I would love to see them more. They remind me very much of my darling Sarah. They had many of her traits. Bright, daring, adventurous. Living life to the full. We do chat often, but they have their own families and lives. I am too old to go gallivanting around the globe. I love them* and they love me. That is good enough. Good enough."

Me: "Did you ever feel like settling down again after Sarah passed away?"

Ernie: *"No. Never. She was the only one for me. I never felt the urge to seek out someone else. I was lucky to have had her. We had nearly forty years together. Nobody else could follow that. No. Sarah was the only girl for me. Cancer is a cruel illness. It killed part of me too."*

Me: "Have you always lived here?"

Ernie: *"My life started here, and it will end here too. It is only a little world, I know, but I love it around here. I feel very settled here."*

Me: "What happened to your brother? (You said you two were very close.)"

Ernie: *"We were. A tremendous bond grew between us. He was my rock. He was older than me."*
Me: "Was?"

Ernie: *"We were parted when we were just young men. We lost contact before we were twenty. It was the saddest time in my life."*

Me: "Have you no idea what happened to him?"

Ernie: *"No. We lost contact with him. We hoped he would get in touch, but he never did. We mourned him. It still aches when I think about him."*

Me: "Can you tell me about any of your life achievements/qualifications/awards etc.?"

Ernie: *"Not much to report to be honest with you. No school qualifications to call upon. A few gardening awards and scouts' badges, but it doesn't amount to much. My greatest achievement was a long and happy marriage."*

Me: "Do you have any regrets in life?"
(Long pause)

Ernie: *"No..."*

At this point he looked up at me and smiled. It was time to go. He didn't have more to tell me. The questions about his brother and the passing of his wife clearly triggered memories he did not want to share with a stranger, and I understood that. I wasn't there to grill him. I was there to gather information. It was time to leave him in peace.

I left him my card and contact details. He didn't have a mobile or an email address, but at least he could contact me if he wanted to. I took his details too, just in case.

We shook hands and wished each other well. He was an old man living out his end days in the place he loved so much. He had spent his whole life here in this unremarkable place and yet, it suited him. He was an unremarkable old man – but a very nice one at that.

6:30 p.m.

The journey had given me plenty of thinking time. Maybe it was just the detective in me, but I felt something wasn't quite right. All the way back I had nagging doubts. I tried to recall everything that had been said and by whom. I have been through my notes and tried to digest it all. Nothing evidential to support this odd feeling of disquiet. I went over it all again to assure myself that I hadn't overlooked something important. I don't want to find that I have done a half-cocked job for Mr. Green.

Who knows? He might know more himself and be testing me.

So, once more, Mr. Grimshaw, no qualifications for a bright man. That got me thinking about school. He never mentioned school. And then there was the dance at Wigton. It was his first time in the town – aged, what, 21? Married two years later at 23? Twenty-one years of living in the same area and not once did he venture into the nearest big town. His story didn't tally either. Now then, in our first chat he said to me that he met Sarah at school in Aspatria – five miles or so from Wigton. He also said he worked on the farm most of his adult life, but Alf told me the farm was lying empty until Billy Turnbull took it over circa 1950. I know memory can play tricks, but surely nothing as significant as where you met your wife-to-be. Especially when she is such an important part of your life.

And David and Mabel? Not Mam and Dad. And what happened to them? Even Alf couldn't recall the family before Billy's ownership.

The brother. He didn't say what happened to him. His prerogative, of course, but no mention of their parting of ways. He didn't mention a death like he did with his wife. Something is not right. I will call him. Just to satisfy my own inner thoughts, clarify his responses before reporting anything to Mr. Green.

6:50 p.m.

No answer. I left a message on his answering machine. I hope he knows how to use it. Just a few questions. Polite, courteous. I wasn't expecting a reply. I wasn't expecting him to listen to it or call back. But he did.

Mr. Diary, where do I go from here?

A voicemail message was left on my mobile when I was out of the room. Recording has been saved. Message below:

"Hello, Mr. Brunskill. I heard your message and thought for a while about whether or not I should call you. I decided to. It could be my last opportunity to be true to myself at last and feel peace before my life ends. Please call me when you get this message."

Bloody hell. What can this be now? I will call him back right away and update you as soon as we have finished talking.

7:15 p.m.

Mr. Diary, it looks like I am off back up to Cumbria sooner than anticipated. Ernie Grimshaw wants to talk to me again as soon as possible.

64

He told me this over the telephone, but no more.

*"David and Mabel were not my parents. Not blood parents anyway. I moved to the farm when I was eighteen. I haven't got a blood brother. Not anymore. David and Mabel have a son... had a son. He was a brother to me. The best. I owe my life to him. I am not Ernie Grimshaw. **He is,** I am too old to be scared anymore. Too old to keep secrets. It doesn't matter now anyway. You came looking for Ernie. You thought you found him.*

I'm not Ernie. We need to speak again soon, Mr. Brunskill. You haven't found your man."

CHAPTER 5
The search for three men

9.2.19

I did not sleep much last night. I lay there staring up at the ceiling and stewed, a mixture of anger and frustration bubbling inside me. At first, I felt used. Taken for a ride. Conned. I felt like a mug again – a fraud. For the second time in a few weeks, I questioned my abilities as a private investigator. This was about two in the morning. By half past, my anger had diluted somewhat. Frustration was still there but, I reconciled myself with the fact that it had not been a wasted trip after all.

My instincts had not let me down. Quite the opposite. I sensed something was not right, and I acted on this suspicion. I reasonably reasoned that, perhaps I was not the only person who had been duped. Those in the Miners' Arms seemed genuine. If this man was hiding behind the name of another, it is fair to assume they would have no reason to know any different, given his age and lifestyle. The history of the farm ownership seemed to tally, and even Alf would not be old enough to know the family at this time. The locals seemingly told me what they believed to be the truth, or had they had me for a fool? If the information Ernie disclosed is not common knowledge, it has been one hell of a cover-up.

And for what reason?

I lay there with a million questions going on in my mind.

Who was this man? Why has he assumed the identity of another? Where is the real Ernie Grimshaw? Who is the real Ernie Grimshaw? Is he still alive? What was David and Mabel's involvement in all of this? Why did he decide to open up to me? Why did he let me into his home? He didn't have to. Did he want to get something off his chest? Did he want to talk? Did he need to? Why me? Why now?

And who is Mr. Green? What does he want to find out? What does he already know? Have I the right to question him? My job isn't to investigate the man who is paying me to investigate. All I can do is gather the information and hand it back to Mr. Green. What he decides to do with it is his own business. So long as he pays what he owes, what do I care?

So where do I go from here? I really do need to speak with this man again; I don't even know his real name. I need some true facts before I can report back anything to Mr. Green.

In the meantime, there is the Fitzgerald case to investigate. That has to take priority this weekend. If nothing is revealed by Sunday that will be the end of it.

Mrs. F. might still be curious, but her funds have run out. If I cannot bring her some news by then, her man's intentions will remain a mystery. I haven't had much to go on. His weekday movements revealed nothing of note. Let's hope his weekends are a little more revealing and exciting. While the cat is away, he has the chance to play. This is what I call a shadow case. Very different from the Grimshaw case. I have to remain anonymous. I can't ask questions or speak with anyone. I can't draw attention to myself – not this weekend, not ever. Even if I find nothing of note, I cannot risk letting him know that he is being watched. These cases can be boring and repetitive but also extremely satisfying, when the watching is worthwhile. An indiscreet meeting. A chance to catch them 'at it', whatever that might entail. I normally have a hunch as to how a case will play out, but I am not feeling anything with the Mr. F. case. He just seems like a nice, normal, boring, middle- aged man. A stale and unhappy marriage does not always mean an affair. Maybe they have just grown tired of each other. Maybe the spark has gone, and she is clutching at straws to either find a way out or simply to put her paranoia to bed. Who knows? Again, it is not for me to question their motives.

I will give the old man until Sunday night to call me and, if nothing, I will call him myself first thing Monday. I won't give Mr. Green anything until I know more. What do I tell him anyway? I thought I found your man, but it is just some other old man pretending to be him. He would hardly be getting value for money for that.

Plan of action for today (for what it is):

11:00 a.m.

Drive to Rochdale and set up position near the house. Mrs F. confirmed that she would not be leaving the house until midday. This will give me time to find a suitable location to park, position and follow.

Await Mrs. F's departure. Go from there.

1:00 p.m.

Well, Mr. Diary, she has gone off to her sister's house. Only ten minutes ago. Typical female timing. Why say twelve if you are not going to go anywhere until nearly one? Nearly two hours I have been crouched down in this cramped van. It is a lovely day too. Sunny and unseasonably warm. I hope she realises that she is paying by the hour. No movement in or out of the house in that time other than a visit from the postman. Visibility of the house itself is good, but with the blinds closed, I have no view of the inside. She assured me that, if he chooses to go out, it will be through the front door as the back only leads to garden with no rear exit available. Update when there is something to report upon.

4:15 p.m.

We have had movement. Just over two hours ago he left the house and set off walking up the Somerset Grove and right onto Edenfield Road. I decided that it would be easier at this stage to follow in the van at a distance. He was dressed in jeans, trainers and a short-sleeved, white shirt. Smart and casual and a little less beige than before. Not exactly a man on a mission (or on the pull) but certainly a lot more relaxed than the Monday to Friday attire. After about half a mile he turned right into Denehurst Park close to Spotland (home of Rochdale FC). He took a seat on a bench there and took out his mobile to make a call. I stayed in the van and observed, at a distance, from Sandy Lane.

The call lasted no more than a minute. I sat and waited. Within ten minutes he was joined by another man. Bearded. Slightly older than Mr. F., I'd guess. Taller too. A smart looking gentleman. Well dressed and confident looking. The two shook hands and chatted together. Whatever they were talking about made them smile. Well, laugh actually. A hearty laugh. It was infectious and made me laugh too. It is amazing what a laugh can do.

Mr. F. seemed to be a different man again. It was then I noticed Mr. Beard had two dogs with him. Two Labradors – one black, one golden. He handed one of the leads to Mr. F. and the two of them set off deeper into the park. I decided to follow at a safe distance. I had a newspaper with me and took it along in case a bench stop was needed.

The two walked at a slow pace which was at odds with my usual jaunty manner, and I had to slow myself down to avoid getting too close. Thankfully, the park was quite busy, and one other walker was unlikely to stand out. The two men walked full circle around the park until the dogs were almost walking at a slower pace than them. They settled on the same bench they started, red-faced and clearly benefitting from the exercise. I made my way back to the van. They were still laughing when they parted, and Mr. F. headed for home.

I needed that. Not just the walk but the dose of normality again. Rochdale, for all its flaws, had pockets of beauty that still brought people together. Families and groups of friends crisscrossed and mingled with dogs, ducks and
squirrels for company. It was the first time I had witnessed laughter and smiles in Rochdale, and it cheered me up too. I cursed myself again for being too cynical. I blame the job.

I didn't need to follow Mr. F. but I did anyway. I knew where he was going. I drove ahead of him and waited back at my starting point near the house. He was a man of routine, and I trusted my instincts. I was right to do so. Through the rear-view mirror, I could see him walking up the street. Still smiling.

He passed the van and walked to the front door, turned the key and went inside.

In the three days I have kept surveillance on him, he has done nothing untoward or out of the ordinary, and yet I am warming to him. I enjoyed this afternoon's stroll as much as he did. Some of us need excitement in our lives. Gossip, tittle tattle, scandal and outrage. I am guilty of being pulled in by it too. Maybe Mrs. Fitzgerald is guilty of it as well. Is she happy with the man she has got? Is he happy? He was today. At least for an hour or so. Paranoia can eat away at a person. Is she paranoid? She is certainly coming across that way. She was/is a lovely lady but maybe a little controlling. He was maybe holding a leash today at the park, but he was off his own for a while, and he seemed to just be enjoying that freedom.

I really do not think there is much more to report today, but I will see it through. I will move the van a little further away from the house to avoid attention and see if there is any other movement in the next few hours.

8:30 p.m.

Mr. F. was on the move again. He walked towards the van – which always makes me worry that I have been discovered – but he carried on by to the end of Somerset Grove before turning left. I

71

followed at a safe distance, but we didn't have far to walk. He entered the club house at the nearby Rochdale Golf Club and settled in the corner with a pint of lager.

Alone. Golf clubs can be strange places. If you are not a 'face' you stick out like a sore thumb, and that's not a good position in my line of work. I returned to the van and parked up on the car park. I could still see inside and had a clear view of Mr. F., so there was no real need to go in and risk blowing my cover.

It was nearly nine o'clock when he moved again. Just to the bar. He bought two pints and returned to the table. There were a few more people in now but hardly what you would call crowded. Either he was very thirsty, or he was expecting another. The poor man sat in the corner on his own for a good hour. Constantly looking at his phone for company.

At nearly 9:45 p.m. he decided to call it a day. He had finished two pints, eaten two bags of nuts and visited the toilet three times before deciding to leave. I really felt for the man. His life was nowhere near as exciting as Mrs. F. thinks it is. He is very much a lonely and lost soul. Stuck in a marriage. Stuck in a job, stuck in Rochdale.

Out of courtesy (and to make sure he was ok), I followed him home. He had lost the smile and his enthusiasm from earlier in the day. He looked thoroughly down as he turned the key to go back inside. It made me think about my own life. Was I that much different?

I will go through the motions tomorrow. I will be back here in the morning for more surveillance at 8:30am. The last day on this case before calling it a day. One more day in Rochdale, then I can turn my attention back to Cumbria and the elusive Mr. Grimshaw.

10.2.19

8:20 a.m.

Ernie Grimshaw is buzzing around in my head, but for now I must push him to the back. Back on the Rochdale trail. Snow today too. There was no sign of much change in the weather from yesterday, but it has fallen quite heavily overnight, making the drive over a little perilous. Snow can be a nuisance for a private investigator, although I am not expecting it to matter much today. Snow leaves tracks. Tyre tracks, footprints – evidence of being followed. Hard to shadow in the snow. This truly will be my last chance to find something on Mr. F., not that I am expecting to find anything. Maybe his behaviour has less to do with infidelity and more to do with something else – money, debt, gambling. That said, his behaviour over the last few days does not have any extravagant traits. He isn't rushing off to the bookies or the shops to fritter away his modest wage or flex the credit card. Two pints in the golf club is not going to break the bank – even with the added cost of the nuts.

Maybe it is Mrs. F. who is having an affair? But why would she pay me to watch him? None of it makes sense. She will be back 'home' later today. I will contact her in the evening with my findings (whatever they might be) along with my final bill. I will be pleased to sign this one off. It is never a total waste of time when I am being paid, but I can think of better ways to fill a day.

A snow day also means a cold day. I can't leave the heater on and the engine running when on watch, for obvious reasons. I will have to rely on coffee to keep me warm today. The waiting begins again. More later, Mr. Diary.

10:25 a.m.

Movement. He is off again. Dressed for the weather. Large, padded coat, heavy boots, scarf and gloves on, which suggests he is staying outside. The park again is my guess. Off we go again.

1:35 p.m.

God, that was cold. My fingers are like blocks of ice. My guess was right, Mr. Diary. The park again. I followed him, staying a good hundred metres behind without any danger of losing him. Keeping a distance was more important today. Due to the weather, there were fewer people in the park, and I'd have stuck out like a sore thumb if I had trailed him around. No need to do this. He found the same bench again and just sat and stared. I watched from a distance. People tend to mind their own business in parks. Lost in their own thoughts. He certainly seemed to be lost in his. He stayed there until just after 1:00 p.m. before heading back home. I made my way back to the van after he went back into the house. I kept asking myself, 'why'?

What was he doing? What was he thinking? I tried to put myself in his shoes. Is that it? Do I need to be in his shoes? Maybe. I will update again soon. It is bloody freezing out there, but I am going to go with my instincts. The coffee is cold anyway. It is worth a try.

2:45 p.m.

I had decided to go back to the park, to sit in the same place that Mr. F. sat in. It was already starting to get dark, and flecks of snow were falling again. I was one of the few people left there, and you couldn't blame the locals for heading back to their homes to toast in front of a warm fire. I wanted to be doing the same, but I felt a need to return. I didn't want to miss anything. I was pleased I had returned. There was nothing obvious as first. The usual teenage scrawls across the wooden bench. 'Courtney for Jack'. 'RFC rule'. 'Bury Bastards', etc.

Not exactly poetic but from the heart, nonetheless. The park was generally well kept, and I was pleased to see a lack of litter or dog muck – signs of neglect so common in places where the community spirit has been broken. Not here though. Mr. F's footprints were still visible, and I sat where he must have sat only an hour or so earlier.

And there it was. Out of the corner of my eye, I saw that folded neatly and wedged tightly in between the iron handle and the wooden slats was a piece of paper. It wasn't really noticeable or easy to see – unless you were looking for something.

By this point, my hands were like ice cubes, but my fingers mustered enough movement to pull it out. It was tightly folded which, in a way, was good, as it helped protect it from the falling snow.

I opened it slowly – more to do with my fumbling fingers than anything else. It contained a handwritten letter – a beautiful, cursive, old-fashioned style of writing. Care had been taken to write this letter. Care had been taken with each word. When I finished reading, I folded the letter and placed it back exactly where I found it and stood to make my way back to the van, but not before taking a photograph of it on my phone. What I do with the photograph I have yet to decide.

I have reproduced the letter below exactly as it was written (in scruffier handwriting, I must confess):

My Dearest M.

It is with a heavy heart that I write this letter.
I so wanted to meet with you again this weekend. Opportunities are few and far between I know.
It isn't anyone's fault – yours, mine, theirs.
*Yesterday afternoon was lovely. Every minute. I know we only had an hour, but it was **our** hour.*
I was at the golf club as agreed. I didn't expect you to make it. I hoped you would, but I didn't expect you to. It was too much of a risk for you, and I would never want you to take a chance like that. Not until the time is right. Will the time ever be right? I hope so. With all my heart.
Kathryn will be back later today. I don't know when we will have another chance to meet. I promise you I will be here at our agreed time at every available opportunity. I hope you can be too. I know the children must come first. I admire your dedication to your family. I applaud your discretion and I would never do anything to put that at risk, but I treasure our moments in each other's company. You make me feel alive again. You make me feel special. You make me feel wanted. I love our time together. I love you.
I will continue to dream of what might be and what already has been. Until next time. You know you are in my thoughts and my heart.

R.

Time to go home. This case has reached its conclusion.

7:35 p.m.

I have felt numb this evening. Yet again, I have proved that I am good at what I do – but at what price?

Can I separate my professional head from my social conscience? Lately, I am finding it harder and harder.

I wasn't expecting this turn of events. It has shocked me. Not so much the unexpected conclusion to my findings but the sheer weight of emotion involved. This 'affair' wasn't conducted through malice, spite or hatred. It wasn't really driven by lust either. The man is lost. He doesn't know how to escape from a life he has locked himself into. He isn't allowed to be himself. He has drifted from her but not for the reason she thinks. He is trying to protect her by denying himself what he wants most of all. He is trying to protect the man he loves. He is trying to protect the family of the man he loves. By doing so, he is sacrificing himself. Am I the man to pull the rug from under him – from them all? That is what I am being paid to do. Morals are all well and good, but these principles don't pay the bills. I am being paid to do a job. My job is to find information and pass on that information. What my employer decides to do with that information is her business. The fallout from my work is not my concern. Or it shouldn't be. Or should it be? I have never felt such a dilemma. I need to contact her.

What do I do? What do I say?

What do I charge? I charge by the hour – she owes me for my time. She owes me a lot. Money I cannot do without.

Does he deserve the consequences? What has he done wrong? Is that for me to decide? Is this job for me?

I need to eat. I need to rest. I need to think.

I will make a decision later this evening and stick to it. It might just dictate what I do with my own life and work from now on.

22:30 p.m.

I have made my decision. Mr. Diary, you and I go back a long way. I have always been honest with you. The truth of me is hidden in your many pages. I have faults – many – but I have always tried to do this job with honesty and integrity. I have always been professional. I have always tried to do my best by my clients, and it is with this in mind that I have decided on the following course of action.

I will not pass on the information gathered to Mrs. Fitzgerald. This job is not for me anymore.

Slowly but surely – death by a thousand cuts – this job has damaged me. I have been an emotional vacuum. I never used to be this way. This case has shaken me. Who am I to play a part in the destruction of lives and relationships for financial reward?

It is sick. It is unforgivable. I cannot justify my part in the lies, the secrets and the hidden truths. Robert Fitzgerald is suffering. He is a man in pain. A man broken. I am not going to make it any worse than it already is.

I will charge Mrs. Fitzgerald. I will have to. I will charge for the hours of surveillance. That guilt will be enough.

In future, the casework for the family trees and ancestral investigations will be enough. The money is great, and it is good, safe work. Nobody gets hurt. There is no shortage of new customers coming my way, so there is no need to take on anymore outside case work. Enough is enough.

Only the loose ends to tie up. This one and Mr. Green's.

Robert Fitzgerald, Ernie Grimshaw and me. Three men. Three very different lives, and not one of us seems to know who the hell we really are.

Tomorrow is a new dawn.

CHAPTER 6
Taken Identity

11.2.19

Invoice prepared for Mrs. Fitzgerald. Final total of £675. It still doesn't sit well with me, but I felt it had to be done. I spoke with her on the telephone, and she was satisfied if not happy. Hopefully, the two of them will come to a natural end and have the chance to live a long and enjoyable life apart. If they stay together, it will be their choosing. I will have a clear conscience. Apart from taking the money.

And now, onto my final case, perhaps, before moving my life on. The case of Ernie Grimshaw. I have looked back at the correspondence between Mr. Green and myself and I am really no further forward than I was at the beginning. Or am I? The old man on the farm clearly knows, or knows of, Mr. Grimshaw. The people in the pub know the man who claimed to be Mr. Grimshaw without knowing who he actually was.

Mr. Green knows Mr. Grimshaw – or enough about him to want to spend a great deal of money finding out something/anything about him.

We know he exists or existed. The birth certificate proves that. We know when and where he was born. We know the names of his parents too. And that is about all, except that I now know another man used his name. Part of me feels that I am being sent on a wild goose chase – looking for a man who doesn't exist. But why? Paranoia on my part, I think. There is clearly something amiss. This old man masquerading as Mr. Grimshaw is strange enough, but he is to be my starting point. Before I can find the real Ernie Grimshaw, I need to find out who the false one really is. I am repeating myself, Mr. Diary, but that is how my head is just now.

I will call him again after breakfast and try to arrange another visit to Cumbria as soon as possible. I need to try to get some semblance of order for this case. The sooner this case is put to bed the better, then I can start afresh without the hassle and moral dilemmas. I already feel better for it. I slept well for the first time in an age.

A fry-up. That's what I need right now. A fry up before my new dawn. I will call after that.

9:50 a.m.

Voicemail left. No pick-up again. A simple polite message. I hope he calls soon. I had a voicemail message of my own. Mother. A typical mother message. Getting in touch because I hadn't been in touch for a few days. Telling me she needed help with the computer as "it doesn't work for me like it does for you" and "if you can afford to go to Germany you can afford to cross town to spend time with your lonely mother" before signing off with a "love you, son. Got to go, I can hear the theme tune starting for *Countdown*".

2:00 p.m.

The call came shortly after one o'clock. The old man's voice seemed hushed and laboured. When we met, he spoke with confidence and humour. That sureness had gone. I got the impression he was struggling to talk. Struggling to say what he wanted to tell me. He sounded frail, if

81

that is possible. I asked him if we could meet soon. He said he wanted to. He wanted to explain. I suggested we arrange a suitable time and date sometime this week. He suggested tomorrow at 2 p.m. So soon? I detected some urgency on his part.

I agreed.

We said our goodbyes, and that was that.

I had some preparation to do. I like to pre-empt what a person might say so that I have extra questions to follow up with. I like to paint a picture in my head (and in my diary) including timelines, places, people and relationships. Whatever it was this old man wanted to tell me, he clearly wanted to get a load off his chest. A burden he had carried with him for some time. I didn't know what to call him. In my haste, I had forgotten to ask his name. In fact, I even addressed him as Ernie when he called. That is the first thing I need. His name. Names are identities. Names have a history. Names open doors. Names have family. Names are traceable. Whoever this man is, he WILL have a past, and I WILL find out who he is/was. And yet, it isn't him I am being paid to find, but he does play a part in this mystery. He might not *be* Ernie Grimshaw, but he has lived in the man's skin for decades. Why? Time to find out.

The Greenhill Hotel had a room available. Fabulous. A little more expensive than the last time, but the bill can be added to my tab. Speaking of which, after this visit I will submit my expenses form to Mr Green with an update.

Hopefully, after this visit, I will have considerably more to tell him.

I will leave early in the morning and take a leisurely drive up.

I have a free afternoon now. No jobs are pressing. I will pack an overnight bag this evening. I think I will go for a drive now to give me time to think and mentally prepare for tomorrow. I know just where I am heading.

7:30 p.m.

It was a beautiful drive over the A680 to Rochdale this afternoon. The hilltops glistened with snow, and the sky was clear blue as far as the eye could see. After taking full and final payment from Mrs F., I didn't envisage visiting the town again any time soon, but curiosity got the better of me. Denehurst Park was my destination and a certain bench within. I parked on Edenfield Road near the golf club so that I could take a leisurely stroll across. I arrived around 3 p.m. There were not many other people around. The icy breeze was biting, and I cursed myself for forgetting to wear my winter coat. It would be dark in an hour or so, and I had no plans to stay until then. I didn't plan to be there long. Just like last time, there was no one on the bench. Remarkably, the outline of Robert Fitzgerald's footprints were still visible. The hard frost was not keen to let them go just yet. It seemed right. Appropriate. This was a special place for him.

His presence deserved to linger. For a moment I forgot why I was there and then I remembered. The note. I looked down to where it had been so tightly folded then squeezed between the wrought iron frame of the bench. It wasn't there anymore.

The wind could not have taken it. The snow or sleet could not have disturbed it. Somebody had found it. Somebody had taken it. I would dearly love

83

to know if it had reached its intended target, but alas, I can only speculate.

And then I did something I had never done before. I knew it was wrong, but it felt right. I committed a terrible crime. A crime I have condemned others for. Graffiti. I defaced the property of the state. Only a little. Not enough to bring the Greater Manchester Police out in force, waving truncheons and spraying tear gas. I took out my black biro and scrawled on the wooden slat near the position the note had been wedged. I stood and admired my creation for a second before making my way back across the park towards the van, looking around to make sure I wasn't going to get caught for my illegal handiwork. I simply wrote, in bold capitals, GOOD LUCK M. AND R.

12.2.19

11:30 a.m.

The drive up to Cumbria was trouble-free, and as I write this lying on the bed of my plush room in the Greenhill Hotel, I have time to jot down some thoughts on the day ahead. I still have a couple of hours before the meet, and I have already thought of a million questions to ask. I think I will take the cautious approach and just let him speak. He wants to speak. Questions might just distract him. There will be some, I am sure, but my role should be the listener, not the talker. I will take the Dictaphone and ask if I may record the conversation. I will take written notes, as I do not want to miss anything. I may only have this one chance to talk with him, and I do not want to waste it. After all this time, I know almost nothing about the man I am investigating. If I am going to find out anything about Mr. Grimshaw – the real Mr. Grimshaw – I need to get a lead, and this chap, whoever he is, seems to be my best chance of finding one.

The real Ernie Grimshaw was born in March 1929. That makes him a month shy of his 90th birthday if he is still alive. I didn't have any reason to question the age of this other man before now, but I am guessing it is similar. As mentioned before, I may not get another chance to interview the man, so I must make the most of this opportunity. I need to leave with as much evidence as possible. I need to take photos of any documents or pictures that might give me a lead.

I think I will go now and get to the village early. I have time to go into the Miners' Arms for a drink. I wasn't going to go in, but if I am only here for today, I have little else to lose. I won't give any secrets away. If anyone asks, I am only here to tie up a few loose ends and take some photographs – not far off the truth anyway. Here goes. Wish me luck, Mr. Diary.

1: 30 p.m.

My last few notes before I meet the man. I am sat in the van around the corner from the house. The visit to the Miners' was not a waste of time after all. Quite the contrary, actually. I hadn't actually noticed before, but the walls in there offered a treasure trove of memories. Photographs of local buildings and local people dating back over 75 years. The pub was quiet – near empty – and other than Sheila, none of the faces from last time were present. I exchanged pleasantries and flirted for a minute or two before taking my pint on a journey around the pub. All those people, all those lives. Who are they? Where are they now? What did they do with their lives? These are the kind of questions I have asked myself a thousand times before on different cases, but there was nothing to gain by browsing now was there? Well, actually there was, Mr. Diary.

In the corner of the lounge was a small collection of photographs dating back to the 1930s. They were all of Harvest Festivals in and around the village. Grand displays of fruit, vegetables and flowers. People dressed in their finest clothes, laughing and posing in front of the camera. Most of the pictures had handwritten captions informing the reader of the place the photo was taken and, if known, the people in them.

The church, the high street, the pub – Greenbank Farm. Dated 1939, the photograph showed a middle-aged couple flanking a young boy. They had their hands resting on his shoulder and the boy stood proud, chest out, holding a trophy.

The black and white image was sharp and in focus - it could have been taken today! The caption underneath read:

GREENBANK, JULY '39, HARVEST F. IN PICTURE (LEFT TO RIGHT: FARMER DAVID 'SHOVEL HANDS' GRIMSHAW, ERNIE - HOLDING ASPATRIA YOUNG WRESTLERS CHAMP 1939 - AND YOUNG MABEL).

My heart raced. There he was – as large as life – right in front of me. I wanted to reach into the photograph and touch the people within. I wanted to talk to them, to question them.

This was evidence.

This was evidence of the man (or the boy at least). Ernie Grimshaw was real. He was there right in front of me. A face. A family. A life.

The picture seemed to say so much. A wrestling champ. He was fit and strong and sporty. He was loved and cared for. He was happy. This was 1939. He was only ten. At that point did he cease to be the Ernie Grimshaw the village knew? How was he replaced by the man I am about to see? Do I mention the picture to him? Would he know? Probably. I took a couple of photographs of the image on my smartphone and another couple on my digital camera. All very good quality – as good as the original. I emailed them to myself to ensure I had enough copies, just in case. After all, this was the best (if not the only) evidence I had.

Nobody in the bar seemed to notice me taking the pictures or if they did, they didn't care. It was time to meet the other Ernie again. I shall update you back at the hotel, Mr. Diary. Dictaphone and notebook and pen at the ready. God only knows where we will go after this meeting, but one thing we now know beyond any doubt – Ernie Grimshaw has a history around here.

6:15 p.m.

Back in the hotel. Back in my room. I am numb. I am not going to write up tonight. I need to gather my thoughts. I need to listen again. Nearly four hours I was there – I could have stayed and listened for another four. Bloody Hell. What on earth is going on here? My mind is spinning right now – where do I start?

I don't feel like eating. I am not tired. I am craving a drink, but I need to keep a clear head.

Coffee. A strong coffee will do for now. I need to listen again and take in what he told me. The dissection, analysis and next step planning can start tomorrow. I am going to sign off for today. I don't expect I will sleep well tonight. I doubt he will either. Or maybe he will. Maybe that is what he needed.

I make no apologies for the tears, Mr. Diary. God help him and, God - please help me. Goodnight.

13.2.19

7:30 a.m.

Good morning, Mr. Diary. I didn't get a great deal of sleep last night as you know. Before I leave the hotel, I want to reproduce part one of the interview. Whilst not word for word, nothing of importance will be left out. The following is taken from the recorded conversation with interjections or points of clarification where necessary. I have also made notes on points I need to follow up on before I write to Mr. Green. I need to vacate my room at 11:00 a.m. and drive home, so I will finish the rest later.

To recap, I sat down to talk with an elderly gentleman I was first led to believe was Mr. Ernie Grimshaw of Greenbank Farm, Prospect, Cumbria. I since found out this man was **NOT** Mr. Grimshaw. This meeting was arranged to clarify who he actually was, what his relationship was to Ernie and his family, and why he was living in the family home. I also needed to establish, if possible, what happened to the real Mr. Grimshaw and his parents, David and Mabel, and why this gentleman's real identity along with the disappearance of Ernie was not known by the wider, and yet close-knit community.

The start of our conversation went as follows:

Him: *"My real name – a name I have not used for nearly 70 years – is Daniel Frankenburg. I am of Jewish decent, as you can probably tell by my name. As far as I know, I have no remaining blood relatives. I have never spoken of my past before, and you must excuse me if I struggle to recall some events or if I am unable to answer some of your questions. I am sure you have so many. I am 91 years old. I was born on 22nd September 1928 in the district of Kleefeld, Hanover, Germany. The Jewish community there was small, and, as a family, we mixed well with our German neighbours. I do not recall any animosity towards us when I was growing up. It was a lovely childhood. I lived with my father, Azriel, my mother, Rebecca and my older sister, Danya. She was three years older than me. We were close."*

There was a silence here on the recording. He had stopped talking to gather his thoughts. This was clearly a traumatic experience for him. His eyes were filled with tears, and he made no attempt to wipe them away. He seemed lost in thought. He took a few moments to compose himself again before clearing his throat and starting again.

Daniel: *"I am not sure what you know about German and Jewish history before the war. In the early 1930s, when I was just a young boy, the politics of the country meant little to my sister and me, and if my parents were worried about the rumours and speculation at the time, they kept it* well hidden from us. I would imagine they had heard enough to worry them.

Before 1936, life in Hanover was normal. School was normal. My father was a chemist, and my mother worked in a baker's shop near where we lived. The school my sister and I attended was relatively small. I think there was only a handful of children from Jewish families, but we were not treated any differently to the others. I was eight in 1936, and my sister eleven. She was a very bright girl – attractive too. She could have been anything she wanted to be, bless her. She had the brains. I was more the sporty type. I loved playing football, but my real talent was as a sprinter. I was the fastest in the school by a long way. I could easily beat the boys much older than me when I was only seven or eight, and the school even entered me into a regional competition, against boys much older than me. I remember coming third and getting a medal for my efforts.

My parents were so proud of me. They were proud of us both.

But it was around that time that little things started to change for us. At first, I didn't really notice or give it much thought. Along with another boy, my table was moved to the back of the class. I didn't ask why. You didn't question the teacher in those days. You trusted them to do right by you. It was a week or so later that my sister told me they had done the same to her. She was the only Jewish girl in that class, and she had to sit alone.

Over the next few weeks, it became more obvious, even to a young naïve mind, I was, or should I say, we were, being singled out. The teachers wouldn't ask us questions in lessons.

We were ignored. They only spoke to us briefly. They kept a distance. We were not getting picked to do jobs or help out. We would be the last to be served at dinnertime, and we were not allowed in the library, or allowed to take books home with us like we always had in the past.

Mother lost her job around that time too. She told us the bakery was not doing so well and they had to make redundancies, but even then, I suspected this was not right. The place was always busy, and no one else lost their jobs. Mother was being singled out.

I can't remember when we were first made to wear the star. We became increasingly aware that our lives were changing and wondered if they would ever be the same again. There was a growing hostility towards us. My friends – or at least the boys I thought were my friends – stopped talking to me. They stopped playing with me. Danya's friends deserted her too. One boy, Fred his name was, told me,

'It's because you are a Jew. Jews don't belong here. My brother told me. He said we can't be with you. You are evil and dirty. That's why. My brother knows.'

Danya told me stories of being spat at, punched and kicked and threatened with violence on her walks home from school. After that, we stuck together. We only had each other. We walked to and from school together – watching each other's backs. It was scary, and yet we still wanted to go to school. It was all we knew.

My father told us to stay hopeful that it would pass. He told us to take any positives we could. He valued education. He used to tell us, 'Learn something new every day and your mind will be richer for it.'

In early 1937, the decision to attend school was taken out of our hands. A law was passed to prevent Jewish children attending the same classes as German children. For a time, the Jewish families tried to form their own classrooms in someone's family home, but this didn't last. It was considered too dangerous to gather together in large numbers in case the Germans considered it a threat to national security. As if a small collection of women and children could bring down the Third Reich.

Anyway, 1937 proved to be a pretty horrific year for us as a family. We rarely left home and if we did, it was only to pick up a few groceries and essentials from those that would still sell to us. The Jewish community elders were still able to buy food, and it was distributed to those in need. My father continued working in the chemist's shop, but his pay was significantly reduced, and he was only allowed to advise on, but not administer medicine.

He had to wear the star too and work out of the back room of the shop. He was not allowed to be 'out front' for fear of losing the shop money.

Nobody, it seemed, wanted to deal with 'the Jew', even though they had taken his advice and help for years."

I hadn't asked any questions. I didn't want to interrupt. I felt he was taking me on a journey that he needed to make himself. More tears rolled down his cheek at this point, and he made no attempt to wipe them away. I wanted to reach out to him. To hold his hand or hug his frail, old frame but I didn't. I was rooted to my chair. I couldn't take my eyes off his face. I was transfixed.

"Anyway, it continued like this for weeks, months. Into 1938. That was a cold winter. After a few horrible months, things got a little better for us. People seemed to leave us alone then. They had their own problems. People were not well off. Germany was still suffering the effects of the depression, and their victimisation of the Jews was almost put on hold while they looked after their own families first.

The image of Adolf Hitler and the imagery of his Nazi Party was becoming more prominent around the country and noticeable in Hanover. You couldn't escape it. As the weather got warmer in springtime, so did the animosity towards the Jews and other minority groups.

The Gypsy population were on his radar as well as us. They suffered terribly too. Random beatings, public humiliations. These people were ostracised. It was around this time I saw my first dead body. It wouldn't be my last. A young man was attacked by a group of soldiers simply for not being able to produce ID when asked. He was Jewish. The star on his arm gave it away. He was beaten so badly that his face was unrecognisable when they had finished with him. They left him where he fell and walked away.

As children, we watched from a distance, stunned and helpless. We stared at his lifeless body for ages until a group of Jewish men came to pick up the body and carry the corpse away. If they hadn't, I am not sure anybody else would have. No one was prepared to help a Jew – alive or dead.

We got used to living that way. By autumn, my father had lost his job too. We were living on handouts from others. My parents sold what they could to raise funds to buy food. We moved from our home into a much smaller flat near the city centre where other Jewish families had gathered.

The only community we now felt part of was the Jewish community. We didn't have much in common with our neighbours, but we tolerated each other because we needed each other. In November, the infamous Kristallnacht showed us just how hated we had become in German society. In a national display of hatred, mobs roamed the street looking for Jews to kill or maim. It was terrifying.

We hid inside hoping and praying we wouldn't be discovered. I remember holding my father so tightly.

He was my protection, and yet I sensed his own fear. What could he have done had they come in? He was only one man. Still, I felt so close to him that night.

I had a lot to learn about the world and what was happening around me, but I knew I was loved, and I knew how much family meant in that one moment of absolute terror.

We survived that night, but the aftermath was an escalation of a vendetta against the Jews and any others considered enemies of the state. Laws were tightened or introduced to make life even harder for us. Passports were taken or amended to make emigration almost impossible. My father wanted to take us to the Netherlands, but we had neither the funds nor the contacts to make that a viable option. We heard stories of 'Ghettos' or 'Hubs' for Jews. People spoke of Jews being evicted from their homes and contained in certain zones until the government decided what do to with them - us. We heard talk of getting rid of the Jews – of prisons or places we would be sent. We even heard stories of 'purifying' the cities. To make them 'German' again.

We lived day to day. We existed rather than lived, and yet we stayed together as a unit. The four of us were strong together. We rarely argued or fell out. We all knew how much we needed each other. By the end of 1938 we knew something was in the offing. We were not allowed to buy newspapers, but we could read the headlines, and from that, we could deduce conflict was not far away.

Hitler had a plan to expand the German Empire. Lots of talk of revenge and retribution following the First World War. The French were damned in particular. Hitler spoke of past glories and the need to ensure the eagle flies high again.

He singled the French out as enemies of the regime. The Russians too. The British would follow. We were not aware that Hitler was planning to invade, but we did sense we were not going to escape his ire.

Over the next two years, we survived. We learned to survive – we learned to live day to day. Some days we would eat, some days we wouldn't, but we stayed strong as a family.

There wasn't a norm anymore. Each day was a challenge. Occasionally, we would be brave and walk around without our star on. To feel free again – even if it was just for a short period – it was worth the risk.

We walked as a family through the park, along the river, or even in the plazas in the centre. We were never recognised or exposed as Jews. It was daring and dangerous, but, on those occasions, we felt alive again.

On the 1st of September 1939, the army invaded Poland, and we knew we were at war. 'Could things get any worse for us?' we pondered. Well, yes, they could. A lot worse. Hitler seemed to

95

have two driving forces. Clean up at home and clean up abroad.

He stopped again at this point. He apologised, and I stressed he had nothing to apologise for. We go at his pace. He thanked me. This was so hard for him, but he carried on despite the grief he was feeling. More tears fell. Some of mine fell too.

Sometime in early 1940, our family unit was lost. They came in the night to get us. I cannot remember too much about it. A knock on the door. My sister answered it. She thought it was one of our neighbours bringing food. She had no reason to be cautious.

Four men in uniform burst through the door. They were waving guns and shouting at us to stand against the wall with our hands in the air. They struck my father with the butt of a gun, but he didn't fall. He stood beside us – trying to protect us even against all the odds. I remember them laughing at us. Mocking us.

They made my mother and sister undress. For no other reason than for their own sick gratification.

Then one of them pointed the gun at my sister. He told my father that she would be shot unless he followed their instructions. I remember my father shaking with anger and fear. They told him to follow the soldier at the door and to take me with him. We were to go outside and board the truck. My father asked what would happen to my mother and sister. The soldier laughed at him but told him not to worry. They would be fine if he followed instructions.

My father looked at them and told them to be strong. To be brave. It was all he could do. He told them he loved them with all his heart. They repeated his words. I didn't say anything. I was too scared. I wanted to. I really wanted to. I wished I had. I have regretted it every day of my life. I wish I had told my mother and my sister how much I loved them.

I did and still do.

I looked at my mother and sister one last time before I was pushed out of the door along with my father.

Our family had been torn apart in a matter of minutes. My father and I were pushed and shoved and herded onto a truck filled with other men.

Other Jews. He held my hand tightly. He wasn't going to lose me as well.

When I looked at him, he was crying. He didn't try to hide it. I needed him to be strong for me, but he was a broken man. He would never be the same again. To this day, I do not know what happened to my mother and sister. I have tried to trace their movements but with no luck. Part of me doesn't want to know. I cannot bear the thought of their suffering. There was talk of Auschwitz. Of the gas chambers. I will never know now. I can only hope and pray that they found a way out. I hope the soldiers let them go. I hope they showed some human compassion.

I have to hope..."

I could tell he was struggling. I asked if he wanted a break, but he refused. He wanted to go on.

"I was nearly twelve at this point. Not a child but not old enough to stand alone either. I needed my father. He needed me. I had no idea where they were taking us. The truck was old and uncomfortable. Some of the men were sat on wooden slats at each side, but the rest of us just had to find

97

room on the floor. We felt every pothole and bump in the road, and the drive seemed to take forever. Hardly anybody spoke. Everybody was tired and drained.

Everyone was frightened. Everyone had their own story to tell but kept it private. It was the only privacy they had left – their thoughts.

When the truck finally came to a stop, we knew we were many miles from our homes in Hanover. The back door creaked and swung open. I remember it being dark, but the sun was rising. It must have been around 7 a.m. or so.

We were told to line up against a fence and await further instructions. The truck pulled away, and we were left facing half a dozen soldiers all pointing their guns at us. Eventually, another soldier arrived. He wore a different uniform and was clearly in charge. I remember him smiling at us. Not a friendly smile. He simply said, 'Welcome to Fuhlsbüttel.' Nobody in our party knew where Fuhlsbüttel was or what it was. It wouldn't take us long to find out.

My father had told me to be polite and respectful at all times – even more so here. He told me to follow instructions. Do whatever they asked of me. I wanted my father to protect me. To keep me safe. But even then, standing alongside that fence, I knew he couldn't. He was just as vulnerable. We all were.

The Commandant of the camp was introduced to us. He told us to follow the guards into the compound. They would lead us to our accommodation where we would be given a uniform, work boots and soup. I remember holding my father's hand incredibly tightly as we walked solemnly into the camp.

The complex was walled with lookout points every hundred metres or so. Each one was manned by an armed soldier. The place had been used as a prison before being transformed into a labour camp for the Nazis.

We were told that it was mainly political prisoners or anti-government protestors that were held there but 'the Jews, queers and gyppos had to go somewhere', so here we were.

I was one of the youngest there, and I felt the threat of violence at every turn. Not only from the guards. Even in the camp there was a hierarchy. Some of the men developed relationships with the guards.

I did not know why at the time, but thinking back, I can only assume it was of a sexual nature as nobody on the inside of the wall had anything else to give or offer the Germans. I remember being beaten by fully grown men. My father was beaten too. I am sure it was because he was trying to protect me. The Germans never tried to stop a brawl. They enjoyed it. They enjoyed watching the enemy tear itself apart from within. No matter how ugly things seemed amongst the prisoners, this was nothing compared to the punishments our captors used against us. For the most part, I escaped their violence, but I witnessed plenty. They would torture..."

He tailed off and again I asked him if he wanted a break. He refused.

"They would tear out fingernails and toenails. Make naked men crawl over broken glass. For their entertainment, they would make people run the

99

length of the camp wall whilst shooting at them for target practice.

Group beatings, hangings, whippings. Anything they could think of to inflict pain. Half the time, they would just do it to pass the time of day. To amuse themselves.

We lived there for over six months, and my father deteriorated rapidly during this time. He couldn't cope with the workload. Hard labour in the forests and the quarry. His fingers were broken, his back severely damaged, and his feet stripped of skin due to the state of the boots he was forced to wear.

What little food we got was not enough to sustain him. I only found out much later that he had given me some of his food to help me stay strong, to his own detriment. The Germans had little sympathy. If he didn't do the work, some other Jew would.

In early 1941, they decided to transfer some of us to another camp. It was explained to us that new armaments factories were being built in central Germany, and I was to be taken to Buchenwald with any other boys under the age of eighteen. The fittest and strongest were needed there to help 'the cause'.

There were eight of us from the group chosen to go. My father was not one of them. He was in a bad way.

I pleaded with them to let me stay to look after my father, but it was no use. As they pushed us onto the transportation, one guard approached me waving his pistol.

'I'll look after your father.' he said, grinning.

I was old enough now to know exactly what he meant. My legs seemed to collapse from under me, and I think I fainted. No one reached out to help me.

The truck drove away. By the time I came to, we were miles away from Fuhlsbüttel. I would never see or hear from my father again. I was alone."

I had so many questions buzzing around in my head, but I stayed quiet. He hadn't finished. His timeline had moved us on to 1941. For my own benefit, my mind was desperately trying to find the links between Ernie and Daniel, but it couldn't. Ernie would only have been thirteen at this point, living out his own wartime in the far north of England.

Daniel asked for a glass of water and took a long drink before continuing.

"I was very much alone now. I had survived so much already, but far worse was still to come. I had lost my family. I had lost my life. I was petrified, hungry and exhausted, but the human spirit is remarkably strong. I must have had a will to live, even though I didn't feel it at the time.

Buchenwald was a camp on a much larger scale than Fuhlsbüttel.

I had witnessed brutal beatings, shootings and even death so far, but Buchenwald was on a different level. When I arrived, it was quite clear that the camp had far more inmates than it was designed to take.

We were allocated a specific hut and told to find a bunk and be ready for roll call. Lateness would not be tolerated. The huts were vile. Stinking cesspits of urine, faeces, vomit and blood.

Each bunk was shared by seven or eight men. The stench stayed with me for years afterwards.

This was another labour camp. Labour designed to kill. The Germans invented new and

101

toxic ways to kill - the screams, wails and cries all drowned out by music they played on the wireless through large speakers.

I stayed at Buchenwald for eighteen months. In this time, I worked in the nearby munitions factory polishing shells. Thankfully, for the most part, we were left alone in there. The dangers were far greater back in the camp.

By the middle of 1943, I was a shadow of the boy I once was. My natural fitness had got me this far, but I was struggling to muster the energy to get up, never mind work. I was approaching my fifteenth birthday, and I felt fifty. Survival was my only goal. We heard rumours of the tide turning – of the Germans losing the war – but these were only rumours. The news - the real world, the wider world – was as alien to us as anything else outside the camp and the factory, but rumours gave us hope. A will to carry on.

My final move, a welcome one at the time, as I feared I would die in Buchenwald – was to Bergen Belsen in north Germany. Close to my family home in Hanover. I was moved, this time, with all the other German Jews in Buchenwald. There were a couple of hundred of us at least. I knew a few names and faces by now, but nobody I would call a friend. We didn't really have time to develop friendships. Friendships could be broken, and the guards took great pleasure in breaking them – often pitting one friend against another for their own amusement. Nobody seemed to know anything about Belsen other than that it was a newly built camp. Another labour camp.

Others told us it was a holding camp – just a place they could put us until they decided what to do with us.

A last stop before Auschwitz and certain death. But we clung on to hope.

We were ushered to the Sternlager or 'Star Camp' for Jews. We were pleased that we were kept together at least. At first, life there was tolerable. The usual SS beatings were carried out, and the regime was strict but bearable.

For the remainder of 1943, the conditions were as good as we could hope for and certainly better than what I had experienced before. However, we couldn't escape the idea that we were only in a waiting room, and soon the trucks would come to take us to Auschwitz.

Things changed significantly throughout the harsh winter months. Prisoners seemed to be arriving by the hundred each day. Hungarians, Poles, Gypsies, Russians, Jews. Each day a new tranche of people herded through the gates.

By the spring of 1944, the camp was dangerously overcrowded, and the violence against prisoners escalated again. The SS didn't want to be there. Their own workload had increased tenfold, and I think they were in fear of some kind of resistance movement – how, I do not know. We had the numbers but not the energy or wherewithal.

In late 1944, I thought I was in hell. The decline over the summer months had been rapid. People were not being moved on, rather, just left to die in that Godforsaken place.

There was hardly any food, hardly any clean water. No medicines. No essentials. People were dying everywhere.

Bodies everywhere. Left to rot. They were stripped of their clothes before they were cold. The old, the young – it didn't matter. If they were weak, they died. People didn't have time for sympathy.

They had to worry about staying alive. Any food would do. Cooked or uncooked. Rabbits, rats, birds – whichever poor creature that had the misfortune to step into the camp.

Rainwater was collected and fought over. Thank God for the rain. The other water available would have killed us as clinically as any SS guard.

By the end of the year, those of us still standing were shadows of who we used to be. We were surrounded by human remains. Emaciated faces. Skin and bones. There was no life in Bergen Belsen anymore – even in us still living. How some of us made it into 1945 is a mystery. How we survived the winter, even more so. But we did.

By now, some of the Germans soldiers were broken too. A few of the guards started talking to us. Talking as if the events of last few months had never happened. They started to tell us that the war was coming to an end, and Germany was going to lose. They told us that we would soon be free. They had heard other camps, like Belsen, had been liberated – freed.

They said they would be arrested. I am sure they wanted our sympathy – our help. They were scared.

It was not until April that the day we had all prayed for finally came. British troops arrived at the gate. The SS did not put up a fight.

Our liberators greeted us not with smiles but with shock and horror. They stared at us, they vomited, and they gagged. Those of us who could, sat up and watched them. We didn't have the strength to be elated. They recorded the scenes on old cine film. It is even on YouTube now, I have heard. I have never had any urge to look. It is still crystal clear in my mind, even now.

104

The scenes were abhorrent. Disgusting. Disgraceful. Evil. There are no words to describe this hell on earth. Whatever they had been expecting – whatever they had imagined – could not have been anywhere near as bad as the reality. I remember their arrival vividly. I was sat on a log near one of the huts. There was a corpse lying not six feet away from me, and I barely gave it any thought.

A British soldier approached me. He was in tears. He spoke to me, but I didn't understand his accent. My English was passable – even then – but I couldn't understand him. I tried to smile at him, but I couldn't. He gave me his water bottle, and all I could muster was a blink to thank him. He wrapped a blanket around my shoulders and scooped me up like a baby in his arms.

I can't have weighed more than six stone by that point. I was dying. He carried me to what I now know was the Red Cross tent set up just outside the camp gates. He placed me down on a bed, and, within seconds, I was asleep. I slept, uninterrupted, for the first time in years."

It was me who insisted on a break now. I didn't give Daniel a choice. I needed it. I went to his kitchen to make a cup of tea for us both. I wanted him to take a break. By the time I returned, he was sat up straight.

He wanted to go on. He thanked me for listening. I thanked him for sharing. He continued.

"It took a long time to recover. Physically, I mean. Mentally, I don't believe I, or anyone who lived through that, will ever forget, nor should they. I am an old man now.

The years since the war have been kind to me.

I feel guilty. Why should I get to enjoy a life when so many others like me did not?

The demise of Hitler and the end of the war came soon after liberation, but that was just a sideshow for me then.

I wasn't really aware of what was happening away from Bergen Belsen.

The nurses and doctors told me I was suffering from dysentery and, more worryingly, tuberculosis. The extent of the damage was going to take weeks to diagnose, and recovery was only a slim possibility in my state, but I was determined to make it after years of struggle and oppression.

My body was a wreck, but they clearly thought I was worth saving. I was just about to turn seventeen. I still had my whole life in front of me, but recovery would take much, if not all, of that time. The Red Cross moved me to a mobile hospital in a nearby town. The British medics were first class. They really cared for me.

Slowly, over weeks, then months, I gained weight and strength. That's when I started to help out in the ward with menial tasks, such as cleaning or making beds. I wanted to give something back. My English improved rapidly – I even developed a bit of a scouse accent from the chaps I worked alongside.

I had nowhere else to go, and the staff were happy to have me there, even when I was considered healthy enough to leave. I approached the orderly and asked if there were any positions within the Red Cross. There was not much paperwork needed to enrol me into the team, and as a volunteer, I did not require payment, which made it an easy decision for them, I'm sure.

I was housed and well fed, and I asked for nothing more.

After liberation, the camp was closed. The remaining bodies were buried or cremated, and much of the site was demolished or burnt to the ground. The British used a nearby German Military School to set up a Displaced Person's Camp or 'DCP' for short.

So many people had nowhere to go. They did not know if any of their family members had survived, and they did not have any idea what to do or where to go next. Myself included.

I continued to work for the Red Cross, and I also spent a great deal of time at the DPC. At work, I could keep myself busy – learn English and help others, but away from the hospital, I felt lost and alone. I had nothing: no family, no home, no identity. It was shortly after this – sometime in Summer 1947, I think – that I met Ernie."

I sat bolt upright at this. It took me by surprise. I was fascinated by Daniel, and, for large parts of the afternoon, I forgot why I was even there. He captivated me. But the name brought me back to the present.

I focused on my job again. I hadn't asked any questions up to this point, but I had to ask him now.

"You met Ernie in Germany? Ernie Grimshaw?" He considered his reply before adding:

"It is important I tell you all of this, Paul. It is important you know my background and what happened to me as a child. It was vital for Ernie to know this too. I wouldn't be here today if Ernie had not studied my life. My past.

107

I couldn't help myself again. I blurted out –

"So, this is when you took Ernie's identity?" He replied, smiling for the first time since we sat down together...

"I think you may have misunderstood, Paul. It was not me who took Ernie's identity. He took mine!"

CHAPTER 7
Sickness and Health

13.2.19

3:15 p.m.

Back home. I have had much to think about on the drive back, but the overriding question I keep asking myself is – Where do I go from here? I am still in shock; I don't mind admitting. Mr. Frankenburg was brutally honest. Equally so in part two of the interview. I will reproduce the rest in the next few pages and then try to make a plan. Tomorrow I will write to Mr. Green with my findings and see which direction he wants me to go next.

The cost to him could be considerable if he wants to find out more. At least now I feel I am making progress of sorts.

PART TWO

Me: "Why would he take your identity? What did he have to gain by doing that? What happened to him? Do you know where he is? Is he still alive?"

I was like a machine gun firing out questions like bullets. Perhaps not the best simile for Daniel but an accurate one.

Daniel: *"So many questions, Paul. I know you must have so many, and I will try to answer them all as honestly as I can, but I need to take you through the chain of events that brought me to England. I will tell you all I know about Ernie, I promise. Hopefully it will give you enough to go on with the next stage of your investigation."*

Again, I was happy with this; it was clear that he trusted that my intentions were honourable, but then what did he have to lose? As he said...

"I am an old man now, Paul. If you choose to report me to the authorities, you are within your rights to do so. I don't suppose it matters now at my age, but I admit I do not regret this.

I feel so much better for having talked to someone about it. Everything I have told you is the truth. Everything I tell you now is the truth to the best of my memory.

I really hope it helps, and I really hope you can find out what happened to Ernie."

I assured him that everything he had told me would remain confidential. I assured him that I protect my sources of information. He seemed pleased to hear this.

"When I met Ernie for the first time, I was only eighteen. Almost nineteen. He was a year younger than me. We struck up a friendship almost straight away. We shared a similar sense of humour. I had almost forgotten what it was like to laugh and joke - but not with Ernie. His sense of fun was infectious.

There we were, in the middle of this hell on earth surrounded by reminders of the most inhumane period in human history, and he provided a chink of light in all this darkness.

In all that misery and sadness, he brought a smile to so many faces – none more so than mine. I was still working and volunteering with the Red

Cross, and in that summer of 1947, the British brought in a number of new recruits to help out. Most were young volunteers rather than medical staff – Ernie was one of them. He had signed up back in England and requested a posting in Germany to support the charity and the army in one of its most challenging hospitals. I wouldn't imagine they would consider such a request these days, but they were different times back then, and any experienced hand was welcome. Ernie was first aid trained and had been a volunteer with the Red Cross ever since his own illness. I will tell you more about that shortly."

Me: "What did Ernie's parents make of this? Were they happy to let him go? It must have been a huge wrench for them."

Daniel: *"From what he told me, they weren't happy, but they understood. The war was over, but it was still a dangerous place to be. To a large extent, though, they wouldn't know that. The media coverage was not as thorough back then. None of this internet or world-wide whatever nonsense. They would have been reliant on letters, newspaper reports and the occasional programme on the wireless.*

I wouldn't imagine they would read or hear anything about what was going on in Germany here in West Cumbria.

I doubt David and Mabel knew much about what it was like there – even two years after the war had come to an end.

Ernie did though. He told me. He studied every newspaper report and listened to every news broadcast.

He read books, journals and press releases.

He wrote to the regiments that liberated the camp.

He read testimonies from the soldiers and survivors of the camps. He studied the history of the conflict and the geography of countries involved. He met with medical staff who had served in Germany during the war.

During his teenage years, he had plenty of time on his hands, but he used it to good effect. He told me of his fascination with the conflict and how he could simply not understand man's inhumanity to man. He wanted, in his own small way, to help. He didn't want to sit at home. He wanted to be there, and when the Red Cross offered him the opportunity to work at Bergen Belsen, he jumped at the chance.

I doubt his parents could have stopped him if they'd tried. They would play their part going forward, but they didn't know this at the time.

By this point, having worked with the British for nearly two years, my English was excellent, and it became my first language. I would spend most of the day in the complex conversing with people who could only speak English so, as you can imagine, I was quite taken aback when I found out that Ernie was proficient in German.

He was mainly self-taught, although he had taken some private tuition – ironically from a German prisoner of war who was based in Cumbria and who went on to settle in Cockermouth. Ernie had met him in the local library there and had struck up an unlikely friendship. I say unlikely – Ernie could befriend anyone. He would never judge.

He never failed to surprise or amaze me.

Some of his pronunciation was shaky, and occasionally the word order was a struggle for him, but in the main, we could converse very well in both English and German.

He wanted me to teach him and correct him when he made mistakes. He was so keen to learn.

It was fun. Refreshing, even.

We spent so much time together. Our nickname in the camp was 'The Twins'. We had so much in common. I'd never really had a friend before. Not like this. I could talk with him, laugh, cry, mess about.

I trusted him. It felt so good. We lived similar early lives. We both had loving parents, and we were both very happy growing up. So much in common.

We looked alike too. Same height, same colour hair, same build. We were both slight and slim – the result of our past illnesses, I suppose.

Like I say, Ernie had such a good sense of humour. Everyone liked him – especially the girls. Neither of us were what I would consider good-looking, but that didn't seem to matter. He could charm the birds out of the trees. There was no arrogance about him. It was all very natural. He courted a few different girls on the camp, but he was a bit unlucky in love on that score. On at least three occasions, just as he felt he had met the right one and they were getting along nicely, they were posted elsewhere and that was that.

I didn't have the same confidence with the ladies as Ernie, but I did have a few dates.

Our double dates were legendary. We would spend whole evenings in stitches. The laughter was such a tonic. After all I had been through, I never imagined I would laugh and joke, but Ernie changed all that for me.

He wasn't daft though. He knew when to joke and when to be serious. The Displaced Persons'

Camp was definitely a place to be serious, and within a month or two of him being in Germany, he asked me if he could help there and could I make the necessary introductions. The fact that he could converse in German certainly went in his favour, and very soon we were working at both the Red Cross hospital and the DPC together.

What an impression he made there too!

Attitudes do not fade overnight, so Germany was still a very hostile environment for any Jew. Even after all that had happened, many Germans still blamed us, and, remarkably, Hitler still had a huge following in the country. The Germans had been beaten, and these people were angry, scared and suspicious.

They had no idea what their own future held. People always look to blame others and find a scapegoat or a target for their anger.

It was a small town with small-minded people, even two years on from the war. The DPC was often targeted by gangs spouting their hatred and bile. Many Jews were attacked and beaten. It was not safe to walk the streets at night or alone. The police were not interested. They would turn a blind eye to such assaults. Some Jews even received death threats. It was not a safe place to be.

Ernie was aware of the mood. He was very protective of the Jewish community. Not just the Jews – any minority group. Physically, he was no match for the thugs, but he didn't need to be.

He seemed to sense danger, and as such, help to avert or avoid it. He was careful. Not so much for himself but for those in his care. He would walk people home if they were frightened. He would plan safe routes to walk or help people with their shopping or bill paying if it saved them from any

114

confrontation or a potentially threatening situation. The community liked him. Trusted him. Even needed him.

He never asked for anything in return. He appreciated life and the lives of those he cared for.

The DPC could be a desperately sad place most of the time, but occasionally there were pockets of joy.

The people who approached the building tended to do so with an air of resignation. Few people were ever reunited with family or friends.

Most of the time, the best they could hope for was closure. Each day, dozens of names appeared on our register of those recorded as entering the camps. They were almost certainly dead, but the lack of anything concrete or final left anyone searching for their loved ones with only a sliver of hope. Deep down they knew. They feared the worst. They tried to come to terms with the worst, and yet, on occasion, that hope was rewarded.

Ernie worked ever so hard to keep that light burning.

We had a system of checking. Registers, lists, files – all linked to places, establishments, prisons, factories and any type of record you can imagine. We collated family trees and collected any type of identification documents we could lay our hands on, from birth certificates to school records. Ninety-nine per cent of the time our efforts would be futile, but systems were in place to help. We would give those enquiring any information we had and wished them well with their search. Even a negative outcome was a result – closure.

Ernie would do over and above his expected duty, though. He would do extra checks. He would go and speak to the families away from the DPC. He would travel to other towns to try to track down individuals to support those unable to do so on their own – the old, the sick or the vulnerable. More often than not, his extra efforts would be without reward, but occasionally, they bore fruit.

Those occasions were memorable. I recall one time, Ernie travelled to Frankfurt to visit a hospital where an old Jewish lady had worked before the war. Her daughter had approached the DPC with the faint hope of finding a trace of her but to no avail. Ernie had talked with her about her mother's life before the war, and she shared memories about those happier days. He asked about where she worked and where she lived.

He made notes and records that the DPC simply didn't have.

On his next weekend off, he travelled nearly 400 km south to Frankfurt on the hunt for someone else's old mother who was presumed dead.

He visited the hospital and found her record there. He located her old address. He spoke to the new residents there. They didn't remember her, but the neighbours did. They not only remembered her but had received a letter from her after the war had ended. The letter indicated that she was trying to find information about her daughter.

The neighbours had written back explaining that they were unable to help. But they still had an address.

The address was in Cologne, so you can guess where Ernie went next. She could not be found at that address – she had moved out only weeks before – but then he was able to find her new address from the landlord who lived in the flat above.

He spent most of that weekend travelling hundreds of miles on a wild goose chase for someone he didn't know. He found her though. I can only imagine the joy on her face when he told her that her daughter was alive and well and had been searching for her. He returned to the DPC late on the Sunday night with the news. He was exhausted but thrilled. I was there when he told the daughter. She broke down in tears at the news. She fell on the floor in front of us and sobbed and sobbed. Ernie sat on the floor with her and held her. He was in tears too. I think I was. We all were. The pair were reunited a day or two later at the DPC. Their embrace was incredible. I can't put it into words. They must have held each other, without any words, for ten minutes. A family reunited. A love reunited. Ernie made it possible. Hope made it possible.

This wasn't an isolated case. Even after DPC intervention and support, on many occasions, against all the odds, Ernie brought together dozens of families and friends, giving up countless hours of his own time for the cause.

I should have done more, I know. We all should. We did help, and we did bring solace to many, but Ernie was special. He didn't seek reward or recognition – ever. He only wanted to help. To do all he could. His reward was seeing the joy and the relief in others. And to think, if fate had been crueller, he wouldn't have ever reached Bergen Belsen in the first place. He was lucky to be alive."

Again, I was jolted back to reality. I had been lost in Daniel's story. A million thoughts had gone through my mind as he was speaking. Would I have done the same as Ernie? Probably not. I would like to think I would have; I would like to think I would

117

have been so thoughtful and dedicated, but deep down I knew I wouldn't have. If I had my time again...

Before I had time to ask any of the questions going through my head, Daniel answered them for me.

"Before this, during his teenage years – around his fourteenth birthday – Ernie had fallen ill. By all accounts, he had always been a fit and sporty child, but he had developed a cough he couldn't shake off. He had gone off food and developed terrible headaches and pains. He was constantly weary.

He would often fall asleep at his desk at school or double up in pain, coughing up thick globules of phlegm.

The doctors had been very quick to identify the symptoms and diagnose consumption – or tuberculosis. TB. According to David, Ernie lost nearly three stone in weight very quickly – a huge amount for one so young. He was wasting away. He was dying. Such a worry for David and Mabel. In the 1930s and 40s, TB was greatly feared. The cure was still in its infancy, and many sufferers did not survive. How Ernie had caught the illness was never established. Ernie told me one doctor attributed it to the animals on the farm, but others dismissed that theory. Either way, at that time, the first stage was to quarantine.

Ernie was sent to a sanatorium near Seaham in County Durham. He was away from home for over two years. For a family-orientated teen, this illness and isolation must have been awful. He was not permitted any visitors for the first six months, and after that, visits were restricted for "everyone's

118

benefit", according to the chief of staff there. His condition worsened in the first year there, and it was touch and go if he would pull through. On two of the visits David and Mabel made to the sanatorium to see Ernie, they had been accompanied by a priest in case the last rites had been needed. So, you can imagine the state he must have been in?

And yet, in spite of all this, Ernie still talked about this time with some fondness – the kind staff, the chance to learn and read more, the stunning seaside views. A few positives in a whole pile of negatives. He craved home, of course, but the one thing the experience gave him was a love of life and a will to live and to make the most of his time on earth.

It was in Seaham that he started to look at life further afield. He probably learnt more about events in Europe at this time than many politicians and government officials. He had a thirst for knowledge – whatever it was - and was fascinated by everything - wanting to learn from others what he couldn't find out for himself through reading. Ernie was an academic but also very practical. As he recovered and regained his strength and physique, he volunteered for more and more. He helped in the library and the local school. He formed friendships with charity workers and supported local sports clubs and services – raising money through fundraising events. It was around this time that he tried to repay the hospital in his own way by doing volunteer work for them.

He trained in first aid and basic care. He helped in the old folks' home and did what he could for others within the sanatorium, such as the disabled or mentally ill.

How he crammed it all in I will never know.

I didn't learn much about this time from Ernie himself, I must admit. The stories came from his parents and the dozens of thank-you letters he received back at the farm after his return home to Cumbria.

David and Mabel showed them to me when I first moved here. Ernie never really talked about his time there, as was typical of him, but others had plenty to say.

Apparently, he has a plaque or a bench or a tree in his honour every fifty yards down the main street in Seaham!

One letter even suggested he should have a bloody statue in the town centre. It made me laugh when I read it, but only because I agreed with the sentiments. He deserved a statue in Bergen too. He was held in such high regard. I don't know what he did when he was in Seaham, but whatever it was it must have been very special to receive so many accolades and such praise.

Ernie was nearly sixteen when he returned home. Still the same boy who had left for the sanatorium in an ambulance.

Fitter, wiser, cleverer and more worldly-wise but still the same boy. His heart was as strong as it ever was, and his good nature could not be killed off – just like his will to battle on.

His parents were delighted to have him home, of course. They were ever so proud of him too. He continued to work on the farm and support them, but, physically, he was not the same and couldn't cope with the labour. This was understandable and expected.

David was very protective of him and brought in a farmhand to take on many of his chores.

The whole community was on hand to help too. Everyone around here seems to be from the same stock. They didn't have much, but what they did have they were willing to share. Time is worth more than money.

David and Mabel were never social animals. They kept themselves to themselves, but I know they had received lots of messages from the villagers over this difficult time, and they really appreciated that support.

Ernie had another further period of isolation on the farm. He rarely ventured out. It was probably a case of his parents being overprotective, but all of this had an effect on him, I am sure. I think he was ready to fly the nest after that. He was so keen to try something new and to see the world. David and Mabel knew this.

'Prospect' didn't offer many prospects for the young Ernie to continue with the good deeds he had become known for in Seaham. He loved his parents dearly, and they loved him, but they knew he was keen to leave and have adventures beyond Cumbria when he was fit and able again. I just don't think they expected him to end up in Germany.

And so, back to Belsen and how we got to where we are today.

Ernie and I continued to work for the DPC and the Red Cross, but by the late 40s, the British were descaling the operation. They wanted out, in short. The Red Cross had other priorities, and the sick were being moved on and treated elsewhere. It was only ever going to be a temporary hospital facility, but it lasted longer than most expected.

The DPC was the same. By the end of the decade, those in charge could not justify keeping the facility open. Records were kept and filed, and

121

copies distributed to the relevant offices and libraries should anyone wish to access them. The general mood was, 'if people haven't been found now, they never will be'. And so, the place was to be closed before the end of 1950.

For many of us, it was a case of what to do next. It was a frightening and unsettling time. Personally, I had not given the future a great deal of thought. I was living in the present. It all took me by surprise. I was very much alone. I was soon to be jobless and homeless with nobody to turn to – other than my friend, Ernie.

One evening, in front of a log fire at the Red Cross barracks, we discussed what might happen. Ernie revealed that he had already been thinking a great deal about the future and what might happen to us all. To my surprise, he told me that he had been thinking about my situation and had been planning what we could do together. Together? Typically, he was thinking of others before himself.

I felt reassured. Wanted – safe even. I wasn't alone. I had my trusted friend, Ernie. That said, I certainly wasn't prepared for what he had planned."

Daniel continued. I was riveted.

"At the time the camp at Belsen was liberated, two of the survivors were twin sisters.

At some point earlier during the war, they had been separated from their parents and eventually found themselves in Belsen. They were eight years old in 1945. Malnourished, suffering from dysentery and riddled with lice. How they pulled through was a testament to the human spirit, and their togetherness. They spent a long time in the hospital. Months.

On a few occasions they were both expected to give up the fight, but we all underestimated them. They fought on and somehow recovered. They became a symbol of the fight for survival. They were inseparable too. When they were strong enough, they helped in and around the hospital and lived on the site. Both girls were shy and insular – totally understandable considering what they had been through. They were called Annabella and Rebecca Kaplan. At some point, they left the hospital and moved into what I can only guess was a type of foster care facility for younger children who had no known family. That must have been early 1946.

We didn't hear from them again until they visited the DPC together in 1948 to try to find out what happened to their family. Thankfully for them, they spoke to Ernie.

In his spare time, he had been working on requests for information.

Ernie took it upon himself to help by searching the records he had access to. He found only one reference to them: probably the worst. Both parents were on a register for passengers, boarding a train to Poland and Auschwitz.

It was fair to assume they did not survive much longer after that, but as I said before, we all clung on to hope. The twins were no exception, but they were at a loss as to what they could do.

But, of course, Ernie felt he could do more. He felt it was too early to draw a line under the query despite the lack of information. He asked the girls to leave it with him, and he would get back in touch with them within a week. At this time, they were staying in a town called Celle to the south of Bergen with a kindly German couple who had taken them under their wing after their recovery.

They were happy there, and they had great affection for the couple, but the desire to find out what had happened to their own parents was strong. Ernie was true to his word. He took it upon himself to travel all the way across Germany and Poland to visit Auschwitz to check the paperwork there. This was a perilous journey at that time for a young Brit. Though, with his Red Cross badge and accreditation, he managed to cut through a lot of red tape and bureaucracy. The site was very different then to the memorial it is today. Ernie passed through countless security checks, border patrols and administrative obstacles before he found what he was looking for. He found their parents.

They had both arrived at the camp in August 1943 and managed to avoid the 'finger to the left', otherwise known as the death line, where people were sent to the ovens as soon as they stepped off the train.

The parents had been split up from each other. At this point, those chosen for work duty were sent to another area of the camp. Women and men were all assigned work duties but were housed in separate barracks. For many, it was as bad as hell itself, and thousands met their end this way, but not the Kaplans. They spent a few months in Auschwitz then, for some reason, they were transferred to Flossenburg in the southeast of Germany with a dozen others.

It was unusual for them to have been transferred as a couple, and Ernie could not find any reason for this in the paperwork. Rumour would suggest they may have offered bribes to guards, but this could not be substantiated.

Ernie continued the search and travelled the long journey east through Poland and

Czechoslovakia, as it was then, on his mission to find out what happened to them. Flossenburg, like many camps, had been initially designed for just a few thousand, but as the years went by and the numbers of prisoners grew, it was expanded to accommodate more 'workers'. Ploughing through more paperwork, he managed to find them - again. They survived the end of the war and were liberated by the Americans in April 1945.

The fact that it was the Americans who had liberated the camp proved to be very significant. As part of the whole issue of resettlement, the Americans offered sanctuary to hundreds of Jewish people there.

The Kaplans were two of the lucky ones. From what Ernie managed to find out, the pair had boarded a ship for New York in August 1945.

The paper trail ended there.

He returned to the DPC with the news, and we met with the girls to explain what he had found out. Needless to say, they were ecstatic. Their optimism had been rewarded – thanks to Ernie. There were still no guarantees of a happy ending here, but the chances were good. Very good. Understandably, the twins wanted to leave and find their parents as soon as possible – if it was possible - but it wasn't that easy. We recognised we would need to formulate a plan, but Ernie had already considered much of this on his return journey. It was quite some plan for all of us. Life-changing, in fact, if we pulled it off.

Ernie was determined to look after us all, reducing the risk to us as much as possible and taking the burden of responsibility on his own shoulders. If this was to happen, the twins, who were still only eleven years old, couldn't travel alone. With his sense of responsibility to the fore, Ernie was insistent that he would be the one to accompany the girls on their search. He would have been their choice too, as they had come trust him wholeheartedly. Further difficulties would need to be overcome.

Their guardians would need to agree; there were many expenses to consider, and also the girls' general wellbeing and state of mind, given what they had already been through.

However, more crucially, there was the even bigger issue of two young Jewish girls travelling with a non-Jewish Brit who had yet to reach adulthood himself.

Ernie was still under eighteen – just – and would not be permitted to travel alone with them. They were German Jews. He was British and unrelated. The chances of them all securing a visa was non-existent. Me, on the other hand, I was also a German Jew - like the twins - and old enough to travel as their guardian. I could take them.

Ernie then put the cat amongst the pigeons by suggesting we swap identities – names, paperwork, IDs – so that he could travel with the girls to America, essentially as an adult Jew, to help them find their parents. I was taken aback. It wasn't the plan I was expecting, but when I had time to think, I could certainly see his logic. He further explained how I could take on his life which would benefit me, and he was certain his parents would understand and support his plan. I was too old for school. I could work on the farm. Ernie had been in hospital and well-hidden since he was thirteen. The family didn't socialise much with the locals. Nobody would really know any difference. As far as anyone in Cumbria was concerned, I would be Ernie. I would have his paperwork, I would live in his family home, and I

126

would assume his identity. I would be David and Mabel's son. Nobody would be any the wiser.

The paperwork was very basic back then. On the grainy images that you would call a photograph, Ernie and I looked very similar. We both spoke German and English very well.

As for me, I was little more than a number and name. My own history and family were lost to the Nazi war machine. I had no birth certificate, school reports, doctor or dental records. For all intents and purposes, I was reborn after the liberation of Bergen Belsen.

My paperwork trail started then. The hospital was closing, the DPC too. We were about to be left to fend for ourselves.

Ernie's paperwork would get me to Britain. It would get me a new life – with people I could trust. He would be able to help the twins and travel to America with them. One day we would be reunited. It was a great plan.

As for the cost of this plan, between us, we had plenty of money saved up for travel and expenses. We had been able to save most of our wages: accommodation had been free and living costs minimal. We were both relatively wealthy young men and were prepared to commit our savings to this cause.

Ernie carefully and cautiously shared the idea with the twins and their guardians, and to his delight, after serious consideration, they gave their consent and approval, as they felt it would be best for the girls. The twins couldn't believe that someone would do all this for them. They could not contain their excitement, but they were well aware that they could not share this plan with others, as it would jeopardise even this slim chance of them finding

127

their parents. It all seemed so simple. So easy. We all agreed to go for it.

Over the next few weeks, Ernie contacted his parents and explained his idea. He asked them if they would help us in principle. After the initial shock of what seemed to them to be a crazy idea, they agreed to back and support their son. It all sounded so bizarre, but there was method in his madness, and his parents trusted their son's instinct and his motivation to do good by others.

By the spring of 1948, we were set to go.

Ernie told me he would write when he could. We had agreed on a period of non-contact – three months to be precise. Just to let the dust settle and make sure all was well.

And that was that.

I boarded a train in Hanover set for Amsterdam. From there I took a ferry to England. As planned, I stayed in London for a night before heading to Cumbria and a new life. I had no idea what would happen, but I don't recall feeling nervous at all. I remember being excited. When I set foot on English soil, paperwork in hand and a new identity to fall back on, I felt free for the first time since the start of the war.

I was met at Carlisle train station by David and Mabel, and they could not have been more welcoming. They were helping their son as much as they were helping me. Life with them was everything I had dreamed and imagined from the moment Ernie had told me of his plan. Within days, I felt like I belonged. They wanted to know everything about me and wanted me to tell them everything I could about Ernie. They were incredibly proud of him.

I had so much to tell them – about our friendship, his achievements and his desire to help others. It was a magical time. I knew they were missing him. I was too. But me simply being there helped them, I'm sure.

Ernie and I had said our goodbyes and good lucks a day before my train departed. He had to get ready for his own journey with the twins. We had purchased all our travel tickets without any problems, and no one had questioned us. It was all so easy. They were going to sail from the port of Hamburg in northern Germany.

We held on to each other so tightly. I didn't want to let go. He was my friend. My brother. He had given me his identity – his life. He could not have done any more than that for me. As the tears filled our eyes and streamed down our faces, we promised we would look out for each other for as long as we were able. We promised to never give in. We promised we would see each other again.

When we parted that day, it broke my heart. He was my best friend. My companion. My brother. Everything and everyone had been taken from me. I didn't want to lose him as well, but I knew it was for the best. He had to help those girls. I understood that.

He boarded that ship as Daniel Frankenburg, and I left for England as Ernie Grimshaw. I was him and he was me.

And here I am. But where is he?"

At this point, we both sat back in our chairs. He stopped talking and looked down at the floor. I looked at this old man and I cried. I am not ashamed to admit it. I cried and cried and cried.

CHAPTER 8
Mr. Green

14.2.19

I had a lot to ponder on my way back down to Lancashire, Mr. Diary. This is not like any other case I have taken on in the past, and even after spending hours in the company of a man who has all but *been* Ernie Grimshaw for the last seventy years, I still don't know much about the real man, last spotted sailing to America with twin girls in search of their parents in 1948.

I know he was going under a new name – Daniel Frankenburg – and I know a little more about his childhood and upbringing, not to mention his battle against TB. I even have a picture of him as a strapping teenager. But what now?

I must admit, it has all been quite an emotional few days. A bit of self-reflection is needed too, Mr. Diary.

Listening to the real Mr. Frankenburg speak has really hit home with me. Do I do enough for other people? Do I do enough to help? What is the purpose of my life? Ever since I started this case, I have found myself analysing everything I do and say. He didn't say anything to shame me. He doesn't even know me. But listening to that man speak touched me like never before. I felt ashamed of myself in a way. Embarrassed. Inspired, even. I want my life to mean something too.

When this is all wrapped up, I am going to start afresh – be a better man.

I will give more to charity or do more (some) volunteer work. I might adopt a gorilla.

I might even adopt a child. No, let's not get carried away.

I have neglected my mother for long enough. I will nip over there tomorrow for a catch-up and an earbashing for something she has imagined I have done wrong. I promise I will listen too. Little steps. I will become a better person.

In the morning, I shall write to Mr. Green with all I have and see if that is enough for him. With a quick calculation, his tab is already over £1,500 with the hotel and expenses, and I really don't have a lot to give him other than a transcript of the interviews and a general overview of dates, times and places. I am afraid the rest of Ernie's history sailed away with him across the Atlantic.

15.2.19

My first day as a new man has hit the rails already. A reply text from my mother to say she is going to the bingo tonight has burst my bubble. I half expected her to jump at the chance to spend some time with her dear son after not seeing me for a good while.

Perhaps I was expecting too much too soon.

Anyway, it is not like I don't have anything to do – starting with a letter to Mr. Green.

I will draft a letter and replicate here, as always. I'll enclose with it a copy of the interview with Mr. Frankenburg, a scan of the photograph and a summary of work done (with costs incurred, of course).

Note to self: If I do not hear back from him by the end of the month, I will chase it up.

The other ancestry work will keep me ticking over through spring and summer, and this payment for Mr. Green's case will be a very welcome bonus when it arrives. Despite the intense self-reflection, I have really enjoyed this case. Something a little different and less, well, sleazy than the usual collection of affairs, theft and abuse cases I have been lumbered with.

Mr. William Green	**Mr. Paul Brunskill**
XXXXX XXXXXX XXXXX	**XXXXX XXXXXXX**
XXXXXXXXXXXX	**XXXXXXXXXX**
XXXX	**XXXXXXXXXX**
XXX XXX	**XXXXXXXX**
XXXXXX	

15th February 2019

Dear Mr. Green,

First, may I thank you for your continued faith in me and my investigations.

I must admit, finding Mr. Grimshaw was not easy. In fact, I am still not sure I have, but the details of my findings will become apparent when you read the documents enclosed.

This has not been a normal search and retrieve case. The birth certificate alone proved to be a challenge. Home births – especially those in a rural setting – are never straightforward, and records kept are both erratic and scarce in the main. Mr. Grimshaw proved to be no different, hence my need to travel to Cumbria.

Age also proved to be a problem. In ninety years, a lot can, and does, change. Unfortunately, there was no one left in the area who knew the real Mr. Grimshaw. By 'real' I

mean just that. Again, the enclosed documents will give more explanation.

Mr. Grimshaw is/was quite an extraordinary man, from what I can gather. Unfortunately, as you will read, circumstances have conspired against us, and the search has reached a premature conclusion.

I hope you are satisfied with the work done. If you require any further information, please do not hesitate to ask. I have enclosed all receipts for expenses and a detailed invoice.

As the bill is quite large, if you wish to spread the cost over a six-monthly period, please let me know, and I will arrange for a standing order to be taken.

It has been a pleasure working for you, and I hope you are satisfied with the outcome.

Yours sincerely,

Paul Brunskill Private Investigator

Enc:
Doc 1: Invoice
Doc 2: Summary of investigation
Doc 3: Copy of interview

18.2.19

Two new offers of work popped into the inbox this morning – both of which I think I will decline. I have reproduced the messages below with profanities crossed out. I would imagine both would be easy to solve, but gut feeling tells me they would be more hassle than they are worth.

Number 1:

*I need a detective to find out what my cheating ******* of a husband is up to and who with.*

*I suspected ages ago that he was up to no good. He has cheated on me before with various ****s where he works, and I think he is at it again. I just need someone to catch him in the act so I can cut his **** off.*

*His name is Tony McNulty. He works for the council – or so he says. He is never ******* there.*

He is 46 years old.

Can I pay over twelve months?

Kerry McNulty

Number 2:

Dear Sir,

I have never had reason to seek to employ the services of a private investigator until now. I am very concerned about my partner's behaviour, and I would like to know what he is doing in his spare time. We are engaged to be married – a commitment and a promise to God that we both take very seriously. Christianity is central to everything we do, but I suspect my intended is struggling to stay on the right path at this moment in time. If my suspicions are correct, with the help of Jesus Christ, I want to help him.

Although close, we are not sexually compatible, and even though this is incredibly frustrating on my part, I do not wish to lose him.

I know he struggles to control his demons – gambling being one, sexual gratification the other.

I know he has frequented adult clubs and strip joints. This makes me feel inadequate, and whilst this is preferable to him having an affair, it is incredibly hurtful.

The gambling addiction is also a curse. He is very protective of his finances and refused to consider a joint account for our bills. When we met, he was a wealthy individual and very careful with his money. I can only imagine the damage this has had on his bank balance.

Through prayer, the good Lord encouraged me to find you. Can you help, Mr. Brunskill?

Are you able to find out the extent of the damage done and help recover his soul? I must do what I can to save him if it is not too late.

God bless you Lesley Andrews

It is funny – a month ago, I would have willingly accepted both cases. I reckon both would take me no more than a couple of days to solve and would be worth at least £600, but now they just aren't worth the hassle.

I will politely decline. Responses noted below.

Number 1:
Dear Kerry,

Thank you for your email. On this occasion, I am afraid I will not be able to provide a service. I am currently inundated with requests for work. I wish you luck during this difficult and worrying time. There are many other reputable private investigators out there. I am sure you will have no difficulty finding a suitable candidate to take on your case.

Thank you for your interest.

Mr. Paul Brunskill

Number 2:
Dear Lesley,

It is with regret that I will have to decline your offer of work. I am presently overwhelmed with cases and simply not in a position to take on any new jobs at this time.

I can empathise with your predicament. Addiction of any kind can be both dangerous and destructive. Your partner is lucky to have such huge support. I can see how important your faith is too. I suggest you approach him with your concerns and - if he is willing - seek counselling.

On this occasion, I can't help. I am sure God can though.

Mr. Paul Brunskill

I hope I didn't sound too flippant at the end there. I am always a little uneasy around religion. I seem fairly hollow when it comes to spiritual intervention, and I suppose that makes me a little too sceptical of others of deep faith. Something else I need to learn.

I think I will have the rest of the day off. Housework, shopping, ironing. The ancestry and a dip into the past can wait until tomorrow.

19.2.19

Nothing to report on the ancestry front. Easy money but boring as hell. Maybe I shouldn't have turned down those other two jobs.

20.2.19

Mr. Diary, you just never know what this job will throw up do you? I am absolutely buzzing right now.

Mr. Green, I could kiss you. It was all set to be another day digging through archives and family trees until the postman dropped this rather unexpected but welcome letter through my door.

Copy below:

Mr. P Brunskill   *Mr. William Green*
XXXXXXXXXXXXXX   *XXXXX XXXX XXXXXXX*
XXXXXXXXX   *XXXXXXXXXXX*
XXXXXXXX
XXXXXX   *XXXX*
XXX XXX
18.2.19

Dear Paul,

Thank you ever so much for your letter dated 15th February 2019.

To be honest, I opened your letter with some trepidation. I had no idea what you might uncover for me – if anything – but I was stunned and delighted by your findings. It certainly was not what I was expecting. You have clearly gone over and above the norm, and for that, I am extremely grateful. You have taken me on a journey through one of the most harrowing times in our recent history with Mr. Grimshaw at its heart.

And yet, our timeline has only taken us as far as 1948. If you are keen, I would like the journey to continue. As you will see, I have enclosed a cheque for £1,828 to cover work and expenses so far. Money well spent.

I have also enclosed a second cheque for £10,000 which will hopefully be enough for the next stage.

If you are willing and able, I would like you to visit Seaham in County Durham and try to find any other evidence of Mr. Grimshaw's time there. After that, I would like you to travel to the USA and stay on the trail.

Please think about my appeal for help. I would understand if you did not have time in your busy schedule to take on such a request, but if you are able, I would be obliged if you could send an outline of your plans and proceed once the cheques have cleared into your account.

If the job is not for you, merely return the cheque to me in the envelope provided. I do hope you cash the cheque. We still have a man to find.

Best wishes and thank you once again for your efforts.

William Green

I have spent the last ten minutes dancing around the living room grinning like a Cheshire cat. Will I cash the cheque and carry on? Of course, I bloody will! Wow. What an opportunity. I have never visited America before, and now I am being paid to go there.

The idea that the case had reached its conclusion at Hamburg docks did not sit well with me. It seemed like a job half done.

Well, not anymore.

Ernie – the real Ernie – I'm coming to find you.

CHAPTER 9
Using your initiative

21.2.20

I couldn't sleep last night with everything buzzing around in my head. I will write back to Mr. Green later today and accept the job, but not before I have put the two cheques in the bank.

£10,000! Wow. That is the biggest one-off payment I have ever had. Return flights won't even cost £1,000 so there is plenty to play with. How long should I go for? Will a week be enough? It is a big country. What if I can't trace him? I will be on foreign soil with no contacts. I have no knowledge of the administration and records systems there. I will have to buy a return ticket and secure a visa. I will fast-track that. By all accounts, they are not very welcoming at the American airports and even less so if you haven't got the proof that you will be leaving soon afterwards.

I will have to do a little digging and prep work before I go. If I look to go this time next week that should give me plenty of time. I have a little trip to County Durham to do first. I will go up there first thing in the morning and make it an overnighter. I can certainly afford it now.

I have not been on the Durham coast since I was a little boy. I just remember it being absolutely Baltic, and that was in the summer. February is going to be worse, so I had better pack accordingly.

Things to do:
Book hotel for tomorrow night.

Write letter to Mr. Green and post it rocket class.

Price up return flights to New York and hotels for the first three nights.

Secure visa.

Ask mother to look after Flea again while I am away (I am sure he is happier at her house anyway).

Contact immigration office to start person trace 8 p.m.

Well, that is the hotel sorted. No need to be extravagant. For £65 I have booked a double room at Number 16 – a boutique room (whatever that is) very close to the coast in Seaham.

Apparently, it is situated at the start of the Durham Coastal Trail and opposite *Tommy*, the famous statue in the town commemorating the fallen soldiers of World War I. Appropriate in a way, what with Ernie's wartime efforts. The rooms look pleasant, and the sea air will do me good. No time for the coastal walk though. I am on a fact-finding mission and with not much time to find the facts. I will set off early in the morning and get there about 10 a.m. That will give me a full day and the best part of another to find out what I can.

If Mr. Frankenburg's recollections are correct, Ernie seemed to have left an impression on the place. Hopefully time hasn't eroded any trace.

Whilst surfing the net, I got an idea of flight prices for the US. Options to fly to either JFK airport or Newark ranging between £650 and £1250 return, depending on best times for departure and arrival. I want to avoid jetlag if possible and make the most of the time I have there. I am not a heavy sleeper, so I don't foresee a problem there. I will

141

confirm times and book when I return from County Durham.

Right, the final job for tonight is to draft a letter to Mr. Green. I will post it in the morning on my way up to the Northeast. I will also cash in those cheques.

Don't forget the cheques.

Mr. William Green   *Mr. Paul Brunskill*
XXXXX XXXXXX XXXXX   *XXXXX XXXXXXX*
XXXXXXXXXXXX   *XXXXXXXXXX*
XXXX   *XXXXXXXXXX*
XXX XXX   *XXXXXXXX*
XXXXXX

21st February 2019

Dear Mr. Green,

Thank you so much for your letter and the enclosed cheques. I am delighted to accept your offer and to continue the search for Mr. Grimshaw. I do admit, I felt that the job was incomplete, and I was a little dismayed at the thought of leaving the trail at the docks in Hamburg.

As an investigator, an unsolved mystery is an unsatisfactory conclusion.

I am so pleased that you are satisfied with the findings so far, and I will endeavour to unearth far more as we move forward. Records dating back to the 1940s are, understandably, often incomplete or difficult to trace, but I am confident there will be evidence of a trail.

I intend to travel to the Northeast tomorrow morning and stay overnight. This should give me enough time to substantiate the story told by Mr. Frankenburg and look for any other traces of Mr. Grimshaw's time in the town.

I intend to fly to New York City early next week (depending on flight times and availability) and stay for one week. If, for any reason, I need more time, I will change the return flight accordingly, but I do not see this being an issue. I am confident I can track, trace and gather what I need in seven days.

I will, of course, keep any receipts and invoices from both trips, and copies will be sent to you to show justification of expenditure.

I will keep a daily record of my plans and movements as always. Any relevant information will be sent to you on my return. Hopefully, we will be able to move the timeline forward beyond 1948.

Mr. Grimshaw clearly means a lot to you. He does to me too now.

Thank you for your continued support. I will strive to do the job to the best of my ability and to your satisfaction.

Yours sincerely,

Paul Brunskill Private Investigator

I have more than enough money in my account to cover the cost of the flight, the hotels for the first three nights and any other expenses before the two cheques clear. I really should wait for them to clear into my account, but excitement has got

143

the better of me, and rational thinking has gone by the wayside.

This cavalier approach is not like me. I don't know anything about this Mr. Green, but instinct tells me I can trust him. I do trust him. Perhaps the giddiness of a trip to America is playing havoc with my usual caution but, what the hell; you only live once.

11:00 p.m.

Bedtime. I have managed to do a little bit of research on Seaham and the sanatorium there. Apparently, it is now a luxury spa facility. The grand house has been extended over the years, but the original building, derelict in the 1970s, seems to have had a heck of a history, entertaining both royalty and the grumpy poet Lord Byron, who married then dumped his wife there to live abroad. He left her to bring up their child alone.

As a sanatorium, its staff cared for many TB infected patients, and others with severe chest problems, when it opened its doors again as a hospital in 1922. Of the few grainy, black and white images of the building at this time, it looks a remote but tranquil place. The huge grounds offering plenty of space to relax and recuperate whilst breathing in the brisk, salty gusts from the North Sea. Ernie certainly seemed to have developed a fondness for the town during his stay there, and if Daniel is to be believed, the residents took to him with great affection too. He was known to join in, and even lead, local fundraising events. He volunteered to help with everything from litter picking to beach cleaning. Daniel was clearly proud of his friend – in awe even.

144

As strange as it sounds, Mr. Diary, I feel like I am on the hunt for one of my own relatives now. I have become quite fond of old Ernie, and I seem to know more about him than I do anyone else. Another jolt to the system highlighting the fact that I have never allowed anyone to get to know me or me them. That is another thing about me I will have to change. This is a lonely job at the best of times, but with this case I feel part of something. I feel part of someone else's life like never before. I want to find him. I need to find him.

Goodnight, Mr. Diary. Another early start, but one I am relishing getting up for.

22.2.19

11:15 a.m.

Seaham Harbour (car park)

I am a little early to check in, which is no problem. Traffic was a bit chaotic and slow on the way up, but I am here now. The northeast coast in February is never the most inviting of places, and today is no exception. It is absolutely glacial. I will have a walk up the promenade and to the Spa hotel (formerly the sanatorium). I am not expecting to find anything there. I wouldn't imagine there is much need for a luxury spa to regale guests with stories of TB and chest infections, and I would not have thought the staff would have any idea of the workings of a hospital in the 1930s and '40s, but it will certainly be worth a visit. It certainly looks impressive from the photos online.

I shall update you again, Mr. Diary, when I check into the hotel. I hope the heating is on. I think I am going to need it.

4:15 p.m.

Well, another day of surprises and shocks on the trail of Mr. Grimshaw. Not what I was expecting at all, but I am buzzing once again. My boutique hotel room at Number 16 is beautiful, by the way – and most importantly, it is nice and toasty. I thought my fingers were going to fall off with the cold by the time I got back to the car, but it was worth it. A friendly host too. Who needs a luxury spa hotel when you have warm people and a warm room?

I left the car at the pay and display car park near the harbour, and there was not a soul in sight. I was not surprised either – the wind chill made it feel like minus 20 degrees, and I was walking into the wind along the exposed, open front. I imagined even the fish out at sea would need their thermals on. Thick, slate grey clouds hovered above, and rain threatened. A truly miserable day weather-wise.

As I made my way along the prom, leaning into the wind, I made a point of checking the bench plaques and inscriptions. There were eight in total along the promenade. All were dedications to lost loved ones. A bench placed on their favourite spot.

'She loved it here', 'It is where he felt most at ease', 'Our treasured place'.

Lovely reminders of happier days. They must have been hardy souls if they ever stood or sat at that spot on wild and windy days like this. One bench, however, had a different inscription. The bronze plaque and bench were clearly very old – much older than the others along the same stretch. The wooden slats had rotted, and the bolts and screws rusted and deformed with age. The bench looked weary and ready for the scrap heap, but for

146

now, it remained. The message was a simple one, but it grabbed my attention and got the butterflies swirling in my stomach.

'TO MARTHA NUGENT. FRIEND AND INSPIRATION. WITHOUT YOUR DETERMINATION AND SENSE OF FUN I WOULD HAVE NOT BEEN ABLE TO SURVIVE. YOUR SEAT IF YOU EVER CHOOSE TO RETURN – E.G.'

Ernie? Possibly? Probably? Who was/is Martha Nugent? No dates or extra information to go on but a welcome surprise indeed. But it made me think of Daniel's words. Part of me expected to see a row of dedications along the front for Ernie, and yet, here was one which appeared to be *from* Ernie. Now I felt I had to find out who Martha was/is. You don't make this easy for me do you, Ernie?

I seemed to forget the cold as I walked on into the wind. My head was filled with thoughts and scenarios. A love interest? It seemed unlikely – he was only a young teen at the time. The message wasn't a love note either – it spoke of a friendship – but who was she?

I turned left, away from the sea, and I was grateful to feel the wind bash the side of my hood rather than my face. I walked up a slight incline towards what was Seaham Hall Sanatorium. The inscription on the bench was still tormenting me, but something else caught my eye. Just off the site of the road was a small gate leading into a garden. There were no summer colours to welcome me as I walked towards the entrance, but there was a sign. Again, my heart skipped a beat as I read.

'WELCOME TO THE ERNIE GRIMSHAW GARDEN OF HOPE. THIS TREASURED SPACE IS DEDICATED TO ALL THE STAFF AND PATIENTS OF THE SEAHAM HALL SANATORIUM. THE GARDEN IS FUNDED AND MAINTAINED BY THE SEAHAM ROUND TABLE SOCIETY IN MEMORY OF ALL WHO SURVIVED, SUFFERED OR SERVED TIME HERE.'

I felt like I had found the pot of gold at the end of the rainbow. Underneath the main text was a separate dedication to Ernie himself.

NEVER DOUBT WHO YOU ARE, WHAT YOU ARE CAPABLE OF AND WHAT YOU MEAN TO OTHERS, ERNIE GRIMSHAW. THIS GARDEN IS DEDICATED TO YOU FOR ALL YOUR HELP, SUPPORT, LOVE AND DEDICATION. YOU GAVE HOPE WHERE THERE WAS NONE, AND WE WILL BE FOREVER GRATEFUL. YOU HELPED SO MANY OF APPRECIATE LIFE. THIS GARDEN IS LIFE.

A FITTING TRIBUTE TO A TRULY ASTONISHING YOUNG MAN. BE SUCCESSFUL IN WHATEVER YOU DO.
THE GOOD PEOPLE OF SEAHAM 1945.

The harsh winter winds had taken their toll on the garden. Only a few evergreens stood firm, but it was clear to see that the garden remained well maintained and would be ready to bloom again when the warmer weather returned. There was no litter or mess. The stonework was immaculate too.

There was clearly a lot of love for this place. I took a number of photographs for the record that can be sent on to Mr. Green as evidence.

The more I found out, the more I wanted to know. I continued up the hill towards Seaham Hall. I didn't expect to find anything there, but I had come this far. At least the wind would be at my back on the return trip to the car.

I was quite taken aback by the splendour of the building. It was huge. The photographs online had not really done it justice; its rebirth as a hotel and spa was quite stunning. I was neither a guest nor a member, and I didn't feel comfortable walking in by the main doors. Judging by the quality of the cars in the car park, it was not the type of place that would welcome bedraggled riff raff from the street, but I had come this far – I had to complete the journey.

The reception was bright, white, open and grand. Thankfully, there were a few people milling about, and I was able to explore the walls for signs of the past. I didn't expect to find any. Instead, large pictures of stones, flowers and running water hung down to help to relax guests. I soaked in the ambiance and warmth long enough to change back to my usual colour before making my way to reception. I asked if I could speak to the manager; I felt like he or she would have a little more local knowledge than the young girl at the desk. She looked me up and down with all the tact an eighteen-year-old can muster, and her smile did not hide her feelings towards me. I couldn't blame her. I was more Brad Shit than Brad Pitt.

She asked me to take a seat, and within a few minutes I was joined by a heavily made-up lady in a tight-fitting black suit. Figure-hugging, you could say. According to the badge, her name was Lynn. I explained briefly why I was there and who I was looking for. She smiled, that same smile the girl on reception gave me, and told me she didn't even know the history of the building before it became a spa. She was from Darlington, she said.

As if that explained it all. I knew I was clutching at straws. She wasn't even aware of the garden down the road. I thanked her for her 'help', and she told me I was more than welcome to come back and try the facilities, with all the sincerity of the wolf inviting one of the three little pigs around to his house for a game of cards and a chat.

I left the way I came in but decided to walk a circle of the building before heading off back to the car. It took longer than I thought. The gardens were huge. At the back, the vast green expanse of grass led down to some steps and a clear view of the sea. I stood right in the middle of the lawn with the gusts battering me, thinking that I could have been standing in the exact same spot that Ernie might have stood. I must have been stood there a while before I realised that I had company.

I turned to face an older man – perhaps in his sixties – staring at me. He smiled and apologised for startling me. He introduced himself as the site manager or general dogsbody. He explained that he had heard the manager talking to the receptionist about me after I had gone and had decided to follow me.

It was a ridiculous situation. Both of us stood there being battered by the wind in the most exposed place possible. Despite that, I introduced myself and repeated what I had said to the manager about why I was there. He said something derogatory about the two blonde and bronzed bimbos in reception, and then said that he might be able to help. My ears pricked up. He introduced himself as Mike Irving. He told me he was busy just now but was not working the next day, and, if I was interested, he could meet up with me and tell me what he knew about the old place. We exchanged numbers (me shivering so much I could barely tap the keyboard), and I promised to call in the morning. He smiled, shook my hand and wandered off pushing a wheelbarrow full of rocks. Another unexpected lead. I was frozen on the outside but warm on the inside.

My mind raced again. What could he possibly know? He was oldish, but not old enough to know Ernie.

He wouldn't know the sanatorium either. But it was another possible lead. The bench, the garden, Martha Nugent and now Mike. Every time I tried to tidy up a few loose ends I found another few pieces stretching out before me.

I made my way back to the car as the light started to fade. In just a few days I would be on a

plane to New York. It felt a world away from Seaham, but it was a journey Ernie had made, and it was one that I must follow.

By the time I made it back to the car, I was freezing again – and hungry. I realised I hadn't eaten a bite all day. I made my way back to the hotel to check in, warm up, shower, book a table in the restaurant and update you, Mr. Diary. All done now apart from the food.

11:15 p.m.

Lovely meal. Not the cheapest, but I can afford it thanks to Mr. Green.

Texted Mr. Irving earlier, and he replied almost straight away.

151

Arranged to meet up with him at the Black Truffle coffee shop a short walk from here at 10:30 a.m.

I'd better sign off for now and get some shut eye. Who knows what tomorrow will bring?

23.2.19

9:30 a.m.

Showered and shaved and looking a tad more presentable than I did yesterday afternoon on the lawn at Seaham Hall. It looks a nicer day out there too. No wind and even a hint of blue sky. Today I plan to just go with the flow.

Mr. Irving has offered an unexpected lead, so I will see where it takes me. It may be something and nothing, but I already feel the journey is vindicated after yesterday's walk up to the spa. It also adds weight to Daniel's words and makes him the credible witness I thought he would be.

Breakfast was nice. Room for another coffee and cake, though in a little while. I will update again when I get back in the room.

1:15 p.m.

Mr. Irving was already waiting at the café when I arrived, five minutes early. He was holding a small box. It looked old. Older than him. We exchanged pleasantries and moved inside, plonking ourselves down at a table near the window. I told him who I was and why I was there. I explained that I had managed to trace Ernie's movements up to 1948, and to get to the next stage, I would have to go to the States, but I felt this trip to County

Durham was important. He nodded as I spoke, tapping the box in front of him. Just as I finished talking, our refreshments arrived. A jolly, plump waitress plonked them on the table and gave me a suggestive wink which caused me to blush. Mr. Irving noticed and chuckled.

"She will eat you alive, lad. Literally."

I sat back in my seat and smiled. He was ready to tell his side of the story. He was happy for me to use the Dictaphone, and so I placed it on the table.

Mr Irving: *"I was born in 1958. The place was being used as a hospital back then after being used as a sanatorium before I was born. It has quite a history and quite a place in my family too.*

My mum worked as a nurse there in the '50s and my grandmother before her. She worked there during the war time, so I am quite sure she will have known the lad you are talking about. Unfortunately, they have both passed on now, but having overheard you talking yesterday, I thought you would like to have a look at some pictures and notes that my mum kept from that time. It is all personal stuff. No patient records or anything like that, but you never know, it might help. Most of the patients were transferred to Newcastle's Freeman Hospital or Sunderland General years later. If any records were kept about the patients, they will be in some vault up there no doubt, but I wouldn't imagine there would be much from the sanatorium days. Maybe what's in here might be of some use to you though."

Mr. Irving then proceeded to open the box and tip the contents onto the table - letters, photos, badges, ribbons and two small notebooks.

'Nurse Elizabeth Moors' it said on one notebook, '1944'.

I reached for the book. Feeling the need to clarify, Mr. Irving told me 'Moors' was his grandmother's surname.

The book itself was a faded green, A5 sized, lined pad. I flipped through a few pages whilst Mr. Irving talked about the other objects on the table and what he could remember about his grandmother when he was young. She sounded like quite a formidable lady in her time but dedicated to her profession and the patients she supported.

The handwriting inside was immaculate. A flowing cursive style in black ink. While Mr. Irving talked, I tried to read. It was a mix of work notes and diary extracts. Weather forecasts, notes about uniforms and a shortage of equipment in the wards. Nothing seems to have changed much.

Her life seemed routine and ordered. One thing that struck me was her concern for the patients. She recorded her concerns of high temperatures, the need to keep them moving, her desire to lift spirits and the monitoring of what they eat and how often. She let her guard down occasionally, showing her human side. The heartbreak she felt when *'Mr.Bellamy could fight on no more',* or the frustration and anger when *'the trip to Durham was cancelled due to the cost of transport.'*

I read on, lost in thought and then, there it was.

"I was delighted to see Martha again when I started the Monday shift. I had fretted all weekend about her condition. I didn't think she would pull through, but there she was. A fighter. No more than six stone of pure determination and will. For one so

154

young she is an inspiration to us all. Selfless too. Also, the way she supported the new boy – to take him under her frail wing the way she did. The two of them get on so well – the ideal tonic for each other. He would have been devastated had we lost her. Good for you, girl."

Although not mentioned by name, it seemed pretty clear to me who the young boy was. Mr. Irving had nipped to the toilet at this point. I took photographs of the pages for the record.

I skimmed the pages looking for more. Six pages on, I found it.

"What a difference a month makes. By the way they behave, you would not know how much pain or suffering those two are going through. Always joking, always laughing. It is infectious and rubbing off on the other patients and staff too. Fellow Cumberland resident, I believe. She is a Carlisle lass. He is from out in the sticks somewhere. I bet they can't wait to get home. This is no place to live out your teenage years, but they are certainly making the most of it. She has taught us all new card games and magic tricks. No poker face though.

She can't hide her emotions, and neither can he. They both brighten the place up no end. Even Bill has started laughing. I never thought I would ever say that."

There was one last reference to Martha. Still no mention of the boy's name in the notebook but, along with the bench dedication it was a fair assumption the person in question was Ernie.

"Martha is leaving us this Friday. She looks so much better than when she arrived. I shall miss her. We all will. Especially the boy. I hope they meet again sometime. I will write to her and ask him if he wishes to do the same. I am sure he will. She has

155

set him jobs in here to keep him busy. He looks so much better now too – stronger, fitter, and healthier. I am sure he will be going back to Cumberland soon. Thanks to Martha. God be with you."

At the foot of the page, there was an address:

MN, 45 Brookside Place, Raffles, Carlisle, Cumberland.

When Mr. Irving returned, I was able to let him know that his little box was a veritable treasure chest for me. He didn't quite understand my excitement at the tenuous link I had found, but he was pleased to have been of help, nonetheless. I thanked Mr. Irving for all his help, and now I had another lead to follow.

It was very unlikely that Martha would still be alive. It was very unlikely she would be at that address. It was unlikely that she would even have lived her life with the same surname. I was off to New York in a few days, and there was so much still to do.

I couldn't just go on a detour and another overnight stay to north Cumbria on a whim with little or nothing to go on, other than hope and instinct, could I?

Damn right I could.

I was loving this adventure more than anything I had ever done before.

CHAPTER 10
Word of mouth

23.2.19

1:15 p.m.

Another room booked thanks to the internet. How did we manage before Google? The Crown and Mitre in the middle of the historic border city of Carlisle. A hotel with history too – previous guests and visitors include the former United States President, Woodrow Wilson (whose mother hailed from the city), and The Beatles.

It wasn't the hotel's status that attracted me – more the price. An absolute bargain at £53 for a double room. Again, I am not expecting to find anything in Carlisle to help with the search, but it will be another nice little jaunt before I head home and prepare for the bigger journey that lies ahead of me. Thoroughness has always been my byword.

Another bout of sentimentality hit me on the way back to the hotel. I bought a bunch of flowers. I will take them to the memorial garden on the way out of town. It felt like the right thing to do.

I will then head north to Newcastle before a turning west over towards Carlisle. With a bar meal somewhere around half-way, I will try to time my arrival just after the worst of the rush hour traffic. I quite fancy a lazy night tonight. A couple of pints in a city centre pub before heading back to the hotel room for nibbles and a bit of TV. I will find out what I can tomorrow and set off back to Lancashire mid-afternoon.

3:45 p.m.

I have found a nice little pub in a place called Corbridge, just off the A69 – The Black Bull. It is a lovely part of the world this. So tranquil and calm. I could retire here. Lovely pub too – this could be my local.

Only myself and two other customers in, so I shouldn't have to wait long to be served. The steak was my meal of choice to be washed down by a large glass of orange juice. I will save the alcohol for tonight.

I am not really sure why I am going to Carlisle. Ernie did not live or work there as far as I can tell, and the only connection to the city was his teenage friendship with Martha Nugent, and I'm not being paid to trace her. Can I justify putting the trip on expenses? Let's see what it reveals, if anything, before I decide that.

The enormousness of my visit to America is beginning to dawn on me. The place is vast. How, in such a short space of time, can I find out anything about a man who arrived on their shores over seventy years ago – and with a false ID at that!

I have decided to allow myself ten days. Flights are booked, but the return is flexible and can be amended for a small fee – if £125 is considered small. Visa sorted.

I fly at 2:30 p.m. from Manchester and arrive 9:30 a.m. local time.

I should get checked in to the hotel by lunchtime, and I have allowed myself two days to acclimatise and get used to my surroundings – as well as enjoy a bit of the city with the New York Sightseeing pass I bought. That can come out of my wages. Who knows when I will get to visit the place

158

again, so I may as well combine work with an unexpected holiday?

From what I have read so far, a trip to Ellis Island seems to be the best starting point. I shall email the museum in the morning with my request for information and help. From what I can gather, diligent records are kept, and access to these is available to the public. Ships arriving from Europe would have been quite regular, but from what I know already, I should be able to narrow the search down considerably.

Note to self: Confirm hotel reservation for the first three nights. Pay on arrival.

Food has arrived. That looks amazing. Mr. Diary, I will update you when we get to Carlisle and check into the hotel.

This, I am going to enjoy.

6:00 p.m.

Arrived and checked in no problem at all. I am doing well with these hotels. I hope the Lexington in New York proves to be just as agreeable as this. It certainly looks like it might be on the photographs on their website.

I have a glorious view here over the market square and old town hall. The shops have just closed, and the city is settling down for the evening. I will have to come back in the summer when it is a bit warmer. At least it is a clear night and no rain. I hate the rain.

I am still stuffed from that steak, but it was worth it. That's the best £15.99 I have spent in a long time. I don't think I will manage more than a snack this evening. Crisps and nuts in a local pub will be sound good enough to me.

I have been thinking about Martha Nugent and her tenuous links to my Ernie on the drive over. What am I expected to find here? I can't go chasing every little lead – I need to tighten up my search. I certainly can't behave like this in the States, I will need to be selective about where I go and make good judgement calls. My window of opportunity is limited, and I need to be focused if we are to find anything about the man after 1948.

Right, quick freshen up and then I will go and find a nice hostelry to relax in. With only a name to go on, I really don't know how much I can accomplish in a few hours tomorrow. Maybe a trip to Births, Deaths and Marriages will reveal something, but I have so little to go on it could take me all day. There is no guarantee she even came back to Carlisle or stayed here. Still, I am here now; I may as well enjoy the evening and start to put a more detailed plan together before my trip to the States. I shall update again later this evening – or in the morning, depending on the condition I'm in.

12:38 a.m.

Mr. Diary, the mission to find Mr. Ernie Grimshaw is just bloody surreal. That was one of the strangest – and most fun – evenings I have had in my entire life. I admit I am a little tipsy right now, but I need to get my thoughts down on paper before I go to sleep. I regret not taking the Dictaphone with me, so these notes are of tonight's conversations and cannot be one hundred per cent accurate, but if I don't write them down now, I will think I have had the weirdest dream possible come the morning.

Location: *The King's Head* pub. Less than one hundred metres from my hotel reception. On

160

arrival, the place was fairly busy: an ancient tavern recently refurbished but retaining its character (and characters) inside and out.

I bought myself a pint of bitter and sat in the top-right hand corner beside a gentle old couple. It was lovely to see them both holding hands. Romance and love were still there. I am not one to strike up a conversation with strangers, and I sat there keeping myself to myself for the first few sips. They were not so backward in coming forward though. The man introduced himself as Frank and then told me his wife's name was Nancy. I told them mine and that was it – friends for life. Before I knew it, I was sat at their table discussing our life stories and we were buying drinks for each other. Frank and Nancy had lived in Carlisle all their lives and had no desire to live anywhere else. He had a razor-sharp, observational wit, and she complemented him brilliantly. For a time, I forgot why I was there. They were such great company I do not think I have laughed so much in years. We talked about everything and nothing. School, football, traffic wardens, drugs, farming, shoes, gardens and dogs. We talked and laughed and talked some more.

About four pints in, Nancy asked about me.

Nobody has asked about me before. I didn't really know where to start. I just opened up and blurted out my life story – loves (or lack of them), family, jobs. They were the kind of couple that you felt you could trust with your innermost thoughts, and so I found myself talking, somewhat unguardedly. They listened and smiled, genuinely interested in what I had to say. They were fascinated about my current job. They had me down as a modern-day version of Sherlock Holmes mixed with James Bond. They made me feel special.

They made me feel wanted. They even called me Sherlock for the rest of the evening. But the best was yet to come.

They eventually asked me how I had come to find myself in Carlisle.

I told them everything (apart from names of sources – I wasn't that drunk) from the first letter to my trip to Seaham then Carlisle. They hung on my every word. Not just them either. Others had tuned into our conversation and my story. They were fascinated. The more I talked, the more people gathered around to listen. When I finished, I was buzzing. I ended by telling them about my weak reason for coming to Carlisle. I felt a little embarrassed about it but certainly not uncomfortable. These people were genuinely interested. Engrossed even. I had never been the centre of attention like this before and it felt amazing.

Thanks, Ernie.

"Well, bugger me," said Frank when I finished. They all burst out laughing. I blushed.

"So, you see," I told them, "this is another leg of my wild goose chase. I have had a bloody good evening so far, but I am not expecting to uncover much here."

"Don't be too sure, son," said Frank, "this is a small city. Every bugger knows every other bugger's business, and if they don't, they will know some bugger who does."

He got up and strolled to the top of the steps that led to the bar.

"Albert," he shouted, "do you know a Martha Nugent?"

"Who?" came the reply.

"Nugent. Martha Nugent – ever heard the name?" Frank asked.

"I know a few Nugents around here. A few rogues among 'em," came the reply, "don't know a Martha though. Do you Keith?"

"Aye, I know a few," came another voice, "most live up Raffles Estate way. Or they did. Don't know a Martha though. There can't be many Marthas about these days."

"I knew a Martha. She wasn't a Nugent though. Used to drink down the road in the Working Men's Club on Fisher Street. It's shut now. She wasn't a Nugent though. Lewis. That's it – Martha Lewis. They were a good crowd in there. Shame that place shut. Shame a lot of them are shutting now."

"Martha Lewis?" said another. "I remember Martha Lewis. Small woman. Thin. Passed away not long ago. Lovely woman. She lived Raffles way, I am sure. Just off Orton Road, I think. I'd often see her at the bus stop there. A strong gust of wind would have knocked her over. My cousin, Bill, used to clean the windows around there. I'll give him a call, hold on."

"She used to go to my church – St Bede's on Wigton Road." shouted another lady. "A great lady. She would do anything for you. She died a couple of years back. I went to her funeral at the crematorium. Popular woman. Huge turnout. Her husband was called Tommy, if I remember rightly. He wasn't a churchgoer. He passed a few years before. I think she lived with her sister for a while."

"Ah, I remember Martha," said another. "She lived with her sister. They looked so alike. Twins almost. You would always see them out and about

163

together. Sally she was called. Can't remember her husband."

"I can. Vaguely. They had a big dog. Daft as a brush. Lovely fella – Tommy Lewis," said another.

"I'm on the phone to Bill." shouted the man with the window cleaner for a brother. "He remembers her well. He cleaned her windows – didn't charge her a penny. I will show you where she used to live if you like. He said she was a scream. He said he took his wages in laughs."

"What's the priest's name at St. Bede's?" Frank asked the lady.

"Father Hayes. He has been there a long time now – he would have known Martha well. If you are going to speak to anyone, he might be a good starting point, son."

"It is amazing who you remember when you get chatting eh," Albert said.

Frank turned to me and said something like, "There you go Sherlock. Let us be your Doctor Watson. I told you everyone knew everyone else around here. Not a wasted journey after all. Martha Lewis, formally Nugent, lived on the Raffles Estate – I am sure these fellas will point you in the right direction if you want the exact address. Died a couple of years back. Buried in the city cemetery beside the crematorium. Lovely lady. Popular. Dog lover. Churchgoer. You didn't expect to find that when you first walked in here, did you?" he laughed.

And here I am. Back in the room with places to go tomorrow, people to see and leads to follow. Just for the record, Mr. Diary, that was one of the best nights of my life. Whatever I find or don't find tomorrow, it was worth coming for that alone. Thank you, Martha. Good night and God bless.

24.2.19

9:30 a.m.

I have not been to church for years. The odd funeral or wedding, maybe, but certainly not because I had any kind of faith or belief in a higher power. I have always admired churches though – and places of worship in general. The love and care that goes into the construction and the upkeep of such monuments to faith should be applauded, I think. Two good qualities and good values, whatever the belief.

I woke with a spring in my step. No hangover from the previous night – just a vigour and enthusiasm to carry on. Then it dawned on me that it was Sunday – a church day.

According to Google, St. Bede's Roman Catholic Church on Wigton Road has a service at 10:30 a.m.

What an ideal opportunity to surround myself with her old friends or acquaintances for an hour or two. If I arrive early, I may even get to chat to a few before the service. It is only a mile or so from here. I can walk that and be there for ten. I can leave my bag and the car here and return straight after. I shall update you, Mr. Diary, on my return, and then we can make tracks back down the motorway.

12:45 p.m.

I am running out of superlatives to describe my state of shock whenever I update you,

Mr. Diary. This dead end, this pointless detour, this wild goose chase has turned out to be anything but. This chance visit to a church service

165

has given me another revelation I wasn't expecting. Could I go so far as to call it a miracle?

Certainly, anything seems possible on this journey.

Let's start from the beginning. The walk up to the church was delightful. A stroll through the city centre, past the cathedral and castle, and down the hill towards Wigton Road.

Hardly a soul about. The city was just waking up. The sweet smell of baking biscuits filled the air as I walked by the *McVities* factory and on up the hill. The receptionist in the hotel had told me I would enjoy the walk back more than the walk there, and I was starting to understand why as the gradient increased. By the time I reached the entrance to the church, I was flushed and a little hot under the collar.

It was 10:10 a.m. when I arrived, and a few people had started to gather at the entrance having claimed their car parking space early. Two older couples were talking to a man who I presumed to be Father Hayes at the door. When they moved inside, I approached him. He greeted me like a lost friend before adding,

"It is always nice to see a new face in the parish." I asked if I could have ten minutes of his time after the service.

"You can have as long as you want – and a cup of tea and biscuit in the Rectory," he laughed, "just give me a few minutes to clear the crowd, and I am all yours. Just wait over there after the service." He pointed to a large house near the church. He didn't ask what I wanted or why. He seemed quite happy to welcome this stranger into his home. I already felt at ease. We shook hands, and I made my way inside St. Bede's.

I sat at the end of a pew two or three rows from the back and soaked in the atmosphere. The church, built in the late '50s, was impressive enough from the outside, but even more so inside. Pristine, high, white walls with plenty of windows to welcome in the sunlight from outside. For such a big place, it was surprisingly warm. The altar stood proud at the front with colourful murals around and above the organ. A smaller chapel stood behind, with two confessional boxes that would have welcomed many a person ready to unburden themselves of sin to the priests who have called this place their home over the years.

I wondered if Martha had had cause to frequent them over the years.

The congregation walked, plodded, hobbled or wheeled their way in depending on their age or mobility. It struck me how old the flock were. More old ram of God than lamb. But they sang with gusto, they prayed aloud, and they laughed and nodded and shook hands in the right places. This was a ritual I was not used to, and I certainly felt like the odd one out despite the welcoming smiles.

Enthusiastically, the organ player started to play out the final hymn. I sat still whilst the congregation filed out of the church behind Father Hayes and the altar boys – one of whom stood out like a sore thumb. He must have been a similar age to the priest and at least fifteen stone heavier than the others around him, but as if it were the most natural thing in the world, he sang and carried his candle out of the door and back into the street. I was one of the last out. I didn't want to interfere or get in the way. I sneaked out unnoticed and sat on the Rectory wall while Father Hayes said his goodbyes and made small talk with the regulars.

He noticed me and waved.

"I'll be ten minutes. Just got to close up and I will be with you."

The fat, old altar boy led his younger charges back in, and Father Hayes locked the door behind them.

By the time he reappeared out of a side door, the car park had cleared, and we were the only ones left. He was dressed rather more casually now but still looked every inch a man of the cloth. You can just tell.

"Come on in, come on in," he said brushing by me and opening the door to his house.

It was beautiful inside. Well appointed, clean, bright and modern. I wasn't sure what I had expected, but it wasn't that. As if he was reading my mind he said,

"I can't take the credit, young man. If it was left to me there would just be a sofa and a TV. Margaret comes in three times a week and has this place looking like a palace. The nearest thing I am going to get to a wife!" he giggled. "So, my friend, what can I do for you?"

Over a lovely cup of coffee, I told my story again. He listened – fascinated – just like those in the pub the previous night. I finished by telling him all about Martha and her friendship with Ernie, and then how the visit to the *King's Head* pub was the inspiration for a visit to St Bede's church. Father Hayes sat back in his chair and exhaled.

"That is quite a tale, young man. Brilliant. I am quite blown away by it, and how it has led you here – to Carlisle, to St Bede's, to me. Maybe I can add another piece to this jigsaw. How it will link into your investigation, only you will know, but I hope it helps."

168

He took another drink of his coffee and sat back in his seat again.

"I knew Martha Lewis. I knew Martha very well. Sadly, I did not know her husband, Tommy, but I feel as though I do, having spent so much time in her company. She was a remarkable lady with a strong faith. Her faith helped her to overcome many of life's challenges. Illness, loss, pain. She suffered an awful lot over the years but never lost faith. She didn't lose spirit either. She was a fighter. In later life, she was in constant pain – sciatica I believe. But she never missed a service. Not once. She needed the church.

I must admit, I did not know she had suffered from TB and had to spend time away from home. That must have been hard for her. She found love though. Tommy was her rock. They didn't have any children, but they had a loving and caring family around them. They knew they were wanted and loved, and you can't ask for more than that in this life."

And then the bombshell.

"I met Ernie Grimshaw. Just the once, but he left quite an impression on me."

I nearly fell off my seat. The butterflies in my stomach raced around again.

"You met him?" I spluttered. Coffee almost escaping my lips.

"I did." Said Father Hayes. "Just the once. Come with me. I have something that you need to see."

I followed Father Hayes through the house and out of the back door. A gate led out to the car park beside the church. He kept walking, and I scuttled on behind.

"That's the primary school attached to the church." he said as he walked, pointing to a large 1960s style structure over a fence and across a field ahead. He stopped before reaching this fence and turned right. In front of us was another small gate leading into a garden flanked by tall evergreens. At the far end of the garden was a large statue of 'Our Lady'. In her arms she held the baby Jesus. I looked around. It was another memorial garden. I was making a habit of visiting these places.

He walked on to the far side, beyond the statue of Our Lady.

"Read the plaque below under that tree" he said, pointing to a relatively young beech.

I crouched down to get a better look, and I could not believe my eyes.

THIS TREE IS PLANTED IN MEMORY OF MARTHA AND THOMAS LEWIS FROM YOUR GOOD FRIEND ERNIE. YOU HELPED TO MAKE ME THE MAN I GREW UP TO BE. I COULD NOT HAVE ASKED FOR MORE. RIP – 2017.

I was rooted more firmly to the spot than that beech tree.

"And that isn't all." continued Father Hayes, smiling.

I couldn't speak to respond to what I could hear him saying, as I had so many thoughts and questions spinning through my head.

"It wasn't just the tree he buried." He continued, with a further mind-blowing revelation:

"Underneath that slab of concrete, beneath the plaque, Ernie dug a hole and placed a small metal box inside. He covered up the box again with the soil and carefully placed the stone back on top.

170

It hasn't been touched since. I have no idea what is inside it. No idea at all."

I wanted to pull up the stone there and then and dig in with my bare hands. Answers could be buried right here. But, as if sensing my excitement and urgency, Father Hayes spoke again.

"I want you to continue your adventure and your quest. That box will still be here when you get back. When Ernie buried it, he indicated to me that I would know when the right time would be for it to see the light of day once more. I don't think that time has yet been reached. Go to America. Find out what you can. Find the Ernie who left these shores in 1948. And when you have discovered all you can, come back here and we can open it together. Is that a fair deal?"

It was. I agreed.

We walked slowly back to the entrance of the church. I was lost in thought. I told him I would return – but only after I had exhausted my search.

He smiled again. Calmness personified.

Before I set off on the walk down the hill and back to the city centre, I asked just one question.

"What did he look like? Ernie. What was he like?"

Father Hayes paused for a few seconds before answering.

"Like an old man. Nothing special. Just an old man."

We both knew that was a world away from the truth.

CHAPTER 11
Following Footsteps

25.2.19

I arrived back in Lancashire a tired but excited soul. My jaunt up to the Northeast, and then to Cumbria, had been more than worthwhile. It had been truly extraordinary. I had not expected to unearth so much – and I still have something quite significant to unearth when I get back from the States.

What on earth could be in that box? I have thought of little else since. Photographs? Personal possessions? Letters? Objects that were special to the three of them? I had no idea. He must have buried them not expecting anyone to ever see the contents again, in spite of what he had said to Father Hayes.

Only Father Hayes knew about it, and he had been happy to leave it untouched until I arrived unexpectedly. Over the last couple of days, I cannot believe that I have stood where Ernie has stood – visiting the places that meant so much to him.

He left this country in 1948, but he returned. He was alive as recently as 2017. He was eighty-eight years old and, as far as I can gather, in good health. So, what happened to him between 1948 and 2017? Another thing that struck me very suddenly on the drive home was his name. He was no longer Daniel Frankenburg. He was Ernie Grimshaw. When did he become himself again?

And so, on to the next chapter of this unfolding adventure. I fly to New York's JFK airport on Thursday 28th February from Manchester at

9:10 a.m. If we are on time, we should land around midday New York time. There isn't much else to do before then. All documentation is in place, taxi booked to the airport, and I will do the packing last minute like a man should.

I will use the next couple of days to catch up on a few loose ends with the ancestry work and make sure there is nothing outstanding that cannot wait a week or so while I am away. I will go visit Mum too.

Right, Mr. Diary, I will put you down and give you a rest. Your pages have taken quite a battering over the last few weeks.

I think it might be a good idea to send a letter to Mr. Green before I go to keep him in the loop.

I am getting quite excited now. New York City. Can't wait.

26.2.19

I posted the following letter to Mr. Green this morning. He should receive it before I fly. I will write again when I return. This is an expensive trip, and I would dearly love to make it worthwhile for him. He certainly seems to trust me and is pleased with my work so far.

Mr. William Green
XXXXX XXXXXX XXXXX
XXXXXXXXXXXX
XXXX
XXX XXX
XXXXXX

Mr. Paul Brunskill
XXXXX XXXXXXX
XXXXXXXXXX
XXXXXXXXXXX
XXXXXXXX

26st February 2019

Dear Mr. Green,

You will be pleased to know that I returned from my trip to the Northeast with an increased enthusiasm and vigour. Not only was I able to substantiate Mr. Frankenburg's story, but I was able to follow a new (and quite remarkable) lead. Ernie did spend a long time in Seaham recuperating from tuberculosis, and it was here he met and befriended Martha Nugent (who became Martha Lewis when she married Thomas Lewis) – another patient in the hospital.

The friendship became a strong one and, from what I can gather, had a huge influence on Ernie and the man he grew to be.

From the people I spoke to and the places I visited, Ernie left a huge impression on all he met there, and his legacy lives on. I have enclosed copies of my diary notes which go into more detail.

Instinct and curiosity led me to Carlisle (Martha's hometown) where I spent the next night hoping to find out more about the lady who had such a positive impact on Ernie. Again, it was a long shot, and I was not

174

expecting to find anything, but that hunch to visit proved very worthwhile.

The notes in my diary explain all, as you will see, but I was bowled over to find out that Ernie had visited the city as recently as 2017!

You can imagine how thrilled I was at this point. I hope you are too.

I fly to America on Thursday for a week, and I will write again on my return.

Now we need to find out what happened between 1948 and 2017. Only sixty-nine years of life to discover, but I am enthused by the task ahead. Let's see where the journey takes us.

Yours sincerely,

Paul Brunskill Private Investigator

(Copy of diary notes and invoices enclosed for your information)

Meeting mum for tea later. She sounded pleased to hear from me on the phone. I will make this a more regular thing when I get back from America. I will get some flowers for her on the way over.

27.2.19

11:00 a.m.

This time tomorrow I should be in the air. The taxi is coming for me at 6:00 a.m., so I'd better get an early night tonight. All packed. The weather forecast is good for the week. Cold but bright and clear. That should be good for the photographs.

I had a reply from the Ellis Island Museum this morning. Bruno Moreno, museum historian replied. It would appear that tracing records or ship arrivals and passenger logs should be fairly straightforward, even from 1948. Records were quite meticulously kept and filed as the government was keen to establish the numbers of new arrivals, the demographic of ages, the mix of men, women and children. They also recorded the nationality of arrivals to ensure 'quotas' were met at this time so soon after the war. America had been accused of closing its doors on the needy at the start of and before the war. The Jewish problem was a European one – not America's. They appeared to turn a political blind eye to the extent of the suffering in the 1930s and early 1940s and were keen to address this after the war by allowing thousands of new immigrants to start a new life in the self-titled home of the free world.

He assured me staff would be on hand to help with the search but advised me to arrive early and be prepared to spend a good few hours there. I had no idea how the records were kept – or how many ships arrived in New York from Hamburg in 1948. The fact I have the names and approximate ages of the three should help. Bruno gave me hope of a starting point too. Many of the immigrants would have been allocated a 'holding' bay in the city where they could stay for a short time while they tried to find work and accommodation of their own. He explained that a number of agencies were set up to help, and there was no shortage of low-skilled, low-paid, manual labouring jobs for desperate newcomers. The worry for me, though, was that Ernie was there to help the twins find their parents who arrived some three years earlier. They could

176

have settled anywhere. He wasn't short of money either. Once the three of them left that terminal, there may be no records whatsoever of where they went after that. Then what do I do?

The twins' parents' ship sailed in August 1945, and Ernie and the girls sailed in the spring of 1948. Annabelle and Rebecca Kaplan and Daniel Frankenburg (Ernie). I didn't even have the first names of the girls' parents, but they were Kaplans too. He was nineteen on the paperwork, and the girls were eleven. And that is all I have to go on. Still, I have a starting point, and I am up for the challenge. This could be fun.

It was fun last night. I forgot just how much Mum and I have in common. Not least our sense of humour. She liked the flowers too – definitely £7 well spent. We both agreed to spend more time with each other on my return. I am a very happy man. I stressed the flowers weren't a regular occurrence.

Well, Mr. Diary, I will sign off now and update you again when we are in the air. Don't worry, you are coming in the hand luggage with me.

28.2.20

10:00 a.m.

Up, up, and away. All good so far. The taxi delivered me to the airport on time, plane departed on time, and I have just been served coffee and biscuits whilst browsing the films and music available. I was far too excited to sleep much last night, but hopefully I can get an hour or two shut-eye on the plane.

I am so pleased I got the window seat and even more delighted that the seat beside me is unoccupied. The air hostesses are all stunners too – what more could a man ask for?

The menu looks good for the main meal – spicy chicken with roasted vegetables for me, followed by a lemon cheesecake and coffee. I may even treat myself to a few beers too. This is how work should be. I could get used to this, Mr. Diary.

When we land, I will get a taxi to the hotel and find my bearings. The Lexington Hotel is in a good location and not far from a number of main attractions in Midtown. If I am not too tired, I will have a walk around and take in the atmosphere of The Big Apple. From what I can gather, it is easy to get about. Much safer than a few years ago. I promised myself a big steak tonight. All on expenses of course. Tomorrow, I am a tourist, and then on Saturday, the work begins. I can get the ferry to Ellis Island at 9:15 a.m., so that gives me plenty of time to investigate. At the very least, I will get to see the Ellis Island, and the Statue of Liberty, so the visit won't be a wasted one. Right, I will sign off now and update again when I get to the hotel. A beer, and three hours of *The Godfather* I think. That will get me in the mood.

2:40 p.m. (New York time)

Arrived at last.

Everything was running smoothly until baggage collection and passport control. I have been through a few airports over the years, but that was a nightmare. Collecting my case was like looking for a needle in a haystack. They changed the belt number for our flight three times. People were running from conveyor belt to conveyor belt hoping to catch a glimpse of their belongings.

Eventually, a few of my fellow travellers managed to locate theirs, and mine showed up just as another half a dozen flights landed, and the next batch of unfortunates were set to go through the same chaos.

Before I had time to calm down and stop sweating, the madness and mayhem of passport control loomed. JFK airport has a reputation for being as welcome as an undertaker in an old folk's home, and I soon discovered it was a reputation well earned. The queue slowly snaked towards the line of officious officials manning each gate. The last obstacle before entering the US of A.

"Stand still!",

"Move into this line!",

"Stay still!",

"Get behind that line and stay there!" – a chunky woman in uniform barked at us, as we closed in on the desk. By the time it was my turn to approach the desk, what little patience she had was exhausted.

"Number 9. You. Yes, you. Now. Step forward. Quicker. Have your passport ready for the officer." She stared at me with contempt as if I had taken her last doughnut.

The man behind the counter was just as aggressive.

"Hand on the sensor. Keep it still." He rolled his eyes and frowned as the machine failed to pick up my fingerprint at the third attempt.

He stared at my passport and then stared at me with apparent hatred in his eyes. My hair was longer on my photograph than it is now, and I had stubble, but it was still clearly me.

I wasn't met with this much suspicion in Germany. They even smiled as they waved me through. Not here though. No "Welcome to America." or "Have a nice day." – he seemed to growl as he tossed my passport back at me, as if to say, "This is New York, I hope you die soon!"

A little shook up, I made my way into the vast foyer and the mood changed again. Me and the other weary travellers were greeted with the more familiar American hospitality.

Overbearing and 'in your face' niceties from dolled up divas ready to fill your case with NYC tat and empty your wallet at the same time. Still, it was a welcome distraction from the aggressive and unfriendly officials I had encountered only minutes before.

I was swept along by the throng towards the long line waiting for taxis into the city. Streams of the familiar yellow cabs stood behind the glass ready to whisk us weary travellers away. The queue moved apace, and I was soon at the front. My driver, a Mexican with no English, tossed my case in the trunk (when in Rome and all that), looked at my hotel address, nodded and beckoned me to get in. The drive from the airport to Manhattan took an age. Traffic jams and roadworks all conspired to slow us down, but whenever there was a stretch of clear road, my driver thought he was Ayrton Senna. If there were any rules of the road, it was obvious they didn't apply to him. No indication, no following the signs or stopping for red lights, or even pedestrians for that matter. I held on to the door handle like my life depended on it – which it quite possibly did – until that famous skyline caught my eye.

As we crossed over the East River into Manhattan, it was impossible not to be transfixed by the sheer size and magnificence of the buildings.

The Empire State Building, the World Trade Centre, The Chrysler Building. They all poked their heads above the dozens of others reaching for the sky on this island of granite.

I looked up at the street signs to work out how far we were from the hotel. East 48th Street was mine. We pulled up behind a bus, and I could see East 62nd to my left. A couple of minutes later, we had arrived. He took my money and zoomed off down the street looking for his next victim.

On entering the reception, the change of pace was welcome. I strolled through the grand, fairly empty lobby to be greeted by a set of teeth on top of a suit.

"Welcome to New York City, my friend. Checking in with us today?" he chattered on, hardly realising I was there. "Anything you require just press '0' and we will do all we can to help. Ah, British. The Brits are always welcome here," (suggesting other nations might not be).

Throughout the check-in process, his toothy grin did not falter once. His jaws *must* have been aching.

I looked at his name badge – Chuck Armitage. What a name. He couldn't have been a more stereotypical American if he tried. Our countries might have some kind of special relationship, but Uncle Sam and Aunty Beeb made for a strange couple. Stars, stripes, sassiness and starlight meets dour, depressed, Dickensian darkness. But they appeared to like us, and we don't mind them, so it seems to work.

My room was on the fourteenth floor, and I was expecting a glorious view. I wasn't to be disappointed. My window overlooked Lexington Avenue, and it was everything I had hoped it would be. I opened the window, crashed on the bed and drank in the sounds of the city.

I had managed to sleep for an hour or so on the plane, so I was not overly tired. If I could stay awake another few hours and go to sleep around 9 p.m. New York time, I should combat the jetlag and be bright-eyed and bushy tailed ready for my touristy day tomorrow. And that steak awaits later. Mr. Diary, you need a break too. I am going to go for a wander for a couple of hours. You get some rest yourself, and I will update you later.

9:20 p.m.

I am stuffed, and I am shattered. A wander up to Trump Towers and the Rockefeller Centre on Fifth Avenue was a nice start. So much to see. It was bitterly cold but not too unpleasant. I felt for the homeless, especially on nights like this. There seems to be so many of them. The forgotten souls. I helped a couple by parting with a few dollars. At least I hope I did. You have to hope.

Still, plenty of tourists out there. The city doesn't sleep, but I will. I found my steakhouse, and it was a good one too. My belly is full, and my eyelids are heavy. Time to sign off and get some sleep.

Just over seventy years ago, Ernie set foot in this city for the first time. I wonder what he would make of it now. So much has changed. As his ship sailed in, was he given a warm American welcome, or were administrators as hostile as the ones who greeted me?

Time will tell. Goodnight, Mr. Diary. Sleep well.

1.3.20

8:30 a.m.

A special day today – Ernie's birthday and look where I am. Up bright and early and ready to follow in his footsteps. You are coming with me today, Mr. D. Today, I am on the tourist trail. For one day and night, I will go where I want to go, and right now, I want to go for a traditional American breakfast. It needs to be fattening, filling and flipping delicious.

What better way to start the day? There is a place just a couple of blocks away and *Trip Advisor* speaks highly of it.

It is called 'Tucker's', and it comes with an appetising five-star rating. After that, I will take advantage of my 'New York City Attraction Pass' and hop on board one of the open top buses. It shouldn't be too busy in this weather – certainly not upstairs and out in the open. According to the map, it is fairly easy to get from Times Square to the Empire State on foot, which will be lovely. This ticket gets me up to the top and even 10% off a statue of King Kong in the shop. I don't expect to see Ernie up there, but you never know, the way this investigation is going.

Come along now, Mr. Diary, my tummy is rumbling and a table at *Tucker's* awaits.

10:15 a.m.

I am going to make a few short notes during the day when I get the chance to remind myself where I have visited, and the people and places I have seen along the way. I have such a terrible memory, as you know, Mr. Diary.

Photographs will help too. Breakfast was as good as expected. Glorious even. A fry-up that could have fed the population of Ecuador, and in true American style it was followed by pancakes with strawberries, cream and syrup, washed down with a barrel of coffee. It is no wonder obesity is rife here. If I chose to stay here, I would be the same. It should be called the Big Arse not the Big Apple.

I am surprised I made it up the stairs of this bus, but I am pleased I did. I'm sitting in the front seat with only an old Chinese couple for company two rows back. It is cold, though, but worth it.

I have my earphones plugged in for the audio commentary. I hope it isn't the bus driver doing it. He could hardly speak English. And he had a lisp. According to the map, Times Square is the fifth stop. If I get back on after my trip up the Empire State, I will head down to the bottom end of Manhattan to take a look at the Wall Street Bronze Bull's balls.

It is lucky to rub them apparently.

I won't walk under a ladder, and I always look out for black cats, but I will be damned if I am rubbing the scrotum of a statue while two hundred tourists look on and take photographs. Ah, here we go, we are moving. Times Square coming up.

Bollocks, it's the driver with the lisp.

10:55 a.m.

Against my principles, I am sat inside a *Starbuck's* soaking in the warmth. In England, I avoid these places like the plague, but I suppose it is quick and easy, even if it is overpriced and bland.

184

Times Square is almost exactly as I expected it to be. Loud, busy, brash and bouncing.

This place makes Covent Garden look like a vicar's tea party in comparison.

I wouldn't like to see the electricity bill for this lot.

Huge screens and flashing lights everywhere you look. Theatres, street entertainers, bars, restaurants, cafés, shops and a million and one other things to catch the eye. New York's heartbeat.

Once I warm up a bit, I will take the short walk to the Empire State Building. Just looking up at it gives me the goosebumps. It is astonishingly high. What a construction. That said, so many buildings around here are simply huge – fifty, sixty, seventy floors high – and they don't even register compared with the tallest ones. London's tallest would be dwarfed by some of these engineering wonders of the modern world.

It truly is some city.

I will reflect on my trip up to the clouds when I get back on the bus again. Here goes, back into the cold.

12:30 p.m.

Well, that was simply incredible. From the moment I walked through the door, to the moment I stepped back out into the street and looked up again. Amazing. What a museum. They have won me over.

What a view from the top. To stand where so many other famous folk have stood before me. Wow, I am in awe.

You can only really appreciate the sheer size and scale of this city from up high.

Wonderment in every direction.

Downtown to the World Trade Centre, Uptown to Central Park then Harlem and the Bronx. Flanked by Brooklyn and Queens on one side to New Jersey on the other, I could have stayed up there all day. It was so busy, and yet I felt at peace. Lost in my own little world.

The tiny yellow taxis below. The echo of police sirens and car horns. The steam, the smoke the sounds, the smells. This is what I had hoped it would be like. This is what I had imagined it would be like.

I looked down at the streets cutting from east to west and the avenues from north to south and wondered just what Ernie thought about this terrific city. Did he ever stand at the top of the Empire State Building?

Am I, yet again, standing in the same place as he once stood? Less than a week ago I stood where he had been as a young teenager.

A day or so after that, I had been in the garden in Carlisle that he had visited at the other end of his life.

And only a few minutes ago, I was standing at the top of one of the world's greatest monuments trying to fathom out just how all these pieces fit together.

It also made me feel so small and insignificant again. Who am I? I am merely a dot on the planet, little more than a speck of dust in the grand scheme of things.

A mere footnote on the human race of all those who have come before and all those who will follow.

When I am gone, these buildings will still be here to thrill the next generation of visitors to the city.

I know I am rambling, Mr. Diary, but I am dumbstruck by the sheer beauty of this loud behemoth of a place. And the bus hasn't even set off yet.

According to the map, we will wind our way down towards Chinatown and Little Italy, past the Flatiron Building and on to Downtown. I will get off at Wall Street. From there, it looks a decent stroll down to the World Trade Centre and Battery Park – the end of the Island, the harbour leading to the Atlantic.

The entrance to America. The waterway that welcomed Ernie - or Daniel as he had then become.

Here we go, the man with the lisp is back on. I better get the guidebook out if I am going to learn anything here.

1:45 p.m.

That is one lucky bull. I am surprised he has got any balls left!

The financial district. Teeming with suits and style – and egos bigger than that bull's balls.

This is the first place, other than the airport, that I have felt unwelcome. I get the impression the tourists are an inconvenience. The only working classes here are cleaning the streets or serving in the cafés.

It could quite easily be London's Square Mile or Canary Wharf or, I suppose, any of the major financial districts in the world's major cities. A young man's game.

And I mean that with all the suggestion of inequality it implies.

Women are here, but they are in a minority. And they dress to look like the men in the office. Power suits and stern expressions.

I may be wrong and judging too early or out of hand, but having worked on instincts and first impressions for over twenty years does tend to give me an eye for these sorts of things. I think I will take my leave.

The bull is welcome to them.

The new World Trade Centre building – or One World Trade Centre – is beckoning me. She is hard to miss. Not so much obese as dominant. She has no wobbly bits or curves out of place. Over one hundred floors of glass and steel reaching for the clouds. Her twin sisters, whose lives were tragically cut short in 2001, have made way for their younger but even taller sibling, and what a sight she is. My ticket doesn't cover a trip to the top, but I am sure I can buy one when I get there. Come on, Mr. Diary, time to leave this money pit and head for the southern tip of the island.

2:15 p.m.

The footprints of the fallen buildings are impressive but sombre. This place is a museum now. A shrine. Another memorial to innocent lost lives – surrounded by a shopping centre and *Starbucks*. The cynic in me rises to the surface too easily. Again, there are many people here, but it has a totally different vibe to it than Midtown, and even Wall Street.

This place seems to be on the up, and I don't just mean the construction work. It is clean and precise. Safe. A nice place to be. A nice place to work. The hum of the city seems a long way away. Perhaps it is the calm of the nearby Battery Park or the lack of cars.

Perhaps it in the gliding boats and ferries or the reassurance of Liberty's statue less than a mile from here, beside Ellis Island.

Was it so calm in 1948? I can imagine a very different Manhattan then. Dirtier. Smellier. More threatening to newcomers. Some would have been excited. Others nervous or even terrified. Many were leaving hell behind for a new life. A new start. Most were alone or at least without the family unit they had enjoyed before the war. Not all were Jews, of course. Ernie for one. America was the escape route for thousands. Germans, Poles, Czechs, French – all heading for these shores, and most hoping to leave their past behind.

The World War II generation are not the first to seek solace across the Atlantic. The American dream has been open to all, and many have had to endure a nightmare or two along the way. The Irish, the Italians, the Latin Americans – if you looked hard enough you would find a footprint from every corner or this world in New York. They come for the opportunity.

The promise of better. And yet, it is an insular place. Cultures and creeds stay with their own. Multiculturalism is, in the main, a politician's manna – a vision of a perfect world. An idealism. The reality is sadly different. Black areas, White areas, Hispanic areas, Little Italy, Chinatown, Irish bars, Gay friendly, Women only, you can't do this, you can't go there. Extreme views, prejudice, religious intolerance, tribal factions, sexist, racism. Sectors. Their estates. No-go areas. Gangs. Cults.

189

The underworld. The underclass. The class system. Rich and poor. The fashionable. The strong. The weak. The fat. The thin. The healthy. The sick. The disabled. The deformed. The blind. The deaf. The midgets. The gingers. The intelligent and the dim. The aggressive and the passive. The extrovert and the introvert.

People. The people who make up the world. All together and yet all apart. Why? Why can't we get on?

When we make the effort, when we look beyond the superficial, there is no reason why we can't get on with everyone. With anyone.

I'm rambling. Thinking too much. New York has done that to me. I'm pleased it has, Mr. Diary. Everyone should have a time to think and to reflect. Everyone should have a chance to meet others. To get to know them. To understand them. To understand their history and who they are.

New York has everyone together. One huge sprawling mass of humankind.

It is a mass. It is a mess. But it can work. Of course, people fall through the cracks. It isn't perfect – far from it. It gives a chance with one hand and takes back with the other. New York offers hope and has done for every ship and person who has sailed in through that channel. Liberty isn't a promise – it is hard earned, if you are prepared to stick at it.

I have just read my own notes back, and I feel a little saddened by them, but it is how I feel at this moment in time, so it is right that I record it.

This moment of reflection in a place of such historical importance is understandable. I won't be the first, and I won't be the last.

I will get up to the top of that tower and then get back on the bus and head back into Midtown and Times Square. You don't have to think there. The thinking is done for you. Maybe that is why it is so popular.

The 'Let me entertain you' culture. I'm pleased I visited this place. In my humble opinion, everyone should if they can.

Get back in the rucksack, Mr. Diary. We are going to head back up to the clouds.

6:45 p.m.

Times Square again. Pleased to get off the bus in the end. Traffic jams meant we snaked along at a pace that would frustrate a snake. It is so different in the dark. The place was lively at lunchtime, but it is positively buzzing now. It is the start of March – hardly the busiest time of the year – but still packed. God only knows what the streets would be like in the height of summer.

The top of the World Trade Centre was fun. More great views. I must admit, I got a bigger kick from the Empire State Building, but it was well worth it, nonetheless.

I have fallen in love with this city as I thought I might.

I know this is my tourist day, and it isn't over yet, but my mind is already on tomorrow. Tomorrow is the most important day. If I am going to find a trail to Ernie, I really need to find it tomorrow. Ellis Island holds the key.

It would be remiss of me not to try a 'dog' in New York. I will go get one soon. Some of them look like dog's dicks rather than sausage meat, and yet I am drawn to one. With onions and mustard too.

191

I think I will walk back to the hotel from here and enjoy the atmosphere of the city at night. One thing did strike me today. How alone I am. Again. In one of the busiest cities in the world, I am alone, but I am happy with it. I have talked to dozens of people. I have passed the time of day and joked with them, and yet I am on my own – and I don't mind one little bit. Life is good.

9:45 p.m.

A lovely walk back to the hotel. So much to see, so much to enjoy – and a couple of bars on the way. They are different from British bars. More noise but less chat. More TVs but fewer dartboards and real ales.

Our barmen are fat and friendly. Our barmaids have big breasts and a welcoming smile. 'Bartenders' here seem efficient, quick, sleek and officious. Both have their merits and flaws. Most importantly, both serve cold, fresh beers after long, enjoyable days.

I am ready for bed. I am ready for sleep. I have had such a wonderful day. The kind of day that stays with you for life. If I leave this city with no new information about Ernie, I won't put the trip down as a failure.

I will raise a glass to the man and return home. Whatever happens now, I am a better man than I was a week ago.

CHAPTER 12
Statute of Liberty

2.3.19

9:15 a.m.

Tucker's has sucked me in again. God only knows where I will be staying tomorrow night, but I doubt they will have this kind of breakfast on the doorstep. Such a comfortable bed too. I didn't want to get out.

No tourist head today – straight down to the point at Battery Park. It is only a fifteen-minute ferry ride across, and I want to arrive before it is swamped by tourists. It will also give me a chance to ride the subway down to the south of Manhattan. Something else to tick off on my bucket list for New York.

From my research, it seems the museum at Ellis Island is well worth a visit. According to the website, 'approximately twelve million immigrants entered America through the golden door of Ellis Island. Today, the descendants of those immigrants account for almost half of the American people.' A purely staggering statistic and one that shows the diversity of the population. America is not so much an individual country, rather a micro-state of the world-wide community.

It also states that the immigration offices opened in 1892 and closed its doors in 1954.

So, for sixty-two years, Ellis Island was the front door to New York, America and a new life for millions of dreamers. The Kaplans were dreamers. They dreamt of being united with their parents again. What was Ernie's dream, I wonder? He was going there for the girls, not for himself. Did he stay with them? Did he make a life out here for himself? How long was he in America before coming back to Britain? How long did he remain as 'Daniel Frankenburg', and how did he rediscover his own identity?

Again, so many questions and so little time to try to find the answers.

I shall sign off for now and update you over lunch. My ship awaits.

12:20 p.m.

Twenty-six dollars for a return ticket on the *Miss Ellis Island* ferry. An absolute bargain. And it included a stop-off and a walk around Lady Liberty herself. She looked absolutely miniscule from the top of the World Trade Centre, but close-up she was a fine sight and much bigger than I imagined her to be.

The view of the skyline looking back towards the ferry terminal at Battery Park was something to behold too. Even back in 1948, it must have been an incredible sight on the approach into New York.

But the journey in was a perilous one. Reading the excellent and informative history pages on the island's official website, immigrants into the States were treated so very differently depending on wealth, status, class and origin. First and second-class passengers were rarely detained or scrutinised on arrival. Port authorities deemed, rightly or wrongly, that if they were rich enough to pay for a better ticket, they were less likely to be considered a drain on the resources of the state and were therefore welcomed with open arms.

'Steerage' or third-class passengers were viewed with more suspicion, and they were often detained for long periods until they proved they were healthy and wealthy enough to enter the US without becoming too much of a hindrance or burden. I suspect Ernie and the twins fell into this category. It would appear that they would have been required to complete a medical examination and some form of interrogation before being allowed to leave the holding bays.

From what I have read, conditions aboard the steam ships would not have been great for passengers of any class, let alone those who did not have the luxury of a cabin. Illness and sea sickness were rife. Days and even weeks without decent food, sleep or a proper wash. Toilet facilities were as basic as could be. God only knows what was out there floating in the Atlantic Ocean.

I have managed to make an appointment to see one of the museum historians, Mr. Moreno, at 1:00 p.m. I am pinning a lot of my hopes on him.

The island is a fascinating place. Such an incredible site of historical importance.

It turns out that, when Ernie was on his way over, President Truman was announcing a significantly important change to the law to help to support the masses of refugees arriving in America following WWII. The Displaced Persons Act of 1948, which offered a lifeline to hundreds of thousands of desperate folk keen to enter into the United States, was sanctioned by congress in the middle of the year. Attitudes towards refugees in the 1930s were ones of scepticism and mistrust. Even when the Nazi war machine started its systematic destruction of all those they deemed inferior, the

US closed and bolted its doors to those who dared to try to flee for sanctuary.

It would appear their conscience was pricked when the extent of the genocide came to light, and the doors were opened again.

On a lighter note, this maple syrup pie is delicious. The Americans may not be known for the best in worldwide cuisine, but they know how to eat for pleasure. Fattening, but fabulous. As the rather chubby waitress said when she saw the look on my face after she positioned the plate in front of me,

"You may as well die happy, sir." How right she was.

I will update again after my keenly anticipated meeting with Mr. Moreno. I'm excited and nervous – scared even. What this man tells me could be vital. In many ways, the next stage of the investigation depends on him. I will nip back in here for a coffee later and update you again, Mr. Diary.

3:40 p.m.

Back in the café with a strong coffee in front of me. I have said it before, and I will say it again – WOW!

To say I am bubbling with excitement and enthusiasm again would be an understatement. Mr. Moreno and all the staff of this fine museum – I doff my cap to you. This place is simply breathtaking.

The compilation and organisation of records here is outstanding, and the staff knowledge and meticulous attention to detail is a joy to behold. An investigator's dream. Part of me envisaged rooms of dusty shelves packed with parchments and files containing faded registers, accounts and archives. I did them a huge injustice. This is record keeping at its finest – and all at the touch of a button or swipe of an iPad. Technology is leaving me behind.

At the information desk, I was first met by Susan Wild (great name). She explained that Mr. Moreno was running a few minutes late, but not to worry, he was expecting me. She led me down the corridor, and then into a large side room filled with computer 'booths'. She explained that all records were held on their database, and this would be the primary centre when searching for ships and passengers. Half a dozen people were in there already, tapping away and staring intently at the screen in front of them. No doubt searching for descendants of their own families.

She found me an empty computer station and explained, very simply, how the search facility worked.

She explained that all passenger records were kept on their database with the original document filed elsewhere in the bowels of the museum. As was common with any kind of nautical record or register, the quality of the records – including the spelling of names and place of origin – were at the mercy of the registrar at the time. This was totally understandable – there could be hundreds boarding a ship at any one time and the condition of their paperwork and ticket was likely to be incomplete, faded or damaged. Their boarding pass containing personal details could therefore contain inaccuracies.

Ms. Wild reassured me though. The computer system was able to filter and narrow down searches, and she was sure that, if I had some details of the passengers in question, they would be there in the system if they arrived in New York around that time. The processing system must have seemed chaotic for the passengers arriving in their thousands, detained in holding bays and questioned and examined along the way, but the administration truly was sound and thorough.

As well as possible administrative errors, Ms. Wild added a caveat that the ships could have stopped at several ports before arriving in New York, and it was likely that the last stop before the US would be the one recorded on the record sheet. She had clearly explained the procedure many times to other hopefuls before me, yet remained calm, jolly and helpful throughout. Her positivity was infectious. Not only would I find them, she boasted, but Mr. Moreno would no doubt be able to shed some light on their next movements. I was told to take my time and see what I could find out before he arrived. She smiled again and left me facing the database search screen.

I had the names of the passengers, the port of departure and the year of departure. I hoped that would be enough. It was.

The first name search I tried was Kaplan. Kill two of the birds with one stone so to speak. This narrowed it down to a possible ten thousand passengers. Thank God I had first names. A search of Rebecca Kaplan narrowed it down to just twenty-eight. I then tried Annabella Kaplan. Just one. Incredible.

I made a note of the ship's number and tried Rebecca again. A match. Both girls on the same ship (the Maasdam). As simple as that. Was it this easy?

I then tried Frankenburg. Twenty-eight of them on the passenger search. I then typed in

Daniel Frankenburg and pressed search. None. Panic.

I tried Ernie Grimshaw too. None. Oh no.

Sitting back in my chair, I suddenly felt a wave of despair wash over me. Where was he? Did he not travel with them? They were too young to travel on their own. He must have boarded the ship. Did they travel with someone else? Was his false identity discovered? Was he arrested or detained? Did he alight at another port along the way?

A million thoughts rattled through my brain, but the overriding one was of disappointment. I was totally deflated. For a few moments I considered this the end of the journey. Nothing more to search for. I was not here to look for the girls, I was here to find Ernie.

I tried to process and focus, but I was struggling at this point. I sat there for a few minutes lost in thought.

A tap on my shoulder brought me back from the hypnotic trance I had found myself in. It was Susan again. She was with a short, dark-haired, middle-aged man. She introduced him as Mr. Moreno, smiled at me, then walked away. He pulled up a chair. He could see that I was looking a little flustered.

"Welcome to Ellis Island, young man." he began. "I hope I can be of some assistance." I just about found the words to explain the results of my search. I didn't try to hide my disappointment, but he didn't seem fazed.

"Don't be so despondent," he laughed. "You have come all this way and you let a little thing like a name put you off? I'm sure Susan explained that it isn't always that simple. To find 'Two out of three ain't bad', as Meatloaf used to say. Your man will be in the system somewhere. We just need to track him down. Now, let's see..."

He pulled the keyboard closer towards him and changed the search option from passengers to ships.

"The important information now is not who he is, but the vessel he travelled in on. You found the girls. They were on the Maasdam."

He searched for the ship and found over 62,000 records. He explained that this is the total number of passengers who travelled on this ship over the year. He used his administration login in order to track the year.

"If you want to look in a more detailed search, you would normally have to register – and pay," he told me. "But, for you, this one is on me."

He searched for 1948. The ship had only sailed to America once that year. It left Hamburg and stopped only at Rotterdam on the way. It was a fourteen-day voyage, and the total number of passengers was recorded as five hundred and forty-three. I couldn't care less about five hundred and forty of them.

He then searched for males. This narrowed it down to three hundred and two.

Males between eighteen and twenty-five – forty-six. There, in front of us, were the names of the forty-six. We already knew the twins were on the ship. Was Ernie (or Daniel)?

Mr. Moreno scrolled down slowly. There he was. Damial Frankingborg. Aged 19. Passenger number 38275.

"There is your man," he exclaimed. "As clear as day."

The euphoria I felt again was palpable. What a rollercoaster of a journey this was.

He then searched for the girls again, and sure enough, they were there. Passenger numbers 38276 and 38277. They boarded together as a threesome.

He asked me to accompany him to his office where he would give me full printouts of the passenger details and try, if he could, to answer any other questions I had.

I had a few.

We walked through the corridors that the tourists don't get to see. I felt important.

Mr. Moreno had a great office. A view right across the harbour with the Statue of Liberty to our right.

"I love my job, Mr. Brunskill. You can't look out of this window every morning and not be in awe of the sights and sounds of this great city."

He wasn't wrong. Again, it was a humbling experience to be stood on the same piece of earth that had meant so much to so many.

I had my Dictaphone with me, and Mr. Moreno was happy enough to let me record the conversation. I gave him a quick overview of the case so far. He smiled and shook his head as I spoke.

"Well, Mr. Brunskill, I truly hope I can help on your quest to find this extraordinary man. This job never fails to surprise and amaze me."

He pulled up another chair for me near the window, and we both gazed out at the numerous ships and boats chugging in every direction across the choppy waters.

It was another cold, crisp day, but the sun was high and the clear and blue sky gave the impression that summer had arrived early. At least, that is how it felt in this heated office looking out at the harbour behind the comfort of double-glazed windows.

I'm sat back in the café now with my earphones in and an endless supply of coffee on tap, I will write down the questions and responses while they are fresh in my mind, along with a few notes and next steps.

Yet again, my mojo is back, and my tail is up. The search confirmed what I had hoped – the three of them had arrived in the city in the spring of 1948. They were, according to Daniel in England, reasonably well off and had the means to be self-sufficient, for a while at least. In some ways, I thought that might make my task even harder, as they had no real need to seek out or register with a job agency straight away. Understandably, their sole focus would have been finding the parents of the twins.

Mr. Moreno had also managed to locate the parents who had arrived in New York in late 1945. Their names were Tobias and Nuria Kaplan. They were both forty-two years old when they arrived. Charitable organisations were set up to help new arrivals, but it was a harsh introduction to life in the States. At that time, the Jews did not really have an 'area' to call their own, and they were dispersed all over the city and into New Jersey. It was unlikely they would have ventured further afield without money, Mr. Moreno said, so it is fair to assume they settled in this area. It gave me something to go on, nevertheless.

Names give an identity, and with an identity I have something concrete to look for.

Below is a rough transcript of our conversation.

I will go over the answers when I get into a hotel and try to plan my next move.

Me: "What would happen to the passengers when they first arrived in the city?"

Mr. Moreno: *"By 1948, the processing of immigrants was fast and efficient. It needed to be. People were arriving every day from all parts of the globe. Unless there was a very good reason for doing so, for example, illnesses or criminal activity, the port authorities did not want to detain people unnecessarily. Truman's new laws were designed to make it easier for immigrants to enter the US, but quotas were still in place to cap numbers. The fear was that the immigrants would become a burden on the Federal Government and take far more than they could give back. The labour market was strong following the resurgence after the 1930s recession, but hospitals and schools were not equipped for such an influx in population growth.*

Anyway, it made sense for the ports to have a quick turnover of people within the compound. Paperwork checks would have been quick and minimal – so long as you could say the name that was on your ticket you would be fine. Each passenger, especially those in the lower classes, was given a short medical examination, as the staff were very adept at spotting the signs of a lingering illness or disease.

If they were happy that you were healthy enough, you would be given the green light to leave and enter the US of A."

Me: "What would they do next? Where would they go?"

Mr Moreno: *"Again, this was very much down to the individual. There were no more barriers. You had a pass into the city. Most would head for Manhattan to start with and start looking for a place to stay. There wasn't a shortage of rooms and cheap labour, although the conditions for both could be dangerous and grim.*

New immigrants would be used and abused. If they were expecting a warm welcome, they would soon realise the grass wasn't always greener. You had to work hard and fight to survive here. It was a new life and a new start, but it wasn't a bed of roses. If you knew someone here already that would have given you an advantage. Perhaps a place to lay your head while you found your feet. If you were alone, it would have been a lot harder. The streets were awash with the homeless during the 1940s. Mr. and Mrs. Kaplan would have been at the bottom end of the food chain, knowing what we know of their background."

Me: "Were there any organisations or charities they could turn to?"

Mr Moreno: *"There were many. Some very unscrupulous ones, but as you can imagine, everyone wanted to access some form of help - people were desperate – but they were not able to help everyone. Many just had to fend for themselves. A lot of the organisations would help families with younger children or the elderly. Some were discriminatory and would only offer support for followers of a certain religion or sect. Some asked for payment or a cut of wages for any employment gained. It was a free for all, and it could be argued that it was the survival of the fittest. Many didn't survive it or chose to return to their own country, if it was possible. The mortality rate for immigrants was high too. Many hospitals simply wouldn't admit them. Truman's intentions were honourable, and the wish of Congress was to reach out to the suffering, but there were not many measures in place to deal with the vast numbers of new arrivals."*

Me: "What kind of documentation were they expected to have?"

Mr Moreno: *"This was a contentious issue and one that proved to be a bureaucratic nightmare for the government. Most people arrived with next to nothing through no fault of their own.*

Especially around the war years. Passport and visa identifications, that we hold so dear now, were non-existent, and with the ports keen to process as many people as they could, as quickly as they could, they were out of the door and invisible to the State before any documentation could be issued. Many people fell through the cracks. Thousands even.

The country did not have the means to track and trace them, and they would only ever be noticed again if they secured registered, paid employment and started to contribute to the tax system. It is highly doubtful that we will ever know the true population of the city at that time. These were balmy years. Nowadays, the accountability is so strict, you can't break wind without appearing on a database somewhere. Then, it was a different matter. So, to answer your question, the majority were not expected to have any documentation – and they weren't given any on arrival either.

Me: "If Mr. and Mrs. Kaplan received no help from a charity and they had no money, where were they likely to go?"

Mr Moreno: *"A good question and one that is not easy to answer, as they could, in theory, have gone anywhere they wanted, but more than likely, they would have congregated with their own. By that, I mean Jews with Jews, or Poles with Poles, etc. There were pockets of Jewish communities spread across the city, and numbers grew considerably with more and more people arriving. At least by doing so, new arrivals could take advice from those already established in the city and from those who could speak the same language. Culturally, it was a shock for the locals as well as the immigrants. Long-standing New Yorkers resented the influx – even though many of their families had arrived in the city in the same way and needed the same kind of support when they did.*

It is likely the Kaplans made for the Lower East side of Manhattan or Borough Park, Brooklyn in the West. Queens and Newark also had a high population of Jews, but both were a little too far for newcomers without the means to explore. Those areas were more likely for those who had 'made it' and had settled in the area for a few years. Away from the glitz and glamour of the central avenues, the East and West sides were notoriously run-down. I would suggest, rather than trail the city looking for a needle in a haystack, you visit the Jewish History Museum. They have their own record system, and now you have the full names of the parents with the date of their arrival, you have a good chance of finding something about them – even if it is just the area they moved into. The same would apply for the girls and Daniel (or Ernie). If they managed to locate the parents, you might find them all in the same place, which would be a real bonus.

There are a number of genealogy websites dedicated to finding Jewish relatives and families of those lost during the war, but I know these things take time – something you don't really have.

I suggest you start with the Jewish Community Centre and synagogue on Garfield Place in The Brooklyn Centre and then venture to the Jewish Heritage Museum near Battery Park. Ask for Assistant Rabbi David Netrukman – an old friend and squash partner of mine – at the community centre. A little bit of name-dropping won't do any harm. Lovely man. If he can be of any assistance, he will do all he can to help you."

Me: "It has been seventy-one years ago since they arrived here. Seriously, what do you think my chances are of finding Ernie?"

Mr Moreno: *"Honestly, I wouldn't like to guess. Some people are found quite quickly, some are never found. People come and people go. Some people leave a bigger impression in life than others.*

Be prepared for anything and hope Mr. Frankenburg or Mr. Grimshaw, Daniel or Ernie, left a big enough impression on New York City for you to find something about him. Hope has got you here, and hope is driving you on. What is it they say? – Where there is life there is hope. This is the city that never sleeps. Plenty of life here.

I wish you all the luck in the world."
Back on the trail. Two leads for tomorrow.

I will head over to Brooklyn in the morning and start there. I have never met a Rabbi before. I hope he is working. I might even challenge him to a game of squash.

It has been another fascinating day, and I even managed to get myself booked into the Lexington for another two nights for only £156. Magic.

Another early morning breakfast in *Tucker's*, methinks.

Come along, Mr. Diary. The ferry will be leaving in twenty minutes, and I want to be on it. Farewell, Ellis Island. Goodbye, Statue of Liberty. I hope we meet again.

Thank you, Mr. Moreno.

Looking over towards Manhattan and Brooklyn as the sun begins to set, I find myself asking the same question over and over again in my mind.

"Where the bloody hell are you, Ernie?"

CHAPTER 13
Start Spreading the News

3.3.19

9:15 a.m.

Tucker's again, Mr. Diary. If I carry on at this rate, I'll be needing to use the next hole along on my belt.

Looking at the subway or bus route to Brooklyn, it would take me over an hour to get there from where I am based. I think I will treat myself to another cab ride there. I can certainly afford it, and I will be there in half the time.

Having read up on the area, the population seems to be made up mainly of Jewish, Chinese and Hispanic communities. It is described as a 'vibrant and safe' area, according to *Trip Advisor*.

Mr. Moreno suggested I seek out the *Congregation Beth Elohim* on 274 Garfield Place, Brooklyn, NY 11215 where his friend, the Rabbi David Netrukman, would be working. I am not sure how he can help me, but it is a start. Kaplan is a popular Jewish surname, and after seventy years, the likelihood of them still being in the area, alive and well isn't great. Certainly, their parents will have died a long time ago.

And what of their surname? If they have married, there is a strong chance they will be going by a different name.

And Frankenburg - whilst not as common as Kaplan – it is still a popular surname in the Jewish community.

After World War II, the number of Jews in New York City rocketed to over two million, and whilst that number has dropped considerably since (mainly due to migration), they still equate to about ten per cent of the population.

My plan of action is a little vague at the moment. I have little to go on and little to tell the Rabbi Netrukman. I just hope he has some ideas of his own. I will update you again when I get there, Mr. Diary.

11:35 a.m.

Another eventful cab ride and another eventful meeting.

I think the cab driver had his eyes shut for most of the journey. How we didn't end up in the East River, I will never know.

Anyway, there I was in the Borough Park neighbourhood. The atmosphere was very different from Downtown Manhattan. It was quiet, calm and peaceful. The Hasidic Jews were everywhere – so noticeable in their traditional dress. This was very much *their* community.

I followed the satnav on my phone across the delightfully scenic Prospect Park.

The sun was out again, and it was another beautiful day. Walking through the park, you could be forgiven for thinking you were not in the middle of a sprawling metropolis at all. The sound of birdsong and the rustling of leaves in the wind drowned out the distant sirens and traffic din.

Even after I had made my way to the other side of the park, the streets were relatively quiet. I soon found myself standing at the entrance of the Congregation Beth Elohim building – a clean and polished granite stone building with the Star of David displayed proudly at the top of the dome on the roof.

A building like this seemed too ornate and too old-fashioned to have a bell, but it did, and I pressed it.

After a few moments, I heard the clatter of keys, and the door opened. I was greeted by a young man (no more than seventeen years old I'd guess) sporting a short beard and side curls (or *payot*, as I later found out). He offered me a warm smile and invited me inside, after I explained who I was and who I was looking for.

Inside, the building was even grander. The echo of our footsteps on the marble floor was the only sound I could hear as I was guided through this holy, sacred place, and into a smaller room at the back where I was offered a seat and asked to wait.

I was soon joined by the Rabbi Netrukman. Not knowing what the correct form of greeting was, I offered my hand, and he shook it enthusiastically. I asked if I could use my Dictaphone, and he didn't seem to mind when I placed it on the table beside us. He just smiled and nodded at me which I took as a 'go ahead'.

"Sit, sit. I spoke to my good friend Bruno last night, and he said you would likely come along and visit our humble place of worship today. I'm so glad to meet you. I hope I am in a position to help." He was a very smiley, jolly chap, and that put me at ease straight away.

"Bruno rarely beats me when we play squash together, so I am happy to help him out in other ways if I can." he laughed.

I explained why I was there and told the story of Ernie and the Kaplans yet again. I enjoyed retelling it.

I enjoyed seeing people's reactions. I even felt part of Ernie's life story now. Rabbi Netrukman clapped his hands together at the end and shouted out,

"Well, well, well. Bravo!".

He continued.

"You have set yourself quite a challenge, Mr. Brunskill. Quite a challenge indeed. But don't be daunted by names and numbers. Our community is large, but also close-knit. After all that has happened to us historically, I suppose we feel safer together. I am sure you understand. This can be a little suffocating at times, but I wouldn't change it for the world. Yes, Frankenburg and Kaplan are common names, and it must seem like you are trying to find a needle in a haystack, but let's just say, if you have a strong magnet, the job is not nearly as difficult. We are interlinked with the other synagogues around the city. Schools and colleges too.

Kaplan, if I am not mistaken, is an Ashkenazi name. That gives us a starting point because many Ashkenazi came to New York from Eastern Europe, Russia and Germany. People tend to stay with their own kind, don't they? We have over seventy synagogues in the city now, but I am guessing, if they gravitated to any area they would have settled where other German-speaking Jews would go. That narrows down our search to certain areas of the city. I am not saying that is where they would have settled, but if I was a betting man, I would wager there is a strong chance they did.

I would like to help you with this. It gives me a bit of a buzz, all this investigating business. It must be all the cop shows on TV now. Leave me your number and your hotel details and I will see what I can find out for you this afternoon. I will make a few calls and enquires of my own. I believe you are going to the Jewish Heritage Museum too? That will be an interesting experience for you, I am sure.

When you are there, study the maps and listen to the real-life audio stories from those who emigrated from Europe. You will get a feel for what life was like for new settlers.

Anyway, leave it with me today, and I shall call you with anything I find this evening. I plan to be in Manhattan tomorrow. It is my day off, and I intend to spend it shopping and chilling out. Even a Rabbi needs to relax," he laughed.

"If you are not too busy it would be nice to meet up for a coffee somewhere. I know a lovely little Columbian place near Pen Station. Fancy it?"

He was such a jovial and positive man. I was enjoying his company, and I enthusiastically accepted his offer. We shook hands again, and he showed me back to the front door.

"We are very much a part of New York City now, Paul" he said, "but for many years Jews were considered as pariahs – even in the land of the free. We have had to work hard to be accepted and appreciated. We are a decent people – friendly and open. This isn't the image the media often like to portray. Our door is always open to you, and I will do all I can to help you. Enjoy the city, learn about our people and our history. Chat later, and may God be with you."

When he closed the door behind me, I was already looking forward to his call.

I will hail another cab shortly and head to the Jewish Heritage Museum. I shall update you after my visit there, Mr. Diary.

4:15 p.m.

I find myself on a park bench in Battery Park, reflecting again. Ahead of me, in the distance, is the Statue of Liberty and Ellis Island. Behind me, the towering skyscrapers of Downtown Manhattan. For the last two hours I didn't feel like I was in the city at all. The Museum of Jewish Heritage and the exhibitions inside took me on a journey to southern Poland and Auschwitz, through the eyes of many who passed through those gates of hell.

I have never been bullied or neglected. I have never been singled out or punished for no reason. I have always had food on the table and clothes on my back. I had a caring family and a nice home. I cannot begin to understand the pain and the loss these people suffered. I cannot understand how anyone could inflict that much pain on another human being.

One thing did strike me, though. I realised it saddened me. Upset me. Even brought me to tears again. I wasn't there, and I didn't know the people in the grainy pictures and video clips, but I didn't need to. I couldn't possibly empathise with them, but I could feel pity for them, and a hatred for their oppressors. The injustice of the whole thing shook me to the core.

And then I realised, I had changed. A month ago, I scolded myself for my selfishness when watching suffering and disaster on television. I

214

couldn't muster any genuine grief. People were numbers to me. Cases. I wouldn't allow myself to be emotionally attached. But look at me now.

I can't hide my feelings. This case has brought them to the fore. I think it is because everything has a context now. Every life matters. Or at least it should. Who the hell are we to be so arrogant as to think one race is better than another?

I'll head back to the hotel shortly. The Heritage Museum was excellent, but I have learnt nothing new about my case, other than how hard life must have been for them.

8:15 p.m.

I am shattered. I think it will be an early night, Mr Diary. I can feel my eyes starting to close on me already. I thought I would have had a call from Rabbi Netrukman by now. He can't have anything of note to tell me. Hopefully, we can catch up tomorrow over a coffee. I will formulate a plan for tomorrow when I wake up in the morning. Signing off.

4.3.19

7:45 a.m.

I can't believe I fell asleep so early last night. I must have drifted off as soon as my head hit the pillow. A missed call and two voicemails from the Rabbi Netrukman. One at 8:48 p.m. and the second at 9:15 p.m.

For the record:

Voicemail 1 - *"Good evening, Paul. I have some news for you. I have had a wonderful and exciting day today on the hunt to find your three. I am quite thrilled. I think you will be too."*

Voicemail 2 – *"Hello again, Paul. I really hope I have got the right number. I would hate to think I have lost you. We have a lot to discuss. Please call me back when you get this message, and I will tell you what I have found out today. Call me. Please."*

Is it too early to call him now? I will wait until 9:00 a.m. and try then. He sounded very eager. I am excited now too. I wonder what he has found out. This is just so bloody surreal. I will go and get some breakfast and call him when I get back in my room.

9:20 a.m.

No answer when I called. I acknowledged his messages with a voicemail of my own to show he had the right number, and I explained that I was free all day.

The hotel was happy to have me for an extra two nights which was good. That will save me having to move my bags from place to place. Now I just need to wait for a call.

10:10 a.m.

Well, that was worth the wait. **Oh, my. God.**

I didn't have my Dictaphone with me, Mr. Diary, so I will have to rely on memory until I meet up with Rabbi Netrukman at lunchtime.

216

The conversation (well, him talking and me listening) went something like this:

"Hello, Paul. I am so glad I got the right number. I spent so long on the phone yesterday; I think I must have an imprint of the receiver on my ear. I think I have found them.

Or at least found where they worship, and the area in which they now live. I made calls to over fifteen synagogues across the city focussing on the areas I mentioned to you. Two or three of them offered hope. Elders in the community returned my calls, and a pattern started to develop. A few knew people with the surname Kaplan, but the descriptions they gave didn't fit the age bracket or profile until...

I had a call back from a Rabbi Netrukman from the Hudson Yards Synagogue on the West Side, just south of Hell's Kitchen. He told me of two Kaplan sisters he knew. Twins. Old ladies. They used the community centre regularly and attended services and prayers in the synagogue.

He couldn't remember their names, but he remembered them moving to Washington Heights in Upper Manhattan less than five years ago. They were memorable because they were always together, and they looked so alike.

When I checked it out, the nearest place of worship for them was the Ansche Chesed Synagogue on the Upper West side, so I called the Rabbi, Jonathan Feldstein, there, and guess what? He only bloody knew them! My apologies for the bad language. Please forgive me. The thrill of the chase has got to me too, I think.

I hope you don't mind, but I made an appointment to meet with him later this afternoon. If you would like to, we could meet for a coffee and

217

make our way up there together? The idea of shopping on 5th Avenue has somehow lost its appeal." He laughed.

"If you can meet me at the Columbian Bakery Café at 1219 Lexington at 12:30 p.m. that would be great."

I didn't need asking twice. A very convenient place for me too. I could get there on foot if I set off around noon. My mind was in overdrive again. Even in a city as big as this, there can't be many female octogenarian twins with the surname Kaplan. I keep having to pinch myself to prove this isn't a dream.

I will update you again this evening when I get back to the hotel. The Columbian Bakery sounds like a fun place to try too. Rabbi David has also been a real tonic. Without him I would have been lost. Maybe God does work in mysterious ways and did intervene after all. Get back in the suitcase, Mr. Diary. I will see you later.

8:15 p.m.

Mr. Green isn't going to believe this. I am not sure I believe this.

Mr. Diary, just when you think you have reached a natural conclusion and there is nowhere else to go, a door opens, and the hunt is back on. Do I have some kind of guardian angel watching over me? Are my pockets stuffed with lucky heather and rabbit's feet? This afternoon has been incredible. Simply incredible. I am not sure where to begin. So, I will start at the beginning. The Columbian Bakery.

I met Rabbi David outside. I was running a little late as I misjudged how far up Lexington

Avenue it actually was, but he greeted me with one of his warm smiles and firm handshakes.

"I'm excited, Paul. I really am. I feel like Columbo or something. Columbo at the Columbian. I'm really grateful to you. I thank God. I think you were brought to me for a reason. Things were getting a little bit stale. I hoped, prayed even, for a new challenge, and here you are. I know you might think me silly, Paul, but I do. I really do believe this was predestined." he giggled. We were drawing stares from passersby who weren't used to seeing a Jewish holy man so enthusiastic.

We moved inside, and a young lady was there within seconds to take our order.

We ordered coffee and sat near to the window looking out at the chaos that is New York.

I set my Dictaphone to record again and placed it on the table. I explained that, as my memory was not what it was and I want to be as accurate as possible, I do this all the time. I hoped he wouldn't mind. He didn't seem to give a hoot. He was too keen to tell me what he had found out to worry about a Dictaphone. This is what he said:

Rabbi David: *"Paul, I started with a blank canvas yesterday. I know quite a few of the Rabbis and synagogues around the city, but certainly not all. There are just far too many. So, I started with the ones I knew, and I asked them to do a bit of networking for me. Most were more than happy to do so. I am not saying a Rabbi's life is easy, but we do have a lot of spare time on our hands. Anyway, I gave out the details of your case and asked them to call me back if they had any information. Within an hour, I was getting calls, emails, faxes and texts from my contacts around the city. Most led to dead*

219

ends. There were Kaplans almost everywhere in the city. In Queens there were Kaplan triplets. All boys and only two years old. There were Kaplan sisters, brothers, grandparents and even pets!

Rabbis were calling other Rabbis they knew. I think you must have had over fifty people making calls and visits on your behalf today, Paul.

And then we struck gold.

I received a call from Rabbi Netrukman at the Hudson Yards synagogue. I didn't know him personally. He had heard about the request from someone else. He knew two elderly ladies with the surname Kaplan. He was almost positive that they were twin sisters. He said they looked alike, their mannerisms were the same and they were inseparable. They used the community centre nearby for reading groups, a sewing club and, rather strangely, table tennis. Everybody knew them, or knew of them, in the community. They were popular characters. That was five years ago. 2014. They would be eighty-four by now.

He said they moved further north to Washington Heights, and they were sadly missed.

He thinks they may have moved into a self-contained ground floor apartment together, and that was the reason for their move. Washington Heights has been cleaned up recently. It used to have a terrible reputation for drug and gang crime, but not so much now. Cheaper than Hell's Kitchen though, so perhaps their move was as much for financial reasons as anything else.

It was then suggested I call the Rabbi Jonathan Feldstein. Most Jews will familiarise themselves with the nearest place of worship wherever they choose to settle, and the Ansche Chesed Synagogue was thought to be their nearest.

I spoke to Jeremy late yesterday evening. I must admit, I was worn out by that point, but when I picked up the phone to call him, I was still hopeful. He listened as I told him the story of my day and who I was trying to find, and why. He then dropped the bombshell. Not only had he heard of them; he knew them personally. He even mentioned them by their first names – Rebecca and Annabella. I nearly fell off my chair. I did mention Daniel Frankenburg and Ernie Grimshaw, but both names meant nothing to him.

I asked if it would be possible to speak with the ladies, and he said he would go personally to speak with them on my behalf. This was all too good to be true, Paul.

He said he would call me back after he had spoken to them. As good as his word, he called me back within the hour. He said he had spoken to Rebecca, and she was very keen to meet us at their house. He suggested we both go the Ansche Chesed Synagogue at 2:00 p.m., and from there, he would drive us to Washington Heights. From the sound of his voice, he was as excited as I was.

So, there you go. When we have finished these drinks, we will make our way over to Hell's Kitchen and hitch a ride north to see the twins. Are you ready, Paul? Are you ready to meet them? Are you excited?"

I just looked back at him and smiled. Inside, I was fit to burst.

Of course, I was ready.

CHAPTER 14
"You didn't come this far,
to only come this far."

8:15 p.m. (continued)

We took the subway across Manhattan to the Upper West Side and alighted at 103rd Street. It was a lot busier here, and the streets hummed with the sound of market stalls and street vendors. It felt alive, but there was an edge to the place. A sense of danger lurking in the back alleys. I don't think I would like to be here after dark.

I let Rabbi Netrukman lead the way a few blocks south, and we were soon outside the entrance to the imposing Ansche Chesed Synagogue. A large cream-brick building standing solidly beside an even taller neighbour.

He knocked loudly on the door and rang the bell at the same time, before turning to me and smiling like he had just won the lottery.

"Exciting, isn't it?" he beamed.

A tall, smartly dressed, bearded man answered the door.

"Gentlemen, I have been expecting you" he said. "Welcome to our humble abode."

He led us inside, and, yet again, I was blown away by the splendour and tranquillity of the place. Even as a non-believer, it was hard not to feel a sense of serenity and calm. He indicated to us to sit down on the nearest pew, and after exchanging a few pleasantries, he began.

"Matthew, when I spoke with the Kaplan ladies earlier on, they seemed very keen to talk to you. They didn't want to waste any time as, in their words 'we don't have time to waste.' They suggested I take you straight over to their house when you arrived. I have my car around the back. May I join you in the meeting? I have nothing on today, and I must say, you have really captured my interest with this one."

The three of us climbed into his aging Toyota and made our way out into the manic midday traffic. I sat in the back, and the two Rabbis sat in the front. We snaked our way through the traffic, swapping from lane to lane whenever a gap was left for a second or two.

Eventually, we arrived at a sign welcoming us to Washington Heights. We can't have travelled more than a mile or two, but we had been on the road for over half an hour.

"If you want to go anywhere in a hurry in this city," Rabbi Jonathan told us, "you need to be up in the air in a helicopter."

We left the main road and turned off onto some quieter streets. Children played outside on the road, but this was clearly a decent area. Gardens were neatly kept and there was no sign of graffiti or decay.

We pulled up outside number 1034 – I didn't even catch the street name.

The house was small but ornate, and beautifully kept from the outside. A small bench sat on the porch surrounded by rose bushes and other assorted flowers. It was clearly a well- loved place. A handrail and a small ramp leading up to the front door suggested the residents were no
longer in the prime of their lives and needed more assistance to manage the simple things in life.

Rabbi Feldstein rang the bell and stood back. We heard someone talking inside, and I could see the silhouette of a small-framed figure approach the door. My heart was beating fast. I was about to meet two people who knew nothing of me. I had knowledge of their early lives and the torment they had endured, followed by their clandestine move to America.

Would they want to talk with me? Was I worthy of their time? How well would they remember Ernie, and would they be happy to talk about him after all these years? Did they find their parents alive? So many questions.

I felt I was intruding by delving into their past. The door opened and a small, frail lady warmed us with her smile.

"Gentlemen, come on in." She beckoned us through. I was the last one in, and as I walked past, she grabbed my arm and halted me in my tracks.

"We may be old and look like we are knocking on heaven's door, but there is life in us old birds yet." She chuckled. "We are still making up for lost time."

I felt a little more at ease.

We made our way into the living room, and the three of us sat on an old leather sofa – me in the middle. I sunk down into the worn cushions and realised I was going to be stuck in that spot for the duration of the visit.

A second lady walked in from another room, and they stood side by side in front of the fire. They were very clearly twins.

"I'm Rebecca and this is Annabelle," said the lady who had greeted us at the door.

They separated, then sat in the two armchairs either side of the hearth. Like bookends. They both looked at me, beaming.

"Well, a man doesn't travel halfway around the world to visit *Washington Heights* for tourist reasons." Annabelle said. "Why don't you tell us why you are here, young man?" Her accent was hard to decipher. American, yes, but with a hint of European.

I explained why I was there and how I had reached this point in my investigation. They wanted to know everything. I was there to question them, but I found myself babbling on for fifteen or twenty minutes, and before I had finished, I looked up to see both the old ladies smiling at me as tears ran down their cheeks.

The two Rabbis didn't say a word. They seemed to be appreciating the moment. It wasn't their stage.

"God be with you, Paul." said Rebecca. "You are a man of integrity. I can see that."

She was smiling again, and she held out her hand. I reached forward and held hers.

I didn't realise at the time, but I was crying too. With their permission, I clicked on the Dictaphone.

"You are referring to events a long, long time ago, and yet they seem as clear to us as though it were yesterday." whispered Rebecca.

"You try and block out those awful times. You try to forget. Sometimes, in busy moments, you forget, but it always comes back to you – especially at night. It always will. And we are the lucky ones."

I kept hold of her hand.

"We met Ernie at the DPC near Bergan Belsen, as you know. By that time, we had all but lost hope

225

of seeing any family members again. We weren't stupid – even at that age we knew the horror of the situation. We knew the chances of finding our parents alive were slim. I wouldn't say we had given up all hope, but we were distraught and lost.

We were no more than children ourselves.

It was a blessing that we met Ernie. It was our fifth time visiting the DPC, and, although everyone was helpful, nobody really gave us time or listened to our story. We were just another number."

Annabelle continued.

"It was so hard to describe the mood around the town at that time. We were hated. By the locals, by the Germans, by the Russians – by anyone who considered us a threat. The British had liberated the camp, but we were still prisoners of sorts, and without anyone to help us. We were just two twelve or thirteen-year-old girls with decimated, disease-riddled bodies, trying to cope with the enormity of war. How we didn't break down, or worse, I will never know. We must have had the will and the hope to fight on.

*Anyway, around that time, we met Ernie. He wasn't like the others. He didn't just want to help – he **really** wanted to help. He wanted to help us believe again – to give us real hope. He wanted to make us realise life was worth living, even after everything we had been through. Daniel too. He had been through it all himself. He had lost his own family. He knew what we had been through. The two of them were our guardian angels.*

When he found out our parents were alive, that they had survived the camps and moved to America, we were just overwhelmed with joy. But the joy was offset by the realisation that America

226

was out of our reach, and not just because of its physical distance from us.

We were only children."

Rebecca carried on.

"Then the boys concocted a crazy, unbelievable plan between them. They were willing to chance everything for us. Us? Who were we to them? That wasn't important to them. They didn't stop to question why. They felt they had to do right by us. It was incredible."

Annabelle: *"It took us months to build up our strength again, but our spirit was always strong. The very thought of meeting and hugging our parents again was our driving force. Daniel and Ernie were realistic, however, and did prepare us for possible failure and subsequent disappointment. Amazingly, the journey over to America was uneventful.*

The paperwork was barely even checked, and although we stopped over on the way, we never felt threatened, vulnerable or exposed. The ship was just so busy. Eventually, when we arrived in New York, we felt like we were in 'Dreamland'. The filth and the squalor didn't even register on arrival. Seeing Liberty for the first time was heavenly. We had arrived.

In hindsight, Ernie was just a young man at the time, but he took on the role as our guardian. He wouldn't let us out of his sight. We knew we were in safe hands. We trusted him to care for us."

Rebecca: *"I remember him linking both our arms and telling us to hold on tight. I loved him like a brother. I knew we were safe with him."*

Annabelle: *"Yes, but he was just a baby himself really, thinking back. He had crossed the ocean with no experience and no idea what to do, but as far as I can remember, he didn't show it. He was always so positive and reassuring. Thinking back now, he must have been terrified, but for us, he kept those emotions hidden.*

I remember our first few nights in the city as though it was yesterday. Ernie had money – not a huge amount – but enough to get us a room for the first month or so, and to feed and clothe us while he formulated a plan.

I can't remember much of that time other than Ernie making sure we were ok. We were just so happy to have regular food and a warm bed. He must have secured some work, probably night shifts somewhere when we were in bed, but I don't remember. He must have been doing twenty-hour days looking after us and earning what he could when we were sleeping."

Rebecca: *"He must also have been trying to find our parents at the same time too. After a couple of months, I remember him coming back one evening with the news that shook our world.*

He had found them. In the Bronx somewhere. Unbeknown to us at the time, Ernie had spent hours, days and weeks trying to track down our parents. Not saying anything for fear of disappointing us. He had been all over the city asking questions, chasing dead ends and clinging onto hope and chance. And then... he found them."

Annabelle: *"Our Dad was working as a waiter in a restaurant, and our mother in a shoe shop. I remember he came back with the news. We were*

228

blown away. He said he had spoken to a friend of a friend who knew them or knew of them. He had travelled to the Bronx and there they were, alive and well. He didn't speak to them or introduce himself. He didn't feel like it was his place to. He wanted that pleasure to be ours."

Rebecca: *"I remember the day we were reunited so well. Ernie made sure we were well dressed and cleaned up for the occasion. We walked the three or four miles to the Bronx together. I was so nervous, but so excited too. We hadn't seen our parents for over five years, but their faces were so clear in my mind. I remembered everything about them from the sparkle in my mother's eyes to the feel of my father's whiskers on my cheek when he gave me those lovely, tight hugs. As we walked, I had never felt so scared in all my life. Not from the Nazis – not from anything. Ernie held our hands and kept telling us it would be ok. He was there for us every step of the way."*

Annabelle: *"We arrived at Father's place of work just before closing time, and we sat on a wall opposite, waiting for the staff to leave. Rebecca and I had always been so close. We needed each other. We relied on each other. We never argued or rowed. That day, we had never felt closer.
And then we spotted him."*

Both ladies were crying. Tears streamed down their faces, and the three of us didn't feel we needed to comfort them or interrupt their flow. These weren't tears of sadness, they were the happiest of tears.

Rebecca: *"He looked so much older. Worn down by burden and worry, but underneath that shell was the man we loved so much. We jumped off the wall at the same time and ran towards him. When he saw us, his face was a picture of terror at first. And... then..."*

Annabelle: *"Everything about him changed. He stood tall. He eyes shone and his face lit up with ecstasy. If I could have captured that moment and bottled it, I would have done. We both ran to him and reached him at the same time. We wrapped our arms around him so tightly. Straight away, that same smell of my daddy consumed me. He held us so tight I thought I was going to explode, but I didn't want him to stop. Not ever. It was magical."*

Rebecca: *"My daddy. Our daddy. Alive. Healthy. In my arms. Few moments in life are treasured to that extent. We held each other for what seemed like forever. Eventually, we parted but kept hold of each other's hands. We were all crying uncontrollably now. I looked around for Ernie. There he was. Back on the wall in the distance. He knew this was our moment. He wasn't going to intrude, and yet, he had made it all possible. I can't remember what we said to Daddy, but he ran to Ernie, collapsed at his feet and sobbed.*

Ernie sat down on the floor beside him and held his hand. After some while, we all set off to the house. We were desperate to see our mother again.

I remember on the way my father and Ernie talking about my mother. When we arrived, Father wanted Ernie to join us. Ernie insisted it was a family matter, and it was not his place to intrude. My father tried to insist, but Ernie was adamant.

230

He promised he would wait outside the house – however long it took – and take it from there."

Annabelle: *"I seem to remember our mother was cooking some kind of stew when Father took us in and introduced us to her again. She fainted there and then. When she came to, we were sat around a table smiling at her. I might be wrong, but I'm sure she fainted a second time.*
When she was able to sit up straight, she stared at us like we were ghosts. It is totally understandable now, but I think at the time we were both a little frightened of her. Or the whole situation."

Rebecca: *"Terrified, you mean. And then the hugs and kisses. It was simply magical. We were together again. Unbelievably so. And Ernie had made it happen."*

Annabelle: *"The four of us went out to find him. My mother couldn't wait to meet him. I realised we must have been in the house for hours – hugging, kissing, chatting, catching up – and yet there he was, propped up against a fence, snoozing. Waiting for us. To this day, I will never*
truly know why he gave so much to us for nothing in return, but I am eternally grateful."

Rebecca: *"When our parents died – of old age, both in 1985 – I didn't feel sadness in the way most people would on losing their parents. I felt so happy that I'd had the chance to spend another thirty-six years with them. I can honestly say without a hint of a lie, we never had one argument in all that time. It wasn't worth it. We appreciated every second we spent with them again.*

Annabelle: *"The bad years of the war will never be forgotten, but I have so much belief in the human spirit and love and family and faith that I will never accept evil can win over good.*

Our guardian angel came in the form of a young Englishman. Without him, I would have lost all hope a long time ago. I would have given up. He never gave up. He never lost hope. He never did. Always positive, always smiling, always happy. It wasn't just us. He made everyone happy – everywhere he went and whoever he spoke to. I have never known such a person before or since. I miss him so much. I do hope he is ok wherever he is."

Rebecca: *"I think of him every day. Every day. He stayed with us on weekends now and again.*

I'm ashamed to say that our new-found family life – and selfish adolescence teenage years – meant we didn't stay in regular contact after a while. It wasn't like it is now with everyone owning a mobile phone. We weren't streetwise or upwardly mobile. We lived within the borough. We didn't truly appreciate what he had done for us until he was no longer there. For a time, he visited regularly and made sure we were all fine. He spoke with our parents often and wrote to them to check we were all ok. It was only when we were older and wiser did we appreciate just how much he did for us – for our family. He was happy that we were happy and reunited.

If I have one regret in life, it is that we never kept in contact with him."

My heart sank again. Was this the end of the line?

Then Annabelle spoke again.

"He kept in touch through letters for some time after, but as Rebecca said, we were too wrapped up in ourselves and our reunited family, to truly appreciate what he had done for us. I don't know. Maybe we took him for granted. Maybe we thought he was always just going to be there and part of our lives.

My father once took us to visit him in Midtown where he was staying. He was quite the local entrepreneur then. That must have been around 1952. That was the last time we met him, I think.

I hope he had an amazing life. He deserved to. He was our saviour. Our hero and our inspiration.

Mr. Brunskill, I hope we have been able to help you. I hope we have been some use to you. And let me just say, you haven't come this far to only come this far. You must have many questions to ask us. Don't give up now. Ernie wouldn't have done, and it seems like there is a lot of him in you."

I had a million and one questions in my head, and we talked and shared stories, but the one question that kept leaping out above all the others was:

"Whatever happened to Daniel Frankenburg, and when did Ernie become Ernie again?"

Rebecca chuckled: *"That's an easy one to start with. Get your paper and pen ready, Mr. Brunskill. Time is of the essence, I believe, and you have work to do."*

CHAPTER 15
Incredible Feet

8:15 p.m. (continued)

Rebecca: *"When Ernie swapped identities to help us, he was also putting himself in danger. For all intents and purposes, he had suddenly become a Jew. Everybody knew what the Nazis thought of us, but we were not held in high regard by many others either.*

Even in America, we were considered the bottom of the food chain, and that was saying something with the amount of prejudice and racism in the States at that time.

Doors opened for you if you were Italian or Irish. Their communities were well-established. Jews were scattered across the whole city, and the whole country, for that matter, and we had to endure a lot of prejudice and hatred. Ernie needed to earn money to support the three of us, and at first, work was hard to come by.

I remember, early on, he was trawling the streets looking for some kind of regular employment. That's when he met Robbie McNulty. Robbie was your typical Irishman. Quick-witted, bubbly and colourful. He was labouring for a construction company on the west side, and when Ernie (or Daniel as he was then) asked him about job opportunities, Robbie persuaded his supervisor to give him a chance."

Annabelle: *"At that point, paperwork was not considered essential. You didn't need a CV to push a wheelbarrow. Ernie said he was just known as*

234

'The Jew' on the site, but there was no malice in the nickname – everyone had to have one on the site. I'm sure you can imagine what a building site is like. I think, after a couple of weeks and over a few drinks, Ernie told Robbie how he had come to find himself in New York, and he explained that he wasn't really 'The Jew' but 'The Englishman'. Robbie joked that being English would put Ernie even lower down the social ladder in his eyes, and he would be better off sticking with his original nickname.

After a while, Robbie advised him to drop the pretence and return to being Ernie. Nobody knew him – this was America, he could be whatever he wanted to be. What better person to be than yourself?"

Rebecca: "It was as simple as that. Ernie was back, and Daniel was somewhere in England pretending to be Ernie. In time, we all became 'official'. I can't even remember how it happened. We registered with doctors and dentists. We secured 'proper' jobs and started to pay taxes and insurance etc. We had numbers attached to our identities. We could get passports and driver's licenses and all the other things you can do when you have an identity."

Annabelle: "Ernie worked around the local construction industry for a couple of years. Robbie knew the scene. He was streetwise, and he had lots of contacts. Ernie and Robbie became good friends. At first Robbie took Ernie under his wing – got him jobs, introduced him to people 'in the know'.

Ernie was such an amiable, likeable character. People warmed to him immediately. Within a month or two, he had more job offers than he could cope with. He was earning a good wage, *and we wanted for nothing. When we moved in with our parents, Ernie kept the apartment on for himself. My father tried to convince him to stay with us, but he stayed in the apartment in the middle of Manhattan. He had fulfilled his promise. He had reunited us, and he wanted us to be a family again. It didn't seem to be a huge issue at the time.*

I don't think any of us were thinking too far into the future. We were just so happy with the present.

It wasn't as easy to stay in touch in those days. Like we said, we didn't have phones or transport. New York was a vast city even then, and we were still very new to the place. People say they will keep in touch. They mean it when they say it too, but life gets in the way, doesn't it?"

"You said Ernie became an entrepreneur - What do you mean? In what way?"

Annabelle: *"Like I said, we kept in touch for a while, and he visited The Bronx when he was able. It was always great to see him. Maybe 'entrepreneur' wasn't the right word to use, but he was certainly doing well for himself, I think. We had received a letter from him, and it prompted my father to plan a visit to see him. My mother was unable to go for whatever reason, but the three of us took a bus into the city and to Midtown. He lived on East 23rd Street. You wouldn't recognise the place now. It is all offices, hotels and trendy café bars. Back then it was a little rough and ready, but we liked it. We had good neighbours, and we were right in the middle of the island. It was only a ten-minute walk from the Empire State Building.*

We hadn't arranged with him to meet. Father wanted it to be a surprise for Ernie. We only had the address to go on, but we took a chance, and we were prepared to wait if he wasn't in.

When we arrived, it brought back a lot of happy memories for us."

Rebecca: *"Indeed. This had been our first proper home in America. Our first proper home since we lost our family home to the Nazis. Remember, Ernie was like an older brother to us. He was only a young man, and he must have been scared and daunted by it all too, but we were only young teens, and to us, he was the adult. We relied on him totally, and he didn't let us down – ever.*

He wasn't in the apartment when we arrived, and father popped a note through the door to say we had come to see him and that we would hang around for the day. We took the chance to explore and be tourists for the afternoon. The city was changing even then. New buildings were springing up all over the place. The place was buzzing.

We popped back to the apartment to see if he was in a couple of hours later. He wasn't, but there was a note on the door. It was from Ernie. He must have returned home at some point and got father's message. It just said that he was working in Madison Square Park, near the Flatiron Building, and we could join him there.

We walked the handful of blocks back up to the park. I remember the streets were very busy. When we arrived, the three of us were all looking around for construction sites.

We just presumed that is what he would be doing for work. We were quite taken aback when we actually found him.

237

He was sitting on one of two raised, comfy, red chairs by the side of the path drinking a can of something. Us young, inexperienced girls had no idea what he was doing there, but my father did.

I remember him laughing out loud, and Ernie laughed too when he saw us approach.

"Ernie Grimshaw – Shoeshine boy!" he shouted.

It was so lovely to see him again. He told us that both he and Robbie had decided to try their luck in business and set up their own shoe polishing enterprise. Robbie was away at a shop somewhere, restocking, and Ernie was putting his feet up for five minutes."

Annabelle: "Both of us jumped up and gave him a huge bear hug. It was great to see him again. It was great to see him looking so well and so happy. I remember sitting on the wall beside him as father jumped up into the unused seat beside him. He was wearing sandals, and we all laughed again when he cursed his luck for losing out on a freebie. Jews had a reputation for being mean, and my father only added fuel to that stereotype. Friends used to joke that Father would go on holiday to the same place twice. The first time for the break, and the second time to make sure he hadn't dropped anything.

There was a sign beside Ernie's chair which said 'Closed until 3 p.m.' He was on his break.

My father asked him about the business.

Was it making him enough money to live on?

Did he enjoy it?

He told us it had taken a while to build custom, but the two of them had soon started to build up a regular clientele base – mainly from the local office workers.

238

They had only been at it two or three months at this point but were earning enough to pay each of them a decent enough salary.

My father was sceptical. Shoeshine boys are down there with newspaper sellers in the land of low earners, but Ernie was never phased by others' perceptions of him. He was convinced that they had found a gap in the market in the right place at the right time.

To be honest with you, I think the two of them could have sold ice to Eskimos. They had the banter and the charm to win over just about anybody. They could read a person like a book. They seemed to know instinctively how to talk to someone or when to stay quiet and listen. They knew how to make someone laugh, but also when to offer kind words or sympathy.

Even more importantly, they were genuine with it. It was never an act. They genuinely cared about, and were interested in, other people. Both of them cared about people. They were in the right business. On a few occasions we met Robbie when he accompanied Ernie up to Washington Heights. I think it is fair to say both of us girls had a bit of a crush on him. He was a handsome man. Confident, but not arrogant. I think he enjoyed the flirting, but he knew the limits. Had father known, I don't think he would have been too pleased with us?"

Rebecca: *"I could imagine customers sitting down for a shine and leaving with nicely polished shoes and feeling ten feet tall. Ernie and Robbie just had that way about them.*

In one of the last letters I read from Ernie, he attached a newspaper clipping from the New York Times with the headline, "INCREDIBLE FEET". The

239

article was written by a popular columnist at that time – Norman Templeton.

It told the tale of two boys living the American Dream. Goodness knows where it is now. Probably in a box in the attic. The two boys in questions, Ernie Grimshaw and Robert McNulty – had set up a shoeshine shop in Madison Square Park and were pulling up trees. Punters were queuing around the block to take their turn in the chair. It used words like 'evangelical' and 'devoted' to describe their customers. Mr Templeton had even interviewed some of those waiting in line, quoting them in the article. It was hysterical."

Annabelle: "It was hilarious. I could just picture the scene. People were quoted as saying things like, 'I wouldn't go anywhere else.' and 'It is well worth the wait.' The boys could not have asked for a better advert. And underneath the headline was a picture of the two of them, sat in the big, comfy chairs, grinning and holding up a brush in each hand. They looked so happy. It was a brilliant picture that captured their personalities wonderfully well.

It was not long after that we lost touch. From what you said earlier, he must have returned to England at some point. I am so glad to hear he was alive and well just a couple of years ago.

He deserved a long life. He made ours worth living again.

I don't know where you would go from here, Paul. We have at least continued the journey until 1952 or 1953 before we lost track of him. Do you know what you will do next?"

It was a question I had been asking myself as they were talking. My knowledge of the city wasn't great, and I didn't have much to go on really. I figured I had only two options. A trip to Madison Square Park, and secondly, a near-impossible task of persuading someone at the New York Times to delve back in their archives to find a minor article from the 1950s about a man who made a living polishing shoes in a park. And just to make things even harder, I only had a full two days in which to do it before I flew back to England.

I would start early again tomorrow and go straight to the *New York Times* headquarters.

I will need to use every ounce of charm to even get past the doorman there I reckon.

When I left Washington Heights, I was kindly driven back to my hotel by the two Rabbis.

I still felt very positive and enthusiastic, despite the odds stacked against me. If this case has taught me anything, it is that you should always expect the unexpected and never give up. The two old ladies were living proof of that.

I checked out the reporter - Norman Templeton - on Google. He had been a journalist with the paper between 1949 and 1968 before moving on to work in TV, behind the cameras.

He was a stalwart of the profession in that era, and highly respected. He penned a number of very famous and controversial articles around that time, and he had even been given a nickname by his peers. He was affectionately known as 'The Ferret'. Famous for not letting go of something once he had gotten his teeth into it. Before he passed away in 1991, he was one of America's best-known journalists – loved and loathed in equal measure.

241

Hardly the kind of journalist to be writing jolly feel-good stories about two young scamps who had fallen on a bit of good fortune with their new shoeshine enterprise.

Maybe he was taking a break from exposing murderers, armed robbers, celebrity affairs and bent bankers.

It could be a make-or-break day tomorrow, Mr Diary. Let's have an early night and be ready for whatever the world throws at us.

CHAPTER 16
The Ferret

5.3.20

9:40 a.m.

The *New York Times* office block on 8th Avenue is massive. I am sat opposite in a chicken house, with a bucket of coffee and a doughnut, looking up and still trying to formulate a plan. I can't just go in there without one. What would they say? What would they think? Who would I ask for?

And then it struck me. I needed an 'in'. Who do I know who could open doors and get me past the security? My old friend, Steve Little.

We haven't spoken since before Christmas, but that doesn't matter. We are due a catch-up. I will give him a call, Mr. Diary.

9:55 a.m.

This could work, Mr. Diary. For the record, Steve and I went to secondary school together, and we have remained good friends ever since – even if we go months without seeing each other or keeping in touch. I had been meaning to give him a call to arrange a meet-up for a drink, but I didn't think I would be calling him under these circumstances.

I feel a bit bad calling just to ask for a favour, but he is my best chance. You see, Mr. Diary, Steve works for the *Manchester Evening News*. I will try him now.

10: 10 a.m.

Now I feel doubly bad. When he answered, I suddenly realised it was 5:00 a.m. in the UK. He was not too pleased at first. Our conversation went something like this, Mr D:

Me: "Hello, mate, long time no speak."

Him: *"Are you drunk?"*

Me: "No why?"

Him: *"It's five o'clock in the ******* morning."*

Me: "Oh, God. I forgot about that. I am in New York."

Him: *"Good for you. Did I need to know that right now?"*

Me: "Sorry, Steve. I need a favour. Are you still working for the M.E.N?"

Him: *"Yes, why?"*

Me: "I'm working on a case over here, and I need your help urgently."

Him: *"What help could I possibly be at this time of the morning?"*

I explained to him what I was doing and where I was. I explained that time was of the essence, and I needed to get to speak with someone with clout in the *New York Times* offices. Steve

244

knew that I was a private investigator. He had even helped me on a case or two in the past. He enjoyed the thrill of the chase. I was hoping he would enjoy this too, but his enthusiasm wasn't noticeable at this point. I put that down to the time of day.

Him: *"It's five o'clock in the bloody morning. Did I mention that?"*

Me: "I know, bud. I owe you for this. Do you think you could help me?"

Him: *"I only work in the offices, pen pushing and playing Minecraft when the boss isn't watching. I am no journalist."*

Me: "I know that, but they don't. Will you call them and pretend you are one? All you need to do is get me in the building. I will do the rest from there. Tell them you need a favour one paper to another. Journalist to journalist. Say you have sent a guy to New York to do some research for a story about Norman Templeton and his links to Manchester."

Him: *"Does he have links to Manchester?"*

Me: "God knows. I wouldn't have thought so, but they don't need to know that. Tell them we just need a little bit of inside information about him from when he worked at the *Times*. I know you. You can bullshit for England."

Him: *"Thanks for the compliment. When do you want me to do it? "*

Me: "Right now."

Him: *"No pressure then."*

Me: "The clock is ticking, mate. I am in a shop opposite their building. Will you call them and call me back as soon as you can?"

Him: *"Yeah, go on then. It will be a giggle. Have I got time for a coffee?"*

Me: "Boil the kettle while you are phoning."

Him: "Yes boss."

Me: "Will you call me back as soon as you have spoken to them?"

Him: *"I will."*

Me: "Don't fall asleep on me, Steve."

Him: *"I won't. I am on the case. Steve Little, Investigative Journalist at your service. They don't need to know I am sat on my bed in just my boxers, do they? I expect a handsome reward for this, Paul."*

Me: "If you get me in there, you won't buy another drink this year."

Him: *"On to it. Let me get the story straight in my head and compose myself then I will call them. I will call you back and let you know what they say."*

Me: "Thank you, thank you, thank you."

Him: *"Now piss off. I'll call you back soon."*

Me: "Good luck, mate."

Him: *"Luck? Who needs luck? I was born for this kind of thing."*

I could tell he had got over the initial shock of the early morning wake-up call. His enthusiasm and positivity had returned. I told him what I knew about Norman Templeton, which wasn't a great deal.

This was going to require a great deal of bluff and bravado, but there was no better person than Steve for the job. If anyone could pull this off, he could.

I had another bite of my doughnut and looked up again at the sheer magnitude of the place. Surely there was someone in there willing to talk to me.

Now I just had to sit back and wait for Steve to call back.

11:15 a.m.

Just off the phone to Steve. The man is a bloody genius. I just hope the *New York Times* aren't currently running an identity check on him. He really does work for the M.E.N., but certainly not in a position of clout or authority. He must have convinced someone that he does though. He was bubbling over with excitement when he called me back.

Him: *"You are in, matey. I have arranged for you to speak with a certain Michelle Goldberg. She*

247

is in the building today and happy to give you some of her time. She is a column writer for the Times and runs her own blog. She sounded very nice too.

Me: "How did you manage to speak to her?"

Him: *"The Manchester Evening News must have a better reputation than we both thought. I spoke to a lady on reception, and she said she would pass me on to someone who might be able to help. I was then connected to Michelle. I asked if she would meet with you on a story we were working on regarding Norman Templeton, and she said to ask you to come in. Just say who you are and who you are visiting when you get to the front desk and that's that."*

Me: "Steve, you are a bloody saviour. I could kiss you."

Him: *"I know I am. And no, you can't kiss me. Try that, even from a distance, and I will call back and tell them the truth."*

Me: "I will stick to getting you drinks, then, on my return. I will let you know what she says."

Him: *"Not for a few hours you won't. I am going back to sleep. Now good luck, God bless, and piss off."*

Me: "Will do. Thanks once again, mate."

Him: *"Anytime. Cheerio."*
I thought it best not to rush straight over there. I will give it half an hour or so and compose

myself. I wouldn't imagine she would know of Mr. Templeton, and certainly not the article in question, but hopefully she would have access to the computer records and archive system or know someone who did. I took the opportunity to check up on her on the internet.

An author and blogger who joined the *New York Times* in 2017, Michelle Goldberg was very popular on social media, and a lady very much in demand. She had quite the profile, and thanks to a cheeky call by an old friend with more balls than Wimbledon, I was going to meet her.

If I strayed too far from the truth, she would smell a rat. In this case, the truth is stranger than the fiction. I needed to know why Mr. Templeton had wanted to run that story.

Did he know them?

Was there a follow-up?

I shall update you again after I speak with Ms. Goldberg.

Note for Steve – don't let him buy another drink this year!

2:20 p.m.

I don't want this case to end.

I really don't. Just when I think things can't get any stranger or more exciting, a new chapter lands on my lap. I think all this might just have given Michelle Goldberg enough inspiration for her next article and blog.

The bluff into the building couldn't have gone any smoother. A simple call from reception to her office, an instruction to sign in and wear a paper badge, and I was in.

I took the lift to the eleventh floor and was told to wait in the foyer until Ms. Goldberg came to meet me.

I sat (or collapsed into) a black sofa near the lifts. She appeared from a nearby office and welcomed me with a warm smile. She was a beautiful lady. I tried to stand up to shake her hand, but embarrassingly collapsed back into the chair. She leaned forward and offered her hand, pulling me up to my feet. As first impressions go, it was hardly what I had in mind, but she just laughed and told me I "*wasn't the first to be swallowed up by that chair*".

She led me through to her office and sat behind her desk.

I explained who I was and why I was there. A journalist working for the M.E.N. running a feature on famous New York journalist, Normal Templeton, who had family links with Manchester and Salford. I also explained that I was looking into the life of another ex-pat, Mr Ernie Grimshaw, whom Mr. Templeton has coincidentally met and wrote about back in the '50s. I think she believed me. It was only half a lie anyway.

I asked if she was able to unearth anything from this time to help with my research, and she said she was more than happy to help. She called in her secretary – a woman in her late fifties I'd guess – to help her use the search facility on the computer.

The name Norman Templeton, unsurprisingly, came up many times – 1,158 to be precise. Most related to his old articles, but there were also a few articles that were written about him after his retirement. More surprising was the result of the name search for Ernie Grimshaw. He

250

appeared, on the New York Times archive database, forty-nine times in eleven different articles.

The two men's names were mentioned together in five of them.

Michelle told me she could print off those articles for me, which was very generous of her. I asked her if she would search for another name – Robbie McNulty (or Robert McNulty). His name appeared forty-three times and also appeared in the five articles with Norman and Ernie.

This alone was absolutely fascinating, but the pièce de résistance was yet to be revealed. Michelle asked her secretary to collect the printouts for her, and I was offered more coffee. We chatted for a few minutes about my thoughts on New York and her work for the newspaper before her secretary reappeared with the printouts.

They had been printed off in date order with the oldest article first. It was the one Rebecca and Annabelle had talked about with the headline, **"INCREDIBLE FEET"**. There they were, Ernie and Robbie, all smiles, in the grainy black-and-white photograph. This was the first time I had seen the adult Ernie. If I am ever lucky enough to catch up with him, I wonder if I will even recognise him. The article told the tale of the two boys' unlikely start in business and the popularity of their venture.

Nothing out of the ordinary, but a pleasant read, nonetheless. The caption underneath the photo used their Sunday names, which made me chuckle – *"Ernest Grimshaw and Robert McNulty take a much-needed break to have their photograph taken."*

They both looked so happy. Young men with the world at their *incredible feet*.

The second article and its headline and sub-heading smacked me right between the eyes.

'STREET MURDER LINKED WITH THE MAFIA' and **'Young Irishman Thought to be the Latest Victim of the Mafia Protection Racket.'**

The piece, by Norman Templeton, told of the murder of Robbie McNulty – a popular and hard-working Irishman from New York's East Side. His body was found badly beaten and bruised following a vicious attack by two unidentified men on 27th August 1954. It said that McNulty, a local small business owner, was brutally attacked and left for dead by two men.

The article went on to say what a great man Robbie was and how, in partnership with his good friend, Ernie Grimshaw, had made *Incredible Feet* the most popular shoeshine business in New York. The motive for the murder had not been established, but it was thought to be related to a protection racket run by one of New York's notorious mob families, The Gambinos. It was suggested that Mr. McNulty had refused to give in to their demands for money and paid the ultimate price.

The third article under the headline, **'MOB MENACE'** exposed the extent of the Gambinos' control over the East Side districts through fear, menace and extreme violence. Ernie and Robbie were named in the article as one of the few businessmen who were willing to speak out against the family, and their methods. Robbie had evidently lost his life for standing up against his aggressor.

The fourth article, written by a different journalist, Sam Thompson, under the headline, **'A BULLET IN THE POST'**, also named the three men, but this time the Mafia had turned their attention to Norman. He had received a death threat in an anonymous letter for his 'haranguing' and 'obsession' with exposing the crimes of the Mafia families – particularly the Gambinos.

The threats were taken seriously by both the New York Police Department and the *New York Times*, and it was big news at that time.

Norman would not be silenced, and in the fifth article with the headline, **'VICTORY FOR THE WORKING MAN,'** it was clear that the Gambinos had decided it would not be worth drawing unwanted media attention to themselves and had slipped back away into the shadows. The protection rackets ceased in that area, and relative calm returned to the streets. People were allowed to get back on with their daily lives without the threat of Mafia violence hanging over them. Templeton again highlighted the work of Ernie and his stand against the bully. He had lost his best friend through it all but hadn't buckled.

He had received numerous threats, but thankfully they came to nothing, in no small thanks to his customers and the local community, who had stood shoulder to shoulder with him. One man was quoted as saying, "We told Ernie, if they come for him, they will have to fight us all. The whole borough. We had lost Robbie, and we weren't going to lose Ernie too."

In the article, there was a picture of Norman sat in one of the shoeshine chairs with Ernie kneeling down in front of him holding a brush and smiling at the camera.

Michelle told me what little she knew about the Mafia influence. The Gambinos were one of five Mafia families who controlled New York and the surrounding area at that time. They had a fearsome reputation and were thought to be responsible for dozens of murders.

Racketeering would have just been one of the many crimes they were associated with, and probably one of the least lucrative compared to their other criminal activities, but they probably considered it important in order to help maintain their reputation of power and control.

I asked about Norman and his work with the paper. Michelle had heard of his name but knew nothing about him before today. Her secretary, on the other hand, did.

"Forgive me for interrupting," she said, interrupting us, "but I have worked here for twenty-five years. Mr. Templeton was before my time, but I do know of him. He was quite the celebrity, and his picture is in our own hall of fame in the lobby. He was the Larry King of his day. I will show you on your way out if you like."

I thanked Michelle for giving up her time for me. She collected up the articles and popped them into a plastic wallet.

"You have certainly given me some food for thought, Mr. Brunskill. I think Norman might need another article about him. What do you say? Have a safe journey back to Manchester, and if you need anything else, just call," she said, handing me her card.

Her secretary, who I found out was called Elaine, took me down in the lift.

In the twenty seconds it took to get down to the ground floor, I found out her husband was called Hank, she had four children – two boys and two girls – and a poodle called Fifi.

We arrived back in the reception area, and she led me to a wall covered in framed pictures. Suited men beamed back at me, holding copies of the newspaper. They were all of journalists past and present. Hardly any women, I noticed. I wondered how long it would be before the beautiful Michelle had her picture up on the wall.

Elaine scanned the pictures.

"I know he is here somewhere." she said. "I am sure there are a couple of him. He was big news back then. Look through the black and white ones."

I scanned them without really knowing what I was looking for, but then she called out,

"Here he is, Paul. Two photographs together."

She pointed at one. The caption at the bottom read, 'Norman Templeton puts pen to paper'. The picture showed a beaming Norman signing a new contract with the *New York Times*. He had a look of Sean Connery about him. Certainly, a handsome and imposing man in his youth.

Elaine pointed to the second picture. It showed him holding a beer in one hand and a newspaper in the other. It was taken in 1989 – two years before he died. He was still a handsome man then, but the years had taken their toll. I looked closely at his face and tried to imagine what he was like to talk to. From what I had been told already, he appeared to have been a strong, determined and brave man. The caption below simply said, 'Norman Templeton enjoys a drink in his favourite bar - 1989.'

I was all set to leave when, suddenly, that thunderbolt shook me to the core again.

Behind Norman in the picture was the bar. In big, clear, gold letters on a bottle green background was its name – 'ERNIE'S'.

CHAPTER 17
Ernie's

2:50 p.m. (continued)

It didn't take long to locate the bar online. Yet again, a quick Google search and there it was – East 26th Street. Less than 200 hundred yards from Madison Square Park where Ernie set up his new business with Robbie. The search didn't reveal much more than the address. No official website, and the images only showed the front of the bar. It was definitely the same as the one behind Norman Templeton in the picture in the New York Times foyer.

The same gold lettering and green background.

That picture of Norman was taken in 1987, so the bar had been there at least thirty-two years.

Did Ernie own it?

From polishing to publican?

He didn't strike me as the kind of man to name a bar after himself though. Only one way to find out, Mr. Diary. I need to go there.

I only have a day and a half left before my flight. When I first set off to America, I had made it as far as 1948. We have at least got up to the mid-50s now, and this bar would suggest a connection beyond that. Whatever happens now, I have made good progress, and Mr. Green is sure to be happy with that.

So far, I have spent less than £3,000 of the £10,000 given, so I am well within budget.

The streets are packed here. By my reckoning it would be just as quick to walk as take a cab.

I don't think I could ever tire of the sights and sounds of this city. It is just so vibrant and alive. I wonder if Ernie felt the same.

I will update again when I get there.

3:20 p.m.

So, there it is. Ernie's Bar. I am sat on a park bench on the northeast corner of Madison Square Park, and there it is across the road – barely a stone's throw from where he would have set up his shoeshine business with Robbie. Surely it is too much of a coincidence to have some random bar bearing his name so close to where he worked. There *has* to be some connection.

I can see why he would have chosen this place to start trading. The location is wonderful. The Flatiron building at one end, and views of the Empire State Building at the other. Prime real estate everywhere you look. Back in the '50s, this park would have been populated by businessmen, shoppers, tourists and locals, all going about their daily business. In those days, nobody wore trainers and sportswear. Shoes and boots were the order of the day.

The boys must have found a real niche in the market. They certainly seemed to have operated a successful little enterprise.

I have always told myself I shouldn't drink on the job, but it would be churlish not to now. I can always raise a glass to Ernie even if this is the end of the line.

I'll take a couple of photos of the place for evidence before going in. To be continued...

5:45 p.m.

Is this *Candid Camera*? Am I being spied on? Is Mr. Green going to jump out from behind a tree and tell me this was all one big trick? I have said it before, and I will say it again – this case never ceases to amaze me.

I am back on the bench opposite *Ernie's* letting everything sink in.

Again, I had no idea what I was walking into, but I certainly wasn't expecting that. Walking through the front door, I was blown away by the interior. Every inch of wall space was filled with photographs and ornaments dedicated to Ernie, Robbie and *Incredible Feet*.

I was rooted to the spot for what seemed like an age, just staring up and around the place. Most of the pictures were in black and white with only a few in colour. In the corner was a small, raised platform. On it were the two comfy chairs used by the boys. The red leather trim was well worn, the varnish all but gone from the handles and legs, and the foot stools were rusted and twisted beyond repair. Above them was, what I guessed to be, the original sign –

'INCREDIBLE FEET – Shoe Shine For All'.

On the shelves around the bar were ornaments and trophies – shoes, brushes, empty tins of polish, certificates and signatures. On one side on the room was a huge canvass with **'INCREDIBLE FEET – WALL OF FAME***'* written in bold across the top. From what I could see from a distance, the board was covered with signatures.

259

I was brought back to the real world by the sound of the lady behind the bar.

"What can I get you, my darling? Would you like a net to help you catch those flies?"

I realised she was talking to me, and I realised I was stood there with my mouth open.

I apologised and made my way to the bar.

"Ah, a Brit." she said, smiling when I introduced myself. "You seem to be quite taken by our interior."

"You have no idea!" I replied, managing a little laugh at the same time. "A lager please. And a large whiskey. Any kind. You choose. I think I need it."

While she served, I walked over to the 'Wall of Fame'. The barmaid called over to me again.

"There are some famous names on there. We never know who is going to walk in next!" she chuckled.

There must have been over a couple of hundred names and messages scrawled on the canvas. Some left simple signatures, other had penned messages to go with their names.

"We even have some of you Brits on there."

I could not quite take in what she was saying. The canvas was a 'Who's Who?' of top celebrities and prominent people from the last few decades. Tom Hanks, Arnie, Michelle Obama, Diana Ross, Mike Tyson, Bon Jovi, Cliff Richard, Tiger Woods, Tina Turner, Spike Lee, Robert De Niro. And so many more besides. I didn't see Churchill, but I don't doubt his name was on there.

The barmaid called over to me again.

"Can you imagine how much we could get for that canvas on Ebay?"

I looked around the bar – almost in a trance. A smattering of customers were sipping their drinks, reading and generally minding their own business. My presence didn't seem to register with them. It was as if this was just normal. Perhaps it was to them. Not to me though. This was incredible. Unreal. Amazing.

I looked back to the canvas and read some of the messages.

"An inspiration." – Spike Lee.

"One of a kind." – Bob Dylan.

"My favourite place to chill and relax." - Morgan Freeman.

"My New York man cave." – Hugh Grant.

At first, I thought I was dreaming, but the barmaid brought me back to reality.

"We have had to insure that for a hefty sum, but it is worth it. A real tourist attraction. The Hard Rock Café wanted to buy it, but we told them where to go. That will be $14, sweetie."

She looked over at one of the elderly patrons sat at the end of the bar and chuckled again.

"To be honest, I haven't even seen most of the folk named on there. I'm sure it is just the handiwork of this mischievous lot when I am not working. That canvas is certainly a talking point though."

I looked over at the old chap. He didn't return my gaze. Instead, he just looked down into his glass and smiled.

I pulled up a stool beside the bar. There were photos behind the optics with both minor and massive celebrities posing in front of the bar or with a glass in their hand, sat in the shoeshine seats.

"We took down the pictures with Bill Cosby and O.J. Simpson on." she continued. "We have a great reputation, and we were not going to jeopardise that for the sake of a couple of celebrities' gone rogue."

I took a sip of my whiskey and let the burn tickle the back of my throat before swallowing. Just what I needed.

I still hadn't found my voice, but she was more than happy to talk for me.

"You look like you needed that mister. Most visitors here gravitate to the Wall of Fame.

Star-struck tourists like yourself. We never know who is going to walk through that door next. We don't make a fuss though. We don't want this place to just be a tourist attraction.

People find us – we don't go looking for them. For all the famous names over there, it is the other walls that mean more to me."

I reached into my pocket and plonked the Dictaphone on the bar. I managed to find my voice at last. I explained briefly who I was and why I was in New York. She listened carefully as I retold my story yet again. I told her of Ernie's journey to America, and of the twins and the *New York Times*. I seemed to be rambling on, but she didn't once try to interrupt me. I looked around at one point and realised the other customers were now staring in my direction. By the time I had finished and told her about my findings in the *New York Times* offices on the eleventh floor, I felt drained.

I asked the question I had asked so many people before.

"Would you mind if I interviewed you, and recorded our conversation on the Dictaphone?"

She stood up straight and smiled the biggest of smiles.

"Mr. Brunskill, it would be my absolute pleasure. Of all the stars that have walked through that door, none have given me such a rush of adrenaline that you have done just now."

She looked up at the clock. It was just after 4 p.m.

"I don't suppose you could hang around for a couple of hours, Paul? Ricky will be back then, and I just know he would love to speak with you too. We come as a pair you see. I'm so excited. This is going to knock him out for sure."

I finished my drinks and said that I would go for a stroll around the area, but promised to return at 6 p.m.

"I'm Deborah. Deborah Hindle. My partner, and co-owner of this little establishment, is Ricky. Ricky Kirby. We have a lot to tell you, Paul. An awful lot. We will be waiting for you. You have made my day ... no, my year!"

I left the bar and wandered around in a daze until I found my way back to this bench. I am still convinced I must be dreaming. But there it is, right in front of me. 'Ernie's' bar. And his pictures are all over the walls. And ... and ... and.

I will go back in shortly and update you when I get back to the hotel later, Mr Diary. This is turning out to be one hell of a day.

6.3.19

10:45 a.m.

I have got a kicking hangover, Mr Diary. I was not in the right frame of mind to be writing in you last night. Again, I thank God for the Dictaphone.

If everything was left to memory alone, I would be lost.

What was meant to be a couple of drinks and a serious interview turned into an all-nighter and a very enjoyable, informal chat. I was ok until the lock-in, and then the spirits started pouring again. It is a good job I wasn't required to start early today. I don't think I could have crawled out

of bed never mind trawled the city. As it is, I don't need to.

Deborah and Ricky. I might be cursing you this morning, but I could have kissed you both last night. Maybe I did. I can't remember.

Listening to the recordings on the Dictaphone and looking through the photographs on my mobile has helped bring back the memories of the night.

I went back into *Ernie's* just after six. It was busier than it had been earlier in the afternoon, Deborah waved to acknowledge my arrival but was too busy at the bar to chat. I took the opportunity to look at some of the pictures on the wall. I recognised Ernie and Robbie in a lot of them, but none of the other people in the pictures looked like celebrities. I certainly didn't recognise them.

In one, Ernie was shaking hands with a tall, black man. The man wore a T-shirt with 'Incredible Feet' emblazoned on the front. Numerous others showed group shots with Ernie and Robbie – or just Ernie – sat in the middle at the front.

The *Incredible Feet* T-shirt was noticeable in quite a few of the pictures, but the people wearing them were hardly good adverts for the brand. Scruffy, toothless and even shoe-less some of them.

Other photos had dates or captions underneath.

'Ernie and Frank – 1957', 'The Featherstone brothers and Ernie – 1958', 'Worth the wait for Carol – 1960'.

In some pictures, there was no sign of Ernie or Robbie, just long queues stretching around the park – presumably customers. I scanned the pictures with dates on looking for the most recent. I could see a 1963 and then a 1965, but nothing more recent than that.

In one section, over the fireplace, most of the photographs were in colour. These showed a much younger Deborah, posing in front of the bar, or in the park opposite. She was with a handsome young man. I guessed this was Ricky and this was later confirmed for me.

These pictures were dated between 1981 and 1989. From what I could make out, the bar must have opened around the start of the 1980s, with a party in Ernie's honour.

I must have been looking at the walls for a good twenty minutes before I felt a tug on my sleeve.

"The landlady is calling you, son." I looked around to see an old gent smiling up at me and pointing to the bar. "I'm pleased you came back. Maybe when you are finished talking to those two, you can come and have a chat with me. I have a story or two for you. I knew Ernie."

Still in a bit of a daze, I promised I would seek him out after speaking to Deborah and Ricky. I wandered over to the bar. There was already a drink waiting for me.

"That's Patrick." she told me. "Nice enough guy, but he can bore a glass eye to sleep."

"Did he know Ernie?" I asked.

"I'm sure he did." she replied. "Everybody did. Those of a certain age anyway." She walked over to the end of the bar and beckoned over a skinny chap, who was engrossed in the baseball on the TV in the corner of the room.

"Joe, watch the bar for me will you. Earn your minimum wage for once in your life. I need to go upstairs with our guest for a while. Make sure you check the notes and count the change out. Use a calculator if you need to. If the till is short at the end of the night, the money will be coming out of your wages. Again."

Joe tutted and walked back behind the bar to do his duty.

"Come on through to the flat, Paul. I love him to bits, that son of mine, but he is a lazy bastard, and the customers will run rings around him when I am not there to keep an eye on him. That said, I can't mother him forever. He has to learn to stand on his own two feet. This is more important than a few bucks anyway. Come on through."

The flat was up the stairs, above the bar. Deborah, a slim, glamorous fifty-something, led the way, flicking switches to light up the gloom.

"It is a bit of a shithole at the moment. I do apologise. We have our family home Uptown, but we use this as a stopover during the week. It is not ideal, but it saves battling with the traffic."

At the top of the stairs, she turned left, and I followed her down a short hallway.

"Hi honey, I'm home!" she called out as she pushed open the door to the flat.

A grey-haired man in jeans and a white shirt stood to greet us, holding out a hand to me.

"This is Ricky. Ricky, meet Paul." said Deborah, getting the introductions out of the way.

When we shook hands, I recognised him immediately from the pictures in the bar.

Older, yes, but definitely the man standing in front of the bar in the '80s photographs.

"Deborah has told me all about you." he said smiling. "Please, sit down."

I sat beside him on the sofa and wondered just exactly what she had said about me.

She came to join us after cracking open a new bottle of malt and started to pour healthy measures into three glass tumblers on the table between us.

I put the Dictaphone down and asked permission to record again. Ricky asked me a few questions about my findings up to this point, and I filled in any blanks that Deborah had omitted.

Deborah was already topping up the glasses again by the time I had finished. Now it was my turn.

The transcript of the interview is recorded below. I have taken out the bad language, as funny as it was:

Me: "When did the bar open? Has it always been called 'Ernie's?"

Deborah: *"We opened the bar in late 1980. It had been closed throughout the '70s and was lying derelict. In a previous life, it was a bar called 'The Iron', named, I'd guess, after the Flatiron Building across the park. It was burnt out sometime in the late '60s, and any nostalgic pictures of the place were lost.*

It is in a prime location, and it was going for next to nothing at the time. It was a gamble for us even then, but it has paid off. We used all our savings and time to make our dream come true, but we got there in the end.

We named the place.

We knew what the name would be even before we even started work on it."

Me: "Why 'Ernie's?'"

Ricky: *"The man was a bit of a legend in this part of town. He still is, as you can see from the décor downstairs. As you know, he set up his business just across the road in the park with Robbie McNulty. The two of them started with nothing in what is normally considered a low paid profession. Outside work in all weathers. Many people viewed a shoeshine boy as a bit of a dogsbody. A bum. A nobody. That is how it must have been for them too, but not for long. Slowly but surely, they changed the perception of the job in this area.*

The two of them were incredibly popular. They just seemed to put people at ease. They made them laugh. They made them feel special and wanted. People gravitated towards them. Customers returned regularly. They brought friends. They spread the word. They even brought extra pairs of shoes to be polished just so they could sit and chat for longer. The queues could sometimes stretch around the park, but nobody complained or moaned.

It became an experience – a novelty – even a community. Even people not getting their shoes polished used to come along to the park to enjoy the atmosphere and chat to new-found friends. It was friendly and fun. A golden age, and a brilliant time for those on the East Side. Rich mingled with the poor, and everybody felt as one. It just struck a chord with the community. In this area, 'Incredible Feet' was as well-known as some of the coffee shop chains we all frequent now. Honestly, that is no exaggeration. The lads must have been working fifteen-hour days at this point, and they were making good money. It even attracted the attention of the New York Times, as you know.

That would have been enough on its own, but I had an extra incentive to dedicate the name of the bar to Ernie. My father worked for him."

Me: "In what capacity?"

Ricky: *"As a shoe-shiner. The '50s was a hard decade for my family. They had nothing. My parents lived in what could only be described as a slum today. He was out of work, depressed and unable to feed the family. He met Ernie one day in the park. Ernie could see he was desperate. Maybe even suicidal at that time. He shut up shop for the afternoon and took my father for a hot meal and a chat. Had they not met, I dread to think what would have happened to him. For the next couple of weeks after that, Ernie insisted my father meet up with him at a set time each day in the park. Whatever he said to him - whatever he did - worked.*

My mother told me that dad found a new determination and desire in life after speaking with Ernie. He sought out and found work wherever he could to get enough money to support the family. No job was considered too menial. His family came before his pride. After dad had been trying so hard for some time, Ernie put forward a proposal for him.

He met up with my dad one afternoon in the park and presented him with a T-shirt with the words 'Incredible Feet' printed on the front. At this point, Ernie's shoeshine business was booming. Both he and Robbie had more work than they could possibly cope with. He was offering my father a job. To say dad was thrilled would be an understatement.

Within a couple of months, he was bringing in a handsome wage, and my family had a lifestyle they could only have dreamt of weeks before.

It was Robbie who first suggested the franchise idea. The 'Incredible Feet' name and logo (a smiling shoe) were very well-known, and the brand was attracting a lot of attention. He suggested my dad set up shop a few blocks down and simply give back ten per cent of everything he made. He could keep the other ninety per cent for himself, but he had to buy his own equipment from his earnings.

He also had to serve with a smile and promote and defend the brand. It was a no-brainer.

My dad set up on a corner of East 21st Street, and he never looked back. When I reached my teenage years, we were living in a fine town house, in a nice area, with no money worries. We were a very happy family, and we didn't have to worry about money anymore.

Dad would make more in tips than he would in wages! Without Ernie, things would have been so different."

Me: "So, Ernie and Robbie had staff?"

Ricky: "First there was dad. Then my older brother. The same deal for him. He worked a few blocks away from my dad and wore the T-shirt with pride. He was such a happy soul – perfect for 'Incredible Feet.' The money was pouring in, but this was never about the money. It was about self-

esteem and self-worth. Nobody ever let it go to their head, and nobody ever took advantage of, or tried to scam, Ernie and Robbie.

These little franchises cropped up all over the place. The boys never advertised for staff – they went out and looked for who they thought needed help, and who would benefit from being part of their enterprise. They even had to convince some people to join them. They targeted the homeless or those struggling with life's challenges. Age was irrelevant. Colour was irrelevant. Religious background was irrelevant. All that was important was the person and the personality.

If they needed money to get them started, the boys would provide it. If they needed help or support, they boys would provide it.

The 'Incredible Feet' family grew to over two hundred and fifty around the city."

Me: "250! All working for Ernie and Robbie?"

Ricky: *"Working for themselves really, but Ernie and Robbie also got ten per cent of everything they earned as well as what they were still making for themselves in the original spot in the park. They still kept on working – they were the actual living and working face of the business. They were the inspiration and role models for the others".*

Me: "They must have been rich?"

Deborah: *"They certainly could have been. They were earning a small fortune. Enough to make them very wealthy men indeed. To be honest, it reached a point where they didn't need to work.*

271

They could have lived off the franchises and been very comfortable with it."

Me: "So why didn't they?"

Deborah: *"Because they didn't keep all their money. They kept enough to live on and gave the rest away."*

Me: "Who to?"

Deborah: *"Whoever needed it - charities, children's homes, schools, collections for the police, the fire service, the doctors and nurses and medical staff. They would look for where the money was needed most at any one time. They didn't advertise what they were doing, but everybody knew. The whole community knew. It wasn't long before the press found out too, but Ernie insisted they leave that angle out of the story. It was nobody else's business but theirs. And then there was the attack on Robbie."*

Me: "The murder? I believe it was linked to the mafia – the Gambino family?"

Ricky: *"They never admitted it, but everyone knew who was responsible. The Gambinos had a fearsome reputation in the '50s and '60s. Nobody messed with them. There were many unsolved crimes. Murders, assaults, arson. Many linked to mob families, but few arrests were ever made.*
They used to run protection rackets across the city. You know the kind – 'pay us 20% each week and your shop will be safe.' It didn't take them long to see how successful Incredible Feet was becoming.

They weren't interested in community, or the charity work associated with the business. They only saw it as another avenue to exploit, another opportunity to amass the bucks. They started putting the squeeze on Ernie and Robbie, but the boys wouldn't pay them a cent. Early on, it was nothing more than threats, but one day a couple of men gave Ernie quite a beating. He was hospitalised, and the business was shut for a few days. It shocked and angered the community. When Ernie came back to work, still bruised and in pain, he was given a hero's welcome. But the threats and intimidation continued.

Ernie and Robbie still refused to pay out, and then they singled out Robbie. One evening, he was dragged off the main street and down into a back alley when he was walking home.

It was clear from the injuries he'd sustained that they had no intention of leaving him alive. It sent shock waves through the community. Robbie was one of the pillars of the community. He was an idol to many. He had never harmed or hurt a soul in his life, and there he was, lifeless and cold in some back alley."

Deborah: *"It was huge news at the time. It was on the radio and in the papers, but the culprits were never identified or found. Ernie took the news particularly hard, as you would expect.*

Robbie was his best friend.

I think the Gambinos underestimated the strength of feeling in the community. They soon became hated by everyone. They prided themselves on respect, but they had lost any respect they once had in this community. People boycotted their clubs, casinos and bars. No one would cover for them or back them. They still had the power and the position, but they had lost the respect, and that hurt them. Incredible Feet continued through its franchise workers, but the prime spot, the two red chairs in the middle of Madison Square Park, remained empty for over a month. Nobody touched them.

No one interfered. And then, one morning, without any fanfare, Ernie returned to polish shoes. Word spread like wildfire, and soon the queues were around the block again. The Gambinos never bothered him or any of his workers ever again. A bitter-sweet triumph for Ernie, - and Robbie. Rumour has it, Carlo Gambino, the head of the family, came to the park and offered to polish Ernie's shoes as way of apology, but Ernie refused.

There were a lot of rumours."

Ricky: *"It is certainly part of New York folklore though. It is stories like that, and the whole fairy tale of Incredible Feet, that brings the celebrities flocking. Especially those in the black community. Out of the two hundred and fifty-odd franchise workers, over two hundred were black. Ernie and Robbie didn't discriminate. Those men and women must have been the ones who needed the most help, but it highlights the inequalities between the races back then just as now. Come with me, I want to show you something."*

Ricky stood up. Instinctively, the three of us picked up our tumblers. Whatever he was going to show us, we weren't going to go without our drinks. We followed him back downstairs and through the bar. Joe called to his mum asking for help, but he was ignored. We walked out through the front door, across the road, and into the park. It was dark now, and only a few people were going about their

274

business along the winding pathways. Ricky stopped by the side of one of them. There, under a streetlamp, were two cast iron replicas of the shoeshine chairs. Underneath them was an inscription.

It read:

'INCREDIBLE FEET WERE POLISHED HERE. INCREDIBLE PEOPLE WORKED HERE. TO ERNIE GRIMSHAW AND ROBBIE MCNULTY – YOU CONTINUE TO SHINE THROUGH US ALL.'

Ricky put his hand on my shoulder.

"Why don't you come back in the bar and get drunk with us tonight. We don't want a dime from you. Just your company. You might even get a few more stories from the regulars. I can't vouch for the accuracy of their tales, though. You can make your own mind up, but I am sure you will have a damn good night."

I didn't need to be asked a second time. And that is why I am sat up in bed with you, Mr Diary, feeling like I have been struck on the back of the head with a sledgehammer.

Once these painkillers kick in, I am sure I will pull through. It was worth it though.

Back to England tomorrow.

One more lead to follow up here in this great city and then I am done. Homeward bound.

CHAPTER 18
London Calling

6.3.20

12:30 p.m.

I am sat back on the same bench as I used yesterday, on the corner of Madison Square Park, facing *Ernie's* bar. The walk down Fifth Avenue blew off the last of the hangover cobwebs, and at last, I am ready to start my last full day in New York City.

I am still astonished at how much I have managed to cram into a week, and even more astonished to find myself still on Ernie's trail, revelation after revelation.

Mr. Green could be forgiven for thinking I have just taken his money, swallowed a pile of LSD tabs and made up the biggest fantasy fairy-tale possible.

Thankfully, I can back up my story with photographs, interviews and numerous contacts around the city.

There was still one pressing matter to follow up on, though, before I left the States to fly home – what happened to Ernie after his exploits with *Incredible Feet*?

Before the effects of alcohol consumed me last night, I spoke again with old Patrick in the bar. He suggested I come back again today for a chat about Ernie. Both Deborah and Ricky would be in too, and a few other regulars who would be able to share their experiences of Ernie with me.

The park was quieter than it was yesterday, probably due to the icy cold wind and slate- grey rainclouds that hovered menacingly overhead. It wasn't a day to be outside.

So, I had better get in. Just soft drinks for me today. I don't fancy another morning like this one for a while, and I have an early start tomorrow.

Dictaphone at the ready – check. Here goes. I will update you, Mr Diary, when I get back to the hotel.

5:45 p.m.

At least I only had four beers. It could have been worse. I asked for a Coke. I am sure I did. Maybe they didn't hear me, or maybe they just didn't want to.

Deborah and Ricky greeted me like an old friend when I entered. They didn't seem to be suffering from our late-night binge. No doubt they are used to it.

The bar was only a quarter full – mainly the same chaps from yesterday. They were all older men. No women. I would guess the youngest was in his sixties. Patrick was there in the same chair as he was yesterday nursing a pint of Guinness.

He nodded and called me over.

Deborah and Ricky came to join us, leaving the bar unattended. No one seemed to mind.

"How you feeling today, Paul?" Ricky laughed, knowing full well how I was feeling.

The pale complexion and the huge bags under my eyes painted an unflattering picture. A photograph of me today with the caption, 'This is what too much drink does for you.' should be sent to every group of Alcoholics Anonymous around the world to use in their promotional campaigns to warn people off drink.

Deborah plonked a large beer in front of me and mentioned the hair of the dog, and, to be honest, that's what it tasted like at first.

I explained that, basically, I was looking for clues as to what to do next. Ricky was the first to share his thoughts with Mr. Dictaphone and me.

Ricky: *"Ernie worked on the business for a good number of years, and for a decade or more, the business boomed. Towards the end though, fashions were changing – footwear was changing – and people were no longer using the polishing service. That isn't to say they weren't visiting Ernie and paying him for his time, but the shoeshine industry was dying out, and he knew it. He decided to call it a day in May 1964. My father took over his position in the park, and Ernie effectively gave him the pitch and what remained of the business.*

He didn't sell it to him – he just gave it to him.

Well, it was still profitable at this point. Ernie suggested he might get another twelve months out of it, and to make the most out of what was left.

Incredible Feet had made my father a wealthy man, and he hadn't forgotten how it had all started. At first, he refused. Then he tried to buy Ernie out, but he wouldn't take any money. He just said he had more than enough, and he didn't need it. My father felt rather humbled and spoke with all the staff working under the franchise name. Every one of them was earning well from the business, and they were all shocked to hear that Ernie had decided to call it a day. They all wanted to give him something back, but he wouldn't hear of it.

As it turned out, Incredible Feet continued to trade successfully for a further five years. My father and brother set up a trust fund for Ernie, but when he found out, he insisted all the money should go to the local charities. They did as he asked.

The business must have helped hundreds of people out over the years. He never sought any kind of publicity, but it didn't go unnoticed in the community."

Patrick: *"Ernie and I used to go fishing off one of the pier heads. We never caught anything much. We didn't have a clue what we were doing, but it was fun and relaxing.*

He used to look out over the harbour towards Brooklyn and beyond. He would often talk about England and home. It was the only time I ever saw a sadness in his eyes.

He had lived away from his homeland longer than he had lived there, but he had never lost his affection for England and his accent was still strong. I think I knew then that he would return to England one day. He was still only in his thirties. A little older than me at that point, but still a youngster himself. He'd packed more into his life than most of us would have in five lifetimes.

After Incredible Feet, he seemed a little more introverted. He didn't socialise as much, and we wouldn't see him around as often. He was still the same Ernie – cheerful, kindly and extremely witty – but something was missing."

Deborah: *"I think he had spent his whole life fighting for a cause and suddenly realised he didn't have to fight anymore at that time. Perhaps he was* drained. Who knows? Though he didn't say, the devastating death of Robbie had taken its toll.

He was the displaced person now."

Patrick: "In late 1964, he confided in me that it was time for him to go home. We had all embraced him as one of us. We all took him for granted. I don't think any of us really stopped to think what he was going through, or what he was thinking. He must have been missing his family terribly. He hadn't seen or heard from them in years.

At first, I didn't believe him, but then he started to make plans. He gave notice on the apartment and sold off furniture and bits and pieces he couldn't take with him. He didn't make a fuss. He just felt it was time. He was still grieving for Robbie on top of everything else. I don't think he ever truly got over his death. His murder.

In January 1965 – the day after New Year's Day – he announced he was leaving to go back to England. He planned to sail in the March. We sort of knew it was coming, but we were devastated when he confirmed it. I suppose we never really thought the day would come. News spread like wildfire up and down the blocks on the East Side and beyond. He was inundated with letters, presents and gifts. This was a poor neighbourhood. People didn't have a lot to give, but they wanted Ernie to know just what he meant to them.

He confirmed his leaving date as the 15th of March 1965. He would sail from New York to the port of Southampton. From there, he planned to find work in London before finding a route back north to reunite with his family."

Another man joined us at the table and introduced himself as Harry.

Harry: *"It is over fifty years since Ernie left us, and I remember that day as though it was yesterday. You have never seen a man have so many leaving parties!*
Everyone wanted to say goodbye and give him their own send off. On the day of his departure, it felt like half of New York had come down to the pier to wave him off. It was like royalty. I don't think the staff, or the other passengers, had any idea what was going on. There was cheering and yelping. Grown men and women were in tears. Young children threw flowers and screamed his name. John Lennon didn't get that kind of reception!"

Patrick: *"No, we shot him dead!"*

Harry: *"It was embarrassing for him really. He was very uncomfortable with it all. Ernie didn't know where to look. He only had a battered old suitcase and a rucksack. Folk were looking around for some big movie star, but saw nothing more than a bewildered Joe Bloggs waving back at the masses."*

Patrick: *"And then the siren blew, and the engines roared. When the ship pulled away from the dock, reality struck. He was going, and we were never going to see him again. We stood there, all of us, waving and hollering until the boat had passed Liberty and was little more than a speck on the horizon. There was a lull for a long time after that. The place was just not the same.*

People got on with their daily lives. We told stories in the bars, and laughed and joked about this strange Englishman who took on and beat the Mafia. He took on legendary status in these parts. A mystical man of mystery. He came, he saw, he conquered."

Harry: *"But the truth is, he was just an ordinary man. An extraordinary man. No ego. No arrogance. No flamboyance. He didn't seek the limelight, and he didn't court publicity. He polished shoes, and he made people happy. Hardly the stuff of legend."*

Patrick: *"That is why he **is** a legend, Harry. That is exactly why."*

CHAPTER 19
Missing In Action

7.3.19

1:30 p.m.

One hour before my flight home. They will be calling our gate soon, I would imagine.

I chose to take my life in my own hands again by requesting a yellow taxi to take me back to J.F.K. Airport. The driver didn't disappoint either. I think this fella left his eyes and ears at home before he set off this morning.

I waved farewell to the Manhattan skyline as we crossed over into Queens, and north to the airport. Then I held on to the door handle until my knuckles turned white.

Despite my concerns, we arrived in one piece, and I checked in. The staff seemed far more pleasant than those on arrival a week ago. Probably because we are all leaving, and they don't need to fear us anymore.

Overall, the trip had been an overwhelming success. It couldn't have gone much better. Ernie was only thirty-six when he left New York in 1965.

Tracking his timeline in England, now that I know so much more about him, shouldn't be anywhere near as difficult.

When I get back home, I will write to Mr. Green as soon as jetlag allows and send him copies of the interviews as before. I can only imagine what his reaction will be when he opens that envelope down in Plymouth.

I still can't fathom the connection between the two men, and why he has sent me on this quest. It isn't really any of my business, but after all this work, I hope he tells me.

This will be my last alcoholic drink on United States soil, and one thing I won't miss is the price. $15 for that beer. I could get five for that in my local and be served with a smile. Still, money isn't an issue at the moment. Long may that continue.

My plan of action for the next few days:
Return home and sleep. Write off the 8th and start again on the 9th.

Write to Mr. Green with an update.

Visit Mum.

Trace the ships into Southampton on the 15th of March 1965.

Contact the ocean liner company headquarters to find passenger lists, and any given contact information (including forwarding address – a requirement in 1965).

Track name and movement from there including places of work, tax and National Insurance records and contributions.

Find addresses he lived in from 1965 to present.

Check births, deaths and marriages for possible spouse or offspring.

Work on ancestry cases to free up Monday 11th to the Monday 18th in order to follow the case leads – wherever that may take me.

Start online dating. It is about time I started to share my life with someone else before I get too old. I am fast approaching my forties – older than Ernie was when he left New York City. I don't want to waste more years wondering what I am, who I

284

am, what I want, and where I am going. You may be my best friend, Mr Diary, but I don't want to take you to bed every night and make you a coffee in the morning. I am willing to give online dating a try anyway. It might be a giggle.

There's the call. Gate number 47. We should arrive back in the U.K. around 2.30 p.m., and I will be ready for bed then. I will try to stay up as late as I can to combat jetlag.

What a great week it has been. I won't forget this city in a hurry.

8.3.19

11:30 a.m.

That was the best night's sleep I've had in weeks. I managed to get an hour on the plane, and stay up until half ten, but I got a solid eleven hours sleep there. Magic. Just what I needed.

The new me starts today. Again. Time to write to Mr. Green.

Mr. William Green   **Mr. Paul Brunskill**
XXXXX XXXXXX XXXXX   **XXXX XXXXXXX**
XXXXXXXXXXXX   **XXXXXXXXX**
XXXX   **XXXXXXXXXX**
XXX XXX   **XXXXXXXX**
XXXXXX

Tel: 07******* 8th March 2019**

Dear Mr. Green,

I have just returned from New York City, and you will be pleased to know the trip was a

285

resounding success. Not only did I manage to locate the Kaplan twins, but I was able to track Mr. Grimshaw's life and movements from 1948 all the way through to 1965, when he returned to England.

I have attached copies of all photographs, interviews and notes taken for your information. Names, addresses, times and dates can all be verified should you require any further information.

I have also enclosed invoices for work done.

Going forward, I plan to continue the search through online and paper tracking systems, government tax and contribution schemes, as well as starting the physical search in Southampton where his ship docked in 1965.

I will update you again in a week's time.

Again, I hope you will agree, the search has been very worthwhile. If you have any questions or queries, you can contact me at the above address, via email:
*(p.brunskill@***********) or telephone.*

Yours sincerely,

Paul Brunskill Private Investigator

Mr. Green seems to be very much a letters man, but it is only fair that he has the option of contacting me via email or phone too. By the time he gets the letter, I will be back on the hunt, so I doubt I will hear from him until I return home again.

I have sent Mum a text. Hopefully she won't mind a visit later this evening. She might even offer to cook for me. I hope so. I have bugger all in the fridge or in the cupboards.

Anyway, it is the least she can do after I bought her an Empire State Building fridge magnet and miniature King Kong teddy.

1:15 p.m.

It would appear that Ernie sailed on the *Queen Mary* cruise liner with the Cunard Company. The Cunard Line was the last of the ocean liners. Passenger services were no longer viable after 1968 with the advent of transatlantic air travel. This seemed to trigger a change of emphasis for the ship companies. Cruises – holidays at sea – were to be their focus from that point on. They were very adaptable and progressive, it seems. I take my hat off to them. Maybe my mother would enjoy a cruise. I might even go with her. I will float the idea later, pardon the pun.

The website describes the *Queen Mary* and the *Queen Elizabeth* as 'superliners', and the 'ultimate expression of art deco style at sea'.

For first class passengers, they offered everything from a library to a soda fountain. I wonder which class Ernie travelled on. I'm guessing he would have been more comfortable with those in economy, even if he could now afford the high life.

According to the ship's profile, the *Queen Mary* could accommodate nearly two thousand passengers with seven hundred places reserved for the first class. It goes to show, even with the economic hardships after World War II, there were still enough wealthy individuals about to justify

287

giving over a third of passenger spaces to those who could afford that bit extra.

Mother has replied. Tonight at 6:30 p.m. would be fine. She can't wait to see me and would I like chicken and chips. Good old Mummy. Yes please. I will have to remember to unpack that fridge magnet and that little King Kong.

2:00 p.m.

It would appear that all passenger lists for ships coming into the U.K. 1965 onwards are now kept at the Cunard Line headquarters on Regent Street. Hopefully that will negate a trip to Southampton if all the records are kept there.

It seems that you can either pay for a search to be done on your behalf or conduct one yourself. As a private investigator of some note, I could hardly justify getting someone to look on my behalf. What if they miss something? No. This is a job for me and me alone. And I can have a few nights in London.

The call to the National Archives and Cunard Line Headquarters just confirmed what I already knew really. The more details I have, the more information I am likely to find, and it will speed the process up too.

Basic information needed:
Date of departure/arrival, passenger name and age.
Extra information that might help – ticket class or number, ongoing address, travelling companions.
I am ok on the first set, but a bit lacking on the second. The lady on the other end of the phone

said the extra information was a likely requirement before travel so that the customs office ran smoothly on arrival. If this is true, I will be able to find Ernie's first address on re-entering the UK.

From the first address, I should then be able to follow a trail, and if he found employment in that area, a combination of forwarding addresses and tax and N.I. payment records should help me find out his movements from that point.

From experience, it is a bit of a long, drawn-out paper exercise, but if it helps me find Ernie it will be worth it.

I will book a hotel later this evening before I go to see Mum.

I also think I will take the train to London. It is a nightmare to park in the centre now.

5:00 p.m.

Train and hotel booked. Four nights at the St. George's Inn, Victoria, for only £230 and a return train journey for £115. All in for less than £450. Some folk would consider that a bargain, but to me that is still ridiculously expensive for just four nights away in my own country. Still, it can go on my list of expenses, so I shouldn't really moan.

I get into Euston Station just before midday tomorrow. I will check in and go straight over to Kew. I should be done and dusted by teatime.

Speaking of tea, I better go and get changed and be ready for Mum.

10:30 p.m.

Great catch-up again. I am really pleased Mum and I are getting on so well. She was delighted

289

with her presents, or at least she pretended to be. Those were the kind of gifts a son gives his mum after a school trip.

The chicken and chips hit the spot. As good as anything I had in the States (*Tucker's* aside).

I offered to return the favour next week and cook for Mum (and my sister) when I get back from London. What was I thinking? – I have no culinary skills. I'm sure they will be happy with a meal deal from the supermarket - or a takeaway. It is the company that counts, isn't it?

Right, bedtime for me. Another early start and a trip to our capital. If I can find out a bit about Ernie tomorrow I can get a couple of touristy days in. I have been meaning to get to a few museums and the odd show for a while now. I could kill two birds with one stone, all being well. Night-night, Mr. Diary.

9.3.19

11:30 a.m.

I am pleased I got allocated a ticket in the Quiet Coach. It wasn't intentional, I must have missed that during the booking process, but it was welcome. No screaming children or inane mobile phone conversations to listen to. Knitting and crosswords I can cope with.

Plenty of thinking time.

We have just trundled through Milton Keynes Central, so we are on time and should get to Euston just after twelve.

I can take the tube straight to Victoria and check in before heading to Regent Street.

They told me I didn't need an appointment as it is all quite straightforward, and everything is computerised.

There is the famous Wembley arch. Nearly there.

12:30 p.m.

No problems on the tube. It seemed a lot cleaner than it did on my last visit a few years ago. Ticket prices have shot up though. It is a great place for a visit, but you just seem to haemorrhage money from the moment you arrive to the moment you leave.

The hotel is decent enough. Basic but clean. It is a bit of a hike to Regent Street from here, but I have time on my hands. The walk won't do me any harm.

I will head along the Thames to Westminster and head up Whitehall to Trafalgar Square. It is only another half a mile on from there.

It will be teatime by the time I pick up what I need from Cunard. There are plenty of places to eat around there. I quite fancy an Italian. I can eat whilst deciding what to do next.

4:15 p.m.

What the hell! WHAT THE HELL!

I have certainly lost my appetite now. What on earth am I missing?

I should have known not to take anything for granted with this case. There must be a fault on the system. There must be. I have double - even triple - checked dates and times. He was meant to be on that ship. It is the only ship that left New York for

Southampton that month. It didn't stop anywhere else on the way. Did I just dream that conversation in *Ernie's* with Patrick, Harry and the others?

Did I fall for some elaborate fairy story? Were they rolling around laughing once I'd left? I feel like a right mug now.

I have just written to Mr. Green with all that information.

Have I been sent on a wild goose chase for no reason? What will I tell him?

Ernie Grimshaw was not on that ship! For the record.

I arrived at Cunard Headquarters at 2:45 p.m.

I explained my situation, and named-dropped the person I spoke to on the phone.

They came to meet me at the front entrance and took me into a side room. She fired up the computer, and I shared what information I had with her.

Date: 15th March 1965. Queen Mary Ocean Liner. New York to Southampton.

All ok so far. Yes, the Queen Mary left New York on time and on that date. Yes, that very same ship arrived in Southampton on time.

One thousand, seven hundred and sixteen passengers boarded that day.

Five hundred and seventy-two in first class. The rest on tourist or economy tickets.

She was even able to break it down further than that:

536 adult females.
632 adult males.
548 minors (under the age of 18).
701 of those on board were between the age

of 18 and 45. 396 of that 701 were men.

And out of the 396 – 216 were registered as White. 128 as Black or Afro-Caribbean.

52 Other.

At this point I was feeling very confident and enthusiastic. I had managed to narrow it down to 216. Even if Ernie had developed a bloody good suntan, he was still in a crowd of less than four hundred. Even if he had had a bloody sex change, he must have been in amongst twelve hundred adults!

BUT NO.

NO RECORD OF HIM.

NO ERNIE GRIMSHAW ON BOARD.

I thought back to my time on Ellis Island.

A spelling mistake surely. A common mistake.

Patiently, the lady beside me checked again. She assured me that the records were very well kept, and it was unlikely that the search would have missed either his first name or surname. No Ernies, no Grimshaws.

"What if both names had been spelt incorrectly?" I asked her out of desperation.

She said I could use the search facility to scan through the names if I wanted to. I was happy to do that. She said she would even nip for a coffee and leave me to it for ten minutes, but when she returned, I was no further forward.

Ernie Grimshaw was not on that ship!

She could tell I was devastated and kindly offered me a drink, but I declined. I was in a daze. I am still in a daze. I thanked her for her time and help, and here I am again, Mr Diary.

Back to square one.

Where is Ernie Grimshaw? Who is Ernie Grimshaw?

And where the hell do I go from here?

CHAPTER 20
Paternal Instinct

9:45 p.m. (continued)

This afternoon has knocked the stuffing out of me. Self-doubt has consumed me. This case has given me unbelievable highs and crushing lows, and this must be the biggest low so far. I quite literally do not know where to go from here.

I mistakenly figured the Cunard Office visit would be the start of a straightforward record trail like the countless ones I have undertaken before. I should have known better.

I need to take stock.

With every case I have ever taken on, I needed to establish truth over hearsay, and fact from fiction. Have I allowed myself to get carried away with the story? Have I believed what I wanted to believe over what is actually happening?

If I strip away the myth and legend, what am I actually left with?

It comes right back to the basic ingredients of every fact-finding mission:

What is certain?
What is probable?
What is unlikely?
What is simply wrong?

I need to make a table. What do I actually know about Ernie Grimshaw?

What is certain?

I have a copy of his birth certificate. That is indisputable evidence of who he is, who his parents

295

were and where he came from. I know that he grew up in West Cumbria and I know he contracted TB when he was a young teen.

I know he had to live in a County Durham sanatorium for two years. I know a man called Mr. Green wants me to find him.

Do I really know anything else? The more I think about it, those are the only key facts about this case, and now I feel pretty stupid. I have fallen for the mystery. I have built my reputation on finding evidence and hard facts. If I had been taken in by every tale or yarn in the past, I don't think I would have solved a single case. And yet.

What is probable or highly likely?

When he was a teen, he recovered from TB. He befriended a fellow patient and made a friend for life.

The garden in Seaham and the bench on the front are connected to an Ernie Grimshaw. The likelihood of it being anybody else is slim.

Was it probable Ernie went to Bergen Belsen? It was certainly more than possible even though he didn't have the correct qualifications, status or experience.

The Kaplans.

Did he help the Kaplans and help Daniel? Unless this whole thing is some elaborate hoax, there is too much evidence to suggest it was not highly likely. My visit to the farm, the interview with Daniel, the actual meeting with the twins. The only other explanation I can think of would be that I have been set up, or the Rabbis concocted a plot to trick me. Why would they do that? It is almost impossible to comprehend.

And then the bar. Was it named after him? Almost certainly. Why? His photos were all over the

296

wall. Am I certain it was real? Could Mr. Green be involved? Now I am being paranoid.

The *New York Times* articles? Not 100% confirmation, but more than probable.

Ricky and Deborah and *Incredible Feet*? They were so genuine. Everything added up. Again, more than probable. Almost certain without being 100% certain. Is it true, or is it me wanting it to be?

The story of Ernie sailing back to England?

That now seems to be the stumbling block. Did he return to England on that ship?

Did they get the date or the ship wrong? That seems to be the most likely scenario, but they seemed so certain. How many passenger lists will I need to check for 1965 if they were wrong? It might not have even been 1965.

This could be a huge task.

What is unlikely?

All of it. No. That's just silly. I have said this since the start. None of it seems real right now. Right now, I feel like I am the centre of one massive joke. But that is unlikely too. Highly unlikely. Why would a stranger from the south coast give me nearly £15,000 to play a trick on me?

Has he been tricked too?

Now that is paranoia.

What is simply wrong?

All of it. None of it.

Am I any further forward? This is the one case I cannot easily sort into those four categories.

As with all cases, I have gone with instinct to a certain extent. You have to. For any investigator, evidence can be superficial or vague. The jigsaw does not fall into place readily. It is a slow process. What am I missing?

My mind is spinning again. I won't sleep tonight; I just know it. Why hasn't Mr. Green given me his telephone number? Why doesn't he want to speak with me?

It is nearly 10 p.m. now. Who would I call anyway? I'm not going to start calling anyone in the States, even though it is only teatime there. What would they think of me? It is too early for that now.

I can't call Mr. Green. No point in calling Daniel Frankenburg (the other Ernie), or whoever the heck he really is. Other than that, my contact list for this case is rather short, despite everything the man has supposedly been through. Most of the stuff I have found out – if it is true – happened fifty plus years ago.

My only option seems to be the passenger hunt through the Cunard Office records, and I don't fancy that. There will be dozens of ships and thousands upon thousands of passengers. Anyway, I can only imagine their reaction if I was to breeze into the office tomorrow and ask if I can spend all day there. She was a polite lady, but I could tell she was losing patience in the end. And yet that is my only lead.

I suppose there is no real guarantee that he arrived in Southampton. That is just what an old man in a pub said. It could have been another port in the UK. Ireland even. Maybe even mainland Europe.

A text from Mum.

"How are you son? Thinking about you. You take care in London. It isn't safe there. Wrap up warm too. x"

I'm suddenly ten years old again. I want her cuddle. She was always so tactile when I was young. At what stage did we lose that?

I realise now that it was me – my job, my lifestyle, my independence – that distanced us. Not her. She hasn't changed a jot – just aged.

But haven't we all? I wish she was here now. She normally goes to bed around this time. I don't want to trouble her or worry her. I'll reply now.

"Thanks Mum. Thinking about you too. I'm in hotel. Safe and sound. Wish you were here with me. x"

Before I had time to put my phone back on charge, I had another message.

"What's wrong? X"

And then the text conversation starts.

"Nothing x"

"Don't lie to me, Paul. I know you better than that x"

"It's nothing, Mum. I am just a bit down with work x"

"I knew it. There is more to it than that. Are you upset, son? X"

"I'm ok Mum. X"

"No you aren't. I know you. You didn't answer my question. X"

"I'll be fine. Just a moment."

"It isn't 'just a moment'. You are upset. I'm worried now.

No kiss in your last text either. I notice these things. X"

"X."

"I won't sleep now until you tell me x."

"I don't want to worry you. It's me. It's work. Long story x."

"I have all night. Tell me. X"

"It will take me ages x"

"I have my hot chocolate. I am sat up in bed.

My book is rubbish. I'm ready for a story. Call me, son. X"

So, I chose to call.

11:30 p.m.

I feel so much better now. That was a mammoth call, but I am so pleased we talked. I felt like her little boy again. She just wanted to know about me. Not work. Just me.

I felt like I was being selfish, but she told me not to be so daft. She wanted to know. She was genuinely interested. Again, I realised just how much she meant to me – means to me. This conversation has brought us closer. Closer than we have been in years.

For half an hour I just opened up. We laughed and cried – both of us. We promised this was a new start for us, and it genuinely is.

Not just words. I need her, and she needs me.

Whatever barriers were built over the last few years were smashed away in that phone call. I told her how much I loved her. She told me – countless times.

Then we talked about my sister, and how I need to keep her close. I promised I would. And then we talked work. The Grimshaw case in particular.

It started off as an overview, but she wasn't content with that. She scolded me for not talking about my work more with her. She said she loved the whole mystery and detective thing, and never missed an episode of *Poirot*. I tried to explain about confidentiality, and that the reality was not quite as exciting, but she was having none of it. I did say the current case was the reason I was feeling so down and a major factor for 'the state I was in', as she put it. She wanted to know more.

I was so used to telling the backstory now, but it wasn't something you could skim over in five minutes. So, there we were – over an hour into the call, and I had just reached the point of my New York experiences.

I stopped talking at one point, and there was no sign of life on the other end of the line. I thought she had fallen asleep.

"No, son," she reassured me, "I'm just taking notes."

This gave me a real buzz knowing how engrossed she was.

When I reached the part of the story where I was sat up in my hotel room in London with the time fast approaching midnight, I asked her what she thought.

After another long pause she excitedly said, "Oooh, you have me hooked now, son. Where the hell is the bugger?"

We both started giggling, and for the first time in a long time, I didn't feel like I was on my own.

"Let me sleep on it." she said. "I will give you a bell in the morning and we can take it from there."

WE? Lovely.

We both agreed that it was getting very late, and we'd both better get some sleep. She said it would be a busy day tomorrow. Maybe she knew something I didn't. Other than another trip to Cunard with my tail between my legs, I didn't know what else I could do.

Goodnight, Mr Diary. I need a Eureka moment, but for now I will settle for a few hours' sleep.

8:15 p.m.

My mother called at 7:15 a.m.

I was enjoying a dream at the time of owning a 'ladies only' gym. I'm only half sure I was asleep when she called.

"Paul, I have had some ideas. Could he have been a member of staff? You said you searched the passenger list. If he was staff, he wouldn't have been on that list."

I hadn't thought of that. That was a possibility. He would have been out of work at the time. It would make sense, and I am sure there were always vacancies appearing for jobs on board ship.

"Also, the ship could have been delayed. It might have been due to sail a day or two before, and only set off on the 15th of March due to bad weather or something."

Again, that was a possibility. Weather conditions were a factor for sailing on time, but it was the right ship on the right date. It was unlikely, but still possible.

"Could they simply have missed him? Records from so long ago must have been paper copies only before being put onto the computer system much later. Could you check the paper records instead of relying on the computer?"

She had a point. Many of the passenger records were copied onto the system much later. Some of the records were scans of original documents. There are bound to be anomalies in the system. The passenger records from so long ago were sure to be incomplete. It is possible, but if that was the case, that would all but end any trace of Ernie through the passenger trace system. Without that, I have no forwarding address, therefore no

302

housing records, therefore no employment history, therefore no tax records etc., etc.

She was very excited, and I didn't want to burst her bubble. She had clearly spent a lot of time thinking about this, and to be fair, she was thinking more clearly than I was.

Her first idea seemed the most plausible. It is quite possible Ernie could have been staff. He was such a sociable bloke. I am sure he could make a good impression with any would-be employer. I will go back into the Cunard offices with that as my focus.

I can always ask about the other ideas Mum suggested if the first option leads to a dead end.

If she carries on at this rate, I will have to start paying her.

I told her I would go back into their offices about ten o'clock, but I'd call in advance out of courtesy. I don't want to overstay my welcome there, but it seems like my only option. After she hung up, she sent me another message.

"Don't give up, son. You have come this far. We will find him. X"

9:45 a.m.

I'm going in, Mr Diary. You can come with me this time in case I need to scribble down some notes. I promised Mum I would keep her in the loop if I found anything.

She said she will be sitting by the phone, and I know she isn't joking. I spoke with the same lady again at Cunard when I called earlier. She was very agreeable and helpful. I think she could sense my desperation.

303

Perhaps I'd misjudged her, and it was me who was getting frustrated with the whole situation and not her.

10:45 a.m.

No luck with the staff idea. Ernie wasn't on that list either. Good shout by Mum though. Sarah confirmed that staff and passengers would have been on separate lists, but unfortunately, Ernie was not one of them.

The same result for her other theories too. Even if he had been ill, it would have been recorded, and the ship was on time on the right day. No enforced delays or adverse weather conditions. All seemed in order.

As for missing passenger lists? Yes, it was possible, and if Ernie was a victim of such an administrative error, there wouldn't be much hope of finding him now.

Sarah, the Cunard staff member with a lot of patience, couldn't think of anything else either. We both stared at one another looking for a spark of inspiration, but we seemed to have exhausted every possibility. I thanked her for her time and effort and made my way down to a little coffee shop near Charring Cross Station. Time to call Mum again.

12:45 p.m.

Back in the hotel room. Back smiling. Confidence and enthusiasm back too. Mother – you are a bloody genius. I have found him.

Sarah found him. Mum – you found him!
Rewind, rewind.
I called Mum after my coffee with the news.

304

No luck. As I headed back down towards the river, I told her I tried all her ideas, but with no success. I told her, as I walked alongside the Cenotaph, that I felt we had reached an end. By the time I was alongside Westminster Abbey, I was telling her that I felt I had let Mr. Green down, and I was scared to tell him that our journey had ended in 1965.

She said to me,

"Be yourself, son. Being someone else won't get you anywhere."

And then I thought, *"But it might get you to Southampton!"*

I said goodbye to Mum and turned around. I turned and ran back. I passed Churchill's frowning statue, up Whitehall and around the crowds gathered at the gates of Downing Street.

I waved at Nelson on top of his Column and skirted past the start of The Mall and up Cockspur Street onto Waterloo Place. I turned left at Piccadilly Circus, and I was back on Regent Street. I must have flown by fifty tourist attractions on my mission to get back to the Cunard Offices as quickly as possible. I burst in through the doors, out of breath and sweating like mad.

The security guard just looked at me with a "You again," he sighed. I asked for Sarah, and he dutifully called her. She arrived, smiling and laughing and asking if I wanted to search again. I did.

We went back into the same little office and turned on the computer.

"Daniel Frankenburg," I said. "Queen Mary, 15th March 1965. New York to Southampton. Daniel Frankenburg – or as near to that spelling as we can find."

There he was. Even spelt correctly. Daniel Frankenburg, Aged 36, white male. Registered address in the UK – 4 Winkley Street, Bethnal Green, London, E2.

How the hell could I have missed that? It makes total sense. The paperwork he arrived with in the States would have been his identity. In New York he worked as a cash in hand contractor, then he was self-employed. His house was rented. No need for a record trail.

He was Ernie Grimshaw in America.

He was coming back to England. He had to be Daniel again because Daniel was him.

He couldn't threaten Daniel's status – even after all these years.

There he was in black and white.

Sarah must have thought I was crazy. I didn't have time to explain. I thanked her profusely.

The trail is back on. All that self-doubt has disappeared again. The confidence and drive are back, and it is down to one person. Not Ernie, not Daniel, not Sarah. My mum. And she doesn't even know how it happened yet, just a random phrase that sent my train of thought down the obvious track.

I bloody love you, Mum.

CHAPTER 21
Integrate Britain

10.3.19

9:15 a.m.

I have a spring in my step once again. An address to go off at last. One thing I do know is that an address opens doors.

It came as no shock (after the shock of finding one) to hear the first known address was in London. People were hardly likely to want to travel halfway around the world to then settle in Southampton. I am sure it is nice enough in parts, but it hardly offers the appeal of our great capital city. Like New York, London offered/offers opportunity, diversity, excitement, multiculturalism, choice and challenge. At least that is what it says on the tin. It also offers poverty, pollution, danger, crime, scams, schemes and swindles.

Nothing much changes. From plague to parasites and gallows to gangsters, London's appeal is as much about its violent and questionable past as it is about its parks and palaces.

So far, I have been safely ensconced in Zone 1, surrounded by picture postcard places of interest. To get beyond 1965, I am going to have to get out of my comfort zone, and into the 'Manors'.

Bethnal Green for a start. I have been to that neck of the woods a few times before, many moons ago, Mr Diary.

An old friend of mine worked at the Royal London Hospital in Whitechapel, and she lived in Bethnal Green. From memory, she lived in a pokey flat just off the Mile End Road.

Time tends to put an attractive sheen on places where you had happy memories, but even now, I remember it being a hell of a dump. I doubt the last ten years will have transformed it into some sort of inner-city utopia.

A Google search of Winkley Street shows a mix of new and old – mainly old – buildings. They were built well before the nineteen sixties (I'd guess the turn of the century), and number 4 is still standing. I would be pretty shocked to knock on the door and have Ernie answer, but one can hope.

With an average house price of well over £300,000 in the area, it would suggest the slums have finally been swept away in this part of East London.

I am going to use this morning to do a bit of legwork around the area. I will go to see the house and the surrounding area, then visit the library and seek out any local historian who may be able to help. Surprisingly, the internet revealed little about the area, with most websites focusing on the rise and fall of the docklands or the exploits of Jack the Ripper and the Kray Twins.

Much of the East End, as it was, has been razed to the ground. At least Winkley Street is still standing. That makes it much easier to find the names of previous owners.

A bit like a used car, the name of those who inhabited the property or owned the deeds will be quite easy to trace. I would imagine, certainly in 1965, Ernie would have been a tenant, which makes things a little trickier, but not impossible.

The British Library near King's Cross might be a good stop-off point after lunch, and then I can do the housing searches on the laptop this afternoon. I am not complaining, but I sometimes wonder why so many people pay to have someone search a family history on their behalf. The process is quite straightforward, and once you have access to the necessary websites and archive links, the information is readily available. I suppose I provide the service to save them having to bother. What a lazy society we live in.

Also, years of being in the business has given me a list of contacts as long as my arm to help cut corners and access information I would otherwise be denied. Perks of the job I suppose. I might just call on one or two of them later to speed up the process.

You are coming with me, Mr Diary. Let's see what we uncover today. I have already got Mum doing some digging for me – the Frankenburgs of London. She is well up for it.

11:30 a.m.

The Common, bakery and café,
Old Bethnal Green Road
Number 4, Winkley Street.

I am always a bit wary doing the cold calling thing. You never know who is going to be behind the door, and how they will respond to a (rather odd) request for information. After all, it could be Ernie. That thought terrifies and thrills me in equal measure.

On this occasion, he was quite a friendly Polish chap (Aleksy) who had been living at the property as a tenant since 2016.

He was quite happy to give me the name and telephone number of his landlord. Thank God it wasn't an agency – they don't like to part with information as they think you intend to use it to steal their business and are also reluctant to pass any messages on to their clients. The landlord's name was Yury Vankin. A Russian.

For a Pole to be at the mercy of a Russian was an irony not wasted on Aleksy, and he spat (not unintentionally, I'm sure) when he told me his landlord's nationality. He told me he thought he had a few properties around Bethnal Green, and that he was a useless landlord, but apart from that he had little to offer other than his telephone number.

I asked if Mr. Vankin lived locally, but he didn't know that either.

"Not if he has any sense he won't".

I am the only customer in this quiet little patisserie, and the staff have left me in peace. I will give Mr. Vankin a call now.

Now call me judgemental and giving in to stereotype, but I suspect he will be suspicious of a call from a sort of British 'spy' or an authority figure. I also have to reckon on his English being a little stilted. He won't want to know Ernie's history either, so I will have to keep it brief. Here goes.

11:40 a.m.

It is not how you get the information; it's getting the information that counts. The conversation went something like this:

Me: "Good morning, Mr Vankin. I am calling you from Bethnal Green Neighbourhood Support Scheme, and you have been nominated as

'Landlord of the Month'. As a result, you are entitled to a number of vouchers worth up to £150, that can be redeemed on your next supermarket shop as a 'well done' and a 'thank you' from your tenants. You were actually nominated by Aleksy, from one of your properties on Winkley Street. Number 4. Is that right?"

Mr. Vankin: *"Hello. Yes. That is my house. Yes. Well, that is good news."*

Me: "Not a problem, Mr Vankin. We pride ourselves on having a strong community spirit, and it is businessmen like you who make the council's job so much easier. You will be mentioned on the Bethnal Green Community website. This is viewed by over twenty thousand people each week. It should be great advertising for you, sir."

Mr. Vankin: *"Brilliant. Good news. My wife and family will be very pleased."*

Me: "Just a couple of questions for you for the article if you don't mind?" Mr. Vankin: "Yes. Please. Go ahead." Me: "How long have you been a property owner and landlord?"

Mr. Vankin: *"Over ten years now. The property on Winkley Street was my first, actually. I have six now."*

Me: "Can you remember who the landlord was before you? Just for our records. How did you become such a fine businessman?"

Mr. Vankin: *"I bought the place and another small flat off Mrs Watt. A lady who owned a pub on Cambridge Heath Road. She was retiring and looking to cash in on her properties."*

Me: "That's brilliant. Do you think you she would remember you? It would be great if she could give us a quote - from one landlord to another, passing the baton on so to speak. That would be great for the 'Housing History' section of the website."

Mr. Vankin: *"Ah, that would be great. Do you need a photograph?"*

Me: "No thank you. Do you know where we can find her?"

Mr. Vankin: *"The pub is still open, I think. Maybe ask there. The Aberdeen Arms. I can be available for a photograph or interview if you need one?"*

Me: "That's great, Mr Vankin. I will send the vouchers in the post and be in touch soon if we need any publicity shots. Ever so grateful. Well done again. Goodbye."

And that was that. If I can't work from 1965 to the present day, I will work from the present day to 1965. Mrs Watt and the *Aberdeen Arms*, here I come.

By the looks of it on Google Maps, the *Aberdeen Arms* is only a five-minute walk away. I may as well have a pint or two while I am there. It is research after all. The place looks like a regular

East End boozer. Hopefully the natives are friendly. I will update when I can once inside, Mr Diary.

12:30 p.m.

Well, here I am – The *Aberdeen Arms*. A bleak, spit-and-sawdust kind of place. Looking around, I would imagine the clientele are the same day in day out. It is a long, narrow pub with little natural daylight allowed in through windows that look like they haven't been cleaned since the blackout. The burgundy chairs are worn and faded, the carpet threadbare. A slot machine and a jukebox take up far too much room, making it difficult to get to the bar without annoying or interrupting the other customers.

At the back of the pub, beyond the bar, stands an ancient pool table – legs propped up with beer mats and fag packets. Two men are playing, butt ends dangling from their mouths, dripping ash onto what's left of the baize as they slam the balls around the table with little accuracy or care. The toilet doors are just beyond them. Thank God they are closed. I hope I don't need to go. The 'Ladies' and 'Gents' signs seem out of place here. Even 'Men' and 'Women' would be stretching the truth.

There must be about twenty people in here right now including the staff. I have been biding my time and working out who to approach.

The barman looks angry with the world. A bald-headed beast of a man with barely a patch of skin left on him that hasn't been violated with ink or scars. The others look either ill or psychotic. No pearly Kings and Queens here. No jolly cockney landlord or cheeky-chappy tinkling the ivories as the congregation bursts into a rendition of 'Roll out

313

the Barrel." No, this isn't your stereotypical East End pub from the black-and-white films.

This place is like a black lung gasping for its last breath, and yet, it is my best hope (at the moment) of tracing Ernie.

I will wait for a chance to speak to the barman when he comes to collect the glasses, rather than disturb his conversations with the locals about salted nuts or pork scratchings.

12:45 p.m.

I am drawing attention to myself with all this writing. The locals seem a suspicious lot, and a strange northerner, sat in the corner making notes, is only likely to unnerve them more.

The barman was of some use at least. He had never heard of Mrs Watt, but he said he would send over 'The Oracle', "after he has finished having a piss" as "he would be able to help me." He assured me that "What he doesn't know about Bethnal Green, ain't worth knowing."

The barman said this man had lived around here all his life and was a "right nosy bastard and would be happy to talk." He also stated that "It would give me a break from the bastard."

I will have the Dictaphone running in my pocket when he comes over. I won't ask permission for this one—he will probably mistake me for the law and pull out a shooter or something.

I will update soon, Mr Diary.

1: 20 p.m.

Back outside in the fresh air. Well, as fresh as London air ever gets.

So much for the smoking ban. Everyone was lighting up in there. My clothes stink like they used to twenty years ago after a night out.

Anyway, I am going to have to brave it again in a couple of hours. 'The Oracle' has invited me back then. He told me he was going to make a call or two. He seemed very confident. He let me tell him the story of Ernie as he worked his way through at least five cigarettes. A number of other pale specimens of human existence looked over his shoulder, eavesdropping, and grinning down at me.

'The Oracle's' real name was Albert Proudlock. A bit of a local celebrity and character by all accounts. He assured me that he knew nearly everyone on the Manor, and if he didn't, he knew someone who would. He didn't seem fazed about the fact that I was searching for someone who arrived in the area in the mid-sixties. When I asked about Mrs. Watt, he just waved his hand in the air and declared,

"Six feet under son. You won't get much out of her. You wouldn't have got much out of her if she was still here either – tight as a duck's arse!" He seemed to be enjoying the attention and assured me that I had come to the right place.

He told me he was eighty-three. He looked more like one hundred and eighty-three. I could smell his rancid breath from across the table, and it was hard not to gag when leaned in closer to talk to me. Anyway, from the Dictaphone recording, this is what I got from him before he requested that I go back in later this afternoon.

I am already dreading it. I just hope it is worth it.

Albert: *"Frankenburg, you say? Jew boy?"*

I explained that his real name was Ernie Grimshaw and he had assumed the other identity in order to help his friends.

Albert: *"Still... Jew on arrival. There weren't many of 'em round here. Tended to find and stick to their own in the north. Stamford Hill, Bloomsbury and Golders Green. That's where they would go. Synagogues as far as the eye can see."*

Although he didn't say it, you could tell in his voice he didn't have much time for Jews.

Albert: *"Daniel Frankenburg, eh? Aged 36. Arrived in '65 from America. Like I said, there weren't many of them around. I will make a couple of calls and see what I can find out. Won't be cheap though. Not if I have to go that far back."*

Me: "Not cheap?"

Albert: *"Yeah. For me services."*

Me: "How much? What am I paying for?"

Albert: *"Information, son. Information. It doesn't come cheap around here. They don't call me 'The Oracle' for nothing. If there is anything to be found, I will find it, son.*
If I can find out what happened to him, let's call it half a monkey."

Me: "Half a monkey?"

Albert: *"£250 to you, my friend."*

I didn't really have a choice here. It was my only lead. Mrs. Watt was dead, and I had backed myself into a corner.

Me: "I don't have that much on me. I only have about fifty."

Albert: *"You won't get much for that, son. Well, give me what you got and bring the rest at 4 o'clock. That will give me enough time, I am sure."*

Reluctantly, I gave him the money and left. I could hardly ask for a receipt. I would have to put it down to expenses, but I felt very uneasy handing over cash to a stranger like that.

I will have to get to a working cash machine, which is not easy around here, and go back into that hellhole later on. I will update again later when I have spoken to him.

6:15 p.m.

Back in the hotel room. What an afternoon. Thankfully, I won't have to visit that place ever again.

I have what I need – even if it cost me £250. Robbing, toothless rogue!

For the record again, here is a transcript of the conversation with Mr. Proudlock.

Albert: *"Have you got the rest of the money? I don't think you will be disappointed, son. I found him."*

I was aghast. Surely not. This was amazing news. I handed over the cash, and he stuffed it into his inside pocket without bothering to count it. A few of the others crowded around the table again to hear him talk. I had to hold my breath. The stench was vile.

Albert: *"Cheers. I've earned that, let me tell yer. Right, the boy Frankenburg arrived in '65 like you said. He got a job working on the buses – a conductor – shortly after arriving. I have a mate who worked for the council. He was able to look back to see who was on their books back in the sixties and, sure enough, a few Jews amongst 'em. Your man was one of them. Can't have been too many thirty-six-year-old Danny Frankenburg's around here in '65. I'm guessing that was him."*

Me: "It does seem possible."

Albert: *"From what I was told, he worked on the buses for a few years. Nothing spectacular. No record of him after 1970. Probably headed up north London with the other Jews."*

Me: "Remember, he wasn't a Jew."

Albert: *"Ah, I know, son. My mate said there was no Eric Grimshaw."*

Me: "Ernie."

Albert: *"Yeah, I meant Ernie. No Ernie either."*

Me: "Can I have the name and number of your friend to verify the details? Will the London

318

Transport Office have records they can share? I need to find out what happened to him after he left them."

Albert: *"I can't share my sources, son. He wouldn't do me another favour again if I passed his name on. He is already going out his way to look. You can go and speak to them if you want, but I doubt they will share records of previous employees. Your best bet is to go up to Golders Green and ask about. Mind you, there are probably facking hundreds of Frankenstein's up there. Hook noses everywhere you look. Hope that helps you, son."*

That was my cue to leave. He didn't have any more to tell me. He started drinking his pint again and talking to those hanging over his shoulder. £250 to find out Ernie worked on the buses.

As they say in these parts, I have been taken for a mug.

At least I had something to go on. I could go to the London Transport Museum in Covent Garden tomorrow and seek out the historian there.

There must be some way of finding out more about ex-staff members. Especially knowing he was with them for more or less five years.

A missed call and a voicemail from Mother.

"Hello son. I have a bit of news for you, but you are clearly not available to talk. Anyway, I am going off to the Bingo with Sandra. It is the big one tonight. £100,000 jackpot. If she wins it, I will be bloody livid. I have been going every week and this is her first trip this year.

I hope you are feeling a little better today.

Don't you worry, we will get to the bottom of this. It is really exciting, isn't it?

Anyway, I hope you have had a good day in London. I'm very jealous you know. If you see the Queen, give her my love.

I will try you again in the morning. You be careful if you are going out. Keep your wallet close. There are pickpockets everywhere down there.

Have a good night. Wish me luck. Love you."

I know all about pickpockets. £250 for something I should really have been able to find out for myself. I will make my way up to Convent Garden when the museum opens in the morning and see what I can find out from them. Good luck, Mum. I hope Sandra doesn't win more than you. I will never hear the end of it.

I think I will stay in the hotel bar tonight and watch the match on TV then get an early night.

The museum opens at 11 a.m. I will get there for when the doors open and make the most of my time. If Ernie worked for the council, he would have been a registered tax-payer – in Daniel's name. If I can establish which branch he worked for, I can look back into employment history and tax records.

It has been an eventful day in East London, but not a place I want to visit again in a hurry. Right, time to switch off and get some sleep.

11.3.19

10:45 a.m.

Well, here I am, Covent Garden. It is raining today, but there are still plenty of tourists and shoppers around. Another expensive coffee shop.

Not much change from a fiver for a cup of brown grit in a cardboard cup. If I don't get out of London soon, I am not going to have much of that £10,000 left.

Another missed call from Mum. I will return her call her at lunchtime after an hour in the museum.

I don't really know what I am expecting to find in here, but hopefully I will learn a little about what life was like in that era if nothing else.

I will update again before calling Mum.

12:15 p.m.

Well, it is a bloody good museum – very interesting. I have learned a lot about the tube, the trams and the bus system, but nothing about who worked for them, other than a display featuring migrant workers from the West Indies. Minimum pay for maximum work and a good dose of racism thrown in for good measure.

The streets were certainly not paved with gold. It must have been hell for those people. If they were confronted by the likes of Albert, they wouldn't have stood a chance.

I am still seething from having to part with that money. I could think of more appropriate names than 'The Oracle' for him, but I won't list them here, Mr Diary.

It was suggested by a staff member that I try the National Archive Office in Kew, South London. That might be an option for later.

I will give Mum a call now and get back to the search.

1:15 p.m.

I am sat back in the coffee shop drinking another cup of brown grit and feeling like an absolute idiot. An elite Private Detective? Who am I trying to kid?

What a fool I am. Bloody Albert and the rest of that collection of streetwise misfits must have seen me coming a mile off. I was so eager to swallow any story he sold me – literally.

I can laugh about it now, but I will never tell anyone of this. My reputation would be in tatters. I'm losing it. I should just hand the case over to my mother.

Daniel Frankenburg *never* worked on the London buses. I really do feel like a mug.

That Jewish phantom with the American passport ceased to be as soon as his foot stepped back onto English soil.

Ernie was back. It seems he used the old identity to get the passport and the paperwork in order to get home, but then discarded that identity as soon as he could.

He was in the wind again.

And how do I know? Because my mother found out with hardly any effort at all! I did not record our conversation, but I will summarise it below.

It went something like this:

"I found him, son. At first, I started with Daniel Frankenburg, but I got nowhere with him. Then I tried Ernie Grimshaw and I found him. Facebook. I know you are not on it, but it is a treasure trove of information if you know where to look. I love it. I joined some of the Bethnal Green social and history groups – there are loads of them. Mostly people

322

sharing photos from the good old days and the like. I put on a post to try to find Daniel, but I got nowhere. I repeated the post and changed the name to Ernie Grimshaw, and it started getting likes and comments. I said I was looking for information about Ernie from when he lived in that area from around 1965. You would be surprised at how many people knew him."

As she was talking, I was thinking two things. Having been through all I have been through this last month, nothing would surprise me about that man.

Albert Proudlock didn't bloody know him—or anyone else for that matter.

She went on:

"A couple remembered him from Winkley Street. One described him as a friendly soul who got along with everyone. I said to myself, 'he is our man'.

He didn't stay there long though. He moved to a flat just off Brick Lane, someone else said. He had a stall on the market. A flower stall. 'Bloomin' Marvellous', it was called. Once that was mentioned the comments came flooding in. I went to bed about midnight and checked first thing this morning. The post had over three hundred likes and nearly seventy comments. Loads of folk remember the stall – and Ernie. Some put pictures on of the market, and someone pointed out another Facebook group to me about the Brick Lane Market itself. I joined it, and I am waiting to be accepted. It doesn't usually take long. It has a few thousand members so I am sure someone on there will know him.

I will keep an eye on it this afternoon and see what we get back. Did you have any joy yourself?"

Yes mother. I met a nice Pole, I tried to con a Russian, I drank beer in a sewer and got ripped off by a lying, conniving, filthy octogenarian.

I didn't tell her that. I didn't tell her anything. I asked her one question – Did they say if he worked on the buses in London?

"No. No one mentioned the buses. I doubt it anyway, I don't think he could drive. Oh, I forgot to mention that part, didn't I? He had trouble with his eyes for a bit. Not sure why.

One local wag called him 'The Blind Beggar' when he first turned up to work on the market.

You know, after the infamous pub in the area that the Kray Twins shot and killed someone in?

Anyway, he didn't seem to have two pennies to rub together when he first arrived, but I think he soon changed all that. He must have been a character on that market. A lot of people remember him, and many have an anecdote to tell.

I will give you a text later on today and let you know what else I find out. You ought to get on this Facebook thing. You can find out all sorts.

Have yourself a lovely day, and if you find out anything, let me know. Bye for now, son."

I looked out the window only to see a juggling clown performing badly. The irony was not lost on me.

I may as well spend the rest of the afternoon in tourist mode and wait to see what she comes back with. I have never been one for social media. Maybe I should. I thought it was all about trolls and keyboard warriors.

Who would have thought that Ernie Grimshaw is on the internet more than I am?

CHAPTER 22
Market Forces

11.3.19

11:15 a.m.

The Bagel House, Brick Lane, London, E1

I spent last night on my laptop reading about the history of different London markets. With Brick Lane being so close to Spitalfields, the two markets have a shared history in terms of the demographic and the services they provide for the community.

The Brick Lane area has been a haven for immigrants over the last hundred years or so, and that pattern has continued to this day. First the Irish, then the Jews, and now those who have moved from Southeast Asia tend to dominate the area. Such is the influx of immigrants from Bangladesh, Brick Lane is now known locally as Banglatown.

The dominant culture of the area might have changed, but the diversity hasn't. In amongst the curry houses and kebab shops, you can still find traditional Jewish fayre and everything else, from Irish pubs to Japanese sushi.

The market is famous for its diversity and for its array of colourful stalls. They boast you can buy everything here. If you want it, someone will be selling it.

Before, during, and after the Second World War, Jewish immigrants settled around Brick Lane as they looked to make a home for themselves in a 'relatively' safe and accommodating city.

The majority moved to the East End where housing was cheaper, and work was plentiful – the busy docks providing most of the jobs. It was safety in numbers, I suppose, with many experiencing persecution first-hand. But a life in London, no matter how miserable and run-down, was better than the place they were fleeing.

As with any influx of migrants, the locals tended to be suspicious and judgemental regardless of skin colour or language. The Jews' period of transition into London life was not without problems. Anti-Semitism was less demonstrative but still prevalent, and prejudice, and in some cases violence, was still common.

Acceptance and tolerance come with time, and a Jewish community around Brick Lane was soon established and thriving. By the 1960s, the scene was changing again. The Jews migrated, – this time to North London – as other new visitors to the city moved in, bringing their culture, colour and cuisine with them. This change did not happen overnight, but it is strange to visit the place now and imagine it to be any different.

It is certainly not hard to imagine Ernie at the heart of it.

Mum sent me the links so I could read the Facebook group comments from her post. It was great to see so many older folk on there, sharing memories and photos. It was even better to read the comments from people who remembered Ernie.

She posted her request for information at 8:45 a.m. yesterday morning, and by 10 a.m. she had over sixty likes and twenty-five comments. Five of which said they knew, or had heard of, Ernie. Every message was a positive one. Everything backed up and reiterated what I already knew about him - "Great guy", "What a character", "A bloody good laugh", "Heart of gold."

Some just commented on the stall or the market in general at that time. "I remember that stall. I bought some flowers for a girl I fancied from there", "It was a busy little place. Very popular.", "I can remember the two of them setting up the stall every morning – ebony and ivory!"

It would seem that Ernie had a business partner on the stall and, without stating the obvious, unless he was a coalman, he was almost certainly black. Or a man of colour, as we are obliged to say now. I think. Or was that last week's term? You know what I mean, Mr Dairy. You can be un-PC whilst trying to be PC.

Mum says she will send me any new links or comments she may receive throughout the day. I've texted her to tell her where I am. I may as well familiarise myself with the market and see if there are any bargains to be had along the way. I shall update you when I have more news, Mr. D.

12:30 p.m.

Well, I have bought an umbrella in the colours of the Jamaican flag, three pairs of black socks from a Turkish ice cream van and a small clutch of 'lucky' heather from a gypsy woman who followed me around for ten minutes until I parted with two pounds in order to release me from her spell.

The fun doesn't end there, Mr. Diary. Mum has sent more links, and the social media world has been in meltdown, it would seem. That same post now has four hundred and twenty-two likes and one hundred and seventy-eight comments. She texted to say she has also had eighteen new friend requests from members of the group. Popular lady.

I am sat on a picnic bench at the side of the road. I am not sure why it is here. It might even be for sale, but no one is bothering me, and it is as good a place as any to write.

Most comments on that link followed in the same vein as the previous compliments, but one revealed the name of his business partner on the stall. Curtis Long. It didn't go into any more detail than that, but it was progress. We had another name to search for.

As I read through the other comments, Mum forwarded me a second Facebook link. It appeared that she had been accepted for the 'Brick Lane Market' group. I opened up that link and I could see she had posted the same request for information on there. This group had a much larger list of members – over thirteen thousand. Her comment had only been posted at 8:30 a.m. and had already drawn a steady stream of likes and comments. This group was very much focused on the market's history and development since its origin back in the seventeenth century.

The group also seemed to be linked to a number of others documenting the history of the East End, and Mum had sent a request to join some of them. She really was getting into this.

The comments on this thread were clearly from older people who had lived and worked in Brick Lane around the same time as Ernie must have. A lot remembered him too. It was great to read. I will keep refreshing the link throughout the afternoon, but the following comments referenced Ernie directly. The post had clearly jogged a few memories, and I could imagine these elderly folk tapping away on their computers to share their thoughts with everybody (or nobody) on the World Wide Web.

"Everybody knew Ernie at that time. He was like a real life Del Boy. 'Bloomin' Marvellous' sold flowers, yes, but it sold everything else as well. I don't know where he got half the stuff from. Whatever you wanted, they could get it. I remember my mum once asked him for a tortoise. He had it for her the following week!" – Saeda Ali, East Ham.

"Ernie provided the flowers for my sister's funeral. He lived just down the road from us. He wouldn't take a penny for them. I remember my dad, in tears, coming back from the market to tell us. We did not have much money, and he wouldn't take any money off us. We never forgot that. What an act of kindness." – Julie Roberts, Stratford.

"Ernie was our neighbour on Hutton Street. He used to come around with Curtis to play cards on a Tuesday night. We only played for biscuits or fags, because we didn't have money to gamble. It was such a laugh. We were all useless and couldn't hold a poker face for love nor money. We just used to crack up laughing. Curtis had the most infectious laugh ever. Other neighbours used to come over to see what the fuss was about and ended up rolling around laughing with us. We couldn't even remember why half the time. Those were the days." – Awesome Dave Sykes, Essex.

"It must have been around 1972 when I met Ernie. We used to have competitions to see who could pick the widest flared trousers from the

market. Fashions were terrible in those days, and we didn't do ourselves any favours. When I look back at some of the photographs from that era, we were lucky to get ourselves a date never mind a girlfriend. We were getting a bit old to try and keep up with the fashions, but it was such a good time. I loved those years. I wonder what he is up to now."
– Alasdair Deakin, Colchester.

"The boys used to bring a lot of flowers up to the church at St. Anne's. Those that had only just started to wilt. We used to use them inside the building around the altar or share them with the elderly members of the congregation. They were always so very grateful. We all were. I sometimes wondered how those two ever made money as they gave so much away. Money wasn't their God, that's for sure. They were just so happy all the time." – Jo Clayton.

My mother posted the question, "When did the stall close? Does anybody know what happened to him?"

I noticed the message had only been posted five minutes earlier. I would have to give it time and refresh the page later to see if anybody could help.

It showed that he was still in the area in 1972 at least. He would have been in his early forties then. We are getting there—slowly but surely.

Records were becoming more sophisticated then. Computers were still in their infancy, but the world was becoming more technologically advanced.

I have been sat here writing for a good half an hour now. Observing people. Watching the world go by.

As I was thinking about record keeping, a nagging thought was going on in my mind. Up to now, other than a few bits of paperwork (under another man's identity), what paper trail has Ernie even left behind?

To get into America, he wasn't himself. Leaving America – presumably with an American passport in Daniel's name, as that is the only way he could have secured legal papers – he wasn't himself. He arrived in England as Daniel and set up in London as Ernie. Just like he did in New York. Throughout his time in America, and from what I have discovered so far in England, he had never had any obligation to register his own true identity.

Ernie Grimshaw existed on a birth certificate and pretty much nothing else official since. From his job history, he has been self-employed – cash in hand. He has had no reason to register to pay tax or National Insurance. He doesn't drive, so he won't have a license. He has a passport from another country, and he doesn't own any property or registered business as far as I can make out.

He is known, but also unknown. He exists in the flesh but not on paper. I still have no idea where this is going to lead me.

I will make my way back into central London. It is a nice day, and the walk will do me good. I could stop somewhere along the way for some food and drink and to refresh the links.

St. Paul's Cathedral perhaps.

Come along, Mr. Diary, let us leave the hustle and bustle of Banglatown. It doesn't look like rain, but I have my umbrella now just in case it does.

Bloomin' marvellous!

2:15 p.m.

I have just sat down with a pint in hand in *The Old Bell Tavern* on Fleet Street. Like any London pub, the prices are extortionate, but it is a tidy little place, and I have managed to get a seat and table to myself in the back room. Fleet Street used to be the hub of printing and publishing and, in the sixteenth century and later, the home of most of the major British Newspapers. In recent years they have taken their empires elsewhere. I would imagine that having a large headquarters in central London was no longer economically viable for them – or viable for Rupert Murdoch and his cronies.

There are plenty of reminders on the walls of the way it used to be. I'm quite happy with the way it is now. I didn't fancy sharing the place with dozens of tabloid journalists looking for their next victim.

I had two text messages from Mum when I checked my phone. One containing an updated link to the Facebook group and the second one simply said, *"Harold Patterson. Sent private message and waiting for response x?"*

I opened the link and read through more comments. It soon became apparent why she'd sent the second message.

Mr. Patterson had also left a message on the thread. Whereas the others merely related good memories or harked back to the good old days, this one offered more.

"Ernie Grimshaw and Curtis Long were very good friends of mine. I ran a stall next to theirs selling carpets and rugs. I got to know the two of them well during the late sixties and early seventies.

332

It was a shame it ended the way it did for them. The market was never the same after that." – Harold Patterson, Enfield.

I sent Mum a message simply asking her to let me know what he comes back with.

He sounded like someone worth talking to. Other comments later in the thread asked Harold how he was getting along. Some remembered his stall too, and even asked about his late wife, Edna. At the time of writing, he hadn't replied to anyone.

Looking through the different threads on Facebook got me thinking about my own attitudes towards social media. I have, in the main, tended to avoid it. Other than name searching – which revealed nothing of note for any of my cases – it did not really hold my interest. People hiding something are hardly likely to broadcast it on social media, and so it proved. Opinion isn't truth either.

Neither Ernie Grimshaw nor Daniel Frankenburg registered on the first few pages on a Google search. Even knowing what I know now with the *New York Times* articles, it was so long ago it didn't even list any mention of their names.

Without actually going to New York, I would never have found out about Robbie McNulty either. Even now, an internet search for his name doesn't mention my 'Robbie'.

His death—or murder—doesn't register as a hit at all.

Ernie's Bar is mentioned on Google Maps, but on Images it only shows the front of the bar—no pictures from within, and the place doesn't even have its own website or Facebook group. I wouldn't have known there was such a bar had I not visited the *Times* offices.

A local place for local people. It may be a celebrity haunt of sorts, but as far as I know, there could be dozens like it across the city and beyond. It doesn't stand out when you are sat outside it, never mind when you search for it online.

Even though we are now unearthing a few leads through this Facebook group, we (I) would never have thought to start a thread based only on a street name looking for a tenant of a house there from half a century ago. And anyway, we private investigators don't exactly want to broadcast our intentions when we are on the hunt for someone. It rather defeats the object. This case is different, though, and I may not be so quick to dismiss such ideas in the future. It has worked out well this time.

Just as shocking as the notion of finding something about Ernie is the fact that my own elderly mother is so 'au fait' with it all. Five years ago, she didn't know the difference between a games console and a calculator, and now she is a social media whizz.

I will carry on the walk back to the hotel and no doubt stop for another drink to break up the journey. I still have the rest of today, all day tomorrow and the morning of the 13th if I need it. Considering all I have done today is walk around London, drink and mess around on my phone, it has been quite a productive day. We know a little bit more about Ernie, and we know he was in Brick Lane until at least 1972. Surely, he has to have settled down at some point. Listen to me, I am now a similar age to what Ernie was then, and how settled am I? Not that I am comparing myself to Ernie again.

4:25 p.m.

Another pub, another pint, another pause. This time I'm in the Red Lion on Parliament Street.

A stone's throw away from the Ministry of Defence—I'd better not test that though.

I chose to get a large glass of white wine for some reason. At £9 a go, I won't be having another.

The place is full of pretentious men in pinstriped suits, garish ties and cufflinks so bright there isn't really a need for any lights to be on in here. They are all competing with each other for the floor.

"Let me tell you about the time...",

"The girls there were simply gorgeous, and I could have had my pick...",

"Wait until you see my new wheels...",

"I will get the next round in. I have had one hell of a good month..."

It is only a small place. If they had a sign requesting patrons leave their egos at the door, they could get twice as many customers in. It doesn't matter where you stand or sit in this place, you can't escape them. I won't stay long.

One rather lanky specimen seemed to be even more dominant in the conversations than the others. He clearly loved himself more than anything else, and his clones seemed to idolise him, but for the life of me I cannot see why. Arrogance seems to be the main quality around here. Not confidence. Confidence can be a good thing. Arrogance rarely is.

The contrast between those on Brick Lane and these suited reptiles in front of me could not be starker. They may share the same city, but they are worlds apart. I could not imagine a time when those in the *Aberdeen Arms* would rub shoulders with Jeremy and Tarquin over there. A clash of classes and cultures. They hail from different worlds.

Could one accept the other?

Would they even try to?

One man who didn't seem to have any problem in any social situation he found himself in was back on my mind as I tried to block out the boasts and the bullshit. Mum had messaged again to say she had had a reply from Harold Patterson. She sent through some screen shots of their conversation. He seemed a little reluctant to engage at first, but Mum won him round.

Her last message was straight to the point.

"Mr. Patterson, if you would be so kind as to speak with, or meet, my son at your convenience, we would be very grateful. He is in London now."

Harold was reluctant to put his telephone number on social media so, without asking, my Mum gave him mine.

He then replied to say he would give me a call on that number later in the evening. He explained that he wasn't sure just how much help he would be, but he was happy to talk with me.

My mother replied with her thanks and even put a kiss on the end of her message, as if that might encourage Harold to call.

I will get back to my hotel room in the next hour or so and await his call. If he worked on the stalls around that time, I am guessing he and Ernie would be of similar age.

I also Googled Harold Patterson to see if he was also more popular on the internet than me. The first search result found a man in America who had been sentenced to 100 years in prison for a double murder in 2008.

The second search link was of a famous American Basketball Star called Harold 'Hal' Patterson who has a sports centre named after him in Arlington.I don't think the Harold Patterson on Facebook, chatting away to my mother, was either of those two. Maybe the internet isn't so revealing and reliable after all.

That is my expensive wine finished. I am off back to my hotel room where I can watch mind-numbing TV for a while. It can't be any worse than carrying on listening to this lot.

I decided to do one more Google search before leaving the pub. Mr. William Green, Plymouth.

The results showed a historian, an artist and a photographer, but alas, none of them could have been my man. The dates simply didn't tally.

The man who was paying me to find Ernie was just as much a mystery as Ernie himself.

CHAPTER 23
"You save everyone, but who saves you?"

11.3.19

7:50 p.m.

I was sat in my room reading the leaflets that I had picked up from the hotel lobby when my phone buzzed. An unknown number. I was ready for it, and I switched on the Dictaphone before answering and turning on the speaker mode on my phone.

I was able to record the conversation with Mr. Patterson. He had an Essex accent but was quite softly spoken. Not what I was expecting from an ex-market trader in the East End.

Our conversation:

Mr. Patterson: *"Hello. Good evening. Am I speaking to Mr. Paul Brunskill?"*

Me: "You are. Thank you for the call. My mother told me about your online conversation. I am very grateful to you for taking time out to call me. I believe you knew Mr. Grimshaw from his time in Brick Lane."

I briefly explained who I was and why I was searching for Ernie. I didn't tell him anything about where I had been so far, or what I already knew. I didn't want to paint a picture of the man from other people's opinions and experiences. I wanted Mr. Patterson to be open and honest, and not hold back for fear of offending myself or others.

Mr. Patterson: *"I haven't heard from or spoke to Ernie since 1979. You will forgive me if my memory lets me down on occasion. I am eighty-six now. My wife tells me I am still as sharp as a tack, but she flatters me. What I wouldn't give for my youth again.*

When we reminisce, we tend to remember the good over the bad don't we? And we also exaggerate the truth to embellish a story. That Facebook group site is full of such tales.

I recall half of the stories talked about on there from my time on the market and, the truth is, there is about thirty per cent truth and seventy per cent legend. But a good story is more thrilling than a true one, isn't it?

When I read your mother's message, I couldn't help but respond. She was referring to a bloke I had not thought about for many a year, and as soon as I read it, all those memories came flooding back. Some of the best times of my life were spent on that market. The best times. We had a cracking community spirit there. We all helped each other. We were all there for one another. We socialised together; we had each other's backs, and we shared what we had.

It wasn't an environment of one-upmanship. We were all just looking to make a living and get by. It was healthy competition, but we all looked after each other. The money was good – there was always a few quid to be had - but it was not our driving force.

In the late sixties and early seventies, I would go so far as to say you would not find a better group of work colleagues and friends the world over.

We were like one big family. Those were golden years.

Anyway, about Ernie. Is there anything in particular you would like to know?"

Like with all my interviews, I like people to talk rather than be guided by me. I told him I was very grateful to him and to just tell me anything he knew. Anything at all. I reiterated that I was just appreciative of anything he cared to tell me. Once assured, he carried on.

Mr Patterson: *"Our stall had been in the family since the early sixties. We had a good pitch on the Lane, and as well as the passing trade, we had a good number of regular customers from the local community. We were an established family business. My father and grandfather ran the stall before me. We didn't need to blow our own trumpet. It was never my style – or my old man's – but thankfully we never needed to either. Our reputation for good service was enough.*

We didn't need to shout about it.

The stall next to ours was owned by an old Jewish guy. Nice chap. He sold trinkets. Nothing special – beads, bracelets, music boxes - that kind of thing. Nice man. When he left, the pitch lay unused for a few weeks. That was a rare thing. On our market, that pitch was prime real estate, but for whatever reason, it stayed empty.

We later found out that the old guy owed money on the rent and was asking too much for it in an attempt to pay his debts off. He was a stubborn bugger and wouldn't sell on the cheap, even when he was in trouble.

It was around then that the boys came along and persuaded him to sell the pitch to them on what seemed like favourable terms.

I think they told him they would clear his debt in the first three months, and if they did, he would sell the pitch to them for half his original asking price.

It was a bold move – a confident one on their part, but he couldn't refuse really. If they failed, he had nothing to lose, but if they were successful, he was free to start afresh.

Needless to say, they were successful. Very successful.

They were just so likeable and approachable. As with any new people, you are sceptical and suspicious. Doubt now, trust later. Wary of newcomers. Strangers.

It didn't take them long to win us over.

My father loved them both instantly. They made his day. He loved going in to work next to them.

He felt alive. They had him in stitches most days. He would have tears rolling down his cheeks when he returned home at night, telling us what they had been up to.

They were so popular, and they made everyone around feel special too. I think they added another couple of years on to my dad's life. He felt wanted and needed again. The boys needed him too. They genuinely sought his opinion and advice. Selling carpets is hardly rocket science, but they made him feel so wanted – he was a mentor to them.

And what a laugh they were.

Half the people gathered around the stalls were there for the banter.

It seemed more of a social club than a workplace, and that was down to Ernie and Curtis.

My mum used to feed them. She would bring them soup or a hot meal for their supper. She would

341

treat them like part of our family, and none of us minded because that is what they felt like to all of us."

At this point, I thought it would be appropriate to ask about Curtis Long. Who was he and how did Ernie know him?

Mr Patterson: *"They arrived together from the States. I seem to recall that Curtis had worked in New York for a time, having arrived there from St. Lucia. I don't think Ernie knew him then though. I think they only just met on the ship. They must have struck up a friendship there. They had a similar sense of humour. Very witty and aware of everyone and everything around them. They seemed to gauge their audience and know what to say and when to say it. They were a right double act. Curtis had family in London. Ernie had his own place, and Curtis lived with relatives somewhere on the Isle of Dogs.*

I know both he and his family suffered awfully from racist abuse. It was commonplace back then. They almost accepted it as something they had to endure. They took it in their stride, so to speak. It wasn't right. Even then, people knew it wasn't right. I won't accept this, 'it was just how it was then' nonsense.

Yes, times were different, yes, people had limited understanding of different cultures, but a good person understands and accepts another good person.

Colour doesn't have anything to do with it.

On the market, Curtis was safe. He had another family there. He was loved. I don't recall one incident where he received any kind of abuse because of the colour of his skin. If he had, and we had known about it, it would never have been tolerated. He was one of us. A market trader. We didn't care where you came from if you were one of us, and both he and Ernie were very much part of the team.

Curtis was such a ray of sunshine. He was so full of beans. Always smiling, always laughing. Like I say, he had one of those really infectious laughs. When he started laughing you couldn't help but laugh along with him. The joke he was telling wasn't important. It might not have even been funny. You laughed because he was laughing.

Ernie could spark him off with a quip or a look. He knew how to play him – how to tickle his funny bone.

I remember one guy, a street cleaner called Colin. He would come through the market, off his designated route, just to chat to Ernie and Curtis. He would leave doubled up with laughter. It made his day. He never bought anything, but we loved seeing him approach our stalls.

I remember my dad saying about Curtis, – 'If he stops laughing, we will lose fifty per cent of our business!'

We didn't lose fifty per cent, but it wasn't far short of that..."

Mr. Patterson tailed off then. He had suddenly reached a point he was always planning to get to. I waited for him to talk again.

There were a few awkward seconds of silence and then he continued.

Mr Patterson: *"One Summer, around 1975 or 1976, Curtis wasn't seen on the stall for a few days.*

Ernie was there and was his usual chatty self, but something didn't seem right. He started shutting up the shop early or asking us to cover. He even turned down jobs.

He confided in me one evening that Curtis was in hospital suffering from chest pains.

He was only fifty-two years old, but it turned out he had a weak heart. We didn't find out much more than that. Curtis died suddenly one night in the August. It must have been 1976, thinking about it. Ernie had been at his bedside along with his close family. It all happened so suddenly. So unexpectedly.

News filtered back onto the streets. The Manor was devastated. In all my time in the East End, I had never seen such an outpouring of grief for one man. We all knew he was popular, but we never knew just how many lives he touched.

To see the recent race riots in London makes me so bloody angry. There is no need. Ignorance is what it is. Curtis was a black man in a predominately white community. It was his personality that mattered. He wasn't black Curtis – he was funny, witty, silly, clever, cheeky Curtis. He won people over with his personality. He didn't have to be anything else. I am still convinced there are enough good people out there you know. Even with everything we see on the television or read about in the papers.

The media doesn't help.

It was never the same after we lost Curtis. Ernie was never the same."

Me: "Can you elaborate on that?"

Mr Patterson: *"The market was stunned. No one could quite get their heads around it. We rallied and we supported each other. We reached out for each other, but we couldn't get our heads around it. How could somebody so good be taken from us? I think we all realised how much we meant to each other after that. It took a death for us to appreciate life.*

The market carried on. Life does, doesn't it? It has to. After a few weeks, to the outsider, things must have seemed normal. The market was busy, the flowers for Curtis around the stalls died and were cleared away – life and trade continued.

People had been ill before. People had died before, but nobody had left a hole as big as Curtis. People were so busy grieving they didn't notice the effect it had on his best friend, Ernie. For understandable reasons, he wasn't expected to be his usual self, and people gave him space. And yet, as the days and weeks went by, people got lost in their own little world. Ernie never did really show how he was truly feeling. Yes, he cried. Yes, he was quiet. But we all were. Nobody judged him, but nobody really stopped to worry about him either. He never asked for help, but we should have been more aware. We should have done more to help and support him."

There was a real sadness in his voice at this point. He was struggling to talk. I let him continue at his own pace.

Mr Patterson: *"It was in January, just after the New Year to welcome in 1977, and I remember opening up one morning to find no sign of Ernie.*

'Bloomin' Marvellous' stayed closed that day - that week.

Dad waited a few days before going around to his flat. No answer.

Nothing on the market remains a secret for long, and suddenly, everyone was worried about Ernie. We realised as a collective that things weren't right. He hadn't been seen in the pubs, he hadn't turned up for get-togethers and nights out.

Some of the lads forced their way into his flat. He wasn't there. The place was all in order. Neat, tidy and nothing missing. He had gone. No note.

We didn't have anything to go on. He hadn't left any message or clue to say he was in trouble. The police wouldn't have cared. An adult off the radar for a week or so was hardly an emergency, but we knew something wasn't right."

Me: "Where was he?" I asked, jumping the gun.

Mr Patterson: "We didn't know. The stall remained closed, the flat remained empty, and yet the landlord of his flat and the market stall were still being paid. Wherever he was, whatever he was doing, money was still being sent to cover the bills.

Life goes on as they say, and we continued to trade. The stall next door remained closed. Months went by. We were doing so well that we expanded to use the space next door to stock and display our carpets and rugs.

I'm sure Ernie wouldn't have minded.

Then one day, totally out of the blue, Dad spotted a familiar figure walking towards us. It was Ernie. We ran to greet him like a lost relative and *embraced him. I remember him smiling back at us and returning our hugs, but he wasn't himself.*

We asked if he was back, if he was ready to start again. We made small talk and jostled and joked, but he wasn't the same. Had I known then what I know now, I would have realised he was going through some sort of breakdown. Outwardly, he was doing his best not to show it, but inside he was suffering."

I asked Mr. Patterson, "Did you find out where he had been for those last few months?"

Mr Patterson: *"From what I remember, he had left to go up to Cumbria. He mentioned he had old friends there. He did tell my mother in a separate conversation, that he couldn't cope anymore. He asked her not to tell anyone, and she promised she wouldn't. She only mentioned it many years later after he had gone, and even then, I think she felt guilty betraying a confidence.*

I remember having a drink with him a few weeks after he returned. He still showed glimpses of his old self, but he had demons inside he couldn't exorcise. Guilt was consuming him. He had to offload, and he chose to talk to me.

He did not know how to cope with the death of Curtis. He mentioned another close friend he had lost in America, but he didn't go into more detail than that.

He said he had gone back up to Cumbria to visit old friends. He kept saying he couldn't go home, but he wanted to see his family. It didn't make any sense to me. We had both had a few drinks. I might have been confused myself. He said he had stayed with friends in Carlisle. I can't remember who they were or even if he told me their names.

He said he wanted to find and see his parents. He wanted to know they were ok. Perhaps when Curtis died, he realised he needed his family. I don't recall him mentioning his family, or where he was originally from, in all the time I knew him.

That night in the pub, he confided in me.

On that visit, he had found out through his friends that his parents had died. Nothing sinister – old age, I think. He took it badly. I don't think he had seen them for years, but he took the news badly. I don't know why he hadn't seen them. I suppose I put it down to his travelling about and working away.

More loss and grief for him to deal with, and maybe some regret. He returned to London a shadow of his former self.

He was never rude or discourteous, but he stopped visiting us and others. The stall was 'given' to the Jackson Family, and slowly but surely, it died too. They didn't have the same drive or desire, and certainly not the personality of either Curtis or Ernie. That kind of business wasn't for everyone."

Me: "What happened to Ernie?" I asked.

Mr Patterson: *"He stayed in the area for a while. He just kept himself to himself. We saw him around occasionally to say hello to, but that was it. It didn't happen overnight. You get caught up in your own little world, don't you?*

As the days go by, you just accept it. People are selfish really. We get consumed by what we consider to be important when, really, most of it is just nonsense. Ernie was always polite. He was always happy – outwardly anyway.

It wasn't talked about then, but I think he was suffering from depression or some kind of mental breakdown. His public face was a show. He wouldn't have been to see a doctor – you just didn't back then, did you?

He moved to another flat in Surrey Quays soon after. It must have been around 1979. Wintertime. I'm sure my brother helped him with some of his stuff. He had started a job over there. I don't remember what it was. We were all so sorry to hear the news that he was leaving. It felt like the end of an era.

It has troubled me a lot over the years. I should have done more to help him. I really hope he is alright, whatever he is doing. Depression is a terrible thing. My own mother suffered from it towards her end. She couldn't explain it. She couldn't explain why she would be down one minute and ok the next. She just seemed to give up in the end. I hope Ernie didn't.

I really regret not being there for him, but I just didn't know what to do. I didn't understand.

I can't help you much more than that, Mr. Brunskill.

If you manage to find out what happened to him, I would be obliged if you would let me know. I am an old man, and I should be over this kind of thing. I have seen enough people come and go over the years. Death and loss become part of life at my age, as sad as it is.

I don't have many regrets in life, but one would be that I didn't do enough for a man that did so much for everyone else. He seemed to save everyone. He cheered everyone up. Him and Curtis.

But who was there to save them?

We are a selfish race, aren't we?"

While I still had him on the phone, I pleaded for any link, any lead that might help me find Ernie beyond 1979.

Mr Patterson: *"I can't really help you with that, Mr. Brunskill. The only thing that was big down there, around Surrey Quays was talk of a regeneration of the docklands. The place had remained derelict since the late sixties, and the government was starting to throw money at it. It was an embarrassment for the city. A dangerous place. I would imagine there were plenty of labouring jobs going at the time. Maybe he got in there? Who knows?"*

It wasn't much to go on, but it was a start. I promised Mr. Patterson I would let him know if I found out anything more.

The Ernie Grimshaw of 1979 was not the man I was now accustomed to hearing about. Life had got to him. He was afraid. He was vulnerable.

He wasn't indestructible.

Suddenly, I felt a surge of sympathy towards him. He was such a strong, resilient character. The life and soul. The backbone. The support and help. The friend.

But who did he have to help him?

He had lost his parents and his two best friends. He had given up his life for others.

Who was there for him when he needed help?

I looked at the tube map for Surrey Quays. It was easy enough to get to.

I'll go in the morning. Why? I don't know yet. Something might crop up. I will keep reading the Facebook group and see if anyone else has anything to add. Perhaps the 'Jackson' family are still in the area. That might be like trying to find a needle in a haystack too, after all these years. The area has changed so much. I doubt many of the residents there now have been there since the seventies.

After the call, I made myself a coffee and sat back on the bed, thinking. I had a gap to fill now. Between 1979 and 2017.

I owed it to Ernie, never mind Mr. Green.

CHAPTER 24
Over and out

11.3.19

10:15 p.m.

I kept refreshing the group page throughout the evening. Mum's post had even more likes, and the occasional general comment, but there was nothing new or revealing that could lead me to investigate. Nearly all the people who had commented had long since left the area and were now residing in Hertfordshire, Surrey, Essex or Kent.

London's East End had changed beyond all recognition since the seventies and eighties. Vast swathes of old dockland had been demolished and replaced by gleaming, glass, high-rise apartments and office blocks, whose monthly rental alone would have been enough to buy a whole street in the same neck of the woods only thirty years earlier.

Before many of the new, high-flying residents had been born, this same land housed some of the worst slums in the country. By the time Margaret Thatcher took up her place in number 10, plans were already afoot to modernise and gentrify the area.

'Out with the old and in with the view' boasted one local estate agent.

The view would be a good one for those who could afford it, but there was no place in the 'New London' for those who couldn't. They would have high-rises of their own, but these wouldn't overlook the river – oh, no – these would be new inner-city estates well away from the corporate eye. People were displaced. Some moved over the river into Bermondsey or Peckham. Others further north or east. Two Up, Two Downs were swapped for boxes in the sky. Flats, fifteen floors up with piss-filled stairwells and broken lifts. Concrete jungles with the 'animals', feral youth congregated in gangs, all hidden under hoods, protecting their wasteland with any means they saw fit.

Drugs were a source of escapism, or profit, depending on your standpoint or status. The rich got richer, and the poorer were abandoned, as usual.

This made my job even harder. London was an ever-changing city, refusing to stand still.

I thought about Ernie and the state he was in then. London was an easy city to get lost in. Ten million people crammed into six hundred square miles – most lost in their own little worlds. A multicultural, cosmopolitan, diverse population of strangers.

Even when the '70s turned into the '80s, and before communities started to become more insular and suspicious of each other, London could still be the ideal place to get lost in if you wanted to be alone.

By moving out of Bethnal Green and over into south London, Ernie may as well have swapped continents, such was the reluctance of the locals to venture out of the areas they knew and felt comfortable in. I suspected Ernie knew that too. Maybe it was his way of making a new life for himself – to start again. Again! Maybe he just wanted to be on his own.

Maybe he didn't know what he wanted, or what he was going to do, or how he would cope.

How in control was he?

How, without help, could he fight an illness few really understood or cared about back then?

Depression has only recently been commonly accepted as an illness. Even in my own younger years – you were told to 'snap out of it', 'man up', or to 'stop being so bloody miserable and down.'

People did cope. People did 'get by', but what mental scars did it leave? Medication has advanced and helped people deal with depression, but I doubt these comforts were available to Ernie – especially if he didn't actively seek them out.

The way forward seems to be closed to me again, Mr Diary.

Leads have dried up. I will sign off now to think. I need to create a mental plan for tomorrow.

What to do? Where to go? Who to approach? Research.

Surrey Quays has, apparently, changed beyond all recognition, but some things are bound to remain the same since the late seventies. Libraries, social and sports clubs – daily, everyday stuff.

I know I won't sleep well tonight.

12.3.19

8:15 a.m.

I didn't sleep well last night. But I have a plan.

I'll start with the Docklands Museum, then make a trip to the Surrey Quays Library to make a list of any local services open since the late 1970s to the present day. From there, I will look for names and addresses of the companies responsible for housing construction in the area following the closure of the docks, as well as those who built the shopping centre and marina. I could easily find out which of these companies are still active and perhaps find out if they had an Ernie Grimshaw – or a Daniel Frankenburg – on their books. Considering Ernie had reached half a century and is yet to leave a paper trail, I would be surprised to find anything in his name.

Looking at images of the area that makes up Surrey Quays now and back in the '40s and '50s, one could be forgiven for wondering if this was actually the same place. Did anything survive the regeneration (or the Blitz)? Not much, it would seem.

It seems a much more sanitised place now. Crime levels are relatively low for inner city London, and the pace of life is slower than its more manic neighbours on both sides of the river. The Docklands Museum looks interesting. A snapshot of industrial London surrounded by all that has replaced it. Reading back over my notes, I sound like I hark for 'the good old days' that I was never even a part of. Perhaps I feel I was born at the wrong time.

Nostalgia is all well and good, but you can't live in the past, and things were certainly not all rosy back then. Stories from the past can be airbrushed. The bad taken out and the fun left in. Is 'Spirit' the same as 'Survival'? The good old days only seemed to be good for those listening to the stories, or those who can't recall the horrors of living through the squalor and desperation. But it is fun experiencing it all through the air-conditioned halls and interactive displays of a museum with a café and 'hands-free' toilets. The concept of a 'hands-free' toilet always makes me chuckle. Maybe it is a man thing.

I doubt Ernie will pop up on an interactive display or be shown playing his part rebuilding the Millwall Docks on a touch screen slide show, but you never know.

The Victoria Line then the Jubilee Line will take me to Canary Wharf. A fairly straightforward trip from west to east London on The Tube. Less than an hour I reckon.

This hotel only offers a continental breakfast. Sliced meats and cheese with a yogurt and a bowl of cereal. London pretending to be Paris. What I wouldn't give for a good fry-up and a builders' tea to wake me up for the day.

I will have a good feast at lunchtime in the café. If I am going to be back to my usual supermarket sandwich meal deal next week when normality kicks in, I may as well treat myself to some proper unhealthy meals and fattening desserts.

Mum has been quiet. No texts or calls. Maybe she has lost interest after the initial 'rush'. Nothing new on the Facebook group again.

I will update you again after eating, Mr. Diary. Last full day in London. Hopefully, by the time I board the train back north, I will have at least taken the case into the 1980s.

10:45 a.m.

Well, this place has changed since I was last here. I am sat on a bench just outside Canary Wharf station. It must be ten years or so since I walked around this complex, and I hardly recognise the place. I'm surrounded by huge, gleaming, glass and steel office blocks, new Lego-like apartments and trendy malls catering for the wealthy and the busy. I'm struck by how clean and sanitised it is too. No litter, no graffiti, no vandalism. A world away from the market world just half a mile down the road. A safe haven for those who can afford it. But it isn't just for the business elite to enjoy. There's plenty here to interest the tourist or day visitor. Continental market stalls, boat trips, riverside walks with great views, parks and information boards, great transport links and, of course, the museum I am here to see.

And it is free to get in. Perhaps the only free thing other than the not-quite-so-fresh air. I will venture over there shortly.

Mum texted earlier. She hasn't forgotten or given up, which is good to hear, but there is nothing new to report. I looked on the Facebook groups again, but there were no new comments, and the thread has slipped down the page with other news stories taking precedence – such as: "Which is the best place to get a coffee on the market?" and "Capri for sale. White. Four previous owners. Babe magnet. £2,000 ono."

I used the time on the train over to read up on clinical depression. I am hardly an expert in it now, but the help sites and many mental health websites paint a vivid picture of the illness and its effects on the individual. While the symptoms and behaviour patterns may be similar, the emotional impact is unique to the sufferer. How they deal and cope with it is personal too.

Depression "may be caused by a combination of genetic, biological, environmental, and psychological factors" one website states. In Ernie's case, none of the above can be ruled out. Genetically or biologically, I will never know. It is more likely his life experiences, sense of loss and any psychological trauma from what he had seen or suffered from, will be the cause and the trigger. To lose two best friends in such horrific circumstances, and then find out your parents have both passed away is traumatic enough, and to top that, he had endured so much more besides. A serious illness during his teen years. A loss of identity. A loss of security – a home and a loving family. He had witnessed the immense suffering of others in Germany. He had dedicated his life to others. Now, or at least in 1979, he is alone.

Through choice? Perhaps not. He had plenty of close friends. He was well liked and loved, but could he see that then?

Did he appreciate what he had?

Did he recognise and know how wanted and needed he was?

Depression isn't immediate. It manifests over time. It may have taken weeks or months to develop in Ernie. How did he cope with it? The medication available back in the '70s and '80s was cruder and not tailored to the individual in the same way as it is today.

People, many of whom didn't understand the extent of the problem, turned to 'pick me ups' or sedatives. Neither of which remedy offered much more than mild or short-term relief and could even trigger an addiction. They were certainly never prescribed or promoted as a cure. Therapy and counselling were for mad people (or Americans) back then. Not for people struggling to cope with the stresses and strains of life in Britain. They were taboo. Something not to be talked about for fear of harming your reputation or being branded a wimp. Stiff upper lip and all that. How times change.

Mental illness and depression are huge issues now. It is being confronted and addressed. The stigma and the shame have lessened. But we are not talking about *now*. We are talking about a different time. A different era. It would be sad to think I could not get beyond this point of Ernie's life. 1979 was clearly a sad time for him. This is no time to end. I need to find out what happened to him, but it isn't going to be easy now. The leads have dried up again.

I am not expecting to find out anything about Ernie in the museum, but I might learn a little about the area. I feel like I am clutching at straws again. Think, think.

I will sign off and update again when I get to Surrey Quays.

2:15 p.m.

The museum was good. I have learnt about the slave trade, shipping channels, the Thames, the type of merchandise, foodstuffs that came through the docks, the effect of the war years on the capital, how the docks have had new life breathed into them through development and even how to tie a good knot.

I didn't find out anything about Ernie, Daniel or even Surrey Quays. I enjoyed the experience, but I have done little other than lose precious time. I go back north tomorrow, and I am still stuck in 1979.

It's like being in Hull.

3:10 p.m.

Surrey Quays. Another bench, another station, another part of London. Out of all the places I have visited, this one seems to offer the least. To me, it is bland. It is relatively quiet, relatively clean and relatively dull. A shopping centre and the usual amenities serve the community, but there is no spark or vibe.

This area died after the dock closures, and regeneration since then doesn't seem to have injected new life into the place. It isn't offensive or unsafe. It isn't unattractive or uninviting. It is just, well, bland. And the library is shut.

Ernie lived around here for a time. I'm sure it didn't look anything like this. What was he doing here?

What kept him here?

Missed call on my mobile. Unknown number but a text.

"Good afternoon Mr. Brunskill. I have remembered something that may be of some help to you. Curtis was an excellent cricketer. He played for a team north of Bethnal green at London Fields. Ernie played there occasionally too. It might be something and nothing. Good luck in your search. Harold."

Something and nothing? That is exactly what I needed. Surrey Quays had nothing to offer, and the place was starting to depress me. I searched for London Fields Cricket Club – it was there. Alive and well and still going. Vibrant even. The opposite of Surrey Quays.

Time is against me now. I will take the train up there and have a look for myself. I don't imagine there will be much going on at this time, but it will be worth checking out. I have the rest of today and tomorrow morning before I have to make my way to Euston Station. Midweek isn't exactly the best time to turn up at a cricket club, but there must be someone who can help. There is even a website and a contact number.

Thank you, Harold – you have thrown me a lifeline!

4: 45 p.m.

There was no direct train line there from Surrey Quays, so I decided to take a cab. I thought it would be quicker. The driver seemed to take all the wrong roads as slowly as he could.

£35 charged! Robbing bastard.

As predicted, there was no sign of cricket life in the park. It was getting dark when I arrived, so I had no choice but to find a nearby pub to plan my next course of action.

The *Pub on the Park* was easy to find. It was clean and recently refurbished with a very enticing menu. I was ready for a pint, and my rumbling stomach told me I was also ready to eat, so here we are, Mr Diary. Another excuse for a drinking dinner.

I will give Mum a call in a minute. She can do a bit of Facebook digging while I tuck into a big steak.

From the contact page on the cricket club's website, I found an email address and sent them a message asking if it would be possible to speak or meet with a senior member of the club.

Hopefully I will get a response before I leave tomorrow. It also mentions on their website that this pub is a popular drinking hole for the team at any time of year. At least I am in the right place, but looking at the clientele, I doubt many were even born when Curtis and Ernie played up here.

I will update again when I get back to the hotel. Time to eat, drink and be merry.

8:30 p.m.

Back at the hotel but...

Progress.

An email back from someone at London Fields Cricket Club.

A certain Paul Turley replied just after seven o'clock to say he would be happy to meet for a drink. It turns out at least half the current first team were on their way to the very same pub I was in whilst I was devouring my mouth-watering steak with peppercorn sauce.

He explained that he had been involved in and around the club for the last few years but knew very little about what it was like as far back as the late '70s and early '80s. He did say he would ask around as "there is always someone who can help".

That gave me some confidence. I emailed back to thank him for his help and left my telephone number. Within ten minutes he had texted me.

"Hello Paul. Great to hear from you. A few of us are in the pub now if you want to join us, or you could give me a call in the morning?"

Time is getting on. Should I, shouldn't I? Before this case I would have said no, and climbed into bed with a hot chocolate, but sod it. You only live once. I fancy a drink; I have the money.

My reply.

"I'm on my way, Paul. I should be there for nine-ish."

He replied.

"Good man. We'll pull up another seat. We are in the corner near the toilets. You won't miss us. Look for the man in the glasses and the flowery, pink shirt. He isn't with us though, thank God."

Mr. Diary, you stay here. I'm calling a cab.

13.3.19

11:30 a.m.

The chances of me getting on my two-thirty train from Euston to Preston are pretty much zero. I am going to need another couple of days here – at least. That is going to eat into the wages, but I have plenty, thanks to Mr. Green, and I don't want to leave now. And I am not getting out of this bed until this afternoon. Bloody hell could those boys drink. They must have had half a dozen before I arrived, and they were just warming up. I'm feeling a little worse for wear now.

I spotted the guy in the pink, flowery shirt. He looked like a cross between Jimmy Savile and Rolf Harris. No wonder he was sat on his own. I don't think I would have needed all my investigative skills to find the team regardless of his presence.

They were all sat around a circular table, drinking and laughing loudly.

But it wasn't the noise than alerted me to them – it was an empty stool in the middle with the words 'SHERLOCK HOLMES' written in thick, black marker pen on a piece of white, A4 paper. I introduced myself and offered to buy a round on expenses. This won them over straight away. I even threw in a few bags of crisps and nuts for good measure.

My social life has been a pretty lonely one this last couple of years. With little effort made on my part, I have allowed myself to drift away from my friends. Last night gave me another much-needed kick up the arse moment, which will hopefully prompt me to rectify that when I get home. It was a great night, even if I am paying for it now.

I have no idea what time I got back in the hotel, but it was definitely after 2 a.m.

I didn't take the Dictaphone – it didn't seem appropriate – but I did take a few notes in my jotter. Thank God most of them were made in the first hour or so, as I don't think much after that would have been legible. Paul introduced himself as the man behind the email.

"We thought it was a piss take at first." he told me. "We get quite a few spam emails – you know the type: 'you have inherited $400,000 from an old relative in Zimbabwe. Can we have your bank details to confirm your identity?' And all those adverts for Viagra and offers to marry beautiful Russian ladies. We respond to them all." he laughed.

I think I reassured them that I was not after any money, and I was not a trafficker, pimp or African gold-digger. A second round of beers helped too.

Paul then introduced me to Dave Krohn, Troy Utz, Ian Charlton and Carl Death (great name) – all current first-team members and all around my age or slightly older. I was given an overview of their contribution (or lack of) to the team and their weaknesses, bad habits and embarrassing traits.

The abuse was flying, and the insults stinging, but it was clear they had a great affection for each other. Troy and Dave sparked off each other often at the expense of others, but there was no malice. They were clearly a team off the field as well as on it. Ian and Carl were highlighted as 'the gurus'. Ian, the oldest around the table, had been on the scene for longer than any of them could remember, and he seemed to take everything in. I had him down as the sensible one, until he suggested trays of shots. After that, had I died, it would have been him the police would have looked to charge with manslaughter.

As is often the way in pubs, a conversation is rarely private, and it wasn't long before a few older heads from around the bar took an interest.

I was given another quick history lesson. It turned out the club hadn't always been called London Fields. Indeed, it was given the name at the behest of Hackney Council in order to secure first call on the in-demand pitch. Before that, it was known as Martello's Cricket Club and, even further back, the Taylor Cricket Club. Ian had joined 'Taylor's' in 1985, and that team included a certain Leroy Golding who went on star in the hit soap opera, 'EastEnders'.

I had to Google him to remember the face. Someone quipped that he was a decent enough batsman but a shite actor, and he should have stuck to playing cricket. They didn't mean it. Ian called over a grey-haired man in his sixties. His name (if I have spelt it correctly) was Colin Heardman. He played in the team before Ian, but he didn't recall playing with Ernie.

But he did remember the name Curtis Long.

He told me that he was a cracking player and thought he could have gone on to play professionally.

I explained that, whilst researching, I found out that Curtis had passed away. We all raised a glass to him.

Colin then called over another friend - Bryan Flynn. Bryan was a Welshman who had made a life in London after marrying an East End girl back in the '70s. He couldn't remember Ernie either, but he had heard of Curtis. It would seem that, on the cricketing scene at least, Ernie's renown and celebrity was eclipsed by his buddy.

By all accounts, Curtis was a great talent lost.

Third time lucky though.

Bryan said he would call another old friend of his. His uncle, another octogenarian. He told me that, *"If Sid doesn't know the man you are after, no one will!"* Bryan gave me his own number, and I gave him mine. He promised to call me after speaking with Sid in the morning. After all that drink, I just hoped he would remember.

Late evening turned into night, and I was in no state to work anymore. By the time I was bundled into a taxi, waving a fond farewell to my new-found friends, I was gone to the world.

I woke with a stonking hangover, but I had the good sense to call reception and book the room for another night. Thank God it was available, or they would have had to carry the bed out with me in it.

I will worry about the train tickets as and when I need to.

I have missed breakfast, but I noticed a very unhealthy-looking café not far from the hotel.

A good, lethal fry-up, six litres of water, and a couple of painkillers should see me right.

1:45 p.m.

Just what the doctor ordered. A nice power shower on top of all that grease, and I am almost back to normal. I had a few texts earlier from the London Field's crowd, which was nice, and also one from Bryan. He had spoken to his uncle and, when I am ready, he will take me over to meet him. I will call him now.

2:00 p.m.

I am meeting Bryan outside Bow Street tube station at 3 p.m. His uncle lives on nearby Alfred Street and is looking forward to meeting up and talking about old times. I love these kinds of meets. I can lose myself in other people's memories – imagining I was there and being part of those times. Most old people make great storytellers.

I had better get a move on. My head is clear now. Notepad and Dictaphone at the ready. Mr. Diary, you can stay here and relax.

6:30 p.m.

Just back at the hotel. After a couple of days losing hope, I am back on the trail.

Meeting Sid (Sidney Barton) was a breath of fresh air. I don't mean that in the literal sense though. His flat stunk of stale cigarette smoke. He proudly boasted that he was a "fifty-a- day man" and still "as fit as a flea". He didn't look as fit as a flea, unless the flea in question was about to keel over whilst coughing its guts out every couple of minutes.

It didn't put him off though.

Sid described himself as 'old-school' and 'not ready for the wooden box just yet'. Bryan clearly had a fondness for the old man and was affectionate and warm towards him. He went to make a cup of tea while we broke bread.

Sid was clearly a cricketing enthusiast, and he knew all the clubs in the area. He knew which league they were all in and how they had performed in recent seasons. He was scathing of the current team at London Fields, but he clarified that with "it's probably because I am just a miserable, jealous, old bastard who wishes he was still playing."

I waited until Bryan was back with the tea before bringing up the names of Curtis Long and Ernie Grimshaw. Sid took a sip of his coffee and smiled.

"Which one first?"

I suggested he tell me what he knew about Curtis.

Sid: *"Black as the ace of spades. Blacker. You can't say that now, though, but he was. Came from the West Indies via America. Many of the new arrivals gravitated towards the cricket clubs from his generation, and the one before him.*

They call them the 'Windrush Generation' now, don't they? They have had a rough deal, poor buggers. It was the government's doing in the main. A cock-up from start to finish.

It never surprises me how heartless and callous they can be. People are just numbers to them. Figures on a spreadsheet.

368

We welcomed them, though. Especially down London Fields. The West Indians – then the Asians - improved the team no end, and no one was better than Curtis Long. He was a dream to watch. What a player. He could bowl, bat, field – whatever was asked of him. And he could do it better than anyone else.

Cricket fans all around the capital soon heard about him, and they would come down to watch us. He was not just the best in the East End, I would say there wasn't a better player in the capital, and I'm not joking when I say that.

We could have hundreds of folk around the boundary watching Curtis play. He was a prized asset – even in his fifties. He could have been a top, top player. And what a nice fella too."

I asked him what it was like for a black player at that time. The 1970s was an unforgiving era.

Sid: *"I won't lie, it can't have been easy for him or any of them. The newspapers didn't help. They whipped up a storm or two to cause trouble. No different from these days. Some didn't settle. Some struggled. Most Londoners were friendly though. We weren't the insular racists they would have you believe. Treat as you find. Those that made the effort were welcomed with open arms. Certainly, the folk in our area."*

Me: "Curtis was living on the Isle of Dogs, wasn't he? How did he land at London Fields?"

Sid: *"He was spotted by someone and invited for a trial. There weren't that many established clubs then, and the standard locally wasn't great.*

369

There was little money, and the facilities were appalling compared to nowadays. We were ok though, and we offered him a game. We made out we were doing him a favour, but it was the other way around really. He was class."

Me: "And Ernie? Did he play in the same team?

"Ernie?" (a loud mixture of coughs, spluttering and laughter) "Ernie was bloody useless. He couldn't swing a bat, he couldn't bowl, and he couldn't catch.
He had about as much chance of getting in a team as my wife – and she has been dead for fifteen years!"

Me: "But he was involved with the team?"

Sid: *"Oh, God yeah. He was involved all right. Yes, he did play on occasion, but only if we were desperate. We would put the boys in before Ernie."*

Me: "Why was he there then?"

Sid: *"Because we loved him. He came along with Curtis at first. He knew he was a top player. Ernie promoted him. It only took one trial to see how good he was. The captain wouldn't let him go until he agreed to play for us.*
Ernie knew he wasn't a good player himself. He never pretended he could play either. He just wanted to do right by his mate and give him a leg up to help him shine. The two of them would come up and join the training sessions and games, but only Curtis had a chance of playing in the first team

really. It was such a shame that he wasn't twenty years younger, or he would have played for the West Indies or England, I'm sure.

   Ernie helped out. Sorted the kit, helped with the ground staff, prepared food and drinks. He didn't need to be there, but we encouraged it. We would pick him for a team just so he would come along sometimes."

Me: "Why?"

Sid: *"Because he was a joy to be around. A real tonic. He fitted in so well. After a few weeks, you would have thought he had been there for years. Not cocky or smart, just really funny and warm. Away from the club, we didn't really know anything about the pair of them. They weren't from the area - many weren't – but it didn't matter. We were a team. A club. Ernie was part of the fabric, and we took him for granted. We loved him."*

Me: "Do you know what happened to Curtis?"

Sid: *"Yeah. It was all of a sudden. Heart problems, wasn't it? A hell of a shock. We didn't recover for a long time after that. I know it sounds selfish, but that was the end of that team. People started to leave. They lost their enthusiasm for it. I stayed on to help the club, but it wasn't the same for a long time after that. The '70s and '80s were bad times, bad for every club, but we really felt it. Times were hard, and it was difficult to keep the club going after that."*

Me: "Did Ernie leave then too?"

Sid: *"He did. He was around for a few weeks after Curtis died, if I remember rightly, but he wasn't himself."*

Me: "I think he started to suffer from depression. Did you notice anything?"

Sid: *"I think he did. We didn't really know it at the time. You have to remember, he lived in a different part of the city. It seems nothing now, but it was a big deal then. Transport wasn't great, none of us had any money. No mobile phones. We wondered where he was, and we tried to stay in touch, of course we did, but we sort of lost touch. It was a sad time. You only really appreciate what you have when it is gone. Both those lads proved that. I don't know what I could have done differently. Hindsight is a wonderful thing. I know I should have done more. I wish I had done more. We all did."*

Me: "Did you hear from him after that?"

Sid: *"Only once. A few months later. I'm guessing around 1980. He came back up to the club to ask my advice. He had moved to South London. It was great to see him. He was much more like his old self. He came up with Tim.*
I think it was Tim who coaxed him out of that bad time - the depression. He certainly helped. The two were inseparable. I think they needed each other in equal measure. He was much more like his old self. Tim was great for him, I think. I got on really well with him that day too. Such a friendly lad. The two of them were perfect together. I don't know where Ernie found him, but the two were well settled. They lived in a flat in Surrey Quays."

372

Me: "Why did he come to see you?"

Sid: *"He might have been pretty useless as a player, but he had become a pretty decent umpire. He came back up to ask for some advice and to see if I could put him on the umpire list to be considered for games.*

He must have been kept busy, though, as I didn't hear from him again after that. I know he used to go to Southwark a lot. He mentioned that. They had a decent enough club there, and I know he got very involved with them. I guess he was in demand there too.

If you find him, Paul, please give him my best wishes. He was a brilliant fella. A good friend too. I hope that whatever he is doing, he is happy. He deserves to be."

I promised I would. Southwark Cricket Club would be my next port of call. It wasn't too late to nip down there and make some enquires. I asked a few more questions and then wished I hadn't.

Me: "Do you know if Ernie stayed with Tim? Did they live together? Marry?"

Sid: *"I bloody hope not. Tim was a Labrador!"*

CHAPTER 25
What's in a name?

6:30 p.m. (continued)

I made my way to Surrey Quays tube station again after speaking with Sid. It was getting dark again, but I thought I would at least locate the cricket club, as it was not far from the station. There wasn't much to see.

The entrance to the park was only a couple of minutes' walk from the station. There, a sign showed a basic layout and the facilities within. There weren't many. I don't know what I was expecting to find. Where I live, every cricket club has its own club house, changing facilities and scoreboard. The pitches are nicely kept by the club's ground staff, and they don't have to compete for space with other sports or recreational activities. Even the council-run facilities are well-suited to individual sports, but in London, space is at a premium. Share it or lose it.

The park was not an attractive one – certainly not at 4:45 p.m., with fading daylight and a chill in the air. I will have to return again in the morning, after doing a bit more digging online.

Mum texted again with a plea to call her. She thinks she has something. I will do that now.

7:00 p.m.

For a split second the other day, I thought Mum had lost interest, but how wrong I was. She had been researching cricket clubs in the east and south of London. She knows more about London Fields than I do. She had also joined various cricket club Facebook groups including Blackheath, Dulwich, Brockley, South Bank and, of course, Southwark Park.

She had received replies from all of them, and she shared the conversations with me. They were all very friendly and helpful, but the messages were from current team players – nobody who would have much of an idea of what the team was like in the '70s and '80s.

She'd had a conversation with 'Johnny W' from Southwark Park Cricket Club. He sent links showing old newspaper reports about the club, but there was nothing in them that would lead me to Ernie. He also suggested that, back then, the park itself was in a much worse state than it is now. You were more likely to hear gunshots than the sound of wickets falling.

The park had been a home for glue-sniffers and druggies, not gentlemen in whites.

Mum also posted a message on their Facebook homepage, and she was pleased to report that she had been sent a personal message from a Kenneth Simpson. He had been the club captain for the team back in the early eighties. He had promised to dig out his old scrapbooks, and he would be more than happy to talk with me. Again, Mum left my number with him and explained that I was in London. She thanked him, and he promised to call me once he had rooted through his cupboards.

She said the messages were sent around 4 p.m. I will nip out for a takeaway and come back to the room. No need to go out again tonight. Hopefully this Mr. Simpson will call sooner rather than later, and I can make plans to see him.

I think a nice chicken Kebab will do for tonight's culinary treat. Near Pimlico station there was a very clean-looking *Abrakebabra*. That will do me.

8:45 p.m.

I have just spoken to Mr. Simpson. He was a bubbly chap. Archetypal cockney. Loud and confident, but warm and friendly. He said he had spent half the evening trawling through folders and boxes. He laughed when he told me that he had even found his wife's wedding ring in there. I didn't enquire as to why it was in a box or as to the whereabouts of Mrs. Simpson.

Maybe she was in there too.

He told me that he had found a number of scrapbooks from the time he played for Southwark Park, and he assured me that his memory was a sharp as it ever was and he "never forgets a face".

He asked me if I would like to come over to his flat in the morning for a coffee and a catch-up. He didn't ask who I was, or what my motives were. I think he was just happy for the company. I could have been an axe murderer for all he knew.

He gave me his address (Flat 45, Grasmere Point, Old Kent Road, South Bermondsey).

I was to get the train to South Bermondsey and head down the Ilderton Road until I reached the tower blocks. He told me to look up at that point – he was somewhere up that tower block.

South Bermondsey – Millwall country.

This case takes me to the nicest of areas.

I told Mr. Simpson I would be over about 11 a.m., and he was happy with that.

I texted Mum to let her know that I was going. She will be buzzing to know she has played a big part in this investigation, and that without her I would have been well and truly stuck.

There is no point in preparing any questions for tomorrow. I will just play it by ear and hope he gives me something else to go on.

That kebab was gorgeous. I am going to go back up north about two stone heavier than when I arrived. I'll sign off for the day. A bit of TV, then sleep.

14.3.19

9:00 a.m.

I love the continent, but I won't miss these continental breakfasts. I know they are healthier for me than a fry-up, but they don't give you the same start to the day. I've booked another night in the hotel. Whatever happens today, I don't want to be rushing around looking for a place to store my bag and having to constantly look at my watch.

This is proving to be an expensive trip. I think I have spent as much here as I did in New York. And what have I got to show for it? Not enough. I am still stuck in 1979. I hope whatever is in Mr. Simpson's scrapbooks can help.

I will leave you here, Mr. Diary. I have my notebook and Dictaphone (fully charged). I will also need my wits about me today. That area has a bad reputation.

3:15 p.m.

Back in the hotel room. Safe and sound. I take it all back, Mr. Diary. The people of South Bermondsey, please take a bow – especially you, Mr. Simpson. What a place – what a man!

I was starting to worry about where this was taking me, but I am back on track once again. What an interview. As usual, I shall reproduce the conversation from the Dictaphone recording below.

Finding his address was easy, and I felt very happy on the way back. Everyone, from the conductor on the train to the locals I asked for directions, was pleasant and obliging. Two of them even walked me the last quarter of a mile to make sure I didn't get lost. I will have a soft spot for Millwall from now on. Not many say that.

Mr. Simpson (Kenny) answered the door with an outstretched hand and a smile as wide as the Thames. A short but stocky man in his early sixties, I'd guess. Arms covered in tattoos. He had a tough aura about him, but he was very hospitable. He greeted me into his lovely little flat and invited me to take in the sights of South London from the fifteenth floor of his high-rise.

There was a great view of some of the famous London landmarks in the distance – The London Eye, The Shard, The Houses of Parliament and St. Paul's, to name but a few.

"See, who needs to pay penthouse prices when Bermondsey Council will give you the same view for a fraction of the price. And, more importantly, you can see right into The Den." he said proudly, referring to the home of Millwall Football Club. He was clearly a fan. *The Lions* scarf hung from the coat hook on the back of his living room door.

"Londoner born and bred, my friend!" he barked before inviting me to sit.

On the table in front of me were his scrapbooks, piled up beside a couple of old photograph albums.

"I've had some fun looking back through those," he continued, "they brought back a lot of good memories, and not many bad ones, I can tell you. Coffee?"

I should say at this point, before I reproduce the interview, I have never heard any man swear as much or as often as Mr. Simpson. He used the word 'fack' (as they pronounce it in London) over two hundred times in the interview. People he liked, people he didn't like, places, equipment, animals and food – they were all fackers, or facking something or other.

I have omitted most of the swearing from the reproduction, but I plan to listen back to the recording on the Dictaphone on many occasions in the next few weeks if I am ever feeling down. He was hilarious.

He insisted at the start that I call him Kenny as in his words, *"...calling me Mr. Simpson makes me think of that fat, yella cartoon fella - and I am not in the least bit yella."*

He sat opposite me, in front of his collection, and invited me to start. I chatted for a few minutes about who I was, and who I was looking for. I explained that the adventure had got me as far as 1979, and I was now a little bit stuck.

Kenny: *"Don't you worry about that, son. I can take you into the '80s and beyond. The things I could*

379

tell you about that **** would fill another ten scrapbooks."

Me: "About Ernie?"

Kenny: *"Yeah. Ernie. The Reaper Man, we used to call him."*

Me: "Why?"

Kenny: *"We all had nicknames and that was his. Once it stuck, it stuck. Grimshaw. Grim. Grim Reaper. Simple as that – the Reaper Man."*

Me: "So, you knew him? You met him?"

Kenny: *"Course I knew him. Course I met him. Everyone knew him. And his dog. Golden Labrador it was. Tim. Happy little bleeder it was. A right soft bastard it was."*

I hadn't given Kenny any information about Ernie or told him what others had said about him, but I didn't need to. He knew him alright.

Me: "So, when did you first meet him?"

Kenny: *"I played for Southwark Park Cricket Club for six years. From 1979 to 1985. It was a right ****hole back then, but we made the best of it. We always had to do a scan of the field for needles and dog****. Can you imagine the stewards doing that at Lords or The Oval? Ernie arrived on the scene shortly after me."*

Me: "Did he play in the same team?"

380

Kenny: *"Play? No, he didn't play. He couldn't play to save his life. He was bloody useless, mate.*

No, he was the umpire. He once volunteered his services when he was walking Tim through the park. We needed an umpire, and he said he was qualified. That was that really – he was with us every week after that. We wouldn't have let him leave even if he had wanted to.

We paid him in beer and dog biscuits.

He almost became part of the squad. We shouldn't say that about an impartial official, but he was. Tim as well. That dog was some character. He used to sit on the boundary during the game. He would sit there for hours while Ernie was at the crease just getting pampered and stroked. Every week, he would take up his position at the side and watch the game. He used to run on the field for a stroke and a cuddle every time we got one of their men out. It was almost as if he knew what was going on. The opposition didn't mind. They all knew him too.

They knew Ernie. Everyone knew Ernie.

They didn't even mind that he was a little biased towards us either. You just couldn't get angry with that man and if you did, it was short-lived. He was the centre of attention at the cricket in more ways than one. He never looked for the limelight – it just seemed to come to him."

Me: "Were you aware that Ernie was suffering from depression at that time?"

Kenny: *"We all were, mate. The country was on its arse. None of us had any money, but we had each other. We were a great team."*

381

Me: "Genuinely though. He was going through an awful time."

Kenny: *"Really? Well, he didn't show it. I suppose he was a little quiet at first, most folk are, but he soon got into the swing of it. What a sense of humour he had. He was razor-sharp, and no one could beat him in a battle of wits. Even me, and I am so ****ing sharp I could cut myself. He could laugh at himself too.*

I remember one time, summer it was. Well, as you may or may not know, it was protocol to give the umpire your sweatshirt to look after if you are bowling. He was so engrossed in the game, he forgot to hand me mine back after I had finished bowling my over. He did the same with the next bowler, and the one after that. We kept adding to the pile on his shoulders every time we sent in a new bowler. He must have had eight sweatshirts wrapped around his neck before he noticed, the dozy ****. He was sweating like a camel's ****. It was over thirty degrees, and he had more wool on him than a flock of ****ing sheep!"

Me: "So, he didn't show any signs of depression or illness?"

Kenny: *"Not with us he didn't. Maybe he had found what he was looking for. What he had been missing in his life at that time. Friends. A community. You can't beat being part of that, and we were a great crowd."*

Me: "Tell me about the cricket club. What was it like? Did you have a good team?"

Kenny: *"We had some good teams and some useless ones. Some great players and some rogues. The trouble with the London scene is people come and go regularly. It isn't like those village teams where the same crowd play year on year, and they all come from the same family – all married to their sisters and the like. Our team was constantly changing. All ages, all ethnicities. It was like the United Nations at times. West Indians, Africans, Aussies, Pakistanis – they all joined the core of white British, and we all got on like a house on fire, in the main. Brixton **was** on fire around that time. The riots. But they weren't fighting us. It was the authorities and the police they had it in for. We didn't have any bother at Southwark Cricket Club. I am sure it was a problem for some people. It still is, isn't it? But not down at the cricket club. We were a family. We looked after each other. The way it should be.*

We only had one really successful year in the six years I played. We won the Surrey Cup in 1983. I found the picture with the team and the trophy. Ernie was on it too – and the dog. He was the umpire, and he was on the team photo! That's the way it was then. Nobody minded. Hold on, I will show it to you."

Kenny started hunting through the scrapbooks to find what he was looking for as I drank my coffee and tucked into the chocolate biscuits he had put on a plate. Nothing seemed to escape his attention.

"Facking hell, do you not have chocolate up north or something? Save me one, for Gawd's sake" he chirped up, laughing away to himself.

After a minute, he pulled out an old bottle-green folder.

"It's in 'ere I think."

383

He flicked through a few pages and then turned the book around and placed it in front of me. There they were. A big, full-page photograph of the team (with Ernie and Tim).

Underneath, at the bottom of the picture, was the caption – **THE SURREY CHALLENGE CUP WINNERS 1982/83 SEASON** – and below that, a list of names. Ernie stood on the far right of the picture. A big grin on his face. That was lovely to see. I just knew he was happy again. Tim sat in front of him facing the camera. In the caption, it didn't say Ernie Grimshaw, merely – *'The Reaper Man.'*

I read some of the others. It was not like a typical list of names, and I pointed this out to Kenny.

"That's because they are all nicknames. This was the picture that we used to hang in the pub. Everyone was known by their nicknames. We rarely used their real names.

I don't think I knew a lot of people by anything other than their nickname. It is still like that around here now. You were quickly given one when you joined, and it just stuck. Shortened even. We used to call Ernie 'Reap' for short. Let me have a look at them and see if I can remember their real names."

Kenny walked around to join me on the sofa, picking up a biscuit before sitting down.

"You had your eye on that one didn't you, you little bastard?" he chuckled.

I did actually.

Kenny: *"Right, let me see. Front row, left to right.*

Elvis. That was Tony Pressley. Good bowler. Bald as an egg. Convict. Alan Cunningham. He was an Australian.

Then me. Mr. Ed, they called me. They said I had a long face – like a horse. Cheeky bastards. Arty. Arthur. A Painter. He had a lovely girlfriend. Everyone fancied her. She used to help make the sandwiches with his mother. He was crap, but we weren't going to tell him that.

Big Ben. Benjamin Holiday. He got that nickname in the shower room. I don't need to tell you why.

That's Moon Face. Jimmy Brown. Just look at his boat race – it's like a facking plate! Then it's Reap – Ernie.

Front row. Limp. Bobby Farrell. He was gay. You probably can't call them that now, but he didn't mind. Great opening bat. Nothing limp about those wrists when he had a bat in his hands, I can tell you.

The Bear. Vince Harrison. Hairiest man I have ever seen. The soap was like a hamster after he finished with it in the shower. Great wicket keeper.

Snail. Thomas Bisset. He was French.

The Stick Man. Tommy Branch. Top player.

Stinger. Old Brian Bainbridge – Bee Bee. Come to think of it, he was rubbish too, but his daughter used to come and help out with the sandwiches. You can see our motives, can't you? Our team selection wasn't built on talent and skill. He was the substitute more often than not. The stand-in.

And the last one on the front row – Henry. Real name was Chris Wallace. He was the strangest member of the team. We called him Henry because he had gone through more wives than our infamous old king.

They are all still alive as far as I know. Some of us still meet up for a drink now and then."

Me: "Is Ernie – Reap – one of them?"

Kenny: *"No, He moved away. South coast. Dorset way. With the wife."*

Me: "Wife? He got married? When did he get married?" I was stunned.

Kenny: *"Did you not know he was married? I don't suppose you would really. Of course, let me tell you about that. Sly old bugger."*

He got up then and said he needed another coffee. He also said he had another packet of biscuits somewhere, but insisted I shared the next lot. He was some man. Not very politically correct, but a joy to listen to.

He had already brought the story of Ernie forward up to 1985, but he wasn't finished there. He was about to take me into the 1990s.

CHAPTER 26
A sight for sore eyes

3:15 p.m. (continued)

Kenny came back with the coffees. I had skimmed through the scrapbooks while he was in the kitchen. There were lots of newspaper clippings with match reports from the local newspaper.

A few of the names he mentioned were there in black and white. He also kept ticket stubs of functions he'd attended, posters of local events, and numerous photographs depicting groups of friends drinking and laughing together.

The fashions of the day brought back memories of my own 1980s wardrobe – brown shirts, parka jackets, balaclavas and cagoules. Snapshots of happy times.

It made me think about my own youth and my own life. Could I fill eleven scrapbooks with my own memories? I doubt it. Another stark reminder not to waste more time being alive but not really living.

Kenny sat down opposite me again and picked up one of the photograph albums. He turned to the first page.

Kenny: *"This is me in 1985. Handsome chap, eh? The girl beside me ended up being my wife. We didn't last long together. Just three years. I don't think I was cut out for marriage. I met her in a bar in Peckham. She told me off for sitting on her bag. I should have read the signs then. Talk about a nag. She was on my back more often than the saddle on*

Red Rum. Even when I told her we should break up, she complained that I should have done it earlier.

Nah, I'm better on my own. Some fellas are not cut out for marriage.

Ernie was though. I just don't understand why it took him over fifty years to find the right one. He had plenty of girlfriends in the time I knew him, but he didn't settle with any of them for long.

They always parted as friends though. He had a knack of being able to break it off with them and still retain their affection. They never had a bad word to say about him, even though it took most of them months to get over him. They all wanted to marry him.

He could have had his pick. It wasn't like he was anything special to look at either. Just normal. But they were drawn to him likes bees to a honey pot. We were all jealous of him on that score, but we never told him. You don't, do you? Some of the lads married his cast-offs, and I think they knew the girls in question had settled for them because they couldn't snare Ernie."

Me: "Someone snared him though?"

Kenny turned the pages of the album and turned it around to show me a picture of a happy couple. Ernie was stood there in a smart black suit, and he was linking arms with a very beautiful lady wearing a cream-coloured dress. She looked radiant.

Me: "Ernie and his bride?"

Kenny: *"Yeah. Well, yes and no. I will come on to that shortly. Bloody strange story."*

Me: "Strange? In what way?"

Kenny: *"There were two weddings that day –
a joint celebration. Ernie and Samantha and Arty
and Mandy. Arty and Mandy married at the registry
office in Bermondsey, and Ernie and Samantha said
their vows on Southwark Park in front of all their
friends and family. There must have been about five
hundred on the park that day. Any passersby must
have thought people were flocking around some kind
of celebrity."*

Me: "Why didn't both couples get married in
the registry office?"

Kenny: *"They couldn't. I'll come on to that in a
minute."*

He took a swig of his coffee and demolished
another biscuit as he flicked through the photo
album.

Kenny: *"I'll tell you the backstory first. How
they met and all that. It was quite romantic really.
As a team – with our umpire – we used to socialise
an awful lot. It was mainly the lads going out for a
few drinks and chatting to ladies. Ninety-nine per
cent of the time it was never more than drinks, but
occasionally one or two of us managed to win the
affections of some lady or other.*
*After Ernie, Limp was probably the most
successful in the pulling department. He used to say
there were more gay men than straight fellas in most
bars, and more straight fellas in gay bars than gays.*

I don't know about that, but he was always with some chap or other at the end of the night.

We had some great nights out on the town, but it was at the cricket club itself that true love was blossoming. Samantha was Brian's daughter. She was best friends with Arty's girlfriend, Mandy.

Arty and Mandy had already been together for a couple of years, and she used to help him with his decorating business. She was good with figures, and she used to do all his accounts and paperwork. It worked well. They were very much in love. You rarely saw them apart.

Arty had been married before and so had Mandy, but things hadn't worked out in those marriages for whatever reason.

They met through the cricket. Mandy's mother used to make us a lovely spread each week. I'm sure she was Stick Man's aunt, thinking about it.

Anyway, Mandy used to help her out, and she soon got chatting to Arty. He was a quiet gentleman and a thoroughly decent bloke. He charmed Mandy over time, and her mother approved of him. He was the kind of lad you could take home and introduce to the family. A safe bet, so to speak. Not like me, ha.

I don't think any of us noticed the relationship developing between Ernie and Samantha. Brian certainly didn't. Sam was a grand lass. Really chirpy. Always happy. A real softy. She wanted to help everyone and everything. I remember one time she wouldn't let us start the game because there was a bird on the field. It was hopping about and falling from side to side. It couldn't get off the ground, and she didn't want us to start in case the ball hit it!

She had been married before when she was a lot younger, but he passed away. I don't know how. She didn't talk about it, so we didn't pry.

She must have been mid-forties when she got together with Ernie.

I think he got so many of his bloody decisions wrong when umpiring because he was watching Samantha and not the game. When the penny dropped with the rest of us that something was going on between them, her old man was over the moon. He actively encouraged it. He thought the world of Ernie.

It was in the summer of 1984 when Arty and Mandy got hitched. They chose Bermondsey because that was where most of her family lived.

They wanted to have a double wedding with Ernie and Samantha, but it wasn't going to be that straightforward. One night, Ernie told us the tale of how he arrived back in England. It was a hell of a story, and he had us in stitches. Samantha was there, and she already knew about his past. They must have discussed it between them, and she was fine with it all.

Basically, as you know, the bastard didn't even exist.

He was who he said he was, but there was no record of him. He came back into the country under someone else's name, reclaimed his own name, and carried on. He never signed on the dole or signed anything that would trigger a paper trail. He worked on the stalls – cash in hand. He worked in construction as a labourer – cash in hand. He even worked as a turnstile operator and steward down the 'The Den', picking up his wage in a little brown envelope after the game. In cash. He was in his mid-fifties and was on no system, register, bank record or electoral roll. He was a facking ghost! The Reaper Man was a bloody good name for him.

Anyway, after all that, it turns out he did propose to Samantha. He was prepared to join the rat race in order to take her hand in marriage, but she wouldn't hear of it. She agreed to 'marry' him without actually getting it done official, like. No priest, no vicar – not even a bloody registrar. They would exchange their own vows in front of us lot, and all their other mates and family, on Southwark Park.

It was crazy. Bonkers. But no one seemed to care about that. It sounded like a great idea, and we all went for it. They got 'married' on the crease. Wickets for an altar! The Bear conducted the service with a can of beer in one hand. Rings were exchanged, photos taken, and when The Bear said, "You may now kiss the bride" a cheer went up right across the park.

It was a glorious, sunny day. Arty and Mandy married in the morning, and everyone from Bermondsey came down for the second service of the day. We had one massive party for both couples, and we all danced and drank well into the night. It was fabulous."

Me: "So, Ernie didn't actually get married?"

Kenny:' "*Course he did. You don't need a man in a dress, or some jumped-up council official, to give your love the seal of approval. That wedding was as relevant and as genuine as any other.*

It was a marriage made in heaven but delivered on Southwark Park.

Even Tim was there with a bright red bow tie on. He looked the part."

Me: "Incredible. Do you have any photographs of the day?"

Kenny: *"I certainly do, son. Here you go."*

Kenny handed me over the photo album from his lap. "SUMMER 1984" it said on the front. Sure enough, there was the wedding day. A dozen or so pictures of everyone enjoying themselves in the park with the two couples centre stage. One snap was taken of Ernie and Samantha hand in hand, dancing together. Behind them, I could see the park was jam packed. Everyone seemed to be looking and smiling at the happy couple.

Kenny pointed to a picture of Arty and Mandy, and another of the four of them together. They looked so in love.

Again, I felt a pang of jealousy and regret. Why hadn't this happened to me? Kenny burst my thought bubble.

Kenny: *"They moved into Ernie's flat in Surrey Quays for a while before finding their own place in Deptford. Samantha worked as a secretary in some solicitor's office, and Ernie kept doing what he was doing – whatever that was. He had so many jobs. He was never out of work. They made a great pair. I don't think I ever saw them argue or fight. They were just head over heels in love with each other. Arty and Mandy were the same. The four of them became very close.*

They were always doing something or going somewhere – the theatre, meals out, sporting events, day trips and holidays. They grew even closer together after the accident."

Me: "The accident?"

Kenny: "At the cricket. We were playing at home one Sunday, and we were getting a right hiding from some team from Croydon. It was a cup match, I think. Anyway, Ernie was umpiring but he was missing even more than usual. We asked him if he was alright, and he just said he had a bit of a headache. Someone threw the ball in from out at the boundary, and it was heading for Ernie. We shouted his name, but it was too late. He didn't see it, and the ball smacked him right on the head, knocking him out cold. We thought it had killed him at first. He just lay there, motionless. We all gathered around wondering what the hell we should do before he suddenly turned over and groaned. We nearly shit ourselves. The Reaper man strikes again!

He took a few minutes to come around, and he was developing a huge shiner on his eye and lump on his forehead. Samantha decided it was best to get him checked out at the hospital, and off they went.

It turned out that the black eye and the lump were the least of his worries. The doctors ran some basic checks on his eyesight and were more than a bit concerned. It turned out that he had glaucoma. He had been suffering from blurred vision for some time. That probably explained some of his umpiring decisions. He needed to have an operation to try and save his sight. The optic nerve to the brain had been damaged at some point, and his eyesight had been slowly failing."

I thought back over Ernie's life. What could have caused the damage? The beating he took in New York? Who knows?

Me: "Did they manage to save his sight?"

Kenny: *"They did, thank God. It was touch and go for a while. Samantha was understandably distraught. She stayed with him the whole time in the hospital.*

When the doctors said he would be able to see clearly again, with the help of strong glasses, she broke down in tears out of sheer relief. He told me later, she was the first person he had seen when they took the bandages off, and he swore he would never let her out of his sight again.

It was the end of his umpiring career, but it was the end of the cricket for a lot of us by then. The park was in a terrible state, and it was proving harder and harder to field a team. The equipment was repeatedly stolen or vandalised, and we couldn't afford to replace it.

It was the end of an era for us.

I'm pleased to see the club is going strong again now, and a new generation have breathed some life back into it again. Ours were good days. Priceless."

Me: "Did you keep in touch?"

Kenny: *"Like I said, a lot of us are still in contact. We meet up and chat on the phone. I gradually lost touch with Ernie and Arty when they moved out of London. We wrote for a while but, you know how it is, you keep promising to call, but other things get in the way. I did go down to stay with them for a couple of holidays, but after that we just drifted apart, sadly."*

I asked him if he still had the address they moved to. He picked up another scrapbook and rooted through a few pages.

Kenny: *"Here we are. This is it. I still have a few postcards. 1989 was one. 1991 another. Weymouth. There should be an address too, hold on. There you are. Numbers 71 and 73 Avalanche Road, Southwell, Isle of Portland, Dorset. They bought the houses side by side. Ernie and Sam in number one and Arty and Mandy next door.*
Lovely little place. Well off the beaten track, if I remember rightly. They were all very happy there."

1991. Ernie would have been sixty-one then. Samantha in her fifties.

Me: "What were they doing in Dorset? Do you know where they were working?"

Kenny: *"Arty's painting and decorating business really took off. He managed to get some good contacts and was making good money. One of those contacts was a building firm who were throwing up new housing estates all over the south coast. They wanted Arty to take on the contract for the Weymouth and Portland developments. It was a huge job for a small company, but he was keen. The four of them often talked about settling on the south coast, and this was their chance. Ernie had been helping Arty out for a while, and it made logical sense to work together. Arty was very good at his job, and he trained Ernie to be, despite the problems he had with his eyesight. Arty was the boss, and that suited Ernie just fine.*

They got on really well, and it was never an issue. The money was rolling in for them.

I don't think they had ever been so well off. They were living quite comfortably when I went down to visit. Arty had even taken on more staff. The business was booming.

I was delighted for them, I really was. They deserved it."

Me: "Do you remember the name of the company?"

Kenny: **"Arty Painter. Painter and Decorator.** *Nicknames stick, ha."*

I smiled at Kenny, and he laughed back.

Kenny: *"I think that's about all I can offer, Paul, hope I have been of some use to you. I have enjoyed our chat. It was nice to reminisce.*

If you get stuck and need any more help, you have my number. Let me know what you find out. Maybe it isn't too late to make contact again, and if you are ever in South Bermondsey, you are welcome to come for a drink or join me down 'The Den'. Just bring your own facking biscuits next time!"

I promised I would. Call and visit. I meant it too.

I now had a lot of very good information. An address, a business name and the names of four people together, not just one. Lots to go on. I was also up to 1991. Twenty-eight years ago.

I'm getting closer.

I need to formulate another plan. I will go home this evening, if I can get on a train, and write to Mr. Green with the latest news. If he is happy for me to do so, and I am sure he will be, I will make plans to go to Dorset later in the month. The sooner the better really, once I get the green light to proceed.

I will give Mum a call now. If she is free tomorrow, I will take her for a slap-up meal. She has certainly earned it.

CHAPTER 27
Southern Comfort

15.3.19

11:50 a.m.

Home. A fairly straightforward train journey back. £128 for a single ticket is a disgrace though. The nice lady on the customer service desk suggested I check out the prices online – after she had sold me the ticket. I'm certainly racking up the expenses. I won't have any money left at this rate. I had better tighten my belt a little.

Mum is up for a meal out tonight. She wanted to go for an Italian. That will be nice.

I will send off that letter to Mr. Green and spend the rest of my afternoon in relax mode. A long, hot soak in a bubble bath sounds just about perfect.

For the next couple of days, I will do some ancestry research work and tie up a few loose ends. Minimum effort for a decent chunk of money.

This last month has been pretty intense. I am emotionally drained, and hopefully I will sleep well tonight. I have arranged to meet Mum at *Romeo's* at half six. The food there is great, and the waiter fancies her like mad, so we always get good, quick service.

I will make some tentative enquires in the morning about Portland and Weymouth. It shouldn't be too hard to find information about housing developments built there since the late '80s.

It will be interesting to see what happened to 'Arty Painter – Painter and Decorator' too. Both Arthur and Ernie were getting on in 1991. Arthur must have been in his fifties and Ernie was over sixty. It is quite a physically demanding job, so they must have had one eye on retirement.

Maybe they had enough staff working for them to allow them to take a back seat and enjoy the profits. Well, Arthur and Mandy anyway. Ernie was his employee, unless things had changed. How could he retire? He would have had no pension, and he couldn't claim a state one either. The government don't tend to pay out for people who don't exist. Maybe Samantha had a good job. Hopefully, I will find out.

Right, time to get a letter off to Mr. Green.

2:15 p.m.

As usual, here is a copy of the letter. I have enclosed copies of the interviews as usual, as well as copies of the photographs I took on my phone from Mr. Simpson's scrapbooks and albums. I have also attached a sheet of known addresses and places of work should he wish to do any future investigation without me.

Mr. Green has a tendency to be quite prompt with his replies. I hope he is on this occasion, as I would like to crack on while it is all still fresh in my mind.

I still have no idea what Mr. Green wants all this information for. His reasons are his prerogative, and I can't go asking him his intentions and motives. What he wishes to do with the information I send him is entirely up to him. I am employed to do a job and follow his guidance and instruction, and yet, I am so emotionally involved in this case, I feel I need to know.

I might end up doing a second investigation of my own on Mr. Green if I don't find out after all this. He is certainly a man of mystery, but he has been a gentleman at every turn, and he pays on time and pays well.

Time will tell. In the meantime, I have a job to do and a letter to write. The letter:

Mr. William Green	**Mr. Paul Brunskill**
XXXXX XXXXXX XXXXX	XXXXX XXXXXXX
XXXXXXXXXXXX	XXXXXXXXXX
XXXX	XXXXXXXXXXX
XXX XXX	XXXXXXXXX
XXXXXX	

*Tel: 07********* 15th March 2019*

Dear Mr. Green,

I hope you are keeping well. As promised, this is my follow-up letter after another week on the case.

I have spent the last five nights in London where Mr. Grimshaw resided on his return to England. He spent the years between 1965 and late 1986 living in the East End, both north and south of the river Thames. You can see from the attachments (Doc 6) a list of addresses where he lived and worked, along with a map.

Unsurprisingly, Ernie proved to be just as popular in London as he was in New York.

I have enclosed full transcripts of the interviews I conducted with old workmates and friends (Docs 1 to 4).

The photographs (Doc 5) are part of Mr. Simpson's collection. He was happy for me to take copies and share them with you.

As you can see, Ernie looked very handsome on his 'wedding day'. You will need to read Mr. Simpson's interview in full to understand the significance of that day.

Sometime in late 1986 or early 1987, Ernie moved to Dorset with his new 'wife', Samantha, and another couple – Arthur and Mandy. Ernie worked for Arthur as a painter and decorator.

You can see from Mr. Simpson's interview that I have an address to check out on the Isle of Portland where the couple lived.

Mr. Simpson stayed in touch with the couples until 1991, before losing contact altogether. If you wish for me to continue with the investigation, I am happy to do so.

I await your instruction, and if there is anything within the attached documents that you wish to clarify, including the invoice list (doc 7), please do not hesitate to ask.

I look forward to hearing from you soon. Yours sincerely,

Paul Brunskill

(Documents enclosed with letter)

I will nip down to the post office and send this by recorded delivery shortly. He should then get the letter in the morning. Then it is bath time.

5:30 p.m.

You can't beat a good bath. I might look like a radish now, but I feel like a new-born baby. I almost fell asleep in there at one point. If it wasn't for my neighbours shouting at each other about the location of a hairbrush, I might have drifted off and drowned.

I feel a lot better now. I'd better get cracking. I don't want to be late for the meal.

9:45 p.m.

That was bloody lovely. I am totally stuffed now. Mum's flirting certainly resulted in bigger portions tonight. I think she might actually fancy him too. That wouldn't be a bad thing. He is a decent chap, and I love Italian food. She deserves a bit of attention and flattery. I do too. The waitress was very pretty, and I am sure I caught her eye when she was pouring the wine.

Mind you, she is probably his daughter. That would be a bit odd if Mum got together with the dad and me the daughter. Perhaps I am getting a bit ahead of myself here. She only poured a glass of wine and dropped a used fork into Mum's handbag by accident.

Hardly the start of a blossoming romance. I can still dream though. I will ask Mum if she would like to go again next week.

Double dating with your mother. Good Lord!

Bedtime for me. It has been a long day, and I want a nice, uninterrupted sleep.

16.3.19

10:40 a.m.

That was a great sleep, but I wish I hadn't turned the television on. Death and disaster everywhere. Even the wildlife story that they normally save until the end was a sad one. A beached whale washed up in the Philippines and was found to have 88lbs of plastic inside its stomach. How sad. What are we doing to this world?

Even the weather was miserable. I now wished I'd just stayed asleep or not bothered to turn the telly on at all.

Ancestry research is my priority today.

Mr. Strong (case 2877), has asked me to look through his family tree to see if he is related to Mozart, and Mr. and Mrs. Harrison (case 2911), from Grimsby want to know if they have any relatives in Bali. Well, I suppose you would if you lived in Grimsby.

I have two timelines to print off and post for Mr. Walton (case 2871) and Ms. Jones (case 2869), and a great grandmother profile for Mr. Reeves. It turns out she was part of the suffragette movement at the turn of the century. She even received a caution for "striking a police officer with a cucumber". I would love to have seen that!

Altogether this work will net me just under £1000 for less than two days' work.

I may as well milk this cash-cow until folk get bored of it and move on to the next fad. By then, I might have to look for a new career. The days of sitting in the back of a freezing cold van on some council estate in Wigan are behind me, if I can save up a nice little nest egg before I am fifty. I will do anything and work anywhere so long as it is safe, easy and stress-free.

If there is nothing else to report today, Mr. Diary, I will update you again tomorrow.

17.3.19

10:15 a.m.

I am up and about and ready for the day. Last night I dreamt I was walking along Southport beach. I might just do that for real today.

This time, I won't bother to walk a crocodile on a lead though. Just how does the mind work? At what point did my subconscious decide to throw in a crocodile into what was a very normal situation. As far as I am aware, there aren't any crocodiles in Southport, and I have no craving to own one as a pet. Neither can I explain why I met Gandhi under the pier. They say all dreams have meaning and tell you a lot about a person's mind-set and character. Well, the experts would have a field day getting their heads around that dream. Last thing I remember before I woke up was the crocodile swimming in the sea, playing with a beach ball, while Gandhi and I ate candyfloss!

I used to dream an awful lot, but that is the first one I can remember for a long while. They always seemed so vivid and real. I have had a cream tea beside the lake in Windermere with Jesus, I've been kidnapped by the Mafia, chased through the town by a shark with legs, and sent to prison for refusing to wear a kilt in Scotland. I never dream about family. I don't ever dream of work. Just daft things.

Things that couldn't possibly (or are very unlikely to) happen.

I might not dream about work, but I find I am constantly thinking about the Ernie Grimshaw case when I'm awake. One thing leads to something else, and then it stops. Nothing is straightforward. Nothing is obvious. It is so frustrating, but so bloody fascinating.

And then there is Mr. Green. Everything comes back to Mr. Green. I will have a bite to eat and head off to Southport beach. If I see a crocodile, I am coming straight back.

6:40 p.m.

That was invigorating. Just what I needed. The wind was strong and right in my face as I walked southwards. Cold, bracing and wild. My cheeks were red and numb. It hardly came as a surprise that I was the only one on the beach. I must have walked into that icy wind for nearly two miles before turning around and retracing my steps with the wind at my back.

Not a crocodile in sight – nor an inspirational, small, bald Indian.

I stopped for a coffee on the way back. My cheeks were still crimson and my nose blue, but I didn't care. I felt alive.

I decided to do a bit of internet research about Weymouth and Portland whilst in the cafe. I had visited the area many years ago on a family holiday. I must have been about ten years old. I remember a man on the beach making sand sculptures. I remember the red clock tower and the harbour bridge. I remember it being really hot and sunny all week.

We stayed in a holiday flat near Chesil Beach – the long stretch of shingle that joins the mainland with the Isle of Portland.

It was a great holiday. Hopefully, if I get to go there soon, I can visit these places again.

I will make some enquires tomorrow regarding any housing development projects in the area throughout the late '80s and early '90s.

According to Kenny, Arthur was employed as a contractor by a larger construction/building company – the one he was already in contact with in London. It was likely that the company in question was London based with ties to the East End. That shouldn't be too hard to narrow down. The chances are, depending on the size of the development in question, they would have taken on more than one local company or contractor to do the job. That might work in my favour, as any established painting and decorating firms still on the go in a small town like Weymouth will be familiar with the competition.

And then there is the address. If they bought the house, it would be under Samantha's name, surely. Arthur and Mandy should be easy enough to trace too. The HM Land Registry will have a historical record of who lived there and who owned the deeds. They will also be able to tell me how old the house is and if it has had any alterations, extensions or planning applications over the years. This should also narrow the search. I should be able to find out when they moved in and when, or if, they sold the house and moved on.

If they rented rather than bought, this would complicate matters a little. The owners could be anywhere. But even if that is the case, there is always the work angle, and as Southwell is such a small village on the island, someone is bound to know the four of them.

I'm feeling a lot more confident than I did this time last week in London. I had very little to go on then.

18.3.19

10:15 a.m.

A text message from Mum gave me a great start to the day. She told me she had bumped into Tina, the waitress from *Romeo's*, in the town square. Apparently, Mum told her I fancied her and asked her directly if she liked me! Our text conversation:

Me: You didn't? x

Mum: I did. X

Me: Bloody hell Mum, what did she say? x

Mum: Nothing at first. She blushed though. x

Me: We won't be able to go in there again! x

Mum: Yes we will. We are. I told her we would be in again next week. X

Me: The poor girl. She will think I am a proper mummy's boy. She is gorgeous! She won't want me. X

Mum: I think she does. I asked her out for you. She didn't say no. x

Me: But she didn't say yes either? X

Mum: No but she didn't say no. Don't be so defeatist. It should be you asking her out anyway, not me. X

Me: I think it is too late for that now. X

Mum: No it isn't. I told her you would next week. x

Me: MUM!!! X

Mum: I think she will say yes. I think she likes you. x

Me: You think so? X

Mum: A mum knows best. x

Me: But what about you and Antonio? He fancies you. x

Mum: I know he does. And if he asked me to go out on a date, I would say that I would. x

Me: As far as we know, Tina could be his daughter. x

Mum: She isn't. I asked her. No relation. She lives in Chorley. Her dad is a plumber. x

Me: Goodness me, Mum. This investigative stuff has taken you over. Is there anything you didn't ask? X

Mum: Well, she hasn't got any kids. Anyway, is that not enough for now? x

Me: More than enough. x

Mum: Good. I will book for next week then. Sunday ok for you? x

Me: That would be lovely x

Mum: It's a date then xx

I felt myself blushing as I was typing. I had butterflies. Tina was gorgeous, and at least ten years younger than me. What chance did I have? Mum thinks she fancies me, but being a mum puts her in a position of bias. I'm still excited though.

Wow. If I ask and she says no, I will never set foot in that place again. What have I got to lose? There are plenty more Italian restaurants in the town.

The new me. I promised myself I would enjoy life and take the bull by the horns. This could be my first real chance to prove it.

1:00 p.m.

Nothing in the post today.

It turns out that there were seven new housing developments built in the Weymouth area between 1986 and 1992. Two smaller estates were built by local independent firms and the other five by *Craven Homes*.

Craven Homes specialised in 'Homes not houses'. The kind of tagline dreamt up in some 'Blue Sky Meeting' by a team of marketing whizz-kids. They built predominantly in the south of England with forays into the Channel Islands and Wales.

Their houses were typical of the flat-pack variety of that time. Smart looking from a distance, but with no substance to them. Walls you could spit through and tiny boxes masquerading as bedrooms.

They were popular because they were cheap. An option for a first-time buyer to get their foot on the housing ladder. This was the south - property was vastly overpriced, but in demand. *Craven Homes* provided an 'affordable alternative'.

Their head offices were near Waterloo Station in London. Their website showed examples of earlier developments in and around London. Surrey Quays being one.

It was very likely that this would have been the company Arthur had contacts with.

I looked at Southwell too.

The village had a long and impressive history, including Roman settlements, a 200 foot deep abandoned quarry, and strong links to the naval base. One primary school, one church and one pub.

410

Surely the gang of four frequented one of them, and my money is on the pub.

Another job request arrived today via email. I haven't had a one like this for a while.

/

"I want you to find Lord Lucan riding on the back of the Loch Ness Monster please."

William Shakespeare.

I couldn't resist a reply.

"Unfortunately, I won't be able to take you up on the job offer. I am currently sailing through the Bermuda Triangle on the Mary Celeste with Captain Hook and the Abominable Snowman."

You get all sorts in this job. Mind you, it would be easier to find Lord Lucan than Ernie Grimshaw.

19.3.19

11:15 a.m.

The post has arrived. A letter from Plymouth. A reply from Mr. Green. As I thought, he wants me back on the case and, once again, he is my financial guardian angel!

411

Mr. P Brunskill   Mr. William Green
XXXXXXXXXXXXXX   XXXXX XXXX XXXXXXX
XXXXXXXXX   XXXXXXXXXXXXXXX
XXXXXXXXXXX   XXXXXXXX
XXXXXX   XXXXX
XXX XXX

Dear Paul,

Thank you for your letter. I am in awe of your work and flabbergasted at the lengths you have gone to in order to trace Mr. Grimshaw.

Of course, I would love you to continue until you find out everything you can about him. I greatly appreciated the attachments. The photographs are fabulous, and the interviews fascinating.

Mr. Simpson seemed to know him extremely well. I was saddened to read about Ernie's illness and troubles with depression, but it seems he was able to put that awful chapter of his life behind him when he found love.

He has certainly led an incredibly eventful life, I'm sure you will agree.

The invoices and receipts you sent are all in order but, from now on, please do not worry about money.

I have enclosed a further cheque for £10,000. This is to cover further expenses and wages. I know you have not requested more recompense, but I want to show you how much your efforts are appreciated. This will hopefully cover wages and any new expenses.

Please continue with the journey and write to me when you find out more. I look forward to hearing from you soon.

Yours sincerely,

William Green

Another cheque for £10,000! TEN THOUSAND POUNDS! I'm only halfway through the last lot he gave me. This is just fantastic. A trip to Dorset beckons. I don't think I even need to wait for the cheque to clear either. I know he is good for it. Amazing.

I will call and tell Mum. I have a full week and more before our next meal. There is nothing to stop me going tomorrow. I will book into a hotel later starting with three nights, and if needed, I can always stay longer. Sod the train. I will drive down. It will be cheaper, and it gives me a lot more flexibility to get out and about if I need to.

8:15 p.m.

Well, that is the hotel booked. Or should I say, bed and breakfast. I decided to avoid the big hotels and support local businesses. The breakfasts are always better in the more traditional, intimate places anyway.

I've gone for the Redcliff on Brunswick Terrace, near the sea front. The fried breakfasts get rave reviews on *Trip Advisor*, and it looks immaculately clean and welcoming. That will do me. It has parking for guests, and it is literally just across the road from the beach. Ideal.

Three nights in a double room for less than £200. In London, you pay more than that for a toothbrush.

I can check in from 2 p.m. which is fine. I'll set off early and have a leisurely drive down in the van. It needs a good run anyway. It will be a four- or five-hour drive depending on the traffic, but I can stop off whenever and wherever I fancy for a bite to eat. I know it is work, but it feels like another holiday.

I won't forget this year in a hurry. I bet 2020 will be pretty uneventful in comparison.

Goodnight, Mr. Diary. I will throw a few things in a bag first thing tomorrow morning and get going.

20.3.19

8:15 a.m.

Packed and ready to hit the road. I was up early this morning to email my old buddy, Darren Martin, at the Land Registry. One of the perks of being a private investigator is getting to know people in certain positions of influence. If Darren gets my message when he gets into work, I will likely get a reply from him later today. He will make sure I skip the queue in return for of a crate of beer. A small price to pay for information.

I have asked him for the deed holders of the two properties on Avalanche Road, Southwell, dating back to 1985. It is much quicker doing a house search than a name search.

Especially if they have owned a number of different properties, or if the names are common ones like Painter or Bainbridge.

It should take him ten minutes or so.

I will get through the Manchester and Birmingham traffic and then look for a suitable place to stop for a late lunch. Somewhere just off the M5 near Worcester will do nicely.

Here we go again. I will update when I get checked in to my B&B in Weymouth.

3:45 p.m.

That was a pleasant enough journey down. The usual traffic congestion around the big cities, but nothing to worry about. I managed to find a reasonable place for a bar meal, so I won't need anything big to eat for the rest of the day.

Maybe some fish and chips on the promenade will be a nice way to end the day. The guest house is as advertised. Clean and homely and right on the sea front. I managed to get a parking spot for the van without any struggle.

My room is a little on the small side, but it has everything I need, including free Wi-Fi and a copy of the Bible in the top drawer, in case I feel the need to brush up on a gospel or psalm.

Nothing from Darren as yet.

I think I will go for a walk along the front and see what I can remember about the place. I bet it has changed an awful lot since I was ten.

8:30 p.m.

It hasn't changed a lot since I was ten. Not the beach front anyway. The clock tower still looks as impressive as it ever did. A focal point of the town. Not quite Blackpool Tower proportions but memorable, nonetheless.

I managed to get some fish and chips and a pint in The Gloucester pub. I'm feeling quite bloated now.

Still no reply from Darren.

Tomorrow morning, after breakfast, I will have a drive onto the Isle of Portland and visit Southwell and Avalanche Road. Plenty of time to do some digging up there. You can come with me, Mr. Diary. Dictaphone too.

You just never know who I might meet and who might be worth talking to. It could be the man himself.

12:45 p.m.

The drive over Chesil Beach brought back a few memories. I will stop there on the way back over and walk on the pebbles. It is a beautiful stretch, and the sun is shining brightly today, despite the bitter cold.

The old naval base has been non-operational since 1996 and was closed completely in 1999. A huge loss for the area. Government cutbacks, I expect. The first village you come to, Fortuneswell, is a little rough and ready, but the scenery changes as you start to climb. At the top, the views over Weymouth Bay and Chesil beach are breathtaking. I had to stop and take a few photographs at the summit.

Not much had changed on Portland either, which pleased me immensely. Large parts of the island remained untouched. It was nice to see vast swathes of rugged countryside as it has been for decades. The bright, white Portland stone was evident all around as I approached Southwell. I stopped and parked up outside the church and decided to walk around the village rather than drive.

It wasn't a big place, and you see so much more on foot. What struck me was how calm and quiet it was. Only a handful of cars drove by as I wandered along the litter-free streets. The locals clearly took a pride in their village. I found Avalanche Road with no problem - it was the main road in and out.

I stopped across the road from numbers 71 and 73, and that familiar feeling of excitement coursed through me when I realised I was only feet away from where Ernie had moved to all those years ago.

I decided to go against my instincts and hold back from knocking on the door. That would be a last resort if I didn't find out anything from Darren, or my own research.

The Eight Kings pub on Southwell Road was just around the corner from where I was parked, so I decided to go in for a sandwich and a lemonade, and that is where I am now.

It is the only pub in the village and clearly a draw for the locals, with adverts for local businesses and social clubs in the entrance hall. I had a look, but there was no sign of any painting and decorating firms. The smell wafting from the kitchen reassured me that I had made the right choice to eat here. Cheesy chips and a BLT sandwich is on its way. Yummy.

I will eat first then work.

2:10 p.m.

Back in the car and suitably stuffed.

417

After eating, I approached the barmaid to explain who I was and why I was there. She was an older lady, and I figured she would have some idea where I could start. She explained that she had lived on the island most of her life, but only in Southwell village for the past six years. She knew the locals and plenty of faces around the village, but she had never heard of Ernie and Samantha or Arty and Mandy.

She called on her husband who was working in the back, but he was none the wiser either. They were both genuine and helpful, but they were not in a position to help. They suggested I return in the evening when a few more regulars would be in, and they would introduce me to a couple of the lifelong residents of the village. Her husband suggested I speak with the vicar at the church. He had been there for a lot longer than they had and may remember something. I thanked them for their time and promised I would call back in later.

I nipped up to the church, but no one was around. I can try there later.

For the rest of this afternoon, I will ring and visit the painting and decorating firms in and around Weymouth. Surely someone remembers Arthur and Ernie.

5:15 p.m.

Back in my hotel room. Another productive day. Surprisingly, there were not that many painters and decorators in Weymouth, and the ones I spoke to had only been operational for the last decade or so. My fifth call, though, struck gold. Chris Harrow based in Bridport had been in the game for over thirty-five years, and, although he

418

lived twenty miles out of Weymouth, he had worked as a contractor for *Craven Homes,* and, more importantly, he remembered Ernie and Arthur.

We chatted about the jobs they had worked on together, and he tried to recall those times. He said he didn't know them well, but what he could remember was all positive, as I had come to expect. He told me they were not in the game now, but he couldn't pinpoint the year they quit – he guessed around the late '90s. He remembered they had an office in Weymouth and another in Exeter in Devon. He said he had dealt with the Weymouth office on occasion. He told me Ernie was in charge there as the manager – Arthur was based in Exeter.

Other than that, he didn't have much more to add, except one very important little nugget. Ernie was responsible for painting the famous lighthouse on Portland Bill. Everyone knew of the lighthouse – it was the island's most famous landmark. I asked Chris if he could remember what year it was roughly. He replied,

"Every year. It was an annual tradition. Ernie was getting on in years, but he carried on with it after he retired, I think. He was a game old bugger. Have a run up to see it. I am sure someone up there will have information about old Ernie. He was a bit of a local celebrity, I believe."

It was too dark to go there now. I still had to make a visit to the pub again. I can make another trip to the island tomorrow and visit the lighthouse. It is staggering to think that a man in his sixties or seventies would take on that job, but nothing seems to surprise me with Ernie anymore. Right, let's see what information I can get from the locals in the pub. I will update before bed.

419

10:50 p.m.

No need to visit the church. The vicar was in the pub. What a fine man he is too. Thanks to decorator Chris and his lighthouse story, it wasn't hard to find people who either knew, or had heard of, Ernie. Everybody knew the story of the lighthouse. The Reverend himself had had a number of dealings with him. It turned out that Ernie had painted the rectory walls for free, as well as the stone walls surrounding the church.

He called over an elderly couple from another table, Margaret and Harry, and they also remembered Ernie and Samantha.

Margaret smiled as she recalled,

"They were a lovely couple. A right good laugh, the pair of them. He used to help out around the village, did Ernie – a proper handyman. He would do anything for anybody without a moan or complaint. He was always smiling."

Another man, Mick, shared his memories of Ernie and the lighthouse.

"Every year he used to paint it. He would join a few other volunteers who gave up their time to keep the place clean and tidy the area around the lighthouse.

Loads of us used to go up and watch Ernie and the others. Tourists too. We would all have a big celebration when they had finished their work. It would take them a week or more to do it. Ernie never asked for extra help. He always volunteered to paint the highest parts. I think he got a great sense of freedom when he was up there – like hanging off the edge of the world.

"I think he has a plaque up at the visitors'

"What happened to him?" I asked.

420

A few people who knew of him chipped in and joined the conversation. People who had lived in the village for a long time. It seemed the other volunteers arranged for a plaque up at the visitors' centre to be dedicated to him. There is a newspaper article framed beside it. **'Earning His Stripes!'** was the headline. The red and white lighthouse is famous all over. That was Ernie.

From what I could gather, he lived on the island until approximately 2005. Someone remembered him leading the conga during the village's celebration for the millennium. Someone else remembered celebrating England's Rugby World Cup win in 2003, when Ernie had re-enacted Johnny Wilkinson's last minute drop kick to win the cup against Australia. He pulled his hamstring as a result. I worked out he must have been seventy-four years old then.

Another customer remembered Samantha – she used to help out at the primary school in her spare time, volunteering to take clubs, organise sports days and run the summer fete. She was also an incredible fundraiser for local charities – especially those that helped support vulnerable or sick children.

"Do you know why they moved?" I asked.

"It was all quite sudden." the Reverend remembered. "They moved to Exeter to be with their friends. I don't think they wanted to go really, but they felt they didn't have much choice. It was a terrible shame. They were so settled here and so happy, but they were needed elsewhere. It is a testament to their character that they would uproot at that age to help others. They sold up and moved on. We didn't hear anything from them after that."

"I kept hoping they would come back." said an older lady. "They don't make them like that anymore. I do hope they are safe and well, wherever they are."

I sat with the group until nearly ten o'clock. It was lovely to see such a close community. I wanted to be part of that too. An extended family really. All there for each other.

But Ernie wasn't there anymore. Sometime around 2005, he moved west to Exeter. Arthur and Mandy were there. Were they the friends in need? It would seem so.

Tomorrow morning, I will have a drive up to the lighthouse. The beacon of light and hope on the island. Ernie's lighthouse.

22.3.19

11:30 a.m.

After another lovely breakfast, I headed back up to Portland and to the southern tip of the island where the lighthouse stands proud over the cliffs looking out over the English Channel. The same channel Ernie sailed through when he returned to England in 1965. I wonder if that crossed his mind while he was sat up there, painting the red and white stripes that hug this impressive structure.

Built in 1906 and standing over forty metres high, the lighthouse is the largest of its kind in the area. It attracts thousands of tourists each year. I wonder how many of them watched Ernie paint it.

Sure enough, in the reception area of the visitors' centre, there was the plaque and framed newspaper report.

It contained a black and white picture of Ernie, dangling precariously about halfway down (or up), waving towards the camera.

The article sang his praises and commended his bravery for taking on such a dangerous task, especially at his age. The article was dated August 2003. The plaque beside it simply read:

"TO ERNIE GRIMSHAW. PORTLAND LIGHTHOUSE VISITORS' CENTRE WOULD LIKE TO PLACE ON RECORD ITS THANKS FOR ALL YOUR HELP, SUPPORT AND DEDICATION OVER THE YEARS. THIS LIGHT SHINES FOR YOU. 2003."

6:30 p.m.

An email from Darren:

"Paul, sorry for the delay. I have been on annual leave for a couple of days. With regard to your request, I can confirm that the deeds to 71, Avalanche Road belonged to Miss. Bainbridge from 15th April 1986 to 8th September 2005. The house was purchased by a Mr. Cross who still resides there to this day. The name you gave me for 73, Avalanche Road does not exist in the system. Can you give me any further information? Speak soon, pal. D."

Does not exist in the system? They lived next door to each other. Mr. Simpson had visited – he had the letters and address. How strange.

I ran an internet search for Arthur's business name but there was nothing. Not in Weymouth, not in Exeter. Nothing. Did he change it? The internet was only coming into its own in the '90s.

The fact that a small, local, family-owned painting and decorating business does not show on the Google search pages is no real surprise, and they are clearly not still in business, but why no record on the Land Registry system? Now Arty and Mandy seem to have disappeared off the face of the earth.

What caused Ernie and Samantha to desert their happy life on Portland? Why did they need to go to Exeter to help out? Where did they move to?

Bloody hell, here we go again.

CHAPTER 28
The Ties that Bind

23.3.19

9:30 a.m.

I have been up for about three hours wondering where I go to from here. I don't need to check out until 11 a.m., but I am not sure what to do next. I could travel down to Exeter. It is about another fifty miles southwest of here, but for what purpose, at this stage?

I don't have any information about Ernie and Samantha, or Arthur and Mandy. But then again, is it worth going all the way back home only to have to come all the way back down again if I find another lead?

No one in the pub mentioned Arthur and Mandy. Come to think about it, neither did Kenny when I interviewed him. I looked back through the notes of that interview, and although he mentioned having a couple of holidays in Dorset, he never talked much about Arthur or Mandy. Only Ernie and Samantha. Why not? They were friends too.

Darren mentioned a Mr. Cross who bought the house from Ernie and Samantha, but he moved there in 2005 – well after Arthur and Mandy moved away. He is unlikely to know anything. I am clutching at straws again. And what could I look for in Exeter? I don't have any information at all. No forwarding address. No work details.

Another trip to the pub might help. I could ask the locals to see what they could remember about Arthur and Mandy, but from what Darren said, there was no record that they ever owned number 73, Avalanche Road, and we are going back to the start of the '90s there.

It is highly unlikely I would find someone who remembers anything about them. I'm going for a walk along the beach to clear my head.

11:30 a.m.

Checked out. I'm sat in the car still wondering what to do and where to go.

I have emailed Darren again to do a name search in the area, and to find out who lived in 73, Avalanche Road at the same time Ernie and Samantha lived in number 71. I also called Mum and asked her to see what she could find, if anything, on social media.

Perhaps she could join a few groups in and around Exeter and ask if anyone remembers my mysterious four.

That's another handful of straws I'm grasping at, but she was happy to be involved. She said she would let me know if she finds anything.

I have made the decision to drive to Devon and stay in Exeter tonight. I will just get a hotel when I arrive.

No point in booking just yet. It may be that, if I find out something else before then, I will have to go to a different location. You just never know where this case is going to take you.

2:00 p.m.

Another fine meal in *The Eight Kings* in Southwell. I will miss this place. I could definitely settle here. Steak and ale pie today, with chunky

426

chips and a decent selection of vegetables. The place is very quiet today, though. None of the faces from last night are in, and even the staff are different – young, pimply teens earning their first wage packet, I'm guessing. They were all very polite and pleasant, I must admit. A credit to themselves and their parents.

I can't stay here all day. I will have a wander down to Avalanche Road and see if Mr. Cross is in, and then have a walk back up to the church to speak with the Vicar.

If I get no joy from either of those two, then it is back on the road for me and a trip to the capital of Devon.

I just hope Mum can unearth something today, or it could turn out to be a wasted journey.

2:45 p.m.

Sat in the car. Stunned.

It started badly. Mr. Cross was in, and he lived up to his name. No, he hadn't heard of them. No, he didn't know anything about them. He said he didn't welcome strangers knocking on his door for no reason, and then he told me to get off his property. He even threatened to set his terrier on me if I didn't.

Cross by name, cross by nature. In fact, throughout this whole investigation, he is the first person I have encountered who has been angry, aggressive or unhelpful towards me. I had forgotten what it felt like to be abused for no good reason. In this job, that kind of thing happens all the time. That's another thing I won't miss when I finish.

As I headed towards the church, I was in a bad mood - still smarting from the abuse from that rude man – but my anger didn't last. The Reverend was trimming the hedge near the church gate, and he greeted me with a huge smile, immediately restoring my faith in mankind.

I explained why I had come back to Southwell, and what I had found out about 73, Avalanche Road. I asked him if he could remember Arthur and Mandy. He said he didn't know them personally but was aware of them, as Ernie and Samantha talked about them regularly, and they often went to Devon to visit them after they moved there.

I told him I had exhausted all my leads and didn't know where to go next, but that I was considering a trip to Devon.

Then he said something that stunned me.

"Ernie and Samantha were always doing things for other people. Always on the go. I don't think they had much time for themselves, which was a shame. They were often nipping down to Devon to help out Arty and Mandy before finally making the decision to up sticks and move down there. I think it was all to do with their son."

Their son? Arthur and Mandy had a son? I quickly worked out the calculations in my head. Arthur must have been in his fifties and Mandy mid to late forties, surely.

We chatted for a while longer, but he couldn't tell me anything more than that. I checked my phone when I got back into the car to see if there were any messages from mum. There weren't, but there was an email from Darren.

"Hi again, Paul. I ran a check on 73, Avalanche Road as requested. The deed owners from 1986 to 1991 were listed as a Mr. and Mrs.

Green. They bought the place on 15th April 1986 – the same day as Mrs. Bainbridge next door. They sold up in May 1991. Hope this helps. D."

Mr. and Mrs. Green! What the hell? I can't process this. What is going on? Green? Were they related to William Green?

The link between William Green and Ernie Grimshaw had never been apparent. No explanation. Is this the link?

this the connection between my paymaster and Ernie?

Arty and Mandy... Green had a child. A son. I can't think straight. I will update soon. I'm going for a walk.

3:15 p.m.

Mr. Diary, I have no idea what is going on here.

I decided to call Mr. Simpson. I logged our conversation for the record below:

Me: "Mr. Simpson? Kenny? It is Paul Brunskill. Remember me?"

Kenny: *"Of course, I do. I'm not bloody senile, ha. How can I help you?"*

Me: "Just a little bit of help. Can you clarify something for me? Arthur and Mandy. You said their surname was Painter."

Kenny: *"Painter? No, no. That was his nickname. Arthur – Arty. Arty Painter. That was his* nickname. *It went with his job you see. I thought of that one."*

Me: "Do you remember his real surname?"

Kenny: *"Yeah, it was Green. Arthur Green. We never called him that, mind you. Have you found them yet?"*

I had a hundred thoughts going through my mind. Somehow all these strands, all these thoughts, all these coincidences – they must link.

Me: "Not yet, but I am making progress - I think. Kenny, that is a great help though. A great help. Can I ask, did you know that Arthur had a son?"

Kenny: *"A son? That's news to me. He didn't mention anything last time I saw him. Randy sod. I didn't know he had it in him. He must have been getting on then. Old dad, eh!"*

Me: "Can you remember when you last saw or spoke to Arthur or Mandy?"

Kenny: *"It must have been that trip in '91. Thinking about it, Mandy wasn't about. I stayed with Ernie. I think Arthur was around. Or was that my first trip down? I honestly can't remember now. It has all faded into one. I didn't know anything about a son, though, and Ernie never mentioned it. Bloody hell. You learn something new every day.*

You make sure you let me know what you find, Paul."

Me: "I will. Thank you for all your help again."

I cannot believe I didn't pick up on that earlier. Arty bloody Painter. Of course it was a nickname. What an idiot.

Arthur and Mandy Green.

I have the address for Mr. William Green in Plymouth, not Exeter. There may be no connection, but it seems too much of a coincidence for them not to be linked.

Do I go to Plymouth or Exeter? Plymouth is a further forty-five miles southwest of Exeter. Decisions, decisions.

Focus – I am being paid to search for Ernie Grimshaw not Arthur, Mandy or William Green. I will set off for Exeter, stay the night, and see what I can find there. If nothing crops up, I will go down to Plymouth and find William Green.

I don't have a telephone number for him, but I do have his address. I feel so close now. What else do I need to complete the jigsaw?

Exeter next.

7:15 p.m.

It was a slow drive down to Devon. Roadworks and delays every mile or so. It gave me plenty of thinking time, though. I found myself getting annoyed with Mr. Green. If he does know something, why has he sent me on this wild goose chase? Why wouldn't he just pick up the phone and talk to me?

Why did he want to know about Ernie? Did he already know about him? And if he did, why did he want to know more? Surely, he wasn't expecting

431

me to find any dirt to dish. Did it need to be so secretive?

And then I calmed down and gave him the benefit of the doubt.

Is he related to Arthur and Mandy? Does he genuinely not know anything about Ernie? I am a private investigator after all – being secretive is what I am all about. I cannot blame my customers for wanting to be the same. Again, it is his prerogative, and he is paying me well for my efforts.

The fact that Arthur and Mandy moved to Devon and William also lives in Devon could be just another coincidence. Green is a common surname. I must remain open to all ideas and paths. But it just seems so weird.

I called Mum earlier to tell her the latest news. She was as shocked as I was.

I got a room at the *Queen's Court Hotel*, about a ten-minute walk from the city centre. They didn't offer parking, which was a bit of a pain.

I should have checked when I booked.

The van is in some multi-story for the night. There doesn't seem much point going out tonight. I have nothing to look for. I will get a bite to eat in the restaurant and retire to my room.

9:30 p.m.

Progress of sorts. Mum messaged to say she had been on Facebook and registered with two groups – 'Exeter Memories' (22,000 members) and 'Exeter Past and Present' (11,000 members). She hasn't been accepted for either yet so she is unable to add a post, but she said she will do as soon as she is accepted as a member.

I'm off to bed. Another stressful day.

24.3.19

8:45 a.m.

Friday. Another great breakfast to start the day. I have been lucky with my choice of hotels over the last few days. Much better than the fayre served up in London. I doubt my arteries would agree, but it won't be for much longer.

Mum sent a text to say she has been accepted by both groups, and she has posted already. I had a look, as non-members could still view the posts.

She wrote:

"I am trying to find information about some old friends who live(d) in the Exeter area. Arthur and Mandy Green and Ernie Grimshaw and Samantha Bainbridge. If anyone has heard of them, and is able to help, please send me a private message. Thank you."

Let's see what comes back from that. In the meantime, I will check the birth records for Mr. William Green or the baby of Arthur and Mandy Green (should they be different). The baby was born in either Dorset or Devon between 1986 and 1991.

I am sure I can unearth a birth certificate based on what I know, and who I know.

I'll do a bit of investigation if I can find a library or internet café. It is all well and good using the phone, but it is no substitute for the world-wide web.

I'll lounge around here until check-out time, then go and put my bag in the van before exploring Exeter's historic city centre. No rush. I'll update you again sometime this afternoon.

Hopefully, I will have some idea where I am going to be spending the night by that point.

1:45 p.m.

I'm sat in a lovely little bar overlooking Exeter Cathedral. I have just spent the last fifteen minutes trying to console and calm my mother. A reminder, if I ever needed one, not to become too familiar with, or reliant on, social media. I think she might think twice in future now.

The post received one or two positive comments early on but was soon hijacked by the trolls and keyboard warriors, hurling obscenities and insults, the likes of which she had never experienced before. She read some of the replies out to me:

"I hope they are dead."

"What do you want to know for – snooping bitch?"

"None of your ******* business!"

Some had sent messages to her own inbox, and they were just as bad. She said she had reported them to the administrators, and they had since been removed, but it left her shaken and upset. A cruel realisation that not everyone out there is good. Not everyone wants to help.

The few politer comments offered us little.

"I hope you find them."

"Good luck with your search."

"I'll ask around."

I told Mum not to look on there again after she had blocked any rude or offensive messages. No point in complaining to Facebook – they don't have a face. I'll keep checking the post myself to see if anything comes of it, but my hopes aren't high.

Now, back to what I am good at. I found a small hotel offering computers and internet access in the reception area.

4:20 p.m.

Back in the van. A fruitful afternoon. I have a birth certificate. The plot thickens. There it was in black and white. William Green is definitely the son of Arthur and Mandy. I am getting closer to unravelling this mystery. I am a bag of nervous excitement.

Name: William Arthur Green Weight: 4lbs 4 ounces
Time/Date of birth: 16th November 1986
Location: St. Mary's Maternity Unit, Poole, Dorset. Father: Mr. Arthur Green
Mother: Mrs. Amanda Green

So that makes William only just less than thirty-three years old. I had him down as an old man. Not many people that young choose to write instead of email or text.
He was a very light baby. Scarily so.
At this stage, I can't see any other option but to go to Plymouth tomorrow. My search for Ernie has reached 2005, but now I am a bit stuck. I'm back to tracking the Greens. I can't be bothered to travel down this evening.
I'm worn out.
I will have another night here in Exeter then go to Plymouth in the morning to actually speak with Mr. William Green.

7:15 p.m.

Mum called. We had a long chat, and I told her about William's birth certificate. She was as perplexed and as thrilled as I was. Neither of us could work out what was going on.

She also had a private message on Facebook from a lady called Louise who thinks she might have worked with Samantha. She was sorry to say that, if it was the same lady, she passed away a few years ago. Again, my mother gave her my number and asked if she would call me.

8:30 p.m.

Louise called. She told me that she worked for Exeter City Council about a decade ago in the same office as a lady called Samantha Bainbridge. She didn't know her very well, but she was sad to say she had died of cancer.

"A lovely, kind old lady." she said.

She guessed it was around 2007 or 2008 but couldn't be exactly sure.

Louise thought Samantha must have been close to pensionable age when she died. When she described her, I was in little doubt that it was Ernie's wife. So, they had lived here, and the trail isn't stone cold yet.

Poor Ernie. He has certainly suffered his fair share of loss over the years. I dread to think how losing his wife affected him. I really hope she didn't suffer for long. I asked Louise if she knew Ernie. She didn't. She didn't have much to add other than that. She seemed genuine. I had no reason to doubt her.

436

I will go the library in the morning and seek out the death certificates in Exeter around that time. They should all be available online. Again, it shouldn't be hard to find. The death certificate will give a place and cause of death. The doctor's name should be recorded too. It might also list the undertaker used.

This was a rather morbid turn that I hadn't really been expecting. Samantha was still a relatively young woman. So very sad.

I didn't feel like eating after that news.

Goodnight, Mr. Diary. Enough for one day.

25.3.19

10:15 a.m.

Mum's Facebook post has been locked by the administrators. No further messages that I could see.

Last night, I thought long and hard about going down to Plymouth and going to see Mr. Green. It felt like I would be breaking a trust by doing so. I hadn't been invited to see him, and his correspondence had all been through letter. But what other options do I have?

I will still go to the library today and find out what I can about Samantha's death.

In 2008, Ernie would have been seventy-nine years old when/if he lost his wife. I wonder where he was living and who was looking after him in his old age. Considering everything must have been in Samantha's name, I wondered how this would affect his bills/mortgage/insurance policies etc., etc.

I feel so close to him now, but I still have no idea where he is. It is gut-wrenching.

I have made my decision, and my plan of action. I will go to the library, find out what I can, and *then* go to Plymouth. I will stay overnight. Tomorrow morning, I will go to the address of Mr. William Green to speak with him. I am prepared to risk getting an unwelcome reception. Our correspondence has always been amiable, so perhaps it's not such a huge risk. Nevertheless, I'm already terrified. Goodness knows what I will be like in the morning. Mr. William Green – I am coming to find you.

CHAPTER 29
In the wind

26.3.19

10:45 a.m.

It wasn't hard to find. There it was in black and white.

Name: Samantha Louise Bainbridge
Age: 65
Date of death: 23rd May 2008.
Cause of death: Cancer of the lung.
Last seen alive by Doctor Munroe at 1:45 p.m.
Place of death: Exeter City Hospital

The doctor's name was hard to read – Monroe or Munroe – something like that. The certificate stated the illness was diagnosed in the February. Nothing more. Only three months or so between diagnosis and death. Not long.

She was a lot younger than Ernie, but she wasn't destined to enjoy a long life. She clearly had a lot of struggles in her own life, and I felt glad that she had found Ernie and enjoyed quite a number of very happy years with him.

Even now, in my forties, I am starting to look towards the end. Going by averages, I am over halfway through my own time on earth. Life is short. We must make the most of it. I need to constantly remind myself of that – especially on the bad days.

I now have butterflies in my stomach, as I know I need to go to Plymouth. There isn't anything else to do. There is nothing left to find here.

I've just booked a room at the Citadel House Hotel. Good facilities, a place to park and good reviews of the breakfast. That will do. I don't think I will need more than one night, and then I can make the long trip home.

It is only about an hour's drive from here, so I should be there in plenty of time before I'm required to check in. I'll park up and have a wander around the city centre. Once I have unpacked and composed myself, I will make my way over to see Mr. Green. Hopefully he won't be too shocked to see me.

1:30 p.m.

What a glorious day. I am sat on a bench on Plymouth Hoe looking out over the English Channel, only metres from the impressive statue of Sir Francis Drake. In 1588, he was getting ready to go into battle against the Spanish Armada from here. He must have been a bit scared, but I bet he didn't show it. I mustn't either. I must stay professional.

I can just explain that the case brought me to Devon, and it seemed rather daft to post my findings when I could simply bring them over (nearly fifty miles further south in the wrong direction).

I'm sure he will be fine. He comes across as a very polite and understanding gentleman. He has always been very grateful and gracious for the work I have done on his behalf. Will he be disappointed, though, that I haven't found Ernie?

440

Is this why I am so nervous?

This is a beautiful place to sit., so calming. The lighthouse to my right is not too dissimilar to the one on Portland that Ernie painted. The red and white stands out against the backdrop of blue sky and green grass. I could sit here all day, but I know I need to go.

Time waits for no man.

2:15 p.m.

So here it is: Mr. Green's house. I don't know what I was expecting, but I have to say, I am very impressed. The house is in a quiet, secluded area on the outskirts of Plymouth called Tamerton Foliot.

It was only a fifteen-minute drive from the busy centre, but it seems like a different world. The house is very big and, I'd guess, very expensive. It seems too big for one man to live in by himself. He never mentioned family. He had no need to. I hadn't really thought about his family until the last couple of days. I hadn't thought about anyone else opening that door but Mr. Green.

Mr. Diary, you stay here. Deep breath, I am going in.

6:30 p.m.

Of all my diary entries, this will have to go down as the most memorable and the hardest one to write.

I'm sitting in the van again after yet another incredible afternoon. For the last fifteen minutes, I have just been driving and thinking and trying to take it all in. I have no idea where I am now. Beside some farm in the middle of nowhere. It is dark and dismal outside.

This isn't the ideal place to sit and write, but I must do it now whilst everything is still fresh in my mind. Thank goodness I had my Dictaphone turned on in my inside pocket.

Oh, my goodness, where do I start? From the knock at the door?

I feel mentally and physically exhausted. I need to write this down, though. I need to get it out of my head, off the Dictaphone and in print. The light isn't great in here, but it doesn't matter – I need to get it down on paper.

I knocked on the door of the house, and it was answered by a woman. I guessed she was in her late sixties, and I presumed her to be Mrs. Amanda Green. I introduced myself and she broke into a huge smile.

"I have been expecting you." she said. Really? I was even more confused then.

I asked if I had the right house, the house of Mr. William Green, and she confirmed that I did. She invited me in. The interior was beautifully appointed, warm and homely.

Spotlessly clean too. It was bright and cheerful. Plush, deep carpets, all bright colours. The large windows let in the sunlight, warming the rooms. I followed her into the conservatory, and she invited me to sit down. The views of the grand gardens outside were gorgeous. Blooms of every colour surrounded rockeries, bird tables and fountains. It was a magical place. The high bushes and trees surrounding the garden gave it an intimate, private feel - like a little piece of heaven away from the demands and stresses of real life.

"Do you like the garden, Mr. Brunskill? It is truly beautiful at this time of year, isn't it?" I think I just nodded in agreement and smiled. I hadn't found my voice at that point.

I scanned the room for signs of Mr. Green and listened for other voices in the house.

She offered tea or coffee along with scones with jam and fresh clotted cream. I nodded enthusiastically. She walked away to the kitchen while I sat back and admired the view. While she was away, I set the Dictaphone to record and placed it back in my inside pocket. After ten minutes or so, she returned with a tray and placed it on the table in front of me.

"Help yourself, Mr. Brunskill. Plenty more in the kitchen if you can manage it." We ate and drank and commented on the garden.

All I could think to say was,

"Call me Paul. Please. Thank you so much."

She must have sensed my nerves.

"Like I said, I was expecting you. We were hoping you would come, William and I." I was relieved to hear his name even if I couldn't see him. Eventually, I managed to collect my thoughts and speak up.

"I hope you don't mind me coming to the house. I thought, with the case taking me to Devon, it made logical sense to drive down and see Mr. Green. I have managed to trace Ernie up to 2005, and his wife up to 2008 but I'm afraid I'm a little stuck now."

She poured herself another tea and sat back, smiling.

"Mr. Brunskill. Paul. You have found and uncovered more than anyone could possibly have expected. More than anyone could have hoped for.

443

You have provided answers to many questions, and you have been worth every penny that we have paid you. We... I... am incredibly grateful for all you have done. You have no idea. To get as far as 2005 is simply incredible. Astonishing. Maybe I can fill in a few blanks for you."

I asked her the question that had been on my mind ever since she opened the door.

"May I ask, are you Amanda Green or a relative of William?"

"No. Mr. Green, William, never married. My name is Miss Mary Graham. I am a nurse. A specialist nurse and carer. Let me introduce you to Mr. Green, but please be quiet as he is sleeping at the moment."

She stood up and walked towards the stairs. I followed. I felt very uneasy but intrigued at the same time. This was a turn of events I hadn't expected at all. At the top of the landing, she turned left and walked slowly and carefully down the hallway to a door at the end that was slightly ajar.

"William is in there - go ahead," she said.

She stepped aside to let me through. I pushed open the door a little further, and I could see what looked like a huge cot. A double bed with safety rails around the side. The bedside table light was on, and I could make out the shape of a man curled up on the bed fast asleep, snoring slightly.

"Let's go back downstairs, and I will tell you more. William has the light on because he finds it hard to sleep in the dark. It scares him." she whispered.

We made our way back to the conservatory and sat down again in the same places as before.

"This is William's house. His home. But he doesn't own it." she said.

444

"It is owned by a trust. We provide care – palliative care – for people coming to the end of their lives. William has been with us for a couple of years now. Before he came here, I was his nurse at the previous home. Suffolk Court in Exeter.

You see, William has suffered from a severe case of cerebral palsy all his life. The condition has got steadily worse over the years. He is nearly thirty-three years old now. Nobody thought he would live this long due to the seriousness of his condition."

She had such a quiet, soothing voice. I was transfixed.

"It is a minor miracle that he has lived this long, according to some of the specialists. He is not in any pain, but the condition has got much worse recently, and the doctors are very concerned, hence the urgency in my earlier letters."

"Your letters?" I asked.

"Yes. I was the one who penned them. I am sorry to confuse you. It was all done with the best of intentions, and with William's consent. I need to explain how and why."

"How bad is William's condition?" I asked her.

"His doctors do not think he has long to live. They have said that before, mind you, and been wrong before, but this time they are fairly sure he will only have weeks. They said they would be surprised if he made it to summer."

"Is he able to talk – to communicate?"

"He is. His speech is very slurred now, and he has lapses when tired. His memory – both short and long-term – isn't good now. It frustrates him. He responds well to visual representations and pictures. He is able to indicate what he wants, such as food or the bathroom. He understands

445

everything you say to him, and can respond with a nod, a smile or a shake of the head. He struggles to form his words now, but the other carers and I have known him for such a long time, we know what he is telling us. We know him better than anyone. We know all his little traits and mannerisms. It was my idea to write to you, but everything was done in agreement with William. He was able to read the letters and agree on the wording. I asked him questions, and he was able to give me answers. A couple of years ago, when William was able to talk more, he kept asking about Ernie. His knowledge of him was minimal, and he was desperate to know more about him. I tried, but it was hopeless.

I'm no investigator, Paul. When William's condition worsened, we thought we would try again. It was obviously very important to him.

I asked William if we should hire someone. A professional. You. He wanted to. He gave his consent. He was very enthusiastic about it. He wasn't stupid. He may have brain damage, but it didn't affect his intellectual capacity. He understood, and he knew what he wanted. Everything you have sent me, I have shown to him. I have shown him all the pictures and read him every single article and interview - several times over. They have had us both in tears, sat out in that garden. We have both been in fits of giggles too. I didn't know much about Ernie Grimshaw before this, but I certainly do now. What an amazing man."

"William is the son of Arthur and Mandy," I said. "Can you tell me more about what happened to them? And why are you, and William, looking to find out so much about Ernie?"

"William's mother, Mandy, wasn't known to me. She had William when she was in her mid-forties. An unexpected pregnancy, you might say. Both delighted by the news, though, by all accounts. But, during pregnancy, she had a blood infection, apparently – sepsis. This prevented the right amount of oxygen reaching the baby. He suffered abnormalities whilst growing in the womb. They wouldn't have known at the time, but the baby will have been brain damaged to a certain extent at birth. It just didn't manifest until later in life. He was a very light baby according to records."

"Just over 4lbs." I added.

"Yes. So, I'm guessing he would have been kept in an incubator for some time until he gained weight. It must have been a stressful time for the family. His father was much older than his mother. Arthur was in his fifties when he became a daddy. When William was finally taken home, things must have seemed normal at first. For the first two or three years at least. It can take that long before the signs become more obvious. You know, things like a lack of balance or blurred vision. He might have been unable to say certain words. He would get bad headaches that could cause endless, sleepless nights. It must have been awful for the family, not knowing what was wrong. William was diagnosed with cerebral palsy around the age of four. There would have been some help from the NHS, but parents were largely left to cope on their own back then.

Incredible to think that was the case at the start of the 1990s. It would have been a battle to get help from the state, and it can't have been easy for two older parents with no experience of the system.

William lost his mum at an early age. She died shortly after turning fifty. He can't have been much more than four or five years old.

The sepsis. The blood infection. It hadn't cleared up. She must have suffered a lot after giving birth, but it was never properly diagnosed. The infection later transferred to her vital organs. On her death certificate, it was recorded as kidney failure brought on by blood poisoning. Such a terrible shame."

"What happened to William then? Did he go into care?" I asked.

"No. Not at all. William still lived with his father. His dad. But the demands were such that Arthur had to quit work and rely on others to run the business for him. William would have required full-time care, even this early in his life."

"That must have been in the early '90s. Arthur and Mandy moved to Exeter," I said.

"Yes, they must have. Exeter was known to have good care facilities. Better than those in Dorset. Exeter was a bigger city with better facilities, I guess. It made sense to move.

I believe Arthur set up an office there for the business, but it can't have lasted more than a few years. The demands on his time must have been huge." I interrupted here as the pieces began to fit together.

"Ernie and his wife, Samantha, used to come down to Devon to help out. They must have been coming to support Arthur and William."

"Yes, I think that would have been the case. William talked about his Uncle Ernie and Auntie Sam a lot. I think they really eased the burden on Arthur. William attended a special school in Exeter. That would have given Arthur time during the day.

His house would have been adapted to accommodate a stairlift and a wheelchair. When William was about ten, the doctors thought he might die. He had a particularly nasty fall, bumping his head in the process, but he recovered from that.

It is a horrible condition, and many specialists have been prophets of doom over the years, but he is still with us.

His life carried on like this throughout his teenage years. It must have been more and more difficult for Arthur, and frustrating for William. Arthur was getting on in years, and the strain and stress to take care of his son must have been enormous. Without the help from Ernie and Sam, I doubt he would have made it.

And then Arthur had his stroke."

"His stroke?"

"Yes. In 2005. He was seventy-one then."

"So that's when Ernie and Sam moved from Portland to Exeter?" I said, clarifying what I had found out from the locals in the pub at Southwell.

"That would make sense. They moved in with Arthur and William. It was a big stroke. It paralysed Arthur down one side of his body, and he lost his ability to speak. He would have needed full-time care from that point. Ernie and Sam gave up everything to look after them both. You can't put a price on that kind of friendship."

"What happened to the business?"

"I think it must have just petered out. Maybe It was already finished before he had the stroke. I don't know. But I'm guessing with the money from the business and the sale of the house in Portland, they were able to get by financially, but the pressure must have been awful."

449

"Samantha died of cancer in 2008. She hadn't been ill long. It seemed to have happened so quickly." I told her.

"Yes, that was a year before Arthur. Arthur died in 2009, leaving William with no one - except Ernie. Although not a blood relative, Ernie took on sole charge of William's care. So much sadness in such a short space of time. Ernie was 80 years old in 2009."

"How on earth could an eighty-year-old care for a twenty-three –year-old man who had such a debilitating illness?" I asked her.

"I have no idea, but he did." she replied.

"William didn't come into the Suffolk Court care facility until 2012. Ernie must have cared for William all by himself for three years or more. When he was able to talk clearly, William would tell me all sorts of stories about his time with Ernie. He treasured him – loved him to bits. Ernie used to take him everywhere in the wheelchair, even at that age. He must have been the fittest eighty-year-old around. They used to regularly go to the coast on days out. They'd visit Dartmoor, Exmoor and Torquay, to name but a few.

They used to take the bus or the train and go all over. William told me they used to sit for hours and hours telling jokes or stories. Ernie could make him laugh like no one else could. I think they helped each other cope after all they both had been through. When William was with Ernie, he never felt restricted, lost or helpless. I can't imagine what it must be like to have such a sharp mind but be stuck in a body that doesn't work as it should.

Ernie gave him that love of life. He loved him and cared for him so much. You can tell so much of this just by the way William talks about him."

She had a tear in her eye but didn't even try to wipe it away.

"Ernie was eighty-three when William was moved to Suffolk Court."

"Was he still able to visit?" I asked after a few moments of reflection.

"Visit? He would visit William every day. Without fail. Sometimes he would stay for an hour, sometimes all morning or afternoon. It was very much dependent on William and what he could cope with. Sometimes he would get very tired and needed to sleep, but Ernie was always there when he needed him. They couldn't go on day trips out anymore. Ernie was too old for that. Don't get me wrong, he wanted to, but we insisted they just use the garden instead.

They would sit out there for hours. Ernie taught William about the different types of flowers and trees, the birds and the insects. They kept scrapbooks together. We often had to drag the two of them back in. I'm sure they would have stayed out there all night if we had let them. But the thing is that, in spite of all of their chats, Ernie told William very little about his own life, and William didn't ask, even though he would have loved to have known more about Ernie. Probably now it's too late. It torments William, I'm sure. He has been desperate to know what made Ernie the man he came to know. The man who was such a loyal and caring friend to his parents and to him." She paused. "That's why we had to find him, or at least find out about him."

We sat quietly for a moment before I continued, changing the subject slightly.

"So, when did you move here? What did Ernie do then?"

"I moved to this house, to this facility, at the same time as William. It was the start of 2017. William was nearly thirty-one. Ernie must have been nearly eighty-seven." she said.

"Where was he living at that time?"

"Still in Exeter, I think. I am not sure where. When Arthur died, his own property was sold, and the proceeds were used to pay for William's care. The bills are astronomical here.

£1700 a week. Any money from Arthur's estate would have all been spent on care costs."

I thought again about Ernie's situation, having lost his wife and close friend.

"Nothing was in Ernie's name. He would have had no income. No pension. Where would he go or where would he live? He had no one else." I could feel myself starting to cry.

"I know, Paul. And I don't have the answer to that question. He did have money though. He still came to visit William, although not every day. There was one week he didn't come at all. That must be the week he went up to Carlisle. 2017, wasn't it?" she said, handing me a tissue.

"Yes, it must have been. How did he seem to you then?"

"He was an old man. He was starting to fade. I don't know where he was living, but whenever he came, he was always immaculately clean and well turned out. It dawned on me around that time that, of all the times he had come to visit William, of all the times I had talked and laughed and joked with him, I knew so little about his life.

In his later visits, I could tell he wasn't himself. I sat him down in this very conservatory once, after he had visited William, to ask him if *he* was alright. He confided in me that he wasn't well.

452

He said he was forgetting things. Normal, everyday things. He had talked to a doctor at the hospital, and she had mentioned memory loss and possible dementia. He was supposed to go to the hospital for treatment. I am not sure he did, though." she said, smiling. "He was very much his own man – even then."

"When was the last time you saw him?"

"It must have been around Christmas time last year. It was a freezing day, but the two of them still went and sat outside in the garden to talk. That is when he gave me a letter."

She stood up at this point and walked over to a chest of drawers. She returned with a small brown envelope and handed it to me.

"Open it. Read it. I'm sure he would have wanted you to."

I opened the envelope and placed the contents on the table in front of me. There were two documents inside. The first one I opened was Ernie's birth certificate. The original of the copy I had back at home. The second piece of paper was a letter from Ernie to William. It had me in tears again. I took photographs of it.

I'm crying again now. I'm shaking, writing this. It said:

William,

I am writing to you now while I still can. While I am still able to pen my thoughts. Slowly but surely, my mind is failing me. I put it down to old age. My brain is full to bursting point, and it can't cope anymore. That's what I reckon anyway.

453

I can't complain. I have had a wonderful life and met so many amazing people. I have lived, and I have loved. You can't ask for any more than that.

When you were born, many so-called experts thought you wouldn't live long, but you proved them wrong.

You are so loved and so special – don't you ever forget that, my lad.

Every day I have spent in your company has made me a better person. More grateful and gracious. I appreciated life more than ever.

I know I will not be with you much longer, but I will be waiting for you on the other side with our scrapbooks and picture books. Remember, you are never alone. You are always in someone's thoughts and prayers.

You keep fighting on until your very last breath. Life is too precious and too short to give up on. My birth certificate is enclosed. You will need this. It is the only piece of evidence that I have left to prove I exist.

It will help you.

I have set up a standing order for you to pay for your care and anything else you need. A sum of £20,000 will be paid, each month, into the care home account, and I trust Mary will ensure the money is used wisely.

If, for whatever reason, you need any further financial support, contact:

'THE FRIENDS OF I.F., 1345 East 26th Street, New York City'. They will be able to help.

All you have to do is show them my birth certificate. I will visit when I am able to, William.

You are in good hands with Mary.

I love you, William. More than you can possibly know. Good luck, and God bless.

Ernie xx

Mary leaned forward to hold my hand. She could see how emotional I was.

"Try not to be upset, Paul. He was, and still is, William's guardian angel. That was the last time anyone saw him. God rest his soul. I have never contacted that address in New York, but the money keeps coming in regardless, and there was plenty. That is how I paid you. I felt that using it in this way was as beneficial for William as his physical care. I could see the positive impact it had on William when your news and updates came through."

"I.F. – Incredible Feet?" I sobbed.

"It must be. I can't think of any other explanation. They must have an awful lot of money," she whispered, giving my hand a squeeze.

I thought back to the pub. The names on the board. The stars. It all seemed so crazy, but then, everything else had been crazy too. It could be possible. Couldn't it?

"You said that was the last time anyone saw Ernie. Do you know where he was going, or what he was going to do?" I asked.

"I have no idea. He was ill, and he knew it. He seemed to know his time was up. I don't know if anyone was looking out for him or taking care of him. I asked around in the local hospitals and care homes, but there was no record of him – as usual. I can only assume he has passed on. In situations like this, where there are no known relatives or friends, the person is generally given a pauper's

455

funeral, which is incredibly sad. He deserved better.

Whatever happened to Ernie at his end, I hope he knows just how much he mattered, and how much he was loved."

We sat in silence for a minute or so, just looking out of the window. Then I said,

"He was the most remarkable man I have ever known, and I never even met him."

"He certainly was," she replied. "There is something he would often say to William. Something that stuck in my mind. He used to say, 'There is no such thing as an ordinary person. Everyone is capable of achieving, but everyone needs help.' He helped. He helped so many people. That's Ernie's legacy. He was anything but ordinary. Ironically, I don't recall Ernie ever asking for others to help him, and you didn't find any evidence of that either, Paul. We planted a tree for him in the garden near to where the two of them used to sit.

It is growing well – growing strong. Another reminder of the man. I wonder how many other plants and trees and benches there are in his memory?"

We both smiled at the thought. Ernie Grimshaw would not be forgotten. Overjoyed, Mary was satisfied that I had reached the end of the search for Ernie. She was delighted that I had amassed such a wealth of information about his extraordinary life. William had now been told so much about his special friend and benefactor, and he was now content.

I left the house. I left Mary. I left William. I climbed back into this van and drove away. And here I am now.

Come on, Mr. Diary. It is time for us to go home.

27.3.19

11:15 a.m.

It was nearly two o'clock in the morning when I eventually got in and crashed on the bed. I completed the long drive in one go. I was on autopilot for most of it.

I haven't got anything to add today. I am not doing any work today either. You deserve a rest too, Mr. Diary.

28.3.19

Nothing to report.

29.3.19

Mum called to remind me about our date night. I had forgotten about that. That is something to look forward to. Something to drag me out of this slump.

I seem to have lost all my enthusiasm, at the moment.

I invested so much time and effort into that case. I am not sure what I have left to give.

I must try to motivate myself to do some casework this afternoon.

I might even join the gym again.

I also must remember to get that crate of ale for Darren.

30.3.19

I am getting more and more excited for tomorrow night. I feel more alive today.

I have my induction at the gym later, and then I'm going to the pub to meet Darren and a couple of the lads. Just a few pints.

The fitness can start for real tomorrow.

Six missed calls on my mobile phone while I was in the bath. Private numbers. Potential fraud, my phone suggests. No messages left. No, I haven't been involved in an accident. No, I don't want to buy life insurance. No, I don't want Viagra – at least not yet.

How do these companies get my number anyway?

31.3.19

That was a brilliant catch-up last night. It was great to see the boys again. I'm going to make this a regular thing from now on. They were very pleased to see me. It gave me a real buzz.

Hopefully tonight will too. I am meeting Mum at the restaurant at half seven. Come on, Paul, you can do it.

10:30 p.m.

I am walking on cloud nine. She said YES! I had the courage to ask, and she said YES! Well, Mum did the groundwork, but I still had the courage to ask.

Tina looked as nervous as I was when we walked in. It was quiet in the restaurant which helped.

There were only a few customers in, and they were well spread out.

Antonio served us, exuding his usual confidence and charm. Mum let him flirt and practically encouraged him. She was enjoying herself.

We ordered wine with the food, and Tina served us. She tried not to make eye contact with me. If she had, she would have noticed me blushing. It went on like that throughout the starters and main courses until Mum's patience ran out.

"I'm going to powder my nose and then I am going to have a drink at the bar with Antonio. Tina – sit down, love. Paul has got something to ask you."

Off she toddled, and Tina did as she was told. I looked over towards the bar. Mum was stood there chatting to Antonio and looking in our direction. The two of them making gestures and mouthing 'go on' to me.

I came straight out with it. Sort of.

"I don't suppose, if you would like to, I mean... if you don't have... erm... what I am trying to say is, I'd love it if you would consider..."

"Going out with you?" she said, finishing my sentence. "Yes, I would love to. I really would love to."

And that was that. We chatted for ten minutes or so before Antonio and Mum returned to the table.

"Did she say she would go out with you then?" asked Mum, bluntly. "She did." I replied, beaming.

"Good. About bloody time. Let's make sure we don't court on the same night then. Antonio has

459

agreed to go out with me too - on the condition we don't go to an Italian restaurant on our first proper date." That broke the ice and we all laughed.

We exchanged numbers and arranged to meet at the weekend when she wasn't working.

I can't believe it. She is gorgeous, funny, witty, gorgeous and gorgeous. I can't believe she agreed to go out with me. I'm so excited, Mr. Diary.

Things are going so well. I have money in the bank, I am getting on better with my mother now than I have in years, I have reacquainted myself with old friends and I have a date with the perfect girl. I feel like a new man. A better man. I don't know if this has anything to do with Ernie and the case, but my eyes have been opened to what is important in life. A burden has been lifted.

But I have one more task to do before I can finally put this case to bed. One last trip to make.

1.4.19

11:10 a.m.

It was a straightforward journey up the M6. The sun was shining again, there were clear blue skies above the mountains in the distance and everything felt right with the world.

I arrived in Carlisle city centre just before 11:00 a.m. and parked up in The Lanes Shopping Centre's multi-story car park. I could have driven straight to the church, but I wanted to enjoy a decent walk after the drive.

I hadn't planned ahead. I hadn't thought to check if Father Allen would be in. I just presumed he would be. I didn't know what I would do if he was out. Probably just go straight back. I will take my

460

chances. You can come with me for the walk, Mr. Diary.

11:45 a.m.

I walked through the city centre and past the old Town Hall. There were plenty of shoppers milling around, minding their own business and going about their daily lives.

I carried on through the Cathedral grounds and onto Castle Way before heading through Caldewgate and on towards Wigton Road, and that steep hill that led up to St. Bede's church. Like last time, I was out of breath by the time I got to the top of the hill. I really do need to get fitter. For once, I need to make use of this new gym membership and not just use it for the first week or so before losing interest, like I normally do.

I'm now sat on a wall opposite the church updating you again, Mr Diary. I can see a car parked outside the house. Hopefully that is Father Allen's. Hopefully he is in.

My phone buzzed again in my pocket. Another missed call to add to the two on the journey north. I'll turn the thing off until later.

Here goes.

3:30 p.m.

I have just spent another delightful couple of hours in the company of Father Allen.

He answered the door after a minute or so wearing a t-shirt and a pair of Bermuda shorts. Not the look I expected to see from a priest. He remembered me instantly and welcomed me into the living room again.

"I wasn't sure you would be back so soon, Paul" he said. "Forgive my appearance, it was the first thing I grabbed when I climbed out of bed. Better this than nothing, I can assure you. Did you find what you were looking for?" he asked.

I told him I had. I also told him that I had managed to trace Ernie's life up to 2018. Father Allen promised to say a prayer and mention him in Sunday's Mass.

He asked if I was ready to do a little bit of excavation work in the memorial garden. I was.

Father Allen slipped on some sandals, and the two of us walked out of the side door and down towards the garden. He picked up a couple of trowels from his own window boxes on the way. "These should do the trick. Hurry up, Paul, let's get this box dug up and we can get back inside again. I don't want any of the parishioners seeing me like this."

We walked to the top end of the garden where the tree for Martha and Tommy had been planted. I read the plaque again.

"Shall we?" Father Allen said, pointing to the earth beneath the tree.

We both knelt down and started digging. The soil was wet and heavy from days of rain, but it didn't take long for the trowels to hit the tin. We dragged it out between us. It was a fair size and quite heavy. There was a handle on each side, we both grabbed one, and pulled it out of the ground.

"Any idea what is in here?" he asked.

"None at all" I replied. "You?"

He smiled.

We left the trowels and the hole in the ground and carried the tin back to the house. Around the back, he had a hose on the wall, and he used it to

462

wash off the dirt and excess soil. It was sealed by a silver padlock, but the key dangled down beside it. Ernie never meant for it to remain sealed forever.

We took the box into the kitchen and placed it on the table. The key was rusty, but it still turned in the lock and clicked open.

Father Allen took off the padlock and looked at me.

"Isn't this exciting?" he said. "Are you ready?"

I nodded, but I wasn't sure if I was. I had no idea what was inside.

He opened the lid carefully, and inside was a large bulk wrapped up in a bin liner, presumably to offer extra protection against the elements. I carefully tore it open to reveal the contents. Books. Eleven of them in total. All identical. Same make, same colour (dark blue) and in mint condition. Underneath the books was an envelope. Father Allen sat back on the sofa. He knew this was for me. He was happy to observe.

I opened the envelope first. It was full of photographs. There must have been over a hundred in there. I skimmed through them. Each one was dated on the back with a caption underneath describing who was in the picture and where it was taken. I skimmed through them like an excited child at Christmas wondering which present to open first.

There they all were – Martha and Tommy, The Kaplans, Daniel, Robbie. Mabel and David, Samantha. The cricket teams. Curtis. Sid. Kenny. Arthur and Mandy. William too. Lots of William. And many more besides.

And the places. Germany - Bergen Belsen. Carlisle and Seaham. Even Prospect and the farm.

New York City. Ellis Island.

London. Brick Lane. The cricket clubs. Weymouth and Portland. The lighthouse and the pub.

It was incredible. Mind-blowing. Everyone that I had found on this incredible adventure. Everyone I had heard about. All the places I had visited and a million more besides. All kept in pristine condition with great attention to detail.

Not for the first time, I was lost for words.

I turned my attention to the books. They were diaries. Like mine. Better than mine. Neater than mine. Diaries dating back to the 1930s. All the way up to 2017. I opened a couple on a random page. They were all handwritten in striking, cursive writing.

Each day dated with specific times and places recorded – just like mine. I read a couple of entries. One on the ship over to New York. Another of an incident with Martha in Carlisle. So descriptive. So detailed. Nothing controversial. Nothing offensive.

Here – right in front of me – in the pages of eleven books, was Ernie's life through his own eyes. Everything I had tried to unearth had been here all along – in the earth.

I collapsed back in the chair and stared at the contents of the tin.

"They are yours to keep, Paul. Take them home with you." Father Allen said.

He gave me an old carrier bag to put them in, and we shook hands at the door. He wished me well and said he would say a prayer for me. I thanked him for his help and support, and even for the old carrier bag.

From the church, I walked down the hill back towards the city centre, carrying this precious cargo.

Along the way, I watched people, young and old, going about their daily lives, unaware of the precious contents inside the carrier bag I was holding.

'What was in their own bags?' I wondered. I'll never know.

I walked back through the Caldewgate area of the city and up towards the Castle, before turning right and into the Cathedral grounds, then pausing to sit on the old Town Hall steps just to reflect. I was in a daze.

What a lovely way to end this quest.

Ernie could rest in peace, and so could I.

It was time to get on with the rest of my life.

Back at the van, I've placed the bag on the passenger seat and turned to you again, Mr. Diary.

If I had found out about the buried treasure earlier, I wouldn't have had to go to America or London, Dorset or Devon.

I wouldn't have had to spend night after night in strange hotel rooms, eating takeaways and getting fatter.

I wouldn't have had to walk the streets of Bermondsey or face the wrath of a man and his dog in Portland.

But do I regret it? Not one bit.

I have got a lot of reading to do when I get back home. I want to sit back and enjoy Ernie's life all over again, but this time through his own eyes, thoughts and ideas.

Time to go home.

4:45 p.m.

I stopped for a takeaway coffee and a chocolate biscuit at a small garage on the way to the motorway to give me sustenance for the journey back. I remembered I had turned off my mobile phone before going to the church grounds. It had been off a couple of hours or more before I remembered. I pressed the 'power on' button and waited for it to kick back into life as I slurped on my coffee.

Messages came thick and fast, as well as emails, adverts and game reminders. How did I ever function without it?

A lovely text message from Tina asking about my day, followed by two kisses. Another from Mum reminding me to send a card for my cousin's birthday. A cousin, I might add, that I haven't seen or spoken to in over a decade.

And then there was another host of missed calls. I was about to put the phone back in my pocket when I realised there was also a voicemail message.

"I don't like talking to these things. Sorry. I know you are a busy man. I just thought you should know – after our conversations and all that. I thought you should know.

Anyway, if you could give me a call. I will be in. I'm always in. Call me when you get this message. I think it has worked. I waited for the beep like it said. Right, I will say goodbye now. Call me when you can. Take care. How do you turn this thing off..."

No name given, but I knew who it was. It was dark outside, but it wasn't too late. I may as well clear up that one final loose end while I am in the area. Come on, Mr. Diary. We are heading west.

6:45 p.m.

It is pitch-black out here. I will keep this entry short and sweet, Mr. Diary. I have just pulled up outside Greenbank Farm in Prospect, West Cumbria.

Mr. Frankenburg won't be expecting to see me tonight, but hopefully it will be a nice surprise for him. I have the diaries with me, and I am sure he would love to see and read them.

The light is on, so I know he is in. I hope he doesn't mind me turning up like this. I'm sure he would prefer this than having to speak over the phone.

Dictaphone at the ready again. Here goes.

10:40 p.m.

When my time is up on earth and new souls take my place, I would like to think I had left a mark. I would like to think my life meant something.

But ultimately, my legacy will be decided by others, not me.

Earlier this evening, I knocked on the door of Greenbank Farm Cottage with the intention of surprising Daniel. When he answered the door, he simply smiled and welcomed me in.

"Come in from the cold, son. It is bitter out there."

I walked through into his living room to be greeted by a roaring log fire and that fine, aromatic smell of a roast chicken drifting from the kitchen.

"Sit down, Paul. I take it my message got to you somehow?"

I apologised for dropping in without warning and sat down on a seat near the fire. It was still warm. Daniel stood with his back to the coals and soaked in the heat.

"You can't beat a log fire." he said, smiling down at me.

I explained that I had brought something to show him, and I opened the carrier bag to reveal the diaries and photographs. I showed him one or two from Ernie's time in Germany, and I searched through one of the books to find the entries where Daniel himself was mentioned.

I suddenly had the guilty realisation that Daniel was stood, and I was sitting in his chair. I stood up and apologised again.

"You are fine, son. I am just enjoying the warmth. I was sitting over there, anyway," he said, pointing to a rocking chair on the other side of the fireplace.

"It isn't me you should be apologising to - that isn't my chair."

It was then I realised we weren't the only two in the room.

I glanced in the direction of the kitchen, and, in the doorway, I caught sight of another smartly dressed old man smiling back at me.

"I believe you have been looking for me, Paul," he said, almost casually. "Well, now you have found me."

My head was suddenly spinning. I was dumbstruck.

468

Ernie continued,

"Daniel was just as surprised as you are now when he opened the door to me last week. I had to return home."

Ernie walked over to me and reached out to hold my hand. I was rooted to the spot and couldn't speak.

"Before you say anything, no, I am not dead. My demise has long since been predicted, but my days aren't numbered just yet, and I haven't lost my mind.

I get a bit confused and dazed now and again, but that is just old age, I'm sure. It will come to us all. Daniel has invited me to stay here.

We can look after each other again. Just like in the old days. No one need ever know there are two Ernie Grimshaws."

Daniel nodded.

"It is your home as much, if not more, than mine. I always hoped you would come back home again. There is only one Ernie Grimshaw."

The two men smiled at each other and enjoyed a few seconds of silence before Ernie spoke again.

"I'm sorry you had to go to so much trouble. I've always tried to keep myself to myself," he said as he continued to hold my hand.

His own hands were warm and his grip firm. He was still strong for his age. His hair was now all white, his eyebrows too. His face was weatherworn, but his piercing blue eyes still sparkled and shone. There was still a sharp mind behind those eyes that had seen so much. You are good at your job, Paul. I see you even found my diaries."

I was still in shock. I could not believe I was face to face with Ernie Grimshaw, after everything.

I was in awe.

"You know, you and I are similar. We are persistent and determined. We don't give up. Some would say these are good qualities to have."

"You are so much more than that." I mumbled, tripping over my words and trying to stop myself from crying. I couldn't.

Daniel brought me a cup of coffee and pulled up another chair.

The three of us sat in front of that fire and talked and talked. We travelled from Belsen to Plymouth and everywhere in between. He was everything I hoped he would be, and more.

Hours passed in a heartbeat. It was a joy and a pleasure to sit in their company.

When I eventually left the two old men and waved goodbye, I promised to return soon. A promise I will keep. There is still so much more to talk about.

Ernie had the same effect on me as he had on every other person he met. I walked away feeling so contented and so blessed to have been able to spend time in his company.

And here we are, Mr. Diary.

Sat under the stars on a cold Cumbrian night in a battered old van, and I could not be any happier.

Never give up. Never give in. Never stop trying. Never stop helping, sharing, supporting and giving. Never stop loving. And never, ever stop living while there is breath in your body.

Once upon a time there was a man - and that man was me. And that man can be anything he wants to be.

Ernie Grimshaw.

Thank you.

ACKNOWLEDGEMENTS

Although I started by dedicating this story to my parents, there are a number of other people who have helped and inspired me to complete this book.

Firstly, I would like to thank Stephanie Grimshaw for dedicating many hours of her precious retirement proofreading and editing my wrok. She ddin't hav a chnce to corect this secshun. I hope she is as proud of the book as I am.

Many of my family and friends appear as characters in the story, and I apologise to the many others I have omitted. I promise that you will be in my next novel – like it or not.

However, not all of the character names included are people I know well. In particular, I would like to thank Mr. Barry Morneo (Ellis Island Historian), the staff at the Museum of Jewish Heritage, and the lads at Southwark and London Fields Cricket Clubs.

Thank you to Emma for your continued love, help and support.

Thank you to Jessica for inspiring me to keep writing.

And finally, thank you to Ernie Grimshaw.

Gone but certainly not forgotten.

All of you are very special to me.

Never doubt your worth.

Once Upon a Time There Was a Man is Peter's debut novel.

Peter was born and bred in Carlisle—a beautiful and historic city in northern England.

Although he has lived and worked in various places around the UK, Cumbria is, and always will be, considered home.

He lives with his young daughter, Jessica and their three goldfish (Toast, Feather, and Ice Cream).

After working as a primary school teacher for over twenty years. Peter recently decided to hang up his chalk and retrain as a driving instructor.

Although teaching is his love, writing is his passion.

As well as Once Upon a Time There Was a Man, Peter has also written a series of children's books, poems, plays, scripts, and short stories—all waiting to be unleashed on the world!

As a huge football supporter, Peter follows his beloved Carlisle United through thick and thin (mainly thin). No glory hunter here!

In an ideal world, Peter would love to live in an idyllic cottage in the Lake District surrounded by Labradors and chilled wine where he could let his imagination run riot. That's not too much to ask, surely.